Praise for *A Most Extraordinary Pursuit*

"*A Most Extraordinary Pursuit* is a most extraordinary new mystery—with a spirited heroine to root for, a disappearing duke, and a murder set on the isle of Crete. Steeped in gorgeous Edwardian detail with plot twists and turns galore, it's a riveting read."

—Susan Elia MacNeal, *New York Times* bestselling author of the Maggie Hope series

"Packed with unforgettable characters, exotic settings, and unexpected twists, *A Most Extraordinary Pursuit* is a delicious adventure from the first word to the last. This book has everything a reader could want: lyrical prose, swashbuckling action, and a heroine worth rooting for. Three cheers for Truelove!"

—Deanna Raybourn, *New York Times* bestselling author of the Veronica Speedwell Mysteries

"Juliana Gray brilliantly weaves historical detail, classical mythology, and unforgettable characters in this magnificent book. A triumph!"

—Tasha Alexander, *New York Times* bestselling author of *The Adventuress*

"If Elizabeth Peters's Amelia Peabody and Deanna Raybourn's Lady Julia had an intrepid younger sister, it would, without doubt, be the heroine of Juliana Gray's new series, Miss Emmeline Truelove. A rollicking good adventure with just a whisper of the supernatural."

—Lauren Willig, *New York Times* bestselling author of the Pink Carnation series

P9-CEY-349

continued . . .

"I fell in love with the winsome, witty, and oh-so-clever Emmeline Truelove. Gray's charming historical mystery flavored by a perfect romance is an utter delight. You'll devour *A Most Extraordinary Pursuit* like a luscious box of chocolates, but without any guilt because it's oh-so-smart."

—M. J. Rose, *New York Times* bestselling
author of *The Witch of Painted Sorrows*

RAVE REVIEWS FOR THE NOVELS OF JULIANA GRAY

"Juliana Gray has a stupendously lyrical voice."

—Meredith Duran, *New York Times* bestselling author

"Charming, original characters, a large dose of humor, and a plot that's fantastic fun."   —Jennifer Ashley, *New York Times* bestselling author

"Fresh, clever, and supremely witty. A true delight."

—Suzanne Enoch, *New York Times* bestselling author

"Fun, engaging, sensual, and touching . . . Gray's lyrical writing, intense emotion, and spirited characters carry the sophisticated plot to satisfying fruition."   —*Kirkus Reviews*

"Emotionally electric scenes between strong characters make this one a winner."   —*Publishers Weekly* (starred review)

"A literary force to be reckoned with."   —*Booklist* (starred review)

"Exquisite characterizations, clever dialogue, and addictive prose."

—*Library Journal* (starred review)

"Extraordinary! In turns charming, passionate, and thrilling . . . Juliana Gray is on my autobuy list."

—Elizabeth Hoyt, *New York Times* bestselling author

A Most Extraordinary Pursuit

JULIANA GRAY

BERKLEY BOOKS
New York

BERKLEY
An imprint of Penguin Random House LLC
375 Hudson Street, New York, New York 10014

Library of Congress Cataloging-in-Publication Data

Names: Gray, Juliana, date.
Title: A most extraordinary pursuit / Juliana Gray.
Description: Berkley trade paperback edition. I New York, NY : Berkley Books, 2016.
Identifiers: LCCN 2015039206 I ISBN 9780425277072 (softcover)
Subjects: LCSH: Missing persons—Investigation—Fiction. I Man-woman
relationships—Fiction. I BISAC: FICTION / Historical. I FICTION / Romance /
Historical. I FICTION / Romance / Suspense. I GSAFD: Romantic suspense fiction.
Classification: LCC PS3607.R395 M67 2016 I DDC 813/.6—dc23
LC record available at http://lccn.loc.gov/2015039206

PUBLISHING HISTORY
Berkley trade paperback edition, October 2016

Printed in the United States of America
1 3 5 7 9 10 8 6 4 2

Cover illustration by Michael Crampton
Cover design by Sarah Oberrender
Book design by Kelly Lipovich

To Maestro Verdi,
for whom great passion was never a mere subplot.

Acknowledgments

If you find this book unusual in certain respects, you (and certainly I) have my editor to thank: the lovely and reckless Kate Seaver at Berkley, who gave me free rein to write whatever I wanted, in whatever style I wanted, based on a disgracefully brief and deliberately vague synopsis. Those of you who have read my earlier books will recognize a few familiar characters—and I apologize for killing off the Duke of Olympia on the first page, an act of creative destruction—but everything else has gone off in a new direction, which will probably end my career as Juliana Gray. To Kate, and to all the well-meaning, talented souls at Berkley who have assisted in the development and marketing of this novel, I offer my endless gratitude and any letters of reference you may soon require, once Management realizes what we've done.

Sharing the blame is that great schemer (and worthy of a novel in her own right) Alexandra Machinist at ICM, who actually got Penguin to write a contract for this novel and its successor, using her Jedi powers of persuasion. Alexandra—assisted by her capable sidekick, Hillary Jacobson—has kept the champagne flowing at Gray Grange for many a year, and if you have any impossible-to-sell manuscripts hiding among the orphaned socks under your bed, I'd recommend you just send them her way. All of them. (You're welcome, Alexandra!)

Speaking of champagne . . . Lauren Willig. Not only a damned fantastic storyteller, but a quaffer of anything bubbly—my kind of girl, in other words—and a Real Help when one's driven one's outlandish omnibus of missing dukes and Edwardian ghosts and Greek myths into a ditch. (Go figure.) By way of thanking her for her invaluable assistance over coffee and omelets at a certain Le Pain Quotidien in midtown Manhattan, I urge you to buy anything she writes. A Lauren Willig book may be just the antidote you need.

We may safely disregard the fractious Gray offspring in any expression of gratitude—without them, which God forbid, this book would have been finished at least a month or two earlier—but Mr. Gray really can't be ignored. Solid and attractive, he performs the duties of a writer's husband without too much complaint, and he's always there for a cuddle when the champagne has run dry.

(Oh, all right. The truth is, I simply can't do without him.)

And finally, to my dear and faithful readers, who have waited so patiently for the next Juliana Gray book, only to discover that there's no sex inside. I'm sorry. Stay with me. I love you.

The distinction between the past, present, and future is only a stubbornly persistent illusion.

ALBERT EINSTEIN

THE HAYWOOD INSTITUTE
RYE, EAST SUSSEX
1 *June 2012*

There was no moon, but the two men stealing through the institute's rear courtyard kept to the periphery wall anyway. They were dressed in dark clothes, and as they neared the metal skip that flanked the service door, the first one stopped and pulled a balaclava over his head. The second did the same.

A battered halogen light illuminated the doorway from one corner, while a security camera blinked a slow red cadence at the other. The first man—medium height and extremely lean beneath his snug black clothes—pulled a pistol from the holster at his waist, fitted a silencer on the end, and motioned to his partner, who stepped to the side and laid his back against the tall brick wall. He fired twice: once at the camera, which expired in a crack of shocked plastic, and once at the light. The bulb splintered, turning the air dark and briefly alive with invisible glass slivers. The sound bounced across the courtyard, and then a tiny rain of glass reached the paving stones.

The two men remained motionless against the wall, waiting for the shower to end. Over the past few days, the weather had turned warm and settled, and the air smelled of cut grass and night jasmine and scorched powder. The first man closed his eyes, as if he were savoring the promise of summer, and leaned his head against the bricks.

The silence resumed, black and rich, except for a soft chorus of crickets in the grass on the other side of the wall. The first man touched the sleeve of his partner, and together they approached the door. The second man felt along the metal surface for the dead bolt. When he found it, he reached into his pocket and drew out a bump key, which he inserted gently into the keyway. A small jerk, and the key turned obediently to the right. He opened the door and allowed the first man to enter.

Inside, the building was cavernous, laden with an Edwardian atmosphere of wood and polish and magisterial damp. The first man extracted a small torch from the belt at his waist, and the beam found the newel post of a long back staircase. He made an upward movement with the torch, and the second man fell into place behind him, climbing the stairs on silent feet.

Either the men were already familiar with the institute, or they had studied its complex floor plan for many hours. They moved without hesitation up the staircase to the first-floor landing, and then the second, where they turned left and proceeded down a high-ceilinged corridor. The first man slid one hand against the wall, counting the doorways, while the other man followed the buoyant track of the torchlight along the worn carpet. They had nearly reached the end of the corridor when the first man stopped and pivoted to face a doorway on the right. He tested the knob: unlocked.

For an instant, he paused, laying one hand on the smooth vertical plane of the door, while the other clenched the turned knob.

The other man nudged his shoulder and spoke in a flat American whisper. "Go on!"

The office inside contained the usual mixture of old and new. A flat computer monitor perched on a battered wooden desk, littered with paper and photographs stuck in cheap plastic frames; a Keurig gleamed atop an oak bookcase, flanked by a sculptural Habitat K-Cup holder, half-stocked, and a couple of white mugs. But the first man wasted no effort exploring the furniture. A cursory survey, and the beam of the torch flashed up twelve feet to the ceiling next to the long sash window.

"There!" whispered the second man.

"Where?"

"Right there! You see the corner?"

He fumbled against the desk until he found the chair, which he scraped across the rug to a position just beneath the flattened yellow oval of torchlight on the ceiling. He climbed onto the seat and stretched his hands upward, while the first man ran the beam along the plaster. "Hold it still!" he hissed, dragging his fingers back and forth, until the tip of his pinkie caught against a small metal latch.

"Got it!"

"Holy shit! For real?"

"Damn, it's stiff."

"Yeah it is. Eighty-five years, bro."

The latch moved, and a rectangular section of ceiling sagged away from the surface, in a tiny creak of old hinges.

"And there it is," said the first man. He directed the torch at the crack in the plaster. "Pull it down."

The second man inserted his fingers into the crack and pushed gently. The hinges squeaked again, louder this time, longer, more like a groan, and the rectangle swung downward, revealing a set of wooden steps folded against the inside.

The second man jumped down from the chair and unfolded the steps. "Saddle up, bro," he said, and mounted into the attic.

The space was cramped and unfinished, triangular, smoky with trapped heat. The first man set the torch upright on the floor, like a lantern, and the glow illuminated only a small writing table, a bookcase, and a file cabinet wedged beneath the slanted wooden ceiling. On the table stood a green-shaded lamp, and the first man stepped forward and pulled its chain. Nothing happened.

The desk was otherwise empty, except for a thick layer of dust. The second man pulled open a drawer in the file cabinet and whistled. "Stuffed."

The first man yanked off his balaclava and knelt next to the bookcase. "Take everything you can."

They worked in silence: pulling out the books from the book-shelf, lifting the files from the cabinet, stacking them on the writing table. The second man also removed his balaclava, and in the macabre underlight of the torch on the floor, a small gold earring flashed in the lobe of his left ear.

When the cabinet was empty, the men placed the files in a pair of dark rubbish bin liners, and the second man straightened and asked, "Anything in the bookcase?"

"Just old history books." The first man stood akimbo beside the volumes stacked on the floor near the bookcase. He looked over the bags and scowled. "Are you sure it wasn't in one of the files?"

"Nope. I checked."

The first man picked up the torch from the floor and shone the beam along the walls. "Damn. It should have been here. We've looked everywhere else."

"We got a lot of good shit here, bro."

"Yeah, but not the book. We need the book." He aimed the torch in the space between the bookshelf and the wall. "Come on, little fucker," he muttered. "Where did you put it?"

"Anso, we gotta go. It's just a book."

"It's not just a book. It's the key to everything. Six chapters, right? Each one revealing the true story of history's greatest myths. How? Because he was *there*, bro. He saw the shit *live*. He made it happen. And that book is proof."

"Yeah, well, it's four o'clock. We gotta go. Sun'll be up."

"*Dammit!*" Anso straightened and kicked the base of the empty bookcase, and a panel fell out from the back of the bottom shelf, making a sharp thud against the century-old wood.

Both men went still. Stared at the bookcase. The slim panel lying flat, like a felled soldier, maybe two feet wide and a foot and a half tall.

"Whoa. What was that?" whispered the second man.

"Shut up!" Anso went down again, on his hands and knees, pointing the torch at the back of the bookcase. The second man crouched next to him.

"See anything?"

Anso didn't answer. He stuck a hand at the back of the shelf, and a ferocious expression took hold of his face. "Hold the flashlight," he said to the second man, and he braced his fingers against the side of the bookcase and maneuvered his other hand in the cavity left behind by the fallen panel.

"Hurry, man! We gotta split!"

"Hold on! Just—damn, damn, *damn*—"

His hand came free from the back of the bookcase, clutching a sheaf of papers bound together by a double loop of plain butcher's twine.

The second man's voice sagged with disappointment. "It's not a book."

"Of course it's not a book, fool. He never published it." Anso drew the papers reverently onto his lap and brushed the dust from the overleaf. The paper was smooth, the twine tough and hardened, catching the dust. He snatched the torch from the second man's hand.

"Well? What does it say?"

Anso looked up slowly. The torch twitched in his hand, causing a nervy glow to flicker along the side of his face.

"Holy shit, man," he said. "This is it. *The Book of Time*, by A. M. Haywood."

"Haywood?"

"Arthur Maximilian Haywood, right? He's our guy. The eighth Duke of Olympia. Born in London in 1874 . . ."

"Died?"

Anso rose to his feet, tucked the manuscript under his black shirt, and tapped the stiff rectangle with his gloved right hand. "That, my friend, with a little more damn luck, is what we're about to find out. Now let's get the hell out of here before the police show up."

They called the King's daughter the Lady of the Labyrinth, for it was she who managed the affairs of that complicated building called the Palace of the Labrys, and who
alone dared to penetrate its deepest interior, where they
kept the King's idiot son.

The Lady was happy with this arrangement, which busied
her from daybreak until midnight, and therefore allowed her
little time to communicate with her father the King—a bitter
drunkard—and her husband the Prince, who was his com-
rade in debauchery.

Our story begins at daybreak, in the fourth year of the
Lady's marriage, when she rose from her couch at the side
of her snoring husband and beheld the new white sails filling the harbour below, except that one of those sails was
pitch black . . .

THE BOOK OF TIME, A. M. HAYWOOD (1921)

One

THE HEART OF ENGLAND

I first met Her Majesty the night before the funeral of my employer, the Duke of Olympia. It was then February of 1906, and she had been dead for five years, but I recognized her instantly. Her eyes, you see. Who could mistake those bulbous blue eyes?

She sat at ease in my favorite armchair when I emerged from the bath. She wore no crown or tiara, nor any distinguishing mark of her rank. Her hair was dark and glossy, parted exactly down the middle, and beneath her dress of sensible blue wool she was no longer stout, but small and plump as a new hen.

As I stood there in the doorway, arrested by shock, still wet and soap-scented from a quarter hour's scrubbing in a narrow enamel tub, she turned her round face toward me and said, "It is really not wise to wash one's hair in the wintertime. We expected a little more sense from you."

"I thought the occasion warranted the effort," I said.

"Not at the expense of one's health. One's health is *paramount*."

I continued to the dressing table, where I took my seat on the cushioned stool and selected a comb. The solid weight of this ancient and wide-toothed ivory object, which had once belonged to my own mother, steadied my nerves. I wore a high-necked nightgown of white flannel, and a lined brocade dressing gown belted snugly over that, but Her Majesty was the sort of person who made one feel as if there weren't enough clothes in the world.

"One does not sit in the presence of royalty, unless invited," said the Queen.

"With all respect, madam, you do not exist."

"You have also turned your back. One never turns one's back on one's sovereign."

"King Edward is my sovereign. In any case, you will observe that in the mirror, we meet face-to-face."

She considered me for some time, while I combed my damp hair into long and careful sheets. As a horse, I might have been described as a liver chestnut, whose coat occupied a muddy middle ground between yellow and brown, neither brilliantly fair nor alluringly dark, remarkable only for its plainness. My employer had at one time expressed approval of this uninspired shade, in such a way that implied I'd had some choice in the matter. A valuable thing, to go about unnoticed, he told me gravely. An advantage not to be wasted.

"You have your mother's hair," said the Queen.

"Not quite. Hers was more fair."

"And how would you know this? You hardly knew the girl."

"I have her portrait."

"The artist flattered her. Aren't you going to offer us a drink?"

"What use would that be?"

"It would demonstrate a certain courtesy, for one thing, a quality in which you appear to be *badly* lacking. One supposes it is your mother's influence. Your father was always a dutiful man." Her fingers were full of rings, and she twisted them about on her lap, one by one, like an engineer twisting knobs on a machine, hoping one of them would do the trick. A look of triumph appeared on her face. "If I don't exist, then why should I appear in your mirror?"

"I expect it is all part of the illusion." I set down the comb and swiveled the stool about to face her. My room was elegant and comfortably furnished but not large—exactly suited to my rank, I suppose—and Her Majesty sat only a yard or two away, while the coals spat on her dress. "Have you got something important to tell me? I really must go to bed."

Scandalized. "But your hair is still wet. You'll catch a chill."

"You are occupying the chair next to the fire, madam, where it is my usual custom to dry my hair."

She harrumphed but didn't move.

"Is this about the ceremony tomorrow?" I asked. "Have you any special instructions? I understand the two of you were close, at one time."

"He was one of my most trusted advisors. I often hoped he would agree to lead the government, but he always refused."

"He hated politics," I said. "The parliamentary kind, at least. He was resigned to democracy, but he hardly relished it."

"And now the grand old Duke of Olympia is dead." She shook her head. "And who is there to replace him, in all my empire? These new young fellows are all beardless fools, every last one. *Soft.* Nothing to the men of my day."

"They'll grow wiser, I'm sure. They always do."

"They will drag us all into general war, mark my words. Or stumble into it, which is even worse. But never mind that. About this funeral tomorrow." She stopped twiddling her rings and placed her hands over the rounded ends of each chair arm, as if she were about to heave herself up. "The duke's widow will attend the service, of course."

"Of course. They were very much in love. I am deeply sorry for her. The death itself was so sudden."

"He was eighty-six years old. She cannot have been surprised." The Queen sniffed and turned to the fire. "She seems hardly bereaved at all. But then, she's only an American."

"I assure you, she is devastated by the loss."

"Yes. Well." She returned her gaze to me, and I had the feeling that she was assessing me, the way she might measure up the man who was to become her next prime minister. Not that she had ever had much choice in the matter, although I am given to understand that she liked to *think* that she did. Don't we all?

"Madam," I said, "I really must retire. There are so many details to which I must attend tomorrow, and I have been working day and night since the hour of His Grace's death."

"Nonetheless, you must listen to me. This is most important. Are you paying attention?"

"Since I must."

"Cheeky little baggage. You will receive a summons tomorrow evening from the dowager duchess, which—"

"I hardly think Her Grace will be in any state to consider her domestic arrangements."

Thump went the imperious little fist on the arm of my chair. "You are wrong. She will summon you tomorrow and ask you to perform a service for her, and you are to refuse."

"To *refuse* her?"

"Yes. Refuse her."

I laughed. "By what right should I refuse? Their Graces employ me to perform services for them. That is the point of my existence. I cannot simply pick and choose which commands to carry out, particularly at such a time, when Her Grace has particular need of me."

"This is not an ordinary service, and I must *insist* you refuse."

"You can't *insist* anything. You don't exist."

The fist struck again. "If I don't exist, why haven't you sat down in this armchair to dry your hair? It's your favorite, after all. Quite the warmest spot in the room. Go ahead, disregard me." She opened her fist and spread out her helpless, jeweled hands. "Squash me to a pulp."

"One must be polite, even to figments of one's imagination."

She sniffed again. From another woman, I might have called it a snort.

"Your Majesty," I said in a conciliatory tone, "I am deeply grateful for your advice, but I have a high regard for the dowager duchess, who has always been kind to me, and I see no reason to refuse any request with which she may honor me. The contrary, in fact. I am eager to be of whatever use I can."

"Ha! Because you're afraid you'll get the sack, now that the duke is dead."

"That's not true."

"Yes, it is. You were the Duke of Olympia's personal secretary, like your father before you—God bless his loyal soul—and now the dukedom falls to a distant cousin—"

"A grandnephew, hardly distant."

She waved her hand. "Off in the Levant or some other beastly place with too much sunshine and too little civilization. In any case, he'll want his own secretary, and one rightly expects you'll be sacked without notice unless you do the pretty to the dowager duchess, bowing and scraping, hoping to catch a crumb as it drops from her table."

"I am not in the habit of either bowing or scraping." I rose from the stool and lifted my nightcap from the dressing table. "And now, if you'll excuse me, I must ready myself for bed."

"Are you really going to bind your wet hair into that nightcap?"

"I seem not to have any choice, since you continue to occupy the chair before the fire."

"Go on, then." She crossed her plump arms, and the rings flashed in the light. Her mouth turned down in that sour, widowed expression familiar to Britons across the empire.

I gathered my hair defiantly into the nightcap and put out the lights, one by one, until only the sizzling coals illuminated us both. I banked the fire, taking care not to brush those regal woolen folds as I went, and crawled into bed with my dressing gown still belted around my waist.

Her Majesty made not a single sound, but I felt the mass of those large blue eyes as I went, disapproving my every move, down to the order in which I turned down the lamps and the side of the bed over which I climbed to my rest. I stared quietly at the shadowed ceiling, at the faint movement of the dying fire on the plasterwork. The sheets smelled of lavender, making me drowsy. Around me, the magnificent old house creaked and whistled into slumber.

When I woke up the next morning, the Queen was gone.

The sight of the sails filled the Lady with sorrow, for she knew they had arrived in respect of a yearly tribute her kingdom exacted on the conquered people of Athens, which required that unfortunate city to sacrifice seven of its fairest young people in slavery to the triumphant Minoans. The annual entry of the tribute ships into the harbour below the palace would be celebrated by seven days of feasting and gamesmanship in the great halls of the port itself, followed by a ceremonial parade of the new slaves from the port into the Palace of Labrys in the hills above. Here they would be taken blindfolded into special chambers, and the outside world would never hear of them again.

But the Lady knew what occurred in those chambers, and the ends to which the innocent Athenian youths were subject. As she watched the tiny ships bob in the distant harbour, her eyes welled with tears at the knowledge of their occupants' fates . . .

THE BOOK OF TIME, A. M. HAYWOOD (1921)

Two

You might wonder why a man so distinguished as the Duke of Olympia chose to employ a humble female, not related to him by blood, as his personal secretary. I can only say that His Grace was a man of great loyalty, and his affection for my father must have guided his choice. In any case, from the moment he offered me the position, two days after my poor father's funeral, I wrung my last nerve in an effort to prove—to the duke and to the world—that I was not a charitable endeavor.

The Duke of Olympia hadn't wanted a grand state funeral. He had told me this five years ago, on the occasion of Queen Victoria's mortal dissolution, while we waited in the black-draped gloom of his London study to depart for the official solemnities at St. George's Chapel in Windsor: a pageant in which England's dukes and duchesses must necessarily play their role. I remember well how the two of them stood in the glorious ermine-trimmed

robes due to their rank, dwarfing even the great scale of the room—
His Grace reached nearly six and a half feet tall, and his wife, though
more than a foot shorter, carried herself like a giant—and how the
duke then asked for a glass of port. I poured one for each of them,
and as the duke accepted the libation from my fingers, he said, "It's
a damned business. I suppose these rituals are good for the public,
but I'm damned glad I shall be dead for the occasion of mine."

The duchess had put her hand on his arm and said, in a voice
of great emotion, "Not for many years."

To which he had patted her affectionate fingers. "I trust,
when the fateful hour arrives, you and Miss Truelove will ensure
that as little fuss as possible is taken with my mortal remains. If
I had wanted a cortege through the streets of London, I should
have elected to become prime minister."

So when His Grace expired without warning in the middle of
his favorite trout stream—about a mile from the door of the stately
pile that had served as the seat of the Dukes of Olympia since the
Glorious Revolution first raised the family to the prominence it
enjoys today—there was no magnificently solemn procession
through the streets of Whitehall, attended by heads of state. The
duke's remains arrived at the nearby church of St. Crispin on a
caisson pulled by a single horse, and were borne to the humble
altar by his grieved grandsons, the Duke of Wallingford and Lord
Roland Penhallow; his natural son, Sir Phineas Burke; and three
nephews by marriage, His Highness the Prince of Holstein-
Schweinwald-Huhnhof and the Dukes of Southam and Ashland.
The county gentry were invited, of course—who could possibly
deny them the pleasure?—along with a handpicked selection of
friends and relations who might reasonably be expected to conduct
themselves with the necessary gravity.

But while the church was filled, it was also small, and when we proceeded to the interment in the family plot, I observed that every last face among us hung with an oppressive weight of grief for this man—this colossus—we had known and admired and occasionally loved. Her Grace the dowager duchess stood veiled on the edge of the newly turned earth, supported by the Duke of Wallingford, the step-grandson to whom she had become especially close, and though her back remained straight, her shoulders curved slightly inward, as if they had begun to warp under the burden of her loss. They had married only twelve years ago, when the duke was already a widower of many decades, and while the marriage had come late in life, and occasioned much sniffing among the more narrow-minded of the duke's contemporaries, it proved as intimate and loving a union as any I had ever witnessed. I shall never forget the sight of the duchess's face when the unhappy news was brought to her at last, at the end of a frantic afternoon's search for her missing husband: the slow way in which her mouth parted and her expression crumpled, as disbelief gave way to despair.

I remember thinking, at the time, that no one would ever mourn me so utterly.

The minister, an elderly man whose own father had first baptized an infant Olympia into the Church of England, wasted few words on the interment itself. It was February, and the wind was bitter with the promise of snow. The air smelled of loam and rot and annihilation, the extinction of a century that had begun with the bloody triumph of Waterloo and was now concluding with the burials of Victoria and Maestro Verdi and, in his turn, the grand old Duke of Olympia.

I watched the polished wood descend into the rough and barbaric earth, and a kind of panic swept over me: not of grief, exactly,

but the sense that a candle was sputtering out, which could never
be lit again.

⁓

By contrast, the reception afterward was almost jovial. I thought
this was exactly as His Grace would have wanted it, and after all,
only a natural reaction of the human spirit when it comes in from
the cold to a brightly lit room, furnished amply with refreshment.

I flatter myself that we did the old lion proud. He had always
appreciated the civilizing effect of good drink and fine food, and
the dowager duchess and I, in consultation with Norton the butler
and Mrs. Greenly the cook, had chosen the funeral meats with
loving care. By the time the guests arrived in carriages and motor-
cars from the churchyard, the servants had laid everything out on
an enormous trestle table along one side of the great hall, while
the footmen circulated to ensure that nobody's glass remained
empty for long. Had everyone not worn an uncongenial black, it
might have been a Christmas ball.

"Not quite the thing for a funeral, however," said my companion, as he surveyed the assembly. "I believe that's Lady Roland by
the punch bowl, squinting her disapproval."

"We did not design the menu with Lady Roland's opinions in
mind," I said.

"We?" His eyebrows lifted.

"I am—I *was*—the duke's personal secretary."

"Oh! My dear. What a dismal sort of job. I suppose you're glad
that's over."

"I quite liked my position, as a matter of fact. The duke was a
generous employer, if exacting."

"Exacting!" He laughed. "Yes, I daresay that's the charitable way to put it. I'm Freddie, by the way."

"Freddie?"

He leaned over my wine. "Frederick, if we must be proper about it. Have you really organized all of this?"

"With a great deal of advice, of course."

"Oh, of course. We mustn't allow anyone to know how capable we are. This wine is excellent, by the way. I applaud your taste. The last of His Grace's seventy Lafite, is it?"

"Yes. You're familiar with it?"

"I don't know much," he said, tapping his temple with one forefinger, "but I do know wine. One's got to be an expert about something, and it might as well be something that gives one pleasure. I say, were you really Olympia's secretary? You don't look like a secretary."

"How does a secretary look?"

"Certainly not like a charmingly constructed young female. Isn't paid employment supposed to be improper and that sort of thing? Have you got to work one of those nasty typing machines?"

"On occasion, when His Grace's personal business demanded it."

Freddie—Frederick—I could hardly call him by either name, so I called him by none—looked at me keenly over the top of his wineglass, which had now fallen dangerously empty.

"I say, you *do* look dashed familiar, though. Have we perhaps met?"

"I don't recall. Did you ever have personal business with the duke?"

"Personal business? Haven't the foggiest. Probably not."

"Then I imagine we haven't met before."

In truth, I would have remembered if we had. I shall not go to such lengths as to call this Freddie an Adonis—the term, I feel, is tossed about too carelessly these days—but in those early days of the century, he possessed the lucky beauty of youth in spades, beginning with a helmet of sleek gold hair and ending in a well-polished shoe, with all manner of blue eyes and straight noses and lantern jaws arranged at regular intervals in between. His shoulders extended sturdily from a somewhat disordered collar. He had a quick, lean way of moving himself about, which he disguised by his lazy expression. If anything, he stood a bit too tall for convenience, but perhaps I quibble; I sometimes suspect I am overparticular when presented with specimens like this self-professed Freddie. At any rate, as I regarded the radiant totality of him in the great hall of the Duke of Olympia's country seat, I expected he was probably very good at the tennis, had left Oxford with a dismal Third in History, went down to Scotland every August to kill grouse in a Norfolk jacket and leather gaiters, was engaged to marry an earl's daughter, and had a mistress waiting for him in a flat in Kensington, to which he motored back and forth in a two-seater automobile.

How this brainless, glamorous creature had come to rest in my proximity, I couldn't imagine.

"And yet," he said, "I can't quite shake the feeling."

"What feeling, sir?"

"That we've met before." A footman passed; Freddie, still frowning, stretched out his glass for servicing. "Do you go to London?"

"Only when His Grace is—was—in town."

"Belong to any clubs?"

"Not your sort of clubs."

"House parties?"

"I have generally preferred to remain at home when Their Graces are called away on social visits."

"I say. How amazingly dull. Well, chin up. You're free now, eh?" He nudged my upper arm with his wineglass, which was already half-empty again.

"Free? I'm in mourning."

"Well, but after a decent interval, I mean. Surely the old chap's left you a nice little remembrance, so you can run off and see the world and all that sort of thing. Smoke cigarettes and gad about on ocean liners, quaffing champagne by the bucketful."

"I haven't begun to think about it."

"Oh, come now. Admit it, it's been in the back of your mind all this time. Why else do we put up with the old duffers, eh? The pot of gold at the end of the rainbow." He leaned close again and winked, and in the copious candlelight—the duke had not yet begun the project of electrifying Aldermere Castle before he died, and perhaps five hundred fine beeswax candles illuminated the great hall this February night—his eyes looked a little too bright.

"Yes," I said. "Exactly so. And if you'll excuse me, sir, I'm afraid I must speak with the butler about the wine."

"The wine? What's wrong with the wine?"

"I suspect there's too much of it."

He laughed at me, and I was about to turn away, when his expression changed to one of recognition. He snapped his fingers. "Now I remember!"

"Remember meeting me?"

"No, alas. Remember that I was supposed to summon you to the library for a desperately important meeting."

"A meeting? With whom?"

"With whom? Why, herself, of course. The dowager duchess.

Wants a word with you, on the chivvy." He shut one blue eye and stared through his wineglass at the ceiling, as if admiring the optical effect. "Better you than me, if you're asking. But then, nobody ever does."

❦

A word about the dowager duchess.

Or perhaps you've already heard of her? I understand the marriage was something of a sensation, a dozen years ago, covered in breathless detail by all the newspapers, though little of that detail actually arose from the couple themselves. They are—*were*—private, by nature. Still, the editors turned somersaults at the news. If *American Heiress Weds English Duke!* never fails to set the blood racing in the veins, then *Penniless American Nobody Weds English Duke!* rings even better. Who was she? How had they met? What cunning American trap had she laid, in the manner of those infamous ladies of the wild western frontier, to get her man and his coronet, too?

At the time I walked into the Aldermere library, on the evening of the Duke of Olympia's funeral, I had few more answers to these burning questions than the general public. Her Grace was then about sixty years old: quiet, elegant, seemly. She had good bones and excellent skin—bones and skin go so far in a woman her age—and her hair, rich as treacle, had only recently begun to take on gray. I had never heard her raise her voice, not once. She read extensively, walked or rode every morning, nursed a small but loyal circle of friends, and took a keen enjoyment in travel. Of her previous life, I knew nothing, only that the couple had met on board an ocean liner and married shortly thereafter. The duke, insofar as he expressed any sentiment whatever, had worshiped the air that fell from her mouth.

She was not alone in the library. An unknown man occupied the enormous wing chair, upholstered in forest-green damask, in which the duke used to read during the winter evenings. His arms were folded across his chest as he watched Her Grace arrange the coals with a long gold-handled poker, and I thought how odd that was, that he should be sitting while the duchess stood, until I realized that his hair was quite white, and his skin made one think of a piece of finely crumpled tissue, stretched back out over his bones. He turned a pair of rheumy eyes in my direction and said, as if I couldn't hear him, "*This* is the girl?"

Nobody had called me a girl for many years. I pushed back my shoulders and looked at the duchess, who returned the poker to the stand and straightened to face me. "Miss Truelove. Thank you so much for attending us. May I present Sir John Worthington, a very old friend of the duke."

I inclined my head. "Sir John."

"How are you holding up, my dear?" she said. "Is everybody behaving themselves out there? Is the punch bowl empty yet?"

"Not yet, but I doubt it will hold out much longer."

"Well, let them enjoy themselves. It's how he would have wanted it. He always hated maudlin displays. Do sit down. You must be exhausted."

No more than a trace of sadness darkened her words. She had gathered herself together with remarkable dignity, for an American. I lowered myself into the indicated armchair and sat at the very edge, back upright, ankles crossed, as I had been taught from childhood, and as I did so I recalled—not that the thought had ever really left my mind all day—last night's extraordinary visitor to my bedroom.

The *imaginary* visitor, I reminded myself, and as if to disprove her existence, I opened my mouth and said firmly: "No more than you, Duchess. I hope you are bearing up, under such a burden."

"One hasn't much choice, has one? Life marches on. I knew we hadn't much time on this earth together, so I made sure to make the most of it. But one is never quite prepared when the ax falls." She placed her hand on the mantel and attempted a smile. "Who would believe the vital spark could possibly be extinguished from such a man?"

"Indeed. I haven't had the chance to think about it, really. I was gratified to see everyone so affected by the service. How comforted you must feel, to see how deeply His Grace was loved among all who knew him."

She allowed a dry little laugh. "Oh, I'm sure that half of them were only there to make certain he was really dead."

"Surely not."

"But never mind. There was one rather glaring absence among the assembled mourners, which has happily given our guests a convenient subject for gossip to go along with their wine. No doubt you know what I mean."

"Mr. Haywood?"

"Yes. Or the Duke of Olympia, as I suppose he's properly styled now. Have you still heard nothing from our peripatetic heir?"

"No reply at all yet, I'm afraid, either to the telegram sent to his business office in London, or to the letter dispatched to his last known address."

"In Crete, isn't that right?"

"To the best of my understanding, he was investigating the lost maze of the Minotaur."

"Very laudable. And when did you last hear from him?"

"A letter and parcel arrived just before Christmas." I folded my hands in my lap and glanced at Sir John, for whose benefit these details were no doubt being rehearsed. The duchess, after all, knew very well where her husband's grandnephew was indulging his latest obsession, and when his last letter had arrived. She and her husband had pored over the missive inside the glow of this very fireplace, if my memory served, laughing and beaming and shaking their heads. The duke and duchess had been unaccountably proud of young Mr. Haywood and his dusty adventures, which took him so far from England that I doubted he even knew the names of half the estates he had just inherited, let alone the tenants and business managers for whose livelihoods he was now responsible. During the six years I had been employed by the duke, and the thirteen additional years I had lived beneath his roof, I had never once met Maximilian Haywood.

At least, so far as I remembered.

Her Grace turned to the man in the chair. "Well, John? What do you think?"

"What do *I* think? By God, I think someone had better head out there straightaway and sort this business out." Sir John lifted the sherry glass resting on the table next to his elbow and drained it without a quiver.

"Head *out there*? Do you mean to Crete?" I said. "Now? In February?"

"Hmm. Yes." The duchess was still watching Sir John, who returned her gaze with his watery own, as if communicating some important idea through the ether, quite outside the limit of my understanding.

Except that it wasn't outside my understanding. Of course not. I hadn't spent a lifetime balanced on the sharp outer edge of what we call Society without developing a sapient sense for the unspoken. For the current of a conversation, independent of the waves rippling its surface.

After all, it is not what's actually *said* that matters. Heavens, no. What matters is what one means.

"There exist a number of private agencies specializing in the search for missing relatives," I said desperately. "I should be pleased to find a suitable candidate. Though I understand there is often some difficulty at the Alps crossings at this time of—"

"My dear," said the duchess, "that won't be necessary. At least, I hope not."

She wore a small suggestion of a smile as she took a seat on the sofa opposite, bringing her face exactly on the level of mine. Her eyes were dark blue, although you couldn't properly see their color except in bright light, and quite large. The funerary black dress only encouraged the opalescent whiteness of her skin.

The smile, I realized, was not happy or even friendly, but expectant.

An imperious voice appeared in my head: *You must refuse her.*

"You wish me to go to Crete?"

"That is our hope."

"But I've never traveled beyond Paris."

She waved her hand. "It's nothing, in this modern age. We'll supply you with all the necessary letters of credit and introduction. You are a clever, capable young lady. And of course you shall have a companion to assist you."

"But why is it necessary? Surely word will reach Mr. Haywood shortly, long before I can reach him myself. It's only a matter of these inefficient Continental mails, or the poor state of the roads, or the lack of telegraph wire . . ."

The duchess was exchanging another of those telling glances with Sir John, and I allowed my words to trail away, waiting instead with an odd crawling sensation in my stomach—dread? anticipation?—for what was to come. The rising current that was about to engulf me.

It is only a simple journey, I told myself. After all, these were modern times. By train perhaps to Venice—first class, yes, I would *insist* on a first-class wagon-lit—and then by steamship to Athens, where Mr. Haywood kept a small flat, largely to collect his post and store his collections. Then, if absolutely necessary, the passage to Crete. A few days spent inconveniently on unpaved roads, eating unwholesome food, traveling perhaps by mule train—here I suppressed an inward shudder—and then I would enjoy the immense moral satisfaction of telling Mr. Haywood just how much trouble he had occasioned by his idiosyncratic habits.

A week or two, then, at the outmost, barring complication.

I looked back and forth between the duchess's inquisitive eyebrows and the frown that deepened the lines of Sir John's face, until Her Grace rose from her place on the sofa and walked to the graceful little cabinet by the window, where a multitude of crystal decanters reflected the light from the guttering candelabrum. She lifted one, removed the stopper, and returned to refill Sir John's glass.

"We have a note," she said.

"Not a *note*," said Sir John.

She returned the decanter to its place. There was the clink of the base on the tray, the chime of the stopper. "A message, then.

It arrived two days ago at the house in London, and reached me yesterday."

"From Mr. Haywood?" I said.

"No. From an official in the Greek government, with whom my nephew has apparently had dealings. It seems he's gone missing."

"Missing? For how long?"

"Since Christmas, when he sent that letter. He had been sending regular updates of his progress to this man, and then he stopped."

I looked at Sir John, whose frown remained exactly as it was, only parting long enough to take in another drink of sherry between his damp lips. He was dressed in an immaculate (if antiquated) black mourning suit, which he wore with such ease I supposed he required it frequently. His hand trembled a little as it balanced the sherry.

"Has this man gone in search of Mr. Haywood? Made any attempt to reach him?"

"No. And I doubt he will, which is why I feel it necessary to send someone myself." The duchess returned to her seat on the sofa and threaded her fingers together on her lap. "Someone I trust, someone who is capable and exacting and has never yet failed us in any task."

My throat had gone quite dry by now. "Madam, with great respect, this is not the sort of errand I am accustomed to performing. I write letters and take dictation and make trivial arrangements; I have never once tracked down a missing man to the far corners of the world."

"Crete isn't that far."

"It is well beyond the boundaries of *my* experience."

Sir John made an elderly harrumphing noise over the top of his glass, starting the remaining sherry to shiver. "My point exactly," he said to the duchess.

I turned to face him. "My good sir, I understand that eyesight is often weakened among the *very* old, but I beg leave to point out that I am actually *sitting* in this room, not five yards away, and demand the courtesy of being spoken to as if I were a living person, and not a cipher."

A coal fell from the pile the duchess had earlier so neatly arranged, popping apart on impact against the grate in a starburst of sparks. From behind the massive library door came a roar of laughter, quickly hushed.

"*Well*," said Sir John.

"Nicely said, Miss Truelove, and I believe he had it coming, as the saying goes. Sir John? Do you see what I mean?"

"She is not without defenses," he said grudgingly, and finished off the sherry. A cane lay against the arm of his chair. He picked it up with his knobble-knuckled left hand and fondled the head, which was gold in color and shaped like a duck.

"You would do much better to send a professional," I said. "In addition, there are so many letters of condolence to answer, to say nothing of the duke's business correspondence—"

"Anyone can do *that*, Miss Truelove, though perhaps not with your efficiency and single-mindedness. But I would not under any circumstances send a mere stranger, however *professional*, into the middle of a delicate family matter such as this."

"A delicate family matter?"

"Imagine the fuss, Miss Truelove, if word of this little trouble reached the newspapers," she said quietly. The pads of her thumbs pressed together.

Sir John banged his cane against the floor. "The girl doesn't want to do it, Penelope!"

"I am not a *girl*, Sir John."

"Yes, quite right," said Her Grace. "You are not a girl at all. Which is why I have asked *you*, of all people, Miss Truelove. You know our affairs intimately, and your discretion is above question."

"Of course."

"And you are aware, no doubt, into whose lap the dukedom falls, should Mr. Haywood fail to appear and claim his birthright? Since my husband is survived by no legitimate heirs of his own body, alas."

"Mr. Haywood's younger brother, I believe."

"Whose reputation for licentiousness and unrepentant irresponsibility is unmatched, even in London, and whose wit I sometimes doubt reaches even that of an average schoolboy."

"The two brothers, I understand, could not be less alike."

She rolled her eyes upward to study the neat geometry of the ceiling plasterwork. "I have often wondered whether they fully are. Brothers, I mean. Their parents' marriage was not a happy one, and Cici never could keep her legs together when a cavalry officer walked past. You will pardon my frankness."

"Naturally," I lied.

"And to make the whole situation even more wretched, there is the matter of the institute."

"The *institute*?"

"You must be aware of it. Olympia's latest obsession. Of course, it was Max's idea to begin with, but they had been corresponding about it for years and—well, naturally you know all that."

"I had the pleasure of transcribing a great deal of correspondence on the matter. It is, if you'll allow me, a subject close to my heart."

She gave me a wise look. "But you didn't approve, did you?"

"It wasn't my place to have an opinion on the subject."

"Of course not. But you don't *believe* in any of it, I expect. You think it's all hokum. Anything that smacks of the extra-natural."

"It's His Grace's fortune. He has a right to do what he likes with it. The institute will provide employment for a number of eminent researchers, to say nothing of the staff and the upkeep. In such a small village as Rye, the economic advantages may be almost miraculous. I have already received many grateful messages from the local residents, on the duke's behalf. The mayor's letter in particular was most touching."

"Damned risky business, if you ask me," said Sir John.

"But that's your trouble in a nutshell, John. We can't sit grumbling in the old century, pushing back progress with both hands, or it will end up engulfing us, and then what?" The duchess spread her palms in a remarkable parody of helplessness.

"I don't say I don't support the damned institute," he said. "But only with the gravest of reservations."

"Duly noted, my dear fellow. In any case, it will all come to nothing, and very soon, if Max doesn't turn up. The project represents an enormous investment, even for an estate so large as ours. Naturally the wretched bloodsuckers at the underwriting bank have already asked me about its continuation—in the letter of condolence itself, if you will!—and I have no doubt they will withdraw their support at once if my nephew doesn't appear soon, all capable and businesslike and ducal."

"But that would be disastrous!" I cried. "The structure is already half-built, and they have begun hiring permanent staff. There is such hope."

Her face turned grim. "Yes, it would be disastrous indeed. And only the nose of the locomotive, were that dolt Marcus to get wind of his brother's disappearance and start causing trouble. They will give us a decent interval, but legally I have no control over the estate, my dear, no control at all. I am only the dowager now, and everything belongs to the new Duke of Olympia. Progress, you know," she said, and I thought her voice broke at last, a small quaver in the center of the word *progress*, quickly recovered.

Sir John, who by now was watching my face with almost unnatural keenness, leaned forward over the top of his walking cane. "Miss—"

"Truelove," I said.

"Miss Truelove. Why this passionate interest in the welfare of a single coastal village?"

My palms hurt, and I realized that I had been digging my nails into the creases just below the finger joints. I opened each damp hand and clasped them around each other with deliberate looseness, so that the tension might drain away. In the past, I had found this an effective means of resolving these irksome knots of anxiety that formed in the various points of one's body, from time to time: one's stomach, one's neck, one's back, one's clenched hands. To concentrate on the physical loosening; the mental always followed the physical, in my experience.

"I was born in Rye, sir," I said. "My earliest memories lie there."

"I see," he said, and I wanted to laugh, suddenly and absurdly, because I couldn't imagine Sir John could see anything behind those clouded eyes, which might once have been blue.

But of course I didn't laugh. I had learned long ago how to manage these inconvenient impulses.

Sir John turned a close and scientific gaze to the duck at the end of his walking stick. "A nice coincidence," he added.

"It was not a coincidence at all. When His Grace first began to investigate the project, several years ago, my father suggested Rye as an ideal location: remote in character, yet within easy distance of both London and the Continent, via the Channel ports."

"I see," he said again.

The dowager duchess drew in a great sigh, as if gathering herself for the final stretch of a racecourse. "All very interesting," she said, turning her thumbs in a windmill, "but I'm afraid we must return to the vital point. Time is short, you know."

Her eyes leveled upon mine, and for an instant I had the unsettling sense that she was not the dowager duchess at all, but someone else. Someone familiar, and yet unrecognizable in her present form, such that I might spend days clawing back the layers of her disguise and come no closer to the stranger within.

Then I blinked, and the illusion disappeared.

"Very well," I said. "Since the errand is of such an urgent nature, and discretion so essential. I shall, of course, need a few days to put everything in order, and to obtain the necessary—"

The duchess was shaking her head. "Oh, dear me. No, no. A few days? Gracious me. The motorcar is already waiting outside."

I startled in my seat and turned my attention to the window overlooking the grand oval drive. An indigo twilight had already settled behind the glass, rendering invisible the landscape beyond, though I knew every tree and stone and stable of it, like a map in my brain. "The motorcar?"

"Yes. Our driver will take you straight down to Southampton docks, where the duke's yacht has just completed a thorough refitting. You will then—"

"His yacht?" I said faintly.

"The *Isolde*. We took our honeymoon tour in her," the duchess said, and an expression of joy came to light across her face, faded, and was gone. "She is now bang up to date, as they say, and is already taking on coal and supplies for the voyage."

"But I can't possibly— An entire steamship, all to myself— What about the train?"

"The train is too public, my dear, and you yourself mentioned the difficulty with the Alpine passes this year. Besides, you would only have to find a steamer in Venice anyway. You will lose no time and much inconvenience by taking the *Isolde*."

"I shall need to pack." I don't remember thinking the words; I existed by then in a kind of dream state, acting and responding as if I were quite human and sentient, instead of the stunned animal I had actually become. I added, "I have no passport, however."

"Oh, that's all been taken care of." She rose from the sofa and went to the door behind me. Her skirts rustled stiffly against the rug. I glanced at Sir John, who was still staring at the duck, eyeball to eyeball. "Freddie!" called Her Grace, in a voice that echoed sweetly down the hallway, encouraging no refusal.

"Freddie?" I whispered.

A brisk pair of shoes shook the floorboards, and then a gust of new air invaded the old library, whistling among the leather and the plaster, smelling of tobacco and spirits and modern frivolity.

"We're all set, Freddie. She's agreed."

The wind began to whir in my ears. I set one hand on the sofa arm and rose. From this height, the view of the drive appeared in shadow through the window glass, and I could just make out the black shadow of the duke's custom Burke open-drive limousine hovering near the front steps.

An unmistakable voice broke out cheerfully behind my head. "Oh, splendid! Was just beginning to lose hope, to say nothing of my virtue, which has been threatened at least a dozen times by your licentious old friends, Penelope. All true what they say about widows, what?" The voice paused. "I say. Are you quite convinced? She looks a trifle blanched, if you ask me."

"I didn't ask you, darling, and she's quite all right. She's just a bit stunned by the suddenness of it all. Aren't you, Miss Truelove?"

"Yes."

Freddie's voice again, like the bark of a young and deep-throated puppy. "What's this, Miss Truelove? Haven't you ever just set out on a lark, that very day, tally-ho and all that, never mind the toothbrush and the hair oil?"

"No."

"Ah, well. As the weasel said to the frog—or was it the other way round?—better to hop—"

I turned at last to face them, shielding my eyes so as not to be blinded by the reckless optimism shining forth from the doorway. "Duchess, is this some sort of joke?"

"Joke, my dear?"

I pointed to Freddie's collar, from which the funerary black neckcloth had somehow come askew. "You're sending me off to Crete with this *millstone* hanging from my neck? I am not a nursemaid, madam, nor yet a chaperone."

The duchess wore a beatific smile. "Miss Truelove, may I present Frederick, the Marquess of Silverton, heir to the Duke of Ashland, who is quite thirty, I believe, and in no need whatever of either nursemaid or chaperone."

"I'm afraid I had the opposite impression."

"Well, I'm dashed," said Lord Silverton.

"Now, Miss Truelove. Freddie's an experienced traveler and very good company, and what's more, he went to university with Max and knows him very well. No one could be more suitable to accompany you."

"It's improper," I said desperately.

"It is not improper at all. These are modern times, Miss True-love, and an independent woman of good character may safely have intercourse with a gentleman—you *are* a gentleman, aren't you, Freddie?—without any sort of impropriety attached to the affair at all. Isn't that right? Freddie?"

Lord Silverton placed his palms together and genuflected. "You are as a goddess to me, Miss Truelove. Our intercourse shall be of the most sacred kind, I solemnly vow."

Behind me, Sir John erupted into a fit of coughing.

"You see?" said Her Grace. "Not even the strictest mind could possibly disapprove."

"Ha!" someone said, over the top of Lord Silverton's left shoulder, and my heart dropped like a piece of coal into my belly.

Go away, I thought.

"I suspect the strictest mind could *well* disapprove, madam," I said. "In fact, I'm certain of it, but given the gravity of the task before me, I see no choice but to—"

"Refuse!" The Queen's head appeared around the corner of Lord Silverton's elbow. Her pale eyes nearly bulged from their sockets. "Refuse!"

"Be quiet!" I hissed.

His lordship blinked. "I beg your pardon?"

"That is, I see no choice but to do what is required of me, whatever my personal objections to the haste and the unsuitable company."

"Very good," said the duchess.

"Fool," said the Queen.

"Right-ho," said Lord Silverton. "That's settled. Let's push off, shall we?"

The Lady spared not a glance for the gross and bloated body of her husband the Prince as she rose from their bed, but stepped instead into the antechamber and called for her handmaids to dress her. When she had dressed and broken her fast, she made her way deep into the intricate chambers of the palace, until she came upon the room that belonged to her idiot brother, which was locked and bolted.

But the Lady had the key to this chamber, and she went inside without fear and greeted her brother tenderly, for they had since childhood been all in all to each other. She told him of the ships' arrival, and her great distress over the fate of the Athenian youths, and her brother said, 'Then why do you not seek to help them, my sister?'

The Lady shook her head. 'But what can I do? Our father will never allow me to deprive him of his greatest sport, nor will my husband the Prince.'

'Then, beloved sister, you must use your clever mind to trick them. Go in disguise to the great halls of the port, and discover among the comely youths one who has the strength and cunning to defeat the King and his depraved ally with your help, and you will surely please the gods . . .'

THE BOOK OF TIME, A. M. HAYWOOD (1921)

Three

Her Majesty did not follow us into the automobile, for which I was grateful. Next to me, Lord Silverton stretched out his long legs, tucked his head into the upholstered corner between door and seat, and went promptly to sleep. He did not awaken until the Burke's wheels began to rattle over the paving stones of Southampton, and the driver took a particularly ambitious lurch around a corner.

"I say." His lordship picked himself up from my lap. "Are we there already?"

"We have been on the road nearly seven hours, your lordship, and stopped for water and petrol three times."

"Do call me Freddie, now."

"I cannot possibly call you Freddie."

"Frederick?"

"I think it best if we continue to address each other in a formal manner, Lord Silverton, in order to prevent any tendency to lapse into familiarity during our travels."

"God forbid *that*," he said. "Silverton, perhaps? Or even Silver, should you feel a momentary thaw coming on."

"Silverton, then. I beg your pardon." I had just fallen against his shoulder.

"Think nothing of it. I've had far worse calamities befall these old bones." He helped me upright and peered out the window at the lurid pattern of the arc lamps against the terraced buildings. His hand disappeared into his waistcoat and emerged in possession of a handsome gold watch. "Half four already! Now there's an odd perspective for you. One doesn't usually see the hour from this angle."

"Which angle is that?"

"The waking-up angle. As opposed to the falling-asleep." He replaced the watch and stretched his apelike arms upward, getting as far as the elbow before clunking against the roof of the automobile. "Jolly nice motor, this."

"His Grace took ownership of it only a month ago."

"Poor chap. I hope he got to ride in it."

"He drove it home himself from the factory. He took enormous pleasure from Sir Phineas's machines."

"You mean his son."

I pressed my lips together. I quite liked Sir Phineas, who lived not far from Aldermere with his wife and children, but one couldn't escape the fact that his mother was a noted adventuress who had once been the duke's mistress, in the years before he met the dowager duchess.

One could only ignore that fact politely.

"Ah, Truelove," said Silverton. "What a jolly voyage spreads out before us."

"I don't think it's jolly at all. His Grace is scarcely a fortnight gone, and the present duke has disappeared—"

"Do you always take everything so seriously, Truelove, or are you just trying to teach me a lesson?"

"I don't quite understand, your lordship."

"Silverton. Never mind. Here we are, then." He turned back to the window. "Glorious Southampton docks in the dregs of night. I do hope they've readied us a drop or two of coffee aboard that old tramp. Or perhaps something stronger. Or the two together, a happy cohabitation."

"Coffee would be welcome," I allowed. The well-cushioned interior of the Burke limousine, supplied at the outset with hot-water bottles and traveling blankets in abundance, had taken on the oppression of a prison after about an hour of Silverton's percussive snoring. Outside the glass, the driver huddled around the steering wheel, wrapped like a Cossack in greatcoat and fur hat and several woolen scarves. "Though certainly poor William should have the first cup," I said. "He seems half-frozen."

"*Poor* William? What's this? Do I detect a note of actual human sympathy in those stentorian tones, Truelove?"

"Only for those who deserve it."

The brakes squealed lightly, and the automobile came to a delicate stop. William climbed stiffly from his seat and opened the door of the cab, charging the interior with dank marine air. No escape now. I took his outstretched hand and levered myself free to step on the dock, one unsteady foot after another, and I thought, *This is the last time these feet will tread on English boards, this is my last sight of England for many weeks.* Only twelve hours ago I was sitting in a pew of solid English heart of oak, and the choir sang "Abide with Me."

The water slapped restlessly against the harbor walls, and from somewhere nearby came a groan of metal, the immense strain of rivets and joints. A few greasy tendrils of mist swirled past the pilings and drifted into my lungs, laden with the sting of salt and of coal smoke, and as I stretched back my neck and looked up and up along the black steel hull before me, I imagined it was actually alive, a thoroughly modern monster waiting to gobble me up and bear me away.

Something brushed my sleeve: Lord Silverton, stretching his arms, shedding sleepy warmth into the fog. "There she bobs," he said. "The faithful *Isolde.*"

❦

I will confess to your ears alone: I have had a terror of steamships since I was a young girl. Why, I can't say. Perhaps news of some great marine disaster appeared in the papers, and the story made a terrifying impression on me as my parents discussed it over the breakfast table, unaware that I could comprehend them. Such things happen, and we don't even remember them. I do recall a painting that used to hang in the duke's morning room in London, depicting a frigate as it climbed toward the crest of an impossibly massive wave, its decks nearly vertical, a plaything in the foamy hands of God. I was only five years old when I came to live under the duke's roof, and used to play in that room when no one else was there.

Now, I quite understand that a modern steamship is not a Napoleonic frigate, and I have studied the design and construction of a twin-screw propeller and the system of bulkheads that renders a vessel almost impervious to the dangers of moderate collision. Moreover, the Marconi wireless has made it possible for a ship in distress to communicate her emergency to a dozen waiting ears in an instant, thus improving the ordinary passenger's chances for survival.

But I simply cannot overcome, in my logic, the extreme fragility of a ship on the ocean. The vessels of today may be larger by many multiples than those of a century ago, built of steel instead of wood, propelled by machine instead of wind and sail, but to the ocean itself, this difference is beneath notice. Against the infinity of nature, we remain but grains of sand. It is folly—hubris—to imagine our machines can prevail against God's will.

Nevertheless, I had been ordered to take ship in search of the Duke of Olympia's missing heir, so to the *Isolde* I repaired, disappearing like an ant into that massive steel hull, to be greeted by the respectful captain and shown to a stateroom by a white-clothed steward. The cabin itself was new and luxurious, having (as the duchess informed me) just benefited from a thorough refitting, and I fell asleep soon afterward on my brass-railed bed, not even noticing our grinding departure from England until I woke, some hours later, to the gray morning light in the porthole, and was promptly sick over a large portion of the expensive new carpet.

⁊

If you have had the good fortune never to suffer the misery of seasickness, I congratulate you.

You can then only guess my vexation at missing the entirety of the ship's passage through the famously temperamental waters of the Bay of Biscay, and the debilitating sense of physical malaise that accompanied my confinement to my cabin. Let me assist you. Imagine that your stomach has been replaced by a butter-churn, and your brain has been removed from its stem and placed upside down in your skull, which has incidentally been filled, in the manner of a rubber balloon, with a mixture of pebbles and bicarbonate of soda. Owing to the severed connection between brain and stem, you are likely unable to move, and if you can, by immense concentration, manage to part your eyelids, the image you see before you will demonstrate an unfortunate tendency to roll about in exact opposition to the churn in your stomach.

Indeed, you are better off not opening your eyes at all.

But I did, eventually. Open my eyes, I mean, to the darkened cabin around me, sometime the next day, because I could no longer bear the sole company of my own overturned brain. The curtains had been drawn over the two portholes, and the lights were off, but when I trained my gaze on the benign gilt-framed painting across the room, ignoring the drunken swing of the room around me, the details of my surroundings began to take vague shape.

The cabin was not large, but it was beautifully furnished. The bed was made of brass and railed on each side, to prevent the sleeping occupant from being turned out of his berth. There was a door on the opposite wall, leading presumably to a private bathroom—all the *Isolde*'s staterooms now boasted individual facilities for the convenience of the duke's guests—and a chest of drawers, secured to the floor. As I lay observing, the ship lurched into another wave, and the room and its furniture held me in firm grasp, coasting effortlessly over the top of the disturbance. The painting, I now saw, was of Arundel Castle on a golden autumn afternoon.

On the table to my left, some unknown steward had deposited a cup of water, made of metal and weighted at the bottom.

I reached out a shaky arm and forced myself to sip. The tempest in my head, I knew, was the result of a drought of vital fluids, not the seasickness itself. The back of my throat welcomed the water's coolness. I sipped again and sat up.

What time was it? I was not wholly certain, but I thought we had left Southampton no more than a day ago. The glow around the edges of the curtains was dim and gray and shifting, but certainly daylight. We must be in the Bay of Biscay, I decided, and the bay was notoriously violent against those ships that dared to cross her. My misery, therefore, would last some time. I might as well find a way to endure it.

Come on, Truelove. Get out of bed.

I lifted my legs free from the covers and discovered I was wearing a nightdress and dressing gown. My slippers had overturned and lay against the wall, near the door to the bathroom. I staggered toward them, clutching the furniture for support, and continued through the door to retch unsuccessfully into the bowl of the convenience.

When I was finished—that is to say, when my stomach gave up attempting to rid itself of nonexistent bile—I wiped my damp forehead with a towel and made my way back into the bedroom, where I settled myself into the armchair next to the porthole and stared at the ceiling.

Mr. Haywood. Mr. Arthur Maximilian Haywood—Max, it seemed, to those with whom he was familiar, like the amiable idiot Lord Silverton—was wholly unknown to me: a ghost who had, until now, occupied a vital yet theoretical role in my life. His letters and parcels I had forwarded unread to my employer's attention, as I did with almost all of the duke's personal correspondence. I knew him only by the handwritten direction on those letters, quick and precise, and by the portrait that hung above the mantel in the duke's Hampshire study. It depicted a serious-eyed young man with dark hair and a thick mouth, and features that resembled the duke's own, except for the coloring. He was not handsome, but his expression commanded attention. I had often felt that he was observing me as I worked at my small desk near the window, though of course the idea was absurd. A painting is only oil and pigment, after all.

In fact, I had only had anything at all to do with Mr. Haywood's affairs since last winter, when he and the duke first conceived the notion of an institute for the study of ancient objects. I had never known His Grace to be especially interested in such things before, but his passion for the subject ignited at once. Perhaps it had something to do with the nature of these objects, which I understood were of an unusual sort. Mr. Haywood, in the course of his archeological investigations in Crete, had discovered a number of artifacts that—or so he insisted—possessed properties that could not be explained by ordinary science. At the time, I had not inquired what, exactly, those properties were. It was not my business.

The Duke of Olympia, however, had been intrigued by his grandnephew's claims, whatever they were, and had spent the past year enthusiastically putting them in the way of further study. Tens of thousands of pounds had already been invested in the institute in Rye, and Mr. Haywood had forwarded regular parcels containing objects for its initial collection. Now, of course, the duke was dead, and Mr. Haywood could not be found. And here I was, roiling atop the sea in my prison of steel, charged with his urgent discovery.

How the devil was I going to do that?

I have every confidence in you, the dowager duchess had said, as we poised on the driveway to make our farewells. She had given me the packet of papers necessary for my voyage and kissed me on both cheeks. The sky had been very black, and her face almost purple in the light from the house. What had she said? *You have a particular talent for detail, my dear, and I know you will not disappoint me.*

An odd way to put things, I thought now, and I forced my torpid limbs to unpick themselves from the cushions and slump to the small writing desk a yard or so away, on which I had placed the packet of papers Her Grace had given me.

A mistake. The documents swam before me: passports, letters of credit, introductions to people I did not recognize. It was beyond my strength even to assemble the words into meaning. I would study everything later, I thought, and I cast about for my traveling desk, which went with me everywhere, and which I could use, if necessary, while sitting up in bed. Should I ever again commit so foolhardy a maneuver as to raise my head, of course.

The stewards had stowed my desk on the floor next to the bed, and I had just unlocked the bottom drawer and placed the papers inside, when the deck began to tilt in the slow, magisterial, vertical manner I recognized too well. An especially murderous series of waves followed, one after another, while the metal groaned from within and the wind raged at the portholes. I closed my eyes and anchored myself to the floor. When I opened them again, I saw that a few of the papers had come loose and scattered across the rug.

For a moment, I simply stared at them. I dislike disorder—my room, wherever it happens to be, remains always in immaculate organization—but I could not summon either the will or the strength to recover these errant sheets. The few feet of carpet seemed an impossible distance, and the ship would go on rolling to one side and then another.

Go on, then, Truelove, I told myself. *You cannot leave the duchess's papers lying on the floor like this. A disgrace.*

I placed both palms on the rug and crawled carefully to where the papers lay, and one by one I gathered them together in a tidy stack. As I did so, I realized they were not documents at all, but photographs, each enlarged to the size of a sheaf of ordinary notepaper.

I turned to lean my back against the wall of the groaning ship, and I held the first photograph up to the faint light from the porthole.

If I hoped to find some clue to the new duke's whereabouts, I was disappointed. The first photograph was of a stucco wall, covered by a series of peeling and disjointed frescoes. I held the photograph closer, but I could not quite make out the images in the paintings. I would require the magnifying glass in my traveling desk to see them clearly.

I turned to the next photograph, which depicted a similar scene, and then the third.

This one had been taken at a closer distance, and I could actually make out the furry gray figures in the frescoes. There was a woman, and an immense man next to her wearing a helmet of some kind, the top of which had been eroded away. Ahead of them stood a man, muscular and warlike though not quite so large as the first, holding a sword in one hand and an object in another, with which he appeared to be beckoning his companions.

I held the photograph higher, and a bar of light from the porthole crossed the image, in such a way that I imagined, for a confused instant, that the object in this ancient man's frescoed hand was a No. 1 Brownie camera, of the type manufactured and sold the world over by the Eastman Kodak Company.

But of course I was mistaken—my God, naturally I *must* be mistaken!—and as the ship pitched back downward, shutting off the meager light, the bile rose up in my throat, and I threw down all three photographs and crawled to my private bathroom, the most miserable creature atop the seven seas.

The Lady did as her brother suggested, enlisting the help of her most trusted handmaid to secure the disguise of a humble peasant, and leaving word for her father and her husband that she had gone into her monthly seclusion. The handmaid borrowed a donkey from her brother, who worked on a small farm near the palace, and together the two women and the donkey walked down the long road from Labrys to the port.

When they arrived, the Athenian youths had already been taken from their ships and housed in great splendour. They were bathed and anointed with oil, and robed in rich silks and velvets. The Lady and her handmaid took up dishes from the kitchens to serve in the banquet hall, and it was there that the Lady beheld the sacrificial youths for the first time, and the man whose fate was already written alongside hers for eternity . . .

THE BOOK OF TIME, A. M. HAYWOOD (1921)

Four

T hat, my dear, is Gibraltar," said Lord Silverton, propping his elbows on the topmost rail of the promenade deck some three days later. "Do you mind if I smoke?"

"I do, but I would not deprive you of the pleasure."

He reached deep into a waistcoat pocket and produced a pipe. "As a cure for seasickness, tobacco cannot be recommended highly enough."

"I doubt any substance so noxious could be called a cure for anything."

"Still cross, I see. Not that I blame you, mind. What a beastly old Biscay she was, this go-around. At her absolute worst." He seemed to be having difficulty with his match, turning this way and that in an attempt to shelter from the draft that rushed along the sides of the ship. "Not that the bay is ever anything less than tempestuous. Ah, there we are." He straightened and dropped the match into the navy water below. "This is more the thing, isn't it? Clear skies, calm seas. Your face is looking decidedly less gray already."

The scent of pipe tobacco filled the breeze. I tried to hold my breath, but you can't avoid the draft of a modern steamship traveling through the February weather at sixteen or seventeen knots; it plows directly into your nose, whether you like it or not. I held my fist to my mouth and said, "So that is Gibraltar. I thought it would be larger."

"Ha! Yes, these things are never so great as we imagine them, eh? But it's a fine old rock all the same. I climbed to the top once, when I was a reckless young lad of seventeen. We had put in for coal, I believe." He paused, sucking gently on his pipe, and patted the rail. "It was my parents' honeymoon trip, in this very ship."

"Your *parents'* honeymoon? And you were there?"

"Well, my father and my stepmother, to be precise. Olympia lent us his ship for an entire year, almost. My half brother was born off the coast of Argentina, in the middle of a hundred-year gale." He laughed. "I don't believe I've ever seen my father so frightened. At one point, my stepmother ordered him off the ship in a lifeboat. Luckily he ignored her and carried on, with the help of a bottle of Scotland's finest, procured for him from the ship's stores by yours truly. One doesn't much listen to women in the throes of childbirth, you see. Anyway, she had another the following year, so I suppose it wasn't as bad as it sounded."

"You shouldn't speak of such things."

"What, childbirth?" He tilted his head to one side. "I never could make that out, actually. What's improper and what's not. Nothing more natural than having a baby, and yet we're not allowed to speak about it. Why is that, do you think?"

"Because it's—because—well, a woman's delicate sensibility demands—"

"Oh, rot. If you had seen my stepmother laboring forth in the middle of a hurricane, you'd have no more regard than I do for this so-called female delicacy." He knocked the ash from his pipe. "It's because babies are the natural consequence of human concourse, I suppose."

I choked into my fist. "Sir!"

"Yes, exactly. And there's nothing dirtier, is there, than a man and woman coming together in mutual— Now, don't flounce off, Truelove. You're a sensible, emancipated woman. If a chap can't have a sensible, emancipated conversation with a sensible, emancipated woman, what's the point of civilization?"

"This is not a sensible conversation, and I don't have the slightest idea what you mean by emancipated."

He made a fluttering motion with his hands, as of wings. "Free. Independent. Able to think and act and decide for oneself."

"I hope you're not accusing me of being a *suffragette*, Lord Silverton."

"Well, are you?"

"Of course not!"

His hands dropped to the rail. "But don't you want the vote?"

"Certainly not. Why should I? It's a nasty business, politics, and we women are well clear of it, in my opinion."

"Oh, nothing more beastly than politics, I quite agree. Pigs in the sty and all that. But it's rather essential, you know, if one wants to get one's way in life."

I looked down and smiled in the general direction of my hands, which were gloved in kidskin and folded, one above the other, on the rail before me. "I don't mean to shock you, Lord Silverton, but women have been . . . *getting their way*, as you put it, for millennia, without recourse to voting for it."

"Are you quite sure of that, Truelove? I can think of a few instances—"

"Such as?"

He pulled at the wisp of golden curl that escaped onto his forehead from beneath the shelter of his woolen cap. "The suttee, for example."

"Yes, a horrifying practice, quite repugnant to our British sensibilities. But do the widows themselves object? Do their families? Very rarely. So it is not the legality of the matter that must change—the politics, if you will—but the moral constitution of the people themselves, of which women are guardians. Once the women decide they want something else, I can assure you, they will shortly have it."

"You dazzle me, Truelove. I'm dashed if there isn't a fatal hole in your logic somewhere, but for the moment you have me at an absolute loss. Drawn, quartered, flopping in the wind." He chewed on his pipe. "Though—and I don't mean to be cheeky—doesn't that make you emancipated?"

"Sir, I gather your notion of emancipation has mostly to do with the freedom to engage in improper conversation, by which definition—"

"I object. I only engage in improper conversation twice a day, at the outmost."

"—by which definition, I insist that I am not emancipated at all."

"Now, where's the logic in that? Just because your rigid old society has decided that certain subjects—sexual relations, for example—are dirty things that must not be discussed."

I said quietly, "You couldn't be more mistaken, your lordship.

We do not restrain ourselves from discussing human love because it is *dirty*."

"What, then?"

"Because it is sacred."

Silverton wrapped his hand around the bowl of his pipe and leaned forward on his elbows, contemplating the coast of Europe. A fishing smack caught the early sun, and its sail turned to gold.

"Now that," he said, "is the kind of logic I can't possibly answer. Have you stomach for breakfast, do you think?"

❧

As it turned out, I did not have the stomach for breakfast, and found myself a short while later back in my berth, attempting to examine the stack of papers in the drawer of my traveling desk without losing what little porridge remained to me.

The desk had been bequeathed to me by my father, together with nearly all of his material possessions. (A naturalist cousin had received his extensive collection of insects, neatly classified and pinned at perfect intervals in a series of glass cases, of which I had a horror: not because they were insects, but because they were dead. I'm told the cousin treasures them still, however.) I believe Papa had had the article specially made for himself, upon his appointment to the post of personal secretary to the Duke of Olympia, around the time of his marriage to my mother, and I have never seen its equal for both usefulness and beauty. There are clever drawers for paper and pens and ink and everything one could wish, and the inner compartment locks in such a way that only the nimblest of lock-pickers could find his way in.

Perhaps, at this point, I should make clear that my father—dearer to me than any living human being—was not my father in the biological sense. He married my mother when I was just past my third birthday, and lavished me from the beginning with such a comforting excess of paternal care that I have never regarded him as a stepfather, or as anything other than my true and devoted parent. When Mama died a few years later, he took me under the shelter of his arm and promised to serve me as both father and mother, and he kept his word faithfully until the moment of his death. Every summer, during the school holidays, he would take me on what he called a journey of discovery: a week in which we might explore the Peaks or the Lakes, the fields of Bosworth or the Outer Hebrides, without a soul for company except each other. As we tramped across the damp meadows and pebbled sun-warmed beaches, discussing history and politics and such books as we had mutually read, I thought how lucky I was to have him entirely and intimately to myself at last, without any other claims on his time and attention.

But always he would bring his beautiful wooden desk and a stack of papers, and as the train clattered along an elderly branch line, or the wind howled softly outside the window of our place of lodging, he would place his spectacles on the bridge of his prominent nose, lift the desk onto his lap, and busy himself in the transcription of letters and the composition of memoranda. I remember the gentle scratch of his pen and the scent of ink and contentment as I sat beside him, immersed in a novel, and even now, as I hold that same desk in place on my own adult lap, I can smell the good British air, the greenness of eternal summer, and it seems as if my father still sits beside me.

Sometimes, in fact, the illusion is so acute that his image actually appears there and speaks to me, interrupting me in my work.

"What a curious coincidence," he said, as I sat with roiling stomach on my berth in the *Isolde*. "I was not a particularly good sailor, either."

I didn't look up. "Lord Silverton said the weather in the Bay of Biscay was particularly severe."

"But the sea is now calm, if a little overcast. Though I suppose it's a common enough affliction, seasickness. I should try *not* to work, if I were you."

"I'm not working, really. Only looking over these papers the duchess has given me. What a wonder, that she could ready all these documents in so little time: passport, letters of credit, and so on."

"She is the Duchess of Olympia, after all."

"Yes."

I waited for him to go away, for the illusion to dissolve— sometimes it did—and when he did not, breathing quietly instead atop the chair next to the porthole, studying me in that scientific way of his, I said, lifting my magnifying glass, "She has also given me a set of photographs, which seem to have been taken in situ by Mr. Haywood last year, according to her note."

"Ah. The frescoes from Knossos?"

"*Are* they from Knossos?"

"So one must suppose."

I peered through the magnifying glass. "One of the figures appears to be holding a modern Brownie camera, manufactured no earlier than 1901 by the Eastman Kodak Company of the United States of America."

"But that would be impossible, wouldn't it?"

"Yes, of course. It must be something else." I paused. "But the resemblance is uncanny. The box, the round hole of the lens, the leather strap for one's fingers. Exactly like the one I purchased last year, which lies, unfortunately, in my bedroom in London."

"But this is only a fresco, and an ancient one at that."

"True. It might represent any number of objects. I am hardly an expert on the subject of ancient Greece." I set down the glass and the photographs. "Did you ever meet Maximilian Haywood?"

"I did. A fine man, a brilliant mind, though not particularly sociable. He has a certain quality of stubbornness, which serves him well in his studies and his archeological expeditions, and less well at other times. I daresay he'll make an excellent duke, if he can reconcile himself to the idea." He paused and stroked his thumb along the crease of his gray trousers. "I see you have met Lord Silverton."

I made a noise of exasperation. "The fool. I wonder that so clever and discerning a woman as the duchess tolerates him at all."

"Perhaps he isn't such a fool as you imagine."

"Obviously you never had the pleasure of speaking with him."

My father took his time to answer, as he often did. I pinched the smooth enamel of the pen between my thumb and forefinger and listened to the distant grind of the engines. Several decks away, three men shoveled unceasing coal into the fireboxes that powered those engines, and six more men waited in shifts to relieve them. Or so the captain had told me over breakfast this morning, perhaps to distract me from the pitch of my stomach. I stared at the passport before me—*name*, TRUELOVE, EMMELINE ROSE; *date of birth*, 18 OCTOBER 1880; *place of birth*, ENGLAND—and imagined those three men now, sinuous and perspiring and unknown beside the inferno below. Laboring for my good speed. "You think I judge him unfairly," I said at last.

"I think that we often judge harshly what we fear most."

I snapped, "Or perhaps I'm right, and he's only a fool, after all."

"A fool he may be, but remember that the duchess considers him a friend. So might you, perhaps, if you allowed yourself."

"I have no wish to become Lord Silverton's friend."

"Why not? It's just as easy to be his friend as not, and our life on this earth is too short and uncertain not to take friendship when it's offered."

"He hasn't offered me his friendship, not as such. I was thrust upon him, or he upon me. Either way, he's hardly the sort of man a decent woman should want as a friend. He speaks too freely, lives too freely—"

"My dear Emmeline. When did you become such a rigid moral character?"

When I describe my father's actions and expressions, I must emphasize that I never actually looked at his face, not directly. Not that I was afraid of the illusion itself, which I knew could not harm me; I think, instead, I was afraid that it might disappear if I turned to address him face-to-face, and in those days, even an illusion of my father—a *hallucination*, as I believe the scientists call them—was better than no father at all. My impressions of him inhabited the periphery of my vision, not quite distinct, and relied as much upon memory and instinct as sight itself. You might say that the illusion itself was an illusion.

I said, into my papers, "You were the one who taught me to do what is right, Papa."

He didn't answer, and when I stole another sidelong glance at the chair beneath the porthole, he had vanished, leaving me alone to wonder what I had done wrong.

There were four young women and three young men on the dais in the center of the hall, and all were dazzling to the eye, richly clothed and anointed in oil, but the Hero shone out amongst them all. He stood as tall as a warhorse, bearing the shoulders of a great ox, and his fair hair was lustrous in the glow of the torches. He refused the wine that the Lady placed before him, and ate only meat and vegetables and water, and when he spoke the men around him grew quiet, for he had the voice of a king.

The Lady knew that concubines were sent to the tributes' chambers in the evening for the pleasure of the male youths, so when the feast concluded she donned the veils of the slave women and knocked upon the door that belonged to the Hero . . .

THE BOOK OF TIME, A. M. HAYWOOD (1921)

Five

The main saloon of the *Isolde* took up the entire width of the ship along a fifty-foot section of her main and upper decks, topped by a brilliant stained glass dome that was presently crackling with rain, though not loudly enough to drown out the voice of Caruso from the gramophone inhabiting a substantial cabinet on the port side.

"What the devil's that?" said Lord Silverton, pausing in the doorway.

"It is Donizetti."

"Damned mournful bloke. Haven't we got anything a bit more cheerful? *Pirates of Penzance*, now that's a jolly farce. Or else— whatsit—that charming little jig a year or two back—*Merrie England*. Marvelous stuff."

I rose to a sitting position. "No."

Silverton strolled to the gramophone and propped his long body against the cabinet. "Still a bit green about the gills, are we?"

"Touch that needle at your peril, sir."

He held up his hands and waited politely for the end of the aria, at which point he raised the arm of the gramophone with a single finger and set it aside, in the same manner he might dispose of a soiled napkin. "Just how the devil do you know what he's caterwauling about? Or does it matter?"

"Of course it matters. Nemorino has joined the army, and he's just seen a tear roll down the cheek of the girl he has always hopelessly loved, so perhaps she cares for him, too, except now it's too late—"

"Oh, I see. The same sentimental rubbish as you get in the music hall, except it's all right because it's sung in Italian."

I folded my arms. "Have you come for any particular purpose, or only to malign a form of art of which you are entirely ignorant?"

"Actually, I thought we might have a little chat about old Max."

"The Duke of Olympia, do you mean?"

"Do you know, I can't quite bring myself to call him that. The last time I saw Max, he was neck-deep in some damned filthy hole in the ground in Mesopotamia, swearing in five different languages."

I shrugged. "I've never met him at all."

"Never? How extraordinary. And now here you are, steaming across the Med to his rescue, in his own private yacht, eating his porridge and listening to his phonograph recordings, except he doesn't know he owns any of it yet." Silverton levered himself away from the cabinet and collapsed crosswise into an armchair, allowing himself a splendid vantage of the rain-dashed dome. "The captain informs me we'll hurtle into the Aegean around daybreak, so it's now or never, so to speak."

"What's now or never?"

"Why, sorting out how we go about this business of tracking down the needle that is Max inside the haystack that is the bloody Mediterranean Sea."

"I thought he was in Crete."

"Ha! You don't know Max." He reached into his jacket pocket and pulled out a small white ball, which he flung into the air and caught with the other hand, before flinging it up again to be caught in the first hand. "If he hears some rumor about a butterfly's wings touching a Rosetta stone in Alexandria, he's off on the next tide, like the cat who . . . who . . ." The ball paused in his hand.

"Ate the canary?"

"No, no."

"Walked by himself?"

"No, dash it. Something to do with yarn." He shook his head and sent the ball back into the air. "Well, it's gone now. But you know what I mean."

"I don't believe I do. In any case, the Rosetta stone is now safe inside the sturdy walls of the British Museum, thank goodness, and— What *is* that?"

"This?" He held up the ball. "It's a cricket ball, of course."

"But why on earth are you flinging it about like that?"

"For sport, Truelove." He tapped his wide golden forehead with the ball. "I find it greases the old gears when the mechanism's got stuck. Perhaps you ought to try it. You look as if you could use a bit of mental focus, at the moment. All pink about the cheeks and green about the gills. Rather ghastly, in a charming sort of way. *Think*, now. Why might upstanding Max leave his Cretan post in the middle of winter, without leaving word to his nearest and dearest?"

"Has he *really* left it? We only know for certain that he's not replied to anyone's messages. Perhaps he's been busy. It's not impossible that he hasn't even received these messages to begin with."

"There is the matter of the Greek official, to whom he's delinquent in sending his regular reports."

"He may have his own reasons for that."

Smack went the cricket ball into Silverton's left palm. "By George, if you're not swimming in optimism this afternoon. Determined not to fear the worst, are you?"

"I see no reason to borrow trouble. There's usually a simple explanation for these conundrums."

"Conundrum." *Smack*. "Now there's a splendid word. I do like a splendid word now and again. Makes one feel as if words actually matter. So I suppose the first person we should interview is this Greek chap who's got his fustanella up around his ears about those missing reports. He'll be as crooked as a mountain path, of course—your petty Mediterranean officials always are—and probably expect a handsome gratuity in exchange for any useful information, unless we can contrive, between the two of us, to make him drunk enough to empty his brain for free."

"Certainly not," I said indignantly.

He tilted his head in my direction and applied his gaze first to my face, and then my bosom. The ball rolled nimbly around his right palm. "There are other ways, of course. But I daresay you'd object to those, too."

I swung my feet to the floor and rose from the sofa. "If you're trying to discompose me, it won't work."

"Perish the thought."

He watched me as I walked across the length of Persian rug to the gramophone cabinet. Lord Silverton had the kind of gaze you could feel between the blades of your shoulders, and down your spine to the back of your legs: not keen or piercing or tingling, but simply heavy. Heavy and quite, quite blue. I turned the crank briskly and lifted the needle.

"If you're right about the corruption, there is always the possibility that these reports from Mr. Haywood—the *former* Mr. Haywood—were not reports at all, but simply payments," I said. "I imagine his explorations in Crete require a certain amount of goodwill from the Greek authorities."

Smack. "The thought had crossed my mind, I will admit."

"Naturally the official would be upset if the payments ceased."

"Incensed, one imagines. Though not so much that he's willing to risk his own comfort to gambol off in search of the missing Max himself."

The needle scratched, the music began. I turned to face Lord Silverton, leaning my body protectively against the cabinet, hands braced against the edge. He was now twirling the cricket ball at the end of one finger. His head tilted to one side, catching an unnecessary radiance from the electric lamp nearby, and I realized that the unsteadiness in my stomach had quite disappeared.

"Nor would he send any men from his own department to investigate," I said, "for fear of arousing suspicion, and perhaps jealousy for his additional income."

A slow smile began at one corner of Lord Silverton's mouth and spread to the other end. He enclosed the cricket ball in the middle of his hand and extended his index finger, *waggle waggle*. "Why, Truelove. What a deliciously devious mind you're hiding behind that mask of oppressive piety."

"I am only doing my job, Lord Silverton."

"A job for which you're singularly suited, I think. Well done, the duchess. I only hope Max keeps you on, once we find him and deliver the awful news."

Caruso sang: *O dolci baci, o languide carezze.*

"Now, there he goes again," said Silverton. "What's the poor fellow lamenting this time?"

"You would neither understand nor appreciate his dilemma."

"Try me. I once wept at the Willow Song, though—to be fair—I *had* just lost a faithful old hound at the Boxing Day meet at Beaulieu the day before. Awfully broken up."

I pushed myself away from the cabinet and wandered to a painting on the opposite wall, depicting the cutting out of the *Hermione.* On the one side, the Porto Cavallo guns made furious orange-pink clouds against the harbor walls; on the other, the silver moon rode at peace in the night sky, casting a path along the agitated sea. In the middle, the frigate herself, young and triumphant.

Sobbed Caruso: *E muoio disperato . . . e muoio disperato . . .*

"He is to die by firing squad at dawn," I said, "and he is remembering how marvelous it is to be alive."

No answer came from the armchair in the center of the saloon. The drum of rain intensified briefly, and then abated. Beneath my feet, the deck was steady and level but nonetheless alive with the grind of the engine, the surge of motion through the water. As if the soles of my shoes were vibrating.

"Well, you're wrong there, Truelove," said Silverton. "I understand the poor fellow's dilemma very well."

I turned in astonishment, but his lordship was already striding toward the door, moving his long legs with remarkable efficiency, having left behind the white cricket ball in the center of the paisley cushion.

We put in to Piraeus at dawn the next day, under a sky that had turned a miraculous blue while we slept. Already the harbor teemed with fishing smacks and cutters and round-bellied sloops, a thousand sails pink and full in the rising sun.

I found Lord Silverton leaning against the starboard railing near the white bow of the ship, looking as if he hadn't a care in the world. He was cradling a porcelain cup in one hand—coffee, I knew, black as pitch and without sugar—and his pipe in the other.

"There you are." He gestured with his pipe to the scene below. "I'm always a trifle shocked by how much of humanity is awake and industrious at this hour, and in such damnable cold."

"Not half so cold as England."

"But cold enough." He drained his cup and turned to face me. "Why, you're all ready to go."

"Of course I am. The captain informs me we shall be secured at the dock within a half hour."

"Which means we have an entire half hour to take in this glorious sight before buckling down to the nasty business at hand."

"I hope you've packed, at least."

Lord Silverton shrugged his shoulders, which were covered in the thick checked wool of a Norfolk shooting jacket, belted at the waist, and looked as sturdy as Britain herself. "That's what valets are for, my dear."

"Have you really brought your valet?"

"Of course I have. I couldn't possibly manage an expedition like this without Brown. For one thing, who would iron my shirts?"

"*I* certainly wouldn't."

Silverton flashed his white teeth. "Why, Truelove, the idea had not occurred to me, I assure you."

I saw the word *you* rather than heard it, because a bellow came forth at that instant from one of the ship's two funnels, nearly vaporizing the bones of my inner ear. I wanted to ask his lordship more about this valet—why hadn't he mentioned him before, why hadn't I noticed him among the crew?—but the noise from the funnel set in motion a flurry of activity from the various members of the *Isolde*'s crew, rendering conversation impossible. Silverton lifted himself from the rail, motioned to his ear, and signaled us inside.

By contrast, the interior of the ship imbued calm, hardly a steward to be seen. I followed Silverton down the staircase to the landing on the main deck, where a vast array of trunks and suitcases had appeared out of nowhere, presided over by an extremely pale man with greasy dark hair that hung over a yellowed collar, and a suit of clothing a chimney sweep would scorn. A white cigarette dangled from the corner of his mouth. I was about to say (incredulous), *Is* this *your valet, Silverton?* when the man straightened from one of the trunks and I realized he had no left arm, but rather a round silver hook, somewhat the worse for tarnish.

"Ah. Brown. Efficient as ever, I see. Have you wired ahead for the car?"

"Yes, sar," said Brown, in a thick northern accent I strained to comprehend.

Lord Silverton turned to me and explained that, among other recent improvements, the *Isolde* had just acquired a brand-new Marconi wireless apparatus, together with an experienced operator, enabling her to communicate with the shore. Terribly useful in cases like this, didn't I think? A car and driver would be waiting for us at the end of the dock, and we were already booked at the Hotel Grand Bretagne in Athens—*separate rooms, of course*, with another flash of those white teeth—and would seek out Mr. Livas at two o'clock in the afternoon. Was that agreeable?

"Yes," I said numbly, trying to avoid the sight of Mr. Brown's gleaming hook and returning to it inevitably. The smell of his cigarette prickled the hairs of my nose.

"Brown, have the stewards brought down Miss Truelove's baggage yet?"

Brown motioned to an obscure corner of the landing. "Over there."

My single meager trunk looked a pitiful thing next to the polished leather and shining buckles of the Silverton luggage. The traveling desk sat on top, honey brown and lonely.

"Ah. Yes. By my soul, that's a fine old desk."

"It was my father's."

"Of course. Miss Truelove, may I present my valet, Brown, who despite all appearance keeps me in elegant trim when he's not stone drunk. Brown, Miss Truelove, whose word is law." Silverton removed the pipe from his mouth and tapped it against the air.

"Delighted," said Brown, or something like it.

"A pleasure to meet you, Mr. Brown."

"It's just Brown," said Silverton. "He doesn't answer to Mister. Do you, Brown?"

"No, sar."

Silverton leaned close. "I acquired him in Venice at two o'clock in the morning of my twenty-second birthday, having nearly come to a bad end at the hands of a somewhat reckless gondolier and required a spot of rescuing. No one's got a clue how he wound up in Venice to begin with, least of all Brown himself, though I daresay we're better off not knowing."

"I see."

"Have no fear, madam. I assure you he's as sound as a silver dollar, and even more valuable. Brown?"

"Sar?"

"Take my cup back down to the galley, there's a good bloke, and ask them whether we disembark on the port side or the starboard."

Off stomped Brown in a swirl of cigarette smoke, and his lordship replaced his pipe in his mouth and rubbed his forehead with a single broad thumb.

"He's the sort of fellow one likes to keep busy," he said.

Before we disembark the *Isolde*, a word about dinner the previous night.

At the time, I thought the conversation too trivial to mention, but now that I reflect more carefully on the events that followed, I realize that perhaps I was wrong. Besides, a dinner on board the *Isolde* is worthy of note in itself, I suppose, since such magnificent spectacles are a kind of moment in history, and should be preserved in some way, whenever possible.

On that final night of the voyage, I joined the three men— Lord Silverton, the captain, and the first officer—for the first time, having felt too unwell during the previous evenings. I admit, I entered the dining saloon with some misgivings. Seamen, after all, are not generally known for their gentlemanly behavior, but when I crossed the threshold into the splendid room, the captain and his mate both rose and greeted me by such polite expressions— pleasure at my returned well-being, regret that only one night remained—that I felt instantly at ease.

As I said, the conversation proceeded along trivial lines, through a succession of beautifully prepared dishes: oysters, veal consommé, poached halibut, filet of beef, roast duckling, potatoes lyonnaise, creamed carrots, lamb in mint sauce, fresh green peas, cheeses, cakes, coffee. Fine wines were decanted; several bottles, I think, though I allowed myself only a few precious sips at each course. (You will understand that a respectable young woman is not fully at ease in such a situation: a formal and elaborate meal with three gentlemen, not one of them entirely familiar to her, and no female company to support her dignity.)

Not to say that I didn't enjoy the dinner. To be perfectly honest, I have never felt entirely at ease at a table of women, either; we seem to have so little in common, perhaps because I tend neither children nor husband. Like me, the captain had served the Duke of Olympia for many years, and he related many stories about the great man and his travels, which illuminated a side to His Grace's character I had never been privileged to witness.

"Their Graces happened to be taking a tour of the Americas when the unfortunate disagreement broke out between the United States and Spain," he said, as a steward solemnly carved the roast duckling into delicate slices, "and we were present in Havana Harbor that terrible night when the battleship *Maine* met her end."

"How awful!" I said.

"The duke and duchess were both ashore at the time, attending a dinner at the governor's residence—"

"Blanco," said Silverton. "Curious chap. Ever meet him?"

"No, sir. My duties were confined to the ship—the duke was concerned about the safety of the vessel and crew, given the various diplomatic and revolutionary tensions—so I was actually on deck at the time of the explosion." He shook his head. "I shall never forget that moment. An utterly peaceful night, such as one often experiences in that part of the world, and then a shattering noise from across the water, followed shortly by another one, even louder, the kind one feels in the interior of one's skull. I turned at once in the direction of the commotion, and saw an immense orange cloud, flying metal, dust, and debris of every kind. The screams of the injured men rent the air."

"Dear God," I whispered.

"For an instant, we were too stunned to move. It was as if the world had ended. But then I realized what had occurred and ordered the lifeboats made ready at once to look for survivors. I captained one myself, and Mr. Wright here took another." His grave face turned to mine. "I shall not describe what we found in that water. Suffice it to say that of over three hundred men on board, less than twenty escaped without injury. We took all we could to the hospital in Havana. A terrible night."

At my side, Lord Silverton muttered something I couldn't quite hear. His knuckles were pale as they gripped his wineglass.

Captain Merriwether exchanged a look with him, a kind of shared male sympathy I had observed before among British gentlemen who were forbidden by breeding and custom to express great emotion. He went on: "I met Her Grace at the hospital, to which she had rushed at once when she heard of the news. She is, as you know, an American herself. I believe she tended the wounded all night, until the duke almost carried her back to the ship. I shall never forget their faces." He shook his head again and picked up his knife and fork to address the duckling. "They were not merely grieved in the abstract. It was as if a child borne of Her Grace's own body had just expired."

"Perhaps she was acquainted with one or another of the officers," said Lord Silverton, whose knuckles had returned to their ordinary golden state.

"Perhaps," said the captain, and the conversation turned to the political state in the Americas, the consequences of the dissolution of the old Spanish Empire, and other general subjects. My pulse began to quiet, my imagination to return to the beautiful paneled room, to its gold leaf and its intricate plasterwork, to the civilizing effect of light from a pair of magnificent silver candelabra. As I went to bed that night, sound on my feet, mercifully free of any lingering sickness, I prayed for the souls of those aboard the *Maine*, and thanked God that my employer and his wife had been able to render aid at the actual scene of the disaster.

It was only much later that I began to wonder if their presence in Havana that night had really been a coincidence.

❧

But we are not in Havana at the present moment. We are in Greece, where the February sun beat down on the crown of my hat with remarkable strength as I descended the gangplank to the dock below.

I had nothing to carry except the small bag that hung from my wrist, containing a few essentials. To my right, the stewards were unloading Lord Silverton's luggage, piece by magnificent piece, into a waiting cart pulled by a donkey with flattened ears and malevolent eyes. I presumed my small trunk was among the stacks. "This way," Lord Silverton said, taking my arm, and I thought for an instant that I should object, until I saw the extreme bustle of the dockyard, the jumble of foreign white walls against the pungent blue sky, and I let my arm remain in the secure crook of his lordship's elbow.

The promised motorcar waited at the end of the dock, or I

should say the beginning. The passenger door stood open, and against the cab leaned a man in a double-breasted uniform of navy blue, topped by a tasseled flat-crowned hat of the type called a fez. He bowed reverently as we approached. I turned and shaded my eyes for a last look at the *Isolde*—"Don't worry, she'll be waiting for us anon," said Lord Silverton—and I ducked inside the automobile.

"I say, it was jolly sporting of Max to disappear in the middle of winter," said his lordship, when we were settled in our seats and lurching about the narrow streets of the port. "Imagine if it were August. I daresay I should have told the duchess to find another chaperone, no matter how fetching the charge."

"You are not my chaperone, Lord Silverton. In fact, I can't think of anyone less suitable for the role." The interior of the automobile smelled of cigarettes and perspiration. The seats were upholstered—if that was the word—in an old and beaten leather that might once have belonged to a boot. I removed my handkerchief from my handbag.

"I protest. I'm a model of respectability," Silverton said. "In any case, as the duchess well knows, it's all very well for a young woman to go larking off by herself in the English countryside, or a steamship bound for America, but it's quite another story in these half-civilized corners of the Mediterranean. So I'm afraid I'm going to have to be useful to you, whether you like it or not. We are a pair, Truelove."

I glanced at his profile and found the expected smile. To my surprise, I felt my own mouth curving upward in reply. Some sort of involuntary human response, no doubt; readily explained by science.

"We are not a pair, Lord Silverton. We are two people thrown together by circumstance—"

"I'll wager yon taxi driver believes otherwise." He nodded toward the man operating the automobile, who had just lit a cigarette and was now happily filling the interior with smoke. "And Brown's convinced I have ulterior motives, though I will allow Brown is the sort of chap who imagines ulterior motives from the cutlery."

"Why on earth are you telling me this? I am quite indifferent to the opinions of others."

"Just so you know what everybody's thinking, Truelove. I find that sort of information useful, from time to time." He raised his fist to his mouth and coughed. "And it's not impossible that we shall have to pretend that there *is* some sort of formal relationship between the two of us when we set out into the hinterlands. Locals can be so disapproving."

"Formal relationship?"

"Marriage, my dear Truelove."

"I shan't pretend any such thing!"

"Possibly you won't have a choice."

"Then we shall be brother and sister. Would you please open the window? The smoke is oppressive."

Silverton turned obediently to the window and forced it downward, allowing a draft of sharp air into the interior. "Oh, brother and *sister*! Of course! Perfectly plausible. Just look at us! I'm sure they'll never think twice."

"So I suppose you're an expert on all this, Lord Silverton?"

He slumped back in his seat, stretching one long leg against the floorboards while the other bent beneath him. He was really too long for the motorcar. How he kept all those ungainly limbs under such strict control, I could hardly imagine. My own body was so neat and compact, so easily contained in the close quarters of the automobile. I shifted an inch to the left, and realized that he hadn't answered me.

"Not that it matters," I said. "I'm sure we shall find a way to jog along in harness, until our mission is completed."

The buildings were giving way to rocks and brown fields. Silverton turned his head and stared out the window, toward the distant hills. The motorcar picked up speed, bouncing over ruts, and his lordship was forced to raise his voice to overcome the gathering roar of the engine, the draft from the window, the rattle of parts as we fought the road beneath.

"About this Greek fellow we're going to meet!"

"What about him!"

"There's every chance he'll turn out to be a rascal of the first order!"

"A what!"

"A RASCAL!"

"Oh! Of course!"

Silverton braced one hand on the seat before him. "You don't sound a bit worried!"

"I'm not!"

"Still, you might want to sit back and let me do the talking!"

"What!"

"Let me do the talking!"

The brakes squealed, the automobile pitched forward. Lord Silverton's long arm swung out to catch me. A few feet ahead in the open front, the driver poked his head over the windscreen and let loose a fluent argument in his native tongue.

"Something to do with goats," said Silverton. "And unnatural acts to do with goats, if I am not mistaken."

His arm was remarkably solid against my stomach. His cheek had somehow angled near mine, smelling of some sort of piquant shaving soap with which I was altogether unfamiliar. I said, or rather gasped, "Do you know Greek?"

"I have retained a lucky word or two from my early schooling," he said solemnly, removing his arm at last. "Alas, mostly ancient."

I craned to see the road, and indeed a herd of angry goats occupied the beaten dirt before us, daring the automobile to do its worst. Amid the distempered chorus of *maa-maa*, a ragged goatherd in billowing trousers exchanged a show of fists with our driver.

"The poor things," I said.

"You wouldn't say that if you'd ever made contact with the wrong end of a goat's forehead."

I reached for the handle of the door. "Is there ever a right one?"

"What are you doing?"

"Getting the goats from the road."

"The devil you are!"

But I was already out of the automobile, shooing the goats with my hat. The air was colder than I expected, but the sun felt pleasant on my hair, like a warm and benevolent hand. The goats stank lustily of unwashed animal, making me think of the stables back at Aldermere Castle, but instead of turning genial brown eyes toward me, as had the Duke of Olympia's livestock whenever I wandered into their presence, the Greek goats regarded me with the shocked resentment one accords to foreigners wandering through one's village market. *Shoo!* I said to one, waving my hat with authority, and *Maa-maa!* he replied indignantly, bolting into one of his neighbors. *Maa-MAAAA!* complained the second goat, bolting in the opposite direction, and like tennis balls released down a flight of stairs, the goats bucked and bounced into one another, swarming past the goat-herd to the opposite side of the road.

I straightened myself proudly and set my hat back on my head, ready to salute Lord Silverton with a triumphant wave, but a hand clamped around my upper arm and a voice yodeled into my ear, smelling of goat and so furious that a fine spray of foam accompanied the words.

I jerked my arm away at once, of course. "How dare you," I began, but it was really the strangest thing.

He didn't let go.

I turned my head and saw the goatherd's face, flushed and wild beneath a springy black beard. He was shouting at me—*shouting!*— a livid garble of words that defied deciphering, and I could only stand there stupidly and stare at him, trapped in the grip of his hand, because this was not how men were supposed to behave. If you exclaimed *Unhand me, sir!* with all the height and heft of good sound British moral authority behind you, why, the man unhanded you. The better sort of man even begged your pardon for his presumption.

But this fellow seemed not to comprehend what was expected of him, that he couldn't simply take hold of a respectable female arm, clothed securely in thick Scotch tweed, and then—to compound his error—continue to enslave that arm after its owner had commanded him to stop. Naturally one expected, when one traveled abroad, to find different customs and accommodations and what the French call *cuisine*; one even girded one's loins to welcome these differences as an enlarging of one's experience. But this! This was an outrage, a violation of human law, an overturning of the familiar moral universe. As if some presumptuous physicist had decided that time was not time, and mass was not mass.

I was almost tempted to raise my voice. "You offend me, sir," I said, in my most scathing tone, almost as if he could understand me, and I reached across my chest with my other hand, took the goatherd firmly by the wrist, and yanked with all my strength.

He struck me so immediately, I never quite knew afterward how he did it: whether backhand with his knuckles, or in a closed fist. Actually, I don't think he had time to close his fist. All I knew was a voltaic blow to my left cheekbone that pushed the air from my lungs and sent me stumbling backward into the chest of Lord Silverton.

(Though, at the instant of impact, I thought he was a goat.)

The Hero's voice bid her enter, and though the Lady's heart was brave she found herself trembling as she passed through the portal, for she was a virtuous woman, and loath to put herself under the power of a man not her husband. The chamber was rich and comfortable, and the Hero stood in the center, dressed only in a simple tunic and bearing his dagger in his hand, as if he had been practicing the use of it.

'Fear not, gentle lady,' he said, 'I am not disposed for company tonight. You may return to your quarters without molestation.'

The Lady removed her veils and said, 'Honored guest, I am not a concubine, but the daughter of the King and the wife of the Prince. I have stolen here today to help you bring an end to this unjust slaughter of your countrymen.'

The Hero tossed aside his dagger and dropped to his knees before the Lady . . .

THE BOOK OF TIME, A. M. HAYWOOD (1921)

Six

His lordship did not stop to assess my condition. He set me back on my feet and stepped forward. "Allow me," he said, and in a motion that managed to convey both boredom and consummate skill, he lifted his fist and delivered a crunch to the goatherd's jaw, propelling that unfortunate man into a kind of drunken spin that ended over the back of an astonished goat.

Silverton shook out his cuff. "The trick, in these cases, is not to knock the chap out cold," he said. He reached forward, lifted the man from his inglorious resting place, and began to speak to him in measured Greek, as one might explain some principle of arithmetic to a child. The goatherd nodded. I wondered how. His jaw was already swollen, and he was moving it about as if to ensure that it was still there.

In my shock, I'd forgotten that I had received a blow of my own. The pain returned with the memory, a sensation that began with a sting on top of my skin and deepened as it traveled inward, so that my cheekbone felt as if Lord Silverton's cricket ball had somehow lodged in the space underneath. I took my handkerchief from my pocket and dabbed it in the general area of the cricket ball. The sting made me jump.

Lord Silverton finished his conversation with the goatherd—that is, the goatherd had nodded sensibly to Silverton's Greek lecture—and turned toward me. "Dear me, Truelove," he said. "One can see you've never taken a fist before."

I wanted to answer, but there was something wrong with my throat.

Silverton reached into his tweed jacket and removed a silver flask and his own snowy handkerchief. He unscrewed the lid and allowed a few precious amber drops to fall into the linen. "Whiskey's the thing, you know." He stepped close, placed his left hand at the back of my head, and applied the handkerchief. "Though it stings like the devil at first."

I jumped, but the two hands held firm, and a few seconds later a wonderful coolness replaced the whiskey's bite. "Is it broken?" I asked.

"Goodness me, no. A bit pink and puffed up, but that will be quite diminished in an hour or two, I should think. Or perhaps a day. Or two. I received worse in the Wall Game. I *gave* worse in the Wall Game, as a matter of fact, and I'm dashed if that's not when I first realized—"

"And the other man?" I said. The side of my face was stiff with pain, making it difficult to speak.

"What, the chap with the goats? What about him?"

I inserted my hand between Lord Silverton's fingers and the handkerchief and pulled myself away. My pulse was so strong and rapid, I felt the artery twitch the skin of my neck. There seemed to be a dream revolving inside my head, slowing my wits. I looked at the goatherd, who had picked up his staff—the staff! That was what he had hit me with—and was staggering to the side of the road, urging the last of his goats with him.

"What did you say to him?" I asked.

"A bit of this and that. Back into the motor, now; there's a clever girl."

He held open the door, and I climbed in, still holding the handkerchief to my cheek. "Thank you," I said.

We settled once more in our seats. Silverton leaned forward and said, "Carry on, Nicodemus," and the automobile lurched forward. The driver was hunched around the steering wheel, making himself as small as possible, glancing back at Silverton from time to time. His lordship handed me the flask, and I added a few more drops to the handkerchief. The pain was dulling into a commonplace ache, and my blood began to cool in my veins, replacing shock with relief. After all, it wasn't a mortal wound. Could, indeed, have been much worse, had the goatherd put a little more time and strength into the blow.

I nodded to the driver. "Is his name really Nicodemus?"

"So he has given me to understand."

I stared at the tanned neck before me, the black curls ending in a thick woolen cap.

"I may have been foolish," I said.

"Not at all, not at all."

"But he was quite in the wrong. I hope you didn't apologize for me."

"Of course not. I simply told him that, as my wife—"

"Your *wife*!"

"—as my wife, you fall to my responsibility alone, and should he have any further admonishments to deliver, he should deliver them to me. After mature consideration, he declined to do so."

"*Well.* Admonishments, indeed."

Silverton shrugged. "My dear Truelove. As I was trying to explain earlier, there are two things a lady should remember when traveling outside the gentle shelter of Anglo-Saxon chivalry. The first is that it's best to have a husband on hand to clear up any misunderstandings with the locals."

I handed him back his handkerchief. "And the second?"

"Never attempt to interfere with another man's goats."

⁂

I waited until I was alone in my room at the Hotel Grand Bretagne in Athens, porter properly tipped and dismissed, before venturing a look at my injury.

By then it was nearly eleven o'clock in the morning, and the elation of landing in an exotic land had fallen apart into exhaustion and a sort of suspicious disillusion. Not even the familiar gilded European opulence of the hotel, echoing the Duke of Olympia's mansion in Belgrave Square, revived my spirits.

The chamber had its own private bathroom en suite, and when I found the courage to raise my eyes and inspect my reflection in the mirror, I saw that the mark was not so bad as I had feared. There was a red patch atop my left cheekbone, more abrasion than bruise, and the skin had swelled lightly beneath it. I worked my jaw in circles, opening and closing my mouth, and every part seemed to move in order, though perhaps more stiffly than before.

But as I stepped back and viewed the whole of my face, the mark inevitably drew my gaze, as it must draw the gaze of any onlooker. That is human nature, I suppose; we notice the fault first of all. It is the imperfection that fascinates us. Until the mark faded, everyone I met would struggle to look politely away, wondering how a respectable woman came by such an injury.

"How unseemly," said a voice behind me.

I closed my eyes, but when I opened them again, she was still there, peering round-faced over my shoulder into the mirror, wearing the same old-fashioned blue dress as before. A matching blue silk ribbon now adorned her hair, stretching over the top from ear to ear. The effect was almost girlish. I thought, *Well, at least she isn't occupying the bathtub. Or, worse yet, the commode.*

"It was not my fault," I said. "At least, not entirely. He had no right to hit me."

"But you were outside of the automobile, shooing away the poor fellow's goats. His *livelihood*, Miss Truelove. Of all the silly things to do."

"Someone had to move them. They were blocking the road."

The little head sighed. "Dear girl, there are certain public maneuvers best left to the gentlemen in one's party. I cannot understand why you must always jump out in front and prove your competence."

I braced my hands on the edge of the sink. "I wish you would go away, Your Majesty."

"Hmph. What an ill-mannered, ungrateful girl you are."

"For what, exactly, should I be grateful? That you see fit to invade my privacy at all hours, for no particular reason? That there seem to be no possible means of ridding myself of your illusion?"

"You are quite wrong. I have excellent reason to visit you, and you would do well, Miss Truelove, to regard these audiences with the proper spirit of humility, although I must presume humility is not in your blood." A royal sniff.

"Are you insulting my father?"

"Of course not. It's your mother's influence I deplore."

I turned from the mirror and swept past her to the door. "I will not listen to this."

She reached out to stop me, and to my relief I did not feel the touch of her hand as it found my arm. "Never mind your silly mother. It's about Silverton."

I went on through the door and into the bedroom.

"He is an unsuitable companion!"

"That is no concern of yours."

"He will ruin you."

I went to my small trunk, which lay open on the floor before the bed, and began to unpack my few belongings into the wardrobe. "He will not ruin me. I have no interest of any kind in his lordship, nor he in me."

"He's much cleverer than you think, and his reputation for licentiousness, even among my son's immoral companions, is legendary."

"All the more reason not to fear for me. I scorn the practice of wanton love."

"Most women find him irresistible."

"I have little in common with most women."

In the corner of my vision—for I would not look at her directly— Her Majesty descended onto the velvet slipper chair by the window. Her skirts spread out against the cushion and spilled over the edges. "He will attempt to seduce you, simply for the challenge."

"He will not succeed."

"I have seen the two of you." She was waggling a finger now, a plump and unwrinkled foremast that bore a large sapphire ring. "He has drawn you into banter, and his conduct in defending you on the road to Athens won your sympathy. You slept against his shoulder afterward."

"I did not."

"I saw you."

I pressed my lips together. I knew I had fallen asleep, soon after the incident with the goats, and that I had woken as the motor lurched to a stop outside the hotel. *Rise and shine, Truelove*, Silverton had said cheerfully, nudging my arm, and though I remembered reacting to his greeting with confusion and embarrassment, I knew with absolute certainty that I hadn't been lying against him.

But *had* I, at some point in my slumber? Lain against him? One cannot, after all, control the movements of one's body while unconscious. Had he only moved me away prior to waking me, in order to spare me further humiliation?

And if he had done this thing while I was still asleep, how would this mere vision of the late Queen—a product, after all, of my own imagination—how would it *know* that I had lain against him at all?

Her Majesty sensed my hesitation and pressed on, in her haughty old-fashioned voice that seemed to grow—this was the image that persisted in my head—from a bubble at the base of her throat. "What is worse, you have your mother's looks."

I closed the wardrobe door and turned to her. "If you wish to be useful to me, perhaps you can use your extraordinary powers of perception to tell me where I might find His Grace, the new Duke of Olympia. Then my association with Lord Silverton will necessarily end, and you need not dread the weakness of my resolve any longer."

The blue eyes, if possible, bulged further from her round face, so that I feared for their security. Just as quickly, the lids narrowed into an expression of utmost suspicion. "I am not privileged to know his whereabouts," she said, and then I must have blinked my own eyelids, for in the next instant she had disappeared, and not the slightest sign remained that she had existed at all.

~∽~

I would have preferred to remain out of sight in my room at the Hotel Grand Bretagne until our meeting with Mr. Livas at the Ministry of Antiquities, but Lord Silverton insisted we first visit Max Haywood's flat, in that warren of streets directly below the Acropolis. I will cast aside pride and concede that he was right.

"As I feared," said Lord Silverton, as he stepped out from behind me to view the interior, "it seems we're not the first ones here."

"Perhaps he's only disorganized."

"Not Max."

He reached inside his waistcoat pocket. I was expecting him to produce his pipe, but instead he drew out a small pair of wire-framed spectacles and unfolded the arms, one by one.

"I didn't know you wore spectacles," I cried.

"I try to avoid the practice, wherever possible."

"But why?" I felt unreasonably affronted, as if he'd been keeping back a vital secret from me.

"Vanity, I suppose. You won't tell a soul, will you?"

He settled the specs on the bridge of his nose, and before I could catch a glimpse of the general effect, he moved forward to pick his way around the scattered books and papers. I released a put-upon sigh and bent down to begin gathering them up, but before my fingers could find the first notebook, his lordship commanded me to stop.

"Stop? Why?"

"I find it's more useful to leave things undisturbed, in such cases, until we've got some idea what we're looking at."

"Such cases? Do you encounter this sort of thing often?"

He made his way to the desk without replying. Mr. Haywood's rooms faced east, away from the Acropolis and its monuments, and the parlor was now quite dark, though I imagined the sun would flood through the windows in the morning. I could still smell the warmth of the trapped sunshine in the wooden furniture, the unmistakable scent of a house that has not been lived in. I folded my arms and peered out between the rooftops to the parkland on the other side. "Is His Grace an early riser?"

"His Grace?"

"The former Mr. Haywood."

"Max? Yes, the devil take him. Wakes at dawn and works until lunchtime. Why do you ask?"

"The windows face east."

Silverton checked his survey of the desk and turned to me. The spectacles glinted briefly. They were small, but they changed his aspect entirely: he now looked like a rather dashing scholar, a rumpled mathematician unaware of his own charm. "Yes. So they do. An astute observation, Truelove."

"Is that the royal palace?" I pointed to the corner of the window, on the other side of the jumble of orange-tile rooftops laid out before me.

His lordship rose and picked his way through the debris to stand beside me. "Yes, the king and queen. It seems they're in residence, if I don't mistake the meaning of that pennant snapping in the breeze."

"And they are not even Greek," I murmured.

"What's that?"

"The king and queen. Don't you think that's precarious? Inviting the second son of Denmark to accept your crown?"

Silverton shrugged. "They seem to be rubbing along all right. It's been—what? Forty years?"

"But what's the point? I don't understand. You might as well have a president, if you're just going to go around inviting suitable candidates to be king. The royal family is meant to be a link to one's heritage, to the nation's past. Its soul."

"The reassuring illusion of permanence."

"Yes, exactly. It gives me great satisfaction to know that a drop of the Conqueror's blood runs in His Majesty's veins."

"I suppose it would be churlish of me to point out that William was a Norman."

"Very churlish."

"And our merry King Edward, God save him, owes his rule to the kind intervention of Olympia's own ancestors—mine, too, come to that—dragging old Dutch William and his wife across the North Sea to replace the Stuarts."

"Yes, but Mary *was* a Stuart by blood, and so was her husband, if I recall. They were both grandchildren of Charles the First."

"Oh, if you like. But you can't jolly well explain away the Hanovers."

I laughed. "Yes, I can. The first George's mother descended directly from James Stuart, as you must know well enough, if you paid any attention at all to your schoolmaster. Just because it's through the female line doesn't make the blood any thinner, you know. It's the women who saved the succession for Britain."

Silverton turned around and leaned against the window frame, bringing his hands together atop the flat stomach of his waistcoat and twiddling his thumbs. As I said, the windows were shadowed at this hour, and the blue of his eyes had faded to a lazy gray behind their glass lenses, but the austere effect of this demi-illumination seemed to suit him, not that a man of his careless beauty needed any augmentation from the surrounding atmosphere. He smiled at me and said, "At least for the Church of England. No lack of Catholic heirs of the male line, after all."

"That isn't the point. The point is that a king should have *some* sort of blood claim to the throne, or he's not a king. You might as well dispense with all the mystery and the ritual and have a proper republic."

"Call a spade a spade, in other words."

"Hmm."

He went on twiddling his thumbs, gazing at me in such a way that I was compelled to gaze back, waiting for him to speak. The sensation was unsettling, the quarters too close. There was, I realized, something intimate about his wearing of the spectacles. They had humbled him, like an admission of guilt. A faint scent of pipe tobacco drifted from his tweeds. I touched the tender side of my face and said, "What's the matter?"

"I was just thinking I should have hit the damned fool a little harder," he said quietly.

I pushed away from the window and turned to face the room. "I don't understand this. Who would ransack Mr. Haywood's rooms? Why? He was a scholar, an archeologist. What were they looking for?"

"Haven't a clue, I'm afraid. But at least we have a start. We know what they *weren't* looking for."

"What's that?"

He came up to stand next to me and gestured grandly around the room. "All this."

After we had made a general inventory of the flat—the bare and shabby parlor in which we stood, which seemed to serve as an office and storage room, and a tiny bedroom in the back, in which a purse containing a hundred and fifteen drachmae was left untouched—we gathered up the papers scattered on the floor and attempted to restore them to order. They were not varied. There were scholarly journals and handwritten notes—Max's handwriting, Silverton said, and indeed it resembled the script I recalled from Mr. Haywood's correspondence with my employer—accompanied by diagrams, almost always in Latin.

"Why Latin?" I said. "Why not Greek or English?"

"God knows. Max was always a bit of a show-off with his languages."

"I wish you wouldn't speak of him in the past tense."

"Ah, yes." He picked up a leather envelope and peered inside. "I nearly forgot we've got a succession crisis of our own. But I don't mean to imply the worst. I've a lingering fondness for the old boy, though he used to ravage me at cards."

"He plays at cards? He doesn't strike me as the frivolous sort."

"He did it for the mental gymnastics, you see, not for the companionship or, come to that, the filthy lucre in the center of the table." Silverton set aside the envelope. "Are you saying I'm frivolous?"

I rose to my feet and carried the last stack to the desk, which was now piled high with neat vertical columns of papers that had held no interest to our apparent burglar. Silverton tossed the envelope on a chair and went to the door.

"What are you doing?"

"Just casting another beady eye on this lock."

"Why?"

"Only to confirm my original impression, which is that there's no sign of its having been picked. Or broken or replaced, for that matter."

"The landlord might have let him in."

Silverton walked to the window and peered down to the street below. "Hmm. Possible, but unlikely. Climbing through the window, I mean." He straightened and turned to me. "As for the landlord, I already asked the fellow if anyone else had been to see the flat, and he said there hadn't."

"Was he telling the truth?"

"Damned if I know for certain. But I slipped him ten drachmae, so I should jolly well hope so." He nodded at the desk. "Nothing but scholarly rubbish, eh? No business matters?"

"No, nothing." I paused. "Although I'd have thought . . ."

"What?"

"Well, Mr. Haywood used to send his correspondence from here. From Athens, I mean, so I suppose he would have been staying in this flat. Not his personal letters—he sent those from wherever he was—but the official reports he sent back every quarter. And the boxes, of course."

Silverton's eyebrows lifted high above his spectacles, like the hair of a hound when it scents a fox. "His boxes, eh? You mean the loot he sent home to Olympia?"

"Yes, he used to send us crates every quarter, along with the reports. Olympia liked to be kept apprised of what he'd found.

He was acutely interested in the progress of Mr. Haywood's expeditions, especially when he came to Crete."

"Yes, I imagine so."

"Because of the institute, you see. The artifacts he was sending back for the institute."

"Exactly. The institute. But do you mean to say he sent them all from here? He would return to Athens every quarter day on the dot, box them up, write up his report, and chuck the whole lot in the post?"

"Actually, he sent them by special courier."

"By special courier! I see. A singular fact that *you*, as His Grace's personal secretary, would be in the best position to know." Lord Silverton cast his gaze about the room. "I don't suppose you'd happen to have his name? The courier, I mean?"

"Why, no."

"Was he English or Greek?"

"Greek, I believe. I never met him. He simply left the shipment with the butler in London and went on his way."

"There's a chap. And this last shipment arrived at Christmas, am I correct?"

"Yes. Just before his last letter." I frowned. "You don't think the intruder was looking for the artifacts, do you?"

"I think it's very likely."

"Why is that?"

Silverton wandered to the cabinet on the opposite wall and opened one door. "Because, Truelove. Unless I'm mistaken, there's no sign of any of his old rubbish here, nor was the intruder troubled to make off with the small fortune in the top drawer of our missing heir's bureau. And that leaves us with two possibilities."

I leaned back against the desk and frowned at the patch of

blue sky across the room. "Either he sent them all to England at Christmas . . ."

"Or else the burglar was good enough to save him the trouble."

⌒

As a consequence of our activities at Mr. Haywood's flat, we were eleven minutes late for our meeting with Mr. Livas at the Ministry of Antiquities, but Lord Silverton assured me the man wouldn't take offense.

"These Mediterranean chaps have it all right side up," he said. "They're not troubled about the tyrant clock the way we English are."

"A sign of spiritual decay."

"Or the opposite." He peered out the window of the motorcar. "There's the Parthenon, if you're interested."

"Oh!" I lurched over his lordship's lap and pressed my nose against the dusty glass. "Oh, it's more beautiful than I dreamt!"

"Surely you've seen photographs."

"But it doesn't compare. My God, the living Parthenon. Look at the endless columns. How magisterial she sits, there on the hill."

He picked me up and set me back in my seat. "Not actually living, you understand, at least by the standards of most of Earth's creatures. And she could bear a spot of cleaning and repair."

"Don't you *dare* be jaded about the Parthenon."

His lordship leaned back against the corner of his seat and regarded me in the beam of winter afternoon that came through the window, as we waited for the street to clear before us. (Athens, I observed, was not a model of organization as regards traffic.) The spectacles were gone now, replaced carefully in his

waistcoat pocket the instant we left the privacy of Mr. Haywood's flat. "Perish the thought. Do you know, Truelove, I can't
quite seem to make you out. You're so frightfully brusque and
practical, until one turns the corner of a Greek street, or plays a
bit of Italian music, and without warning you're a romantic fool."

The motor thrust forward again, while the driver stuck his
entire torso out the window and hurled reckless invective at a
man pushing a cart piled high with dung. I placed my handkerchief over my nose. The Parthenon sped past Silverton's golden
head and disappeared behind us.

"There's nothing contradictory about it. I simply appreciate
beauty, Lord Silverton."

"You don't appreciate *my* beauty," he said.

"Why should I? You worship it well enough without my help."

"Oh! Well played, Truelove. The point is yours."

Nicodemus released a burst of noise from the automobile's
horn and swerved to the curb, nearly oversetting a carthorse and
its indignant driver. We roared to a dizzying halt outside a smart
new building, and the driver blew the horn again, scattering
another dozen astonished souls from the adjacent sidewalk.

Satisfied, Nicodemus popped out of his seat, tassel swinging
jauntily, and came around to open the passenger door.

The building reeked simultaneously of newness and decay, or
perhaps that was only the mildew growing in tiny dark spots in
the corners of the ceiling. Hastily built structures, I am told, are
subject to this complaint, especially in such climes where the
summer heat reaches oppressive heights.

"Grand but cheap," I whispered to Silverton, as we followed a
clerk down a red-carpeted corridor lined with doors.

"What's that?"

I pointed to the plasterwork, which was crumbling in patches. His lordship nodded. "Rather like the newer London suburbs."

The clerk made an abrupt right turn and disappeared through a doorway. I darted through after him and found myself inside a large square white-walled office, upholstered in patriotic blue and white, where a compact man was rising from a desk and preparing to greet us. The clerk whispered in his ear and stood back.

"Good afternoon," I said. "I apologize for our late arrival, Mr. Livas, but—"

The man frowned and turned to the clerk, asking a question in rapid Greek.

"Dear me," said his lordship. His hand touched the small of my back.

The official turned back to us, cleared his throat, and spoke in smooth accented English. "I am afraid, sir and madam, that there has been some terrible mistake. I regret very much to say that my colleague Mr. Livas departed this mortal realm unexpectedly a fortnight ago, God rest his soul."

He crossed himself. I pressed my hand against my stomach.

"Well, I'll be damned," said Lord Silverton.

The Lady stared in amazement at the Hero's bowed head before her. 'My lady, you have been sent by the gods,' he said, 'for I am the son of the King of Athens, and I have taken the place of one of the tributes in order to defeat this yearly summons upon my country, which feeds the appetites of the King's beast-made son.'

'Then rise, Hero,' she said, 'and I will tell you what you must do to save yourself and your people. But before you agree, be warned that I ask a boon in return, which you may not wish to grant.'

He replied, 'Lady, before the gods, I will do whatever you ask of me, for since I saw you tonight at the banquet I have thought of nothing else but you, and when you removed your veils before me I knew that my prayers had been answered.'

The Lady knew not whether to speak or to weep, for her tender heart had known nothing but sorrow since the night of her nuptial rites. She knelt to join the Hero on the fine rug before the brazier, and she placed her hands upon his cheeks and said, 'I will tell you the secret of the Labyrinth and the Beast at its heart, if you will promise to carry me away with you when you leave . . .'

THE BOOK OF TIME, A. M. HAYWOOD (1921)

Seven

I told you so," said Her Majesty. "I told you, in clear and exact language, that this expedition would prove a grave mistake."

I went on brushing my hair. "On the contrary, I am convinced my presence here is of the utmost importance. Imagine if Lord Silverton were left to deal with the affair himself."

"I think that would be a very good idea indeed. I advise you to take the next steamship back to England, and leave this sort of grubby investigation to those best suited to soil themselves in it."

A sharp double knock sounded on the door to my room. "Heigh-ho," said a cheerful and muffled voice.

"Speak of the devil," muttered the Queen.

I set down the hairbrush, gathered my hair in a rapid braid at the nape of my neck, and rose from the dressing table.

"You don't mean to answer the *door*!" Her Majesty exclaimed. "In your *nightgown*!"

"I'm wearing a dressing gown above all. It is hardly improper."

"Your hair is wantonly loose."

"Nonsense. I have braided it. If you'll excuse me."

I marched to the door and flung it open.

"I say," said his lordship. "Abed already? What about dinner?"

"I plan to take a tray in my room. Have you something import-ant to communicate? Could you not have used the telephone?"

"I meant to whisk you downstairs to the hotel restaurant, but I'm perfectly happy to dine here instead."

"Certainly not."

His lordship edged past me into the room. "A fine chamber you've got here, Truelove. Overlooking the square and whatnot. My window looks into the alleyway, which is endlessly enter-taining but not precisely healthy for one's morals."

"I should think your morals would hardly know the difference."

"Ah, Truelove. You have the most confounded notions about me. I'm as tame as a pussycat, really. Stories all false. Or at least exaggerated to a great degree." He shoved his hands in the pock-ets of his trousers—he was wearing immaculate dinner dress—and turned to offer me a broad and toothsome grin, of the sort a female hyena might find alluring. "Your virtue is perfectly safe with me."

I heard a faint harrumph, though the slipper chair was now empty.

I folded my arms across my chest. "Be quick, your lordship. I wish to order my dinner now."

"I shall take that as a rejection of my very kind offer, and be accordingly offended," said Silverton, looking not offended in the least, but rather amused.

I said nothing.

Silverton walked to the fireplace and removed one hand from his pocket to lay his elbow on the mantel. "Oh, very well. You're a hard woman, Truelove, very hard. The thing is, I've been thinking rather thoroughly about this matter, gears grinding squeakily and all that, and I wonder if—now, don't raise your nose at me—I wonder if you're better off taking the *Isolde* back home to England, while I delve into this Cretan matter on my own humble power."

Indeed! said a haughty voice, from the direction of the slipper chair. *Just what I think. The first sensible thing he's said in days.*

"I see. You think it's too dangerous for me."

"I wasn't going to say *dangerous*, exactly. The contrary. I expect it's all just a jolly queer coincidence, Mr. Livas shucking off his mortal coil just now. Wintertime is notorious for . . . well . . ." He waved a hand.

"Men having their throats cut at half past five in the afternoon, on the way home from an honest day's labor?"

"I was going to say incidents of a violent nature, since the hours of darkness are much increased. And Greece, I regret to report, is notable for its lawlessness, even in this modern age. Might a fellow have a drink, do you think?"

"I haven't got anything."

"Ring something up, I mean. Perhaps a spot of dinner, while you're on the telephone."

"I'm not dressed for dinner."

"I think you look charming." The smile flashed out once more, white enough to match his shirt. He had brushed back his hair with a touch of pomade, so that it positively burnished in the electric light. No one could deny that Lord Silverton was a glossy, well-polished animal, in the absolute prime of its health and strength, and that, as impressive as he looked in his travel tweeds, he appeared even more remarkably resplendent in dinner dress.

"Your lordship," I said, closing my ears to any possible comment from the slipper chair by the window, "you have come here to ask me a question, and my answer is no. Frankly, I am now convinced that Mr. Haywood may stand in real danger, and my participation in this search has become even more urgent than before."

"*More* urgent? I say, that's humbling. You think I'll foul things up on my own, do you? Where's the *trust*, Truelove?"

"It's not a matter of trust. I simply believe—as does the dowager duchess, I should like to point out—that my intimate knowledge of the duchy's affairs may prove essential to discovering the whereabouts of Mr. Haywood."

"The dowager duchess was not aware that flats had been ransacked and chaps murdered in Athenian alleyways."

"Why should that make any difference?"

Silverton's elbow fell from the mantel. "Because you're a gently bred female, Truelove, not a trained agent! I'm going to ring for a drink. If you want one, speak now."

He strode to the telephone on the desk, muttering under his breath, and I thought, as I watched him, that there was nothing lazy about Lord Silverton in this particular moment. That his movements had, without warning, turned quick and competent, and that his voice—well, not commanding. Not entirely divested of its languid aristocratic drawl. But perhaps . . . authoritative.

Yes. That was it. Authoritative. The way he had sounded, from time to time, while we were searching Mr. Haywood's flat. The way he had spoken Greek to the goatherd—not a broken schoolboy word or two, but fluently.

The way he had taken the shocking news of Mr. Livas's death:

nonplussed, even methodical, asking questions as if he already knew exactly which questions to ask.

Because you're a gently bred female, Truelove, not a trained agent.

His lordship stood beneath the electric chandelier, and it is no more than the truth to say that the light touched his golden head like a nimbus, an effect so splendid that it caused a smaller spark to flicker into being inside the chambers of my own mind.

Or perhaps I have not properly expressed the instant of revelation. Perhaps it was more like the lifting of a curtain, the opening of an eyelid that had, until now, remained willfully shut.

"A trained agent," I said slowly. "A trained agent, did you say, sir?"

He picked up the telephone and brought the receiver to his ear. "Hello? Hello? Front desk?" Pause. "I say, would you speak a little louder?"

He toggled the switch hook, muttered again, and frowned. "Hello? Yes, yes. Room three hundred and—" He raised an eyebrow in my direction.

"Twelve," I said.

"Room three hundred and twelve. Yes. Yes. Yes, I quite understand that's Miss Truelove's room. No, no. I am not Miss Truelove."

I was not a fool, nor did I lack the rudimentary powers of observation. From the earliest days of my employment with the Duke of Olympia, or at least as soon as I had emerged from the fog of grief that surrounded my father's death, I had had some inkling of His Grace's involvement in certain confidential affairs of the kingdom of Great Britain. Couriers had sometimes arrived in the middle of the night, requiring immediate attention; His Grace might disappear for a few days, entirely without warning or explanation; the odd gentleman, dressed in dark and nondescript clothing, would hustle inside through the service entrance and confer with the duke behind a locked door. Once, I had entered His Grace's study at my usual hour of seven o'clock in the morning, and found a few tiny spots of blood on the rug, which had disappeared by the time I returned from lunch.

Lord Silverton was still gazing at me from that sideways aspect of his, eyebrow arched, sly smile curving the lips. One hand held the transmitter to his chin, the other secured the receiver to his ear. The skin of his neck was tawny against the sharp white collar of his shirt. "No, not her brother. Let's just say she's a friend of mine, shall we? A very dear friend who so happens to require my company at the present moment."

I had never inquired into those occasions, nor allowed myself to speculate on their meaning. His Grace employed me to carry out the duties of a personal secretary, not to involve myself in affairs he clearly wished to keep private. I merely presumed, using the logic with which God had granted me, that a man so wise and so influential should naturally become privy to any number of the nation's secrets, and that I might best serve him—and my beloved Great Britain—by allowing myself to discover no more about them than the duke saw fit to relate to me.

"Why, what an insinuating question, my good man. I don't see that it's any of your business, to be perfectly frank. No, you may not speak to Miss Truelove yourself. She's not receiving visitors, either by sight or sound. Well, except me, of course." A dashing wink.

But now it seemed to me that those secrets were being thrust upon me, one by one, in the manner of what I believe the professionals at Scotland Yard call *clues*. There was, for instance, this institute: a collaboration between the Duke of Olympia and his heir. There was the quarterly shipment of mysterious objects and the official report from Mr. Haywood to the duke. There was a dead body, and a missing man, and a ransacked flat, and a sense of urgency I had understood from the beginning.

There was the Marquess of Silverton, who was—as the Queen herself had rightly observed—a little more clever than he let on.

"I say, what the devil sort of establishment are you running, where a fellow has to endure the Spanish Inquisition in order to have a bottle of brandy sent to his room? Yes, yes. You're quite right. In point of fact, it's not *my* room, at least as a matter of legal tenancy. But—"

I marched across the rug, reached between Lord Silverton's glossy black arms, and pressed down firmly on the switch hook.

His lordship set down the device and turned to me with an expression of great affront. "Now, why the devil did you do that? I'll have to start all over from the beginning."

I know not from what hidden reserve of daring I found the courage to reach inside Lord Silverton's jacket, grasp the expected pipe, and draw it forth from the warmth of its pocket. Perhaps I was simply angry at myself: angry that I had not assembled these clues together at the outset and produced the truth; angry that I had, in short, allowed this fool to fool me. My pride was wounded, and wanted to assert itself before the man who had wounded it.

Or, if I am scrupulous, and with the benefit of hindsight, I will allow the possibility of another explanation: that Her Majesty was perhaps more wise—or at least more perceptive—than I was willing to admit at the time.

Whatever the reason for my actions, however, I could see that while I had surprised Lord Silverton by this uninvited and deeply personal gesture, he minded my brass not a bit. He placed his thumbs into the slim pockets of his waistcoat and gave me the sort of look men give to women who are flirting with them.

I held out the pipe to his starched white chest. "I think that's an excellent idea, sir. I should like you to make yourself comfortable and start all over, from the very beginning, and *this* time tell me *exactly* what the devil is going on."

'Dear Lady,' said the Hero, 'this is not a boon you ask of me, but the wish of my own heart, and I will obey you in this and in all things. But if I am destined to carry away the wife of another man, and to take her for my own, I must know whether she is determined in our course, and whether the crimes of her husband are equal to the sin of abandoning him.'

Said the Lady, 'You would not ask me this, if you knew what he is. The Prince himself is the author of this cruel custom we have inflicted on your country, and it is he, *and not my poor brother,* who feeds his perverse lusts with the flesh of your Athens youth. He is not a husband to me, but a jailer; he has not honored the majesty of my blood, but rather used it for his own gratification. He has deceived and corrupted my father and defamed my beloved brother, and his time is spent chiefly in drink and in carnal heat, wherein his only pleasure flows from the agony of others.' She unfastened her tunic and bared her limbs to the Hero's gaze, and said, 'These are the scars I have earned on our nuptial couch . . .'

THE BOOK OF TIME, A. M. HAYWOOD (1921)

Eight

In the same spirit of recklessness, I allowed myself a tumbler of brandy from the squat bottle that arrived in the company of a cold supper and a scandalized waiter. Lord Silverton assured me it was a fine old cognac from a reputable cave in the north of France. I forget the name. In any case, it didn't matter. I was not drinking the brandy for the pleasure of it.

"There's not much to tell, really," said his lordship, settling his long shanks into an armchair that could only just accommodate them. He held his pipe in one hand and his own glass in another; the remains of the supper littered the round white-clothed table between us. (He had refused to speak business on an empty stomach: an elegant piece of bribery.) "I was cursed at birth with a bit of a head for numbers, and Olympia caught wind of it from my father, who *would* boast about these things whenever you gave him a bottle of wine and a good cigar. So they brought me a snatch of code to decipher, really a most elementary thing, and I suppose they must have been hard up for help at the time, because the next thing I knew, I was on the boat train for Paris and thence to Leipzig, the most confounded balls-up. Lucky to escape with my hide intact, but there you have it. Caught. Once you start, it's fantastically hard to stop." He stuck his pipe in his mouth and sucked thoughtfully.

"Why?"

"The excitement, Truelove. The ecstasy of danger."

I was drinking my brandy in careful sips from the comfort of the slipper chair by the window. I had half expected to hear an outraged gasp as I settled myself into the cushion, but Her Majesty was either mute or gone entirely. My father had fed me my first taste of liquor when I was eighteen, and a heavy fall of snow had caught us unawares during the journey from Petersfield station to Aldermere one winter, the last winter of his life. The cart was stuck fast, the driver drunk and cursing, the horse unable to go on. We had taken shelter in a gamekeeper's cottage a mile or so away, and Father had found a few bottles in the larder, covered in dust. He poured me a glassful while the driver attempted to start a fire in the dirty grate. *Never mind the bite, my dear,* he said. *It will warm you from the inside out.* And he was right. Then the old coals had taken hold at last, and my outsides had warmed, too, and before long we were a jolly threesome, right through that winter night, waiting out the storm in the gamekeeper's cottage with our brandy and our sizzling dirty fire. When the sun rose the next morning, my head ached like the devil, but I thought it had been worth it, to laugh like that with my father and the cart driver, whose name I cannot now recall.

As I swallowed my first drink from the tumbler Lord Silverton had poured me, I thought I could hear my father's voice: *Never mind the bite, my dear.* The brandy burned down my throat and settled, fuming, in my stomach.

"Have you ever killed anybody?" I asked.

Silverton blew out a shapely cloud of smoke. "Only when the bloke deserved it."

Another sip.

"I suppose it doesn't matter, your history. What matters is what we're doing now. Who put you up to this, and why? What does Mr. Haywood's disappearance have to do with—well, with whatever it is you do?"

"I haven't a clue, actually."

"Don't play the idiot, your lordship."

He laughed. "I'm not *playing* the idiot, my dear Truelove. I'm quite in the dark. Her Grace told me the bare facts of the matter—Max missing, Olympia dead—and asked if I would—"

"Wait a moment." I shook my head, because the pungency of the brandy was already blunting the edges of my intellect. "*Olympia?* Do you mean to say that His Grace—that his death—" I couldn't say the word.

"Well, it *is* suspicious, isn't it? Coming to a bad end like that, in a half-frozen trout stream in February. What was he doing there? How had he gotten in? Her Grace didn't like the look of it, not a bit, and when it emerged that Max was missing, and up to his ears with Olympia in this dashed institute of theirs, why, she called me in at once. That was the day before the funeral." His brandy was gone. He reached for the bottle. I stared at his wrist as he poured, at the band of golden skin stretching out below his cuff, and the fine hairs springing out from his pores in amazing detail. I thought I could count each one.

"The institute," I repeated.

"Yes, the institute. Olympia's final passion." Silverton lifted his glass to the light and shut one eye. "Not even the duchess could tell me exactly what it was about. Perhaps you can enlighten me."

"Not really. I understand—*understood*—that it's meant to be a special research laboratory, for the study of certain objects that Mr. Haywood had encountered in the course of his many expeditions. But the duke never explained what they were, exactly. The objects. They would arrive in those quarterly parcels, and he would open them all himself."

"And you never asked?"

"It was not my place."

"Your *place*, Truelove? Now there's a good question. The crux of the matter, the mystery that is Truelove. What exactly *is* your place?"

I didn't answer. My insides were now quite warm and cozy, and my glass was empty. His lordship glanced at it and rose, carrying the brandy bottle with him. I covered the glass with my hand.

"Only one, Truelove? Tsk, tsk. That's no way to get properly tight."

"I don't wish to become inebriated." I looked up at his looming face, which had taken on a hint of flush, not unbecoming. There was something loose about him now, some tiny screw that had become unbolted, and yet he seemed to conduct himself under perfect control. His pupils were steady, his words precise.

"Why not?" he asked.

The answer to this question was perfectly obvious, and yet when I opened my mouth, I found there was no argument inside. "Because," I said feebly.

His face came closer. I smelled the brandy on his breath, the weedy note of his tobacco. The pipe nestled in his other hand, brewing quietly. "Because why?"

"Because it isn't seemly."

His lordship straightened and smiled, slipping the very tip of the pipe into the corner of his mouth. "Ah, well. You've got me there, right enough. It's not seemly at all, getting tight. But it's jolly good fun, from time to time, especially when one happens to like one's companions in debauchery. And I like you, Truelove." He removed the pipe and pointed the stem in my direction. "I like you. I really do."

The brandy's warmth had spread outward to my skin, making it singe, making each hair stand erect in its follicle. I imagined I must be quite pink. I looked upward at Lord Silverton's face, which was not so close now as at its unnerving apogee, but still hovered within the reach of my arm. I could, if I wished, stretch out my hand and touch the small, smooth cleft at the end of his chin.

"About the institute, your lordship."

"Yes. About that. Damned curious. I mean, what sort of objects?" He returned to his chair, swinging the brandy bottle at his side, chewing on his pipe, and fell back into his seat as the toppling of a black-and-white tree. "I've known Olympia for years. Never a more practical fellow on the face of the earth. So what's old Max been digging up that interests a man who, I dare guess, never glimpsed an archeological treatise in his life?"

"Don't you know?"

He shook his head. "Do you?"

"But the photographs. Didn't the duchess show you?"

"What photographs?"

His lordship wore his blank face: the expression that I could not yet determine was genuine or feigned. It was a neat trick, I realized, a genius ploy. You always took away more information than you gave.

"Do you always answer a question with another question?" I said.

A smile stretched slowly from the corner of his mouth, the opposite of the one that held the pipe. He leaned forward, balancing the tumbler of brandy between his forefingers, and said, "I really don't know about the photographs. What are they?"

I rose and placed my empty tumbler on the table, next to the plate that had once held my supper. A cold Greek supper: pickled fish and olives, rice stuffed in tangy grape leaves. I had expected to endure it, and found instead that I was reaching for more. I presumed I must have been hungrier than I realized.

The photographs still lay in the bottom drawer of my traveling desk. I took the key from my satchel and unlocked the drawer. As I did so, I considered the note that I had found among the papers, written in the duchess's exquisite hand: *To be kept strictly confidential.* Surely she had not meant *kept from Lord Silverton?* She would not have sent him with me if he weren't to be trusted.

On the other hand, the duchess hadn't seen fit to share these photographs with Silverton *before* our departure, had she?

Well, it was too late for doubts. I drew the photographs from their drawer and returned to Lord Silverton, who had risen politely and now stood next to the table, draining the last of his brandy. The pipe lay propped against his plate. He set down the glass and held out his hand.

"These are from Knossos. Is that right?" he said, holding the first photograph up for inspection, squinting ever so slightly.

"I presume so, yes."

"I don't quite understand. It's a painting, obviously. Three figures. Very lovely, fine rendering and all that, somewhat the worse for wear. Did they find this on a wall somewhere? Is it an original, or have they restored it?"

"I don't know. What I *do* know is that the object in the first man's right hand did not exist three thousand years ago."

Silverton brought the photograph another inch closer to his face and turned it to the light. For a moment, his expression remained puzzled: the squint deepened, the lines of his forehead compressed in concentration.

And then the doubt fell away.

"I'll be damned," he said, and as the word *damned* left his mouth, a pair of sharp knocks sounded on the door.

"Room service!" sang out a cheerful voice.

Silverton met my gaze above the edge of the photograph, glanced at the littered table, and then returned to me. A small kink had developed in his left eyebrow. "Peculiar," he said. "I'd swear that didn't sound like a Greek."

⌒⌒

When I began my employment with the Duke of Olympia, he and the duchess had, perhaps, already passed the absolute zenith of life, but they nonetheless maintained a wide and active circle of friends, who arrived in their dozens for parties in town and Friday-to-Mondays in the country.

In the course of my duties, I often accompanied Their Graces into Hampshire (during the winter season) and the hunting lodge near Dundee (during the grouse season) and such was their generosity—or perhaps it was the duchess's American egalitarianism—I was always given a room on the splendor of the second floor, among the guests, though at the quietest end of a minor corridor. As a matter of habit, I retired to this room directly after dinner, read for an hour or two, and then turned off the lamp no later than eleven o'clock and went to sleep, glorying in my independence and my self-discipline.

As you might guess, however, mine was not the general habit of the rest of the house party, particularly in those long-ago days of furtive hedonism, when one changed clothes five times a day and lovers nearly as often. The midnight hour was then famous for assignation, which was why the duchess always kindly situated me so far away from the well-trafficked corridors, in a small and beautifully furnished room with a private attached bathroom. I can picture that room still, and the rose-colored drapes on the magnificent windows, which overlooked the yew maze. The bed was new and quite wide, so that I could stretch my limbs almost into infinity without reaching the edge of the mattress.

But never mind that. I had always felt secure and hidden in my tucked-away room, listening to the faint creaks of the busy floorboards as I drifted to sleep, until one evening, perhaps a quarter hour after I had turned down the lamp, a knock came softly on my door, and the rattle of a doorknob.

I remember freezing beneath the sheets, quite afraid to move.

A mistake, of course. Someone had mistaken the room. I should ignore the knock, and the visitor would shortly realize his error and stumble off (one naturally assumed he was drunk) to the room that contained the lady of his choice.

But there is something so imperative about a knock on one's door, so pregnant with opportunity. One is drawn irresistibly to wonder what is on the other side. The sensible course, naturally, is to pretend an uninvited visitor does not exist. But human beings are not always sensible, are they? Particularly during the midnight hour. Just as we convince ourselves to play dead, the urge rises inside us to come alive. To discover what exists on the other side of the door: waiting, knocking, rattling your doorknob.

Opportunity or disaster.

♪

So, in the spirit of recklessness, now enhanced by a tumbler of fine French brandy, I tightened the belt of my dressing gown and marched across the room in the direction of the summons.

"Nonsense," I said. "We are inhabiting a room inside the finest hotel in Athens, not a back alley."

I turned the knob and flung open the door, and there in the dim electric glow of the hallway stood a handsome dark-haired man in monochrome dinner dress, every detail crisp and immaculate and identical to the gentlemanly kit of Lord Silverton, except for the small gold stud that adorned the lobe of his left ear.

"Miss Truelove?" he said, and I had just enough time to recognize his accent as that of America, before his right hand appeared from behind his back to reveal a slim black pistol such as I had never seen before.

I stumbled backward. "Good God!"

"Just as I thought," said a bored English voice behind me, and a pair of long arms took me by the shoulders and set me firmly aside from the doorway.

The intruder's face registered shock; he had not, presumably, expected Miss Truelove to be entertaining a male visitor at this late hour. (A reputation for virtue, I have often maintained, has innumerable uses.) Silverton wasted no time to press his advantage.

He knocked the pistol from the man's hand in one quick blow, and in the second, delivered almost immediately with his left fist, struck the jaw of the man himself.

Under the surprise of this assault, the intruder spun and crashed into the doorjamb. The impact, a rather sickening crunch, caused him to lose his feet and crumple to the floor. I screamed and ran for the brandy bottle. I am not sure whether my original intent was to drink or to strike.

I found, however, that the bottle was empty, which made my decision straightforward. I turned back to the doorway, where his lordship had hauled the intruder upward by his lapels and flung him, groaning, into a chair. "For God's sake, Truelove," he said, chest heaving, "would you kindly restrain yourself, in future, from opening your door to strange men in the middle of the night?"

"How could I have known that he had a gun?" I bent to pick up the pistol.

"Don't touch that. Because it is the middle of the night, and because at least two men have already died in connection with this affair. A healthy sense of caution, my dear, is all I ask." He placed his hands on his hips and stared at the stranger, who lay sprawled in the chair with his head canted awkwardly to one side, exposing the gold earring to the light. "At least we have him now, however."

My heart still struck against my ribs. I glanced back down at the gun on the floor. "You see? If I hadn't opened the door—"

"Yes, yes." Silverton leaned closer to peer at the earring. "Come look at this, Truelove. Tell me what you see."

I stepped carefully around his lordship and bent, squinting, in the direction of the intruder's ear.

"It is an ax, I believe. A double-bladed ax."

"What I thought. Right-ho. Let's see about this gun, then," he said, and bent over to pick it up from the floor.

In the instant he turned away, the intruder's eyes flew open.

"Watch out!" I shouted, lifting the brandy bottle, and Silverton whipped around just as the intruder launched himself from the chair.

I am sorry to say that his lordship was caught flat-footed, despite my warning. The two men went sprawling across the floor, Silverton beneath, while the stranger wrestled to get in a blow. He struck once, on Silverton's chin. I brought down my brandy bottle, which glanced against that dark-haired skull and rolled to the floor. Silverton swore and heaved upward, but while his lordship was longer and perhaps even stronger, the other man enjoyed a heavy burliness that Silverton could not quite shake off. They rolled instead, over and over across the rug, like an ungainly pair of mating insects, grunting and swearing at each other. The room filled with the sweat of masculine combat. I found the brandy bottle and swung it again, just missing Silverton's shoulders, but the momentum of the swing caused me to lose my balance and tangle my legs in the voluminous folds of my dressing gown, and I went down in an inglorious tumble of damask and cotton.

When I lifted my head an instant later, I saw that the intruder—now underneath—had taken hold of the brandy bottle in his large palm. Silverton saw it, too, and uttered a vulgarism I shall not dare to record. I heaved myself forward, reaching for the bottle, but I had too little leverage from my tangled legs, and only succeeded in deflecting the man's silky black arm as it descended, armed with bottle, toward the back of Silverton's head.

The bottle shattered, I screamed, the men rolled over, and the intruder leapt to his feet. My foot nudged against something hard:

the gun. I bent down, grasped the handle between my palms, and brought it up before me almost as if I knew how to fire it.

"Stand back!" I said sharply, and the man jumped around and gazed at me, eyes wide and wary. In that instant, Silverton leapt to his feet and delivered a crunching blow to the left side of the intruder's jaw.

The man staggered back, turned, and ran out the door.

"You're bleeding!" I exclaimed.

"The devil take it!"

Silverton snatched the gun from my hands and ran after the man, disappearing around the edge of the doorway in a flash.

I uttered an exclamation of my own, which I fear does me no credit, and hesitated between following the two men into a public hotel corridor in a state of undress, and finding the telephone to ring the front desk. (To tell them *what*, I was not quite sure.)

I had just chosen the former course of action and spun around the corner of the doorway, when a shattering bang reached my ears, unlike any sound I had ever heard, so precise and mechanical and *terrible* that I stopped where I was, impaled by mortal terror, recording the crash of my heart in my fingertips and unable to move a single limb.

⁓

I cannot determine how many minutes I stood there in the hallway. It was perhaps not even one, but it seemed like hours. The hotel had gone quiet in shock. Not even the floorboards dared to creak. I smelled something faintly acrid.

Silverton? I whispered, or perhaps I only said the word in my head. I started forward down the corridor, but I had only taken a few steps when the marquess himself trotted around the far corner, shaking his head, examining the gun in his hands. He looked up, and I gasped at the sight of his face, smeared about the neck with bright blood.

"He's gone," said his lordship.

"Dead?" I gasped.

"No, just gone. Away. Fled round the corner. I knocked away most of a pilaster with this, however." He stopped before me and turned the pistol in his palms. He reeked of copper, of blood and pipe tobacco and brandy and *smoke*, that awful scorched smell.

"You're hurt."

"I'm all right. Come along." He took my arm and pulled me back into the hotel room and shut the door in a bang behind us. I jumped. He tossed the gun onto the bed and turned to me. "Are *you* all right, Truelove?"

"Yes," I lied.

"No, you're not. You've never been in a fight before, have you? A real one, I mean, not that dustup on the road today." He took out his handkerchief, wiped his neck, and frowned at the result. "Might I perhaps enjoy the use of your lavatory sink?"

"Of course."

When he emerged a minute or two later, his jacket off and his collar pink and loosened, I was sitting on the extreme edge of the slipper chair, staring at the gun where it sat on the bed.

"My collar's ruined," he said, "but I believe Brown can save the shirt. It's a shame we drank all the brandy already. You look as if you could use a glass or two."

"Yes. I mean no. I don't want any brandy."

He grinned. "First thing tomorrow, I'm going to instruct you in the proper swing of a brandy bottle. In the meantime, pack your things."

"Pack my things?"

"We're leaving for Piraeus this instant. I'll wire the ship so they can get the steam up by the time we've arrived." He crossed the room to the bed and picked up the gun.

I felt that faint, wobbly enervation that follows a great shock, and I only wanted to crawl into bed and pull the covers over my head. "This instant? It can't wait until morning?"

"What do you think, Truelove?"

"I don't know what to think."

His lordship ran a finger along the barrel of the pistol. His jacket was slung over one elbow. Beneath his white waistcoat, his shoulder blades appeared and disappeared with the movement of his arms. He said, without looking at me, "Either we leave tonight, my dear, or I sleep in your room with this gun in my lap, cocked and ready to fire. Does that clear up the matter for you?"

I thought, *A man just tried to kill us.* But the words did not quite penetrate my understanding. Like the blow from the goatherd this morning, it was all too unreal: a story one had heard but not actually experienced for oneself. I put my hand to my cheek, which had begun to throb.

"Quite clear. Obviously the matter has grown quite—quite urgent. It's just that I don't understand why. Why Mr. Haywood's affairs have become a matter of such—of such deadly earnest."

"Neither do I," he said. "It's a damned peculiar case, that's all. I find I've become a trifle anxious to see my old pal Max standing safe and sound before me, wondering what all the bloody fuss is about. You'll pardon my language." He slipped the gun into a jacket pocket and turned around. "You're worried, Truelove. Don't worry. Leave it all to me."

"I can't do that. For one thing, I suspect you can't see past your nose without those spectacles."

His smile blinded me. "I shan't let anyone hurt you, you know."

"It's easy for you to say. You're used to all this."

Silverton shook his head slowly and took a step in my direction. The jacket still hung from his arm, weighed down by the newly acquired gun, and his smile had begun to fade, like a falling sun. When I found his eyes, I saw that they had lost their brightness, that he looked as if he had lived in them forever.

"My dear Truelove. One never gets used to this."

A firm voice came from the corner of the room: *Just as I warned you, Miss Truelove. You're losing your head already.*

But no. That was ridiculous. If that voice had really spoken, Lord Silverton would surely start and turn in amazement, and he did not. No, he did not even twitch that flexible left eyebrow at the words I heard so clearly. So it was all in my imagination, wasn't it? A figment, a hallucination of my disordered brain.

I stood in the center of the room: silent, white, trembling. Lord Silverton was looking at me as if he expected me to speak. When I didn't, he reached out and placed a heavy, warm hand on my shoulder.

"Now pack your things, before the hotel staff comes out of its shock and bursts into this room. We've got enough explaining to do already, eh?"

I turned around to gather the photographs from the white-clothed table, and thought, *You have no idea.*

The Hero cried out when he saw the marks upon the Lady's fair body. 'Indeed I will deliver you from this evil man,' he said, 'and it shall be the honor of my life to sink my dagger into his heart for your sake.'

'Let it not be for my sake,' she replied, 'but for the sake of those youths he has destroyed, and for the sake of my brother, whom they call a beast, and whose honor and youth have been stolen from him.'

The Hero scored his palm with his dagger and swore by his own blood that he should free her brother as well as herself, and when he saw that the Lady was shivering from the audacity of her deeds this night, he took her to his bed and soothed her fears . . .

THE BOOK OF TIME, A. M. HAYWOOD (1921)

Nine

By the time the *Isolde* steamed into harbor in Heraklion,
some thirty-six hours after the incident in the Hotel Grand
Bretagne, I was thoroughly in love with her.

Not because I was any less sick this time. Goodness, no. My
innards had forgotten all they ever learned from the Bay of Biscay, and reverted to their original state of disarray almost as
soon as I climbed the gangplank. During the hours of the voyage, I neither ate nor slept, but existed in a kind of miserable
netherworld, bearable only because it wasn't inhabited by a med-
dling and officious regent, imagined or otherwise.

"I say, you're not going to be sick again, are you?" asked Lord
Silverton, as we stood bravely on deck in a brisk wind, watching
the awed boats scatter before our prow. His face was drawn with
worry; whether for my health or for the sanctity of his nearby
breeches, I didn't care to ask.

"I shall give you fair warning, I promise."

"That's the spirit. I imagine you'll want to lie down at the hotel for a few hours, while I head out to make inquiries—"

"Certainly not."

"Very dull sort of work, making inquiries." He was wearing his spectacles, and the salt spray was getting the better of them. He removed his handkerchief, pinched the specs from his nose, and wiped the glass clean. "Especially when one doesn't speak Greek."

"Nonetheless, I should like to accompany you."

"What, have I still not gained your trust?"

"No, it's the opposite. You don't believe I have anything to contribute to this investigation. You consider me a millstone around your experienced neck."

"And you wish to prove me wrong." He replaced the spectacles on his nose and aimed his face at the solemn ochre lines of the Venetian fortress at the mouth of the harbor. "You think it's all glamour and derring-do, don't you? Blakeney and that rot?"

"You *are* masquerading as an idiot, after all."

"I protest. I'm not masquerading at all." He spread his hands. "Simply born this way, I'm afraid. Only I happen to have a talent for mathematics and languages, which others seem to think is useful in this line of work."

"You have more than that." I propped my elbows on the railing and gazed down at the fitful uncurling of the white-capped waves below. My head swam with them. "What sort of inquiries are we making? Where do we start?"

Silverton's tweedy arms appeared next to mine, atop the polished wooden rail. His hands were encased in snug black leather gloves, which strained against the enormity of the flesh and bone within. He knit his fingers together and pressed the thumbs into a steeple. "We start with Mr. Arthur Evans, don't we? He's the chap in charge at Knossos, after all, and a managing sort of fellow at that, from all accounts. If anyone knows where Max is, or ought to be, Evans will have caught wind of it."

"*How* do you know that Mr. Evans is a managing sort of person?"

He looked surprised. "Common knowledge."

Of course. I imagined the leathery interior of a London gentlemen's club, filled with smoke and common knowledge in magnificent gassy clouds, where some corpulent Royal Society fellow was leaning back in his wing chair, lighting a cigar, and shaking his head: *Oh, that Evans, he's a managing chap, right enough.* Then accepting a glass of cream sherry from a passing waiter.

"I suppose that depends on how one defines the word *common*," I said.

"Am I about to be lectured again?"

"No. You can't help what you are. Where can we find Mr. Evans, do you think? In town, or at Knossos itself?"

Silverton lifted one finger. "That, my dear, is what I mean by making inquiries."

We had slowed to a crawl now, maneuvering around the shipping to find a berth against the multitude of docks thrusting out into the harbor waters, and this was why I loved the *Isolde*, even though she made me sick. She was so solid and protective. She had waited for us so faithfully in Piraeus, and borne us across the seas while we lay safe in our berths, free from any danger of gun-toting intruders, and now used her power and dignity to secure us the most advantageous position in the harbor, so that we might disembark without any injury or even inconvenience. Without the competition of other passengers striving alongside, each bent on a separate goal.

Because of *Isolde*, we were ourselves mighty. We could do anything.

⟊

Except we could not secure lodgings. This was my fault, for which I cannot apologize. I insisted on scrupulous honesty as regards my relation to Lord Silverton—none—and the clerk's expression of open greed turned instantly grave.

"Explain to him that we will take separate rooms," I said to his lordship. "Quite on opposite sides of the hotel, if necessary."

"My dear Truelove, have you already forgotten the events of the night before last? I must insist on your keeping a room next to mine, though I should naturally prefer to share accommodation, just to be quite safe."

"Sir!"

"I should sleep on the floor, of course."

"Impossible."

"Impossible that I should sleep on the floor, or impossible that—?"

"Just secure us two rooms, sir. Two *separate* rooms."

He shook his head. "The chap won't allow it, now that you've spilled the beans. I had him quite convinced and happy, and you *would* refuse to sign the register as Lady Silverton—"

"I can't tell a lie, your lordship."

"It's not a lie, precisely. Well, I suppose it is. But when one goes gallivanting across the globe, dodging assassins and ducking bullets, one's naturally put to the wall. In extremis. One's forced to commit a few petty sins simply in order to—"

"Pretending to be united before God is *not* a petty sin, sir. If necessary, we can resume our berths on the *Isolde* each evening. Knossos is only a few miles away."

"Hardly convenient. What about our baggage?"

"Perhaps the proprietor will be so good as to allow our trunks temporary accommodation, even if he will not extend the invitation to their owners."

Lord Silverton heaved an aggrieved sigh and turned back to the hotel clerk, who was regarding our exchange with haughty Mediterranean disapproval. After some deliberation, he conceded that our luggage faced no moral temptation from cohabitation, and allowed us—or Mr. Brown, rather, who was lurking near the entrance, keeping watch on the street outside while stifling his evident amusement—to place the trunks in a single dark room at the back of the lobby. For a fee, of course, which Silverton delivered in jingling five-drachmae coins, casting me dark looks as he counted them out.

"Ask him if he knows where Mr. Evans can be found," I said, when he had finished.

"Already have, Truelove." He removed his spectacles from his inside pocket and set them in place. He was wearing a Norfolk suit of gray British tweed, perfectly pressed, and a cap of matching tweed that settled comfortably over his gold hair. A pair of smart leather gaiters topped his sturdy shoes. He looked like a man off to denude a Scottish glen of its grouse. "He's up at the ruins, overseeing restoration, and mine host is happy to loan us a mule to assist our journey."

"Why, how far is it?"

"A few miles only. The roads aren't up to snuff, however. Years of civil war and all that. Evans's show is about the only reliable source of employment at the moment. Come along, then, and look sharp. I don't suppose you happen to be on familiar terms with mules?"

∽

I was not familiar with mules, and especially not the beady-eyed, rough-haired specimen presented to us in the alleyway behind the Hotel Alabaster. "You can always change your mind later," Silverton said as he led the reluctant animal up the road in the space between us. The sky had cleared to a brilliant Greek blue, and the wind blew steadily in the gaps between the rocky hills around us. By now the hour was approaching noon, and a brave winter sun stood high above the peaks, shedding what feeble warmth it could.

"I am an excellent walker, I assure you," I said.

"Yes, I expect you are. I say, I'm rather looking forward to this. Max's mysterious doings aside, one hears of such astonishing things emerging from the old stones up there."

I thought of the photographs, which were presently tucked inside the small leather satchel that bumped along the side of my leg. "What sort of things?"

"Why, the palace itself, to start. Who would have thought that Knossos actually existed? They say the complex is very like a maze, just as the Greeks had it in their myths."

"Myths often begin as actual events, don't they? I believe I read that somewhere. Nobody makes things up out of whole cloth."

"Do you believe that, really? You think there was an actual Minotaur kept in the labyrinth? Theseus and Ariadne and the ball of string?"

"Not all of that, of course. But surely there might have been some kernel of truth in the middle of it all, some actual beast that was defeated. Why not?"

Silverton had resumed his spectacles, presumably to better negotiate the rocky ground, and he now drew his pipe from his jacket pocket. "Hmm. Yes. Then the story gets handed down, and the poets layer it all over with magic and gods and turn it into myth, until we've got Theseus the magnificent nobly volunteering to sail to Crete among the annual tribute of Athenian youths to King Minos. Naturally, being such a strapping young fellow, he inspires instant passion in the tender breast of the king's daughter—"

"Ariadne."

"—who with fiendish cleverness gives him a simple ball of string so he can find his way through the labyrinth—odd that he couldn't think of that one himself, mind you—to defeat the Minotaur and end the annual sacrifice. The fellow then goes on to perform endless acts of derring-do, aided by the gods, and goes down as one of the great heroes of history."

"I have never considered Theseus a great hero," I said. "It's abominable, the way he treated Ariadne."

Silverton held a match to the end of his pipe, cupping one hand lovingly around the bowl. "Oh, do you mean that bit about how he leaves the poor girl in the lurch, stranded on Naxos, while he heads back to Athens and a hero's spoils?"

"Abominable. And then he married her own sister."

"Oh, but Ariadne *did* settle herself well, in the end. You can't deny that. You could do far worse than marriage to Dionysus. Think of the jolly times."

"Only a man would say that."

"Just what have you got against laughter and pleasure, True-love? Frankly, I believe she's better off with old Bacchus. Damned tiresome, I should think, to be married to a hero. His time's not his own. He's got all these bloody public duties. He probably thinks he's entitled to a mistress or two, to keep up his spirits, and then you're stuck home with a couple of heirs squalling round your feet, while he goes off cleaning out the Augean stables and whatnot . . ."

"That was Heracles."

"Irrelevant. The point is, Truelove, if a woman's got to be married at all, she might as well be married to a chap who's going to treat her to a night on the town once in a while. Who doesn't give a damn if she likes a bit of wine to go with her meat. Who'll laugh along with her when the gods chuck those little thunderbolts their way."

Our shoes crunched together along the road, which was rutted by cartwheels and illuminated almost to whiteness by the noon sun. We had passed out of town, and the buildings had long given way to elegant columns of native cypress. Silverton held the mule's rope in his left hand and the pipe in his right, and his face, when I glanced his way, seemed to be tilted slightly upward, knit with contemplation.

"But you're forgetting the main point, Lord Silverton," I said. "The only point. She was in love with Theseus."

"Ah, well." He sucked on the pipe. "I can't answer that. But it seems to me that if a fellow hasn't the good sense to return a woman's love, she should the devil find herself another chap who will."

The air slipped from my lungs. I pressed my lips together and counted my steps, *crunch crunch crunch*, and when the passage of oxygen returned, I said, "It is rarely so straightforward as that, I understand."

Silverton had left his pipe in his mouth, and his hand swung carelessly by his side as he marched along the road, leading the mule.

"Why, now, Truelove," he said gently, from the corner of his mouth, "one would almost suspect you've been disappointed in love."

I waited an instant too long before I replied, "Then one would be quite mistaken," and I knew by his silence that he did not believe me.

༄

The climb was steady but not steep, and in little more than an hour the scrubby brush gave way to pale quadrangles of excavated earth. A cart rolled out from a beaten path onto the main road, laden with lumps draped in canvas, and Silverton hailed the elderly driver. I sat down on a nearby boulder and gazed back down the hillside, where the square buildings of Heraklion massed together around the mouth of the harbor. The air smelled of dust and a peculiar spicy scent I didn't recognize.

Silverton turned from the driver. "This is the place, all right. Right up that path. How are you holding up?"

I took in a long breath of cool air. "Magnificently."

"Carry on, then." He tugged at the mule, and I rose from the boulder to follow him along the path.

I don't quite remember what I was expecting when the ruins of Knossos opened up before us. Naturally I would not have imagined an actual palace gleaming in the sunshine, flags snapping from the turrets, but I thought there ought certainly to be something recognizable as a building, instead of a jumble of haphazard stone walls and staircases that ended in midair.

Silverton removed his pipe from his mouth, knocked away the ash, and said, "I say, where's all the fuss? It looks remarkably somnolent, for the greatest ancient discovery in modern times."

"Perhaps they're all indoors."

"Indoors where?"

But we continued toward the gravitational center, a series of dun-colored walls that stretched higher than the others, lined with what might once have been columns. I said to myself, *These are ancient columns, these are the relics of Minos*, but my imagination failed me. The expected tingle failed to gather at the back of my neck.

"Just the sort of place one expects to find Max," Silverton said. "With any luck he'll emerge from a grotto any moment, covered in dust, wondering what the devil we're doing here."

"So absorbed in his work, he's neglected to read or reply to his post?"

"It's happened before, I assure you."

I thought of the ransacked flat and poor dead Mr. Livas, and the intruder in the hotel with his lethal pistol, and I didn't reply. We skirted gingerly around the crumbling walls, and at last, carried on the wind, came the sound of human occupation: a raised voice, speaking in Greek, coming from the central structure.

"There we are," said Silverton.

"It's Mr. Haywood?"

"It's somebody, at any rate." He led the mule to a nearby cypress tree and tied the rope to the trunk. I found the spicy scent again, stronger now, and I realized that it came from the cypress itself. I filled my lungs and thought, *This is the same smell that Homer knew. This is the smell that perhaps filled the lungs of some genuine Theseus, as he approached these palace walls three thousand years ago.*

A faint tingle at last.

Silverton turned from the mule and slipped his empty pipe back into the large pocket of his Norfolk jacket. "Right-ho," he said, a little too cheerfully.

More voices joined the first as we made our way to the building in the middle. We turned a corner, and a new front appeared to us, covered with ropes and scaffolding and a few hardy figures. A man stood at the bottom of a ladder in a worn brown suit, looking up fiercely at the workmen above. His hands were cupped around his mouth.

"That's not Max," said Silverton. "Or Evans, come to that."

"How do you know?"

"Evans is a short little fellow, not five and a half feet. I saw him once at a lecture in Oxford, this museum he directs. The Ashmolean. You can't mistake him."

"Then who is this?"

"Let's find out, shall we?"

The man at the bottom of the ladder turned in astonishment at Silverton's halloo. He was about thirty years old, with olive skin and curling dark hair beneath his beaten cap: a native, evidently.

"Hello, there," said Silverton. "Speak English?"

"Yes, I do." The man adjusted his cap and placed his hands warily on his hips.

"Good morning, then. My name's Silverton, and this is my colleague, Miss Truelove. We're looking for a man named Haywood. Max Haywood. Friend of ours. I believe he's been working with Mr. Evans this past year."

One by one, the workers on the wall lowered their tools and gazed down at the three of us. I became conscious of my dusty shoes, my hair slipping untidily from my hat. Next to me, Lord Silverton stood close, in a pose that appeared negligent but wasn't. In fact, the arm that brushed mine was as taut as a magnetic wire, and his position—a quarter step ahead, legs slightly apart—I recognized as protective.

Before us, the foreman took in Silverton's stance with steady and intelligent eyes. He did not waste his gaze on me; I was quite invisible to such a man, in my plain clothes and serviceable wide hat. The silence widened and took on weight, until someone muttered a few words from the wall above.

"Well?" said Silverton. "Never heard of him? I understand he's been working on Knossos for some time."

The foreman's hands fell away from his hips. He tilted his head upward and shouted something to the workers on the scaffolding, who picked up their tools in unison and turned back to the stone face of the building, which I now saw was unnaturally perfect.

The foreman looked at us, and though his mouth curled in a welcoming smile, the rest of his face remained grave.

"Come inside, please," he said. "I will make us some coffee."

For three days and three nights the Lady remained in the great hall by the sea, in communion with the Hero, until their souls were fully joined and there was no joy left that had not been revealed to them. On the morning of the fourth day, the Lady's handmaid knocked on the door and said that the period of seclusion would soon end, and they must return to the Palace before the Prince's suspicions were raised.

So the Lady prepared to depart from her love, and though she knew he would soon arrive at the Palace and deliver them from the wickedness of the Prince her husband, she felt great fear at the thought of their separation. 'Remember to do exactly as I have taught you,' she said, 'and do not forget your promise to me.'

'My own Lady,' said the Hero, 'every word you have spoken to me is graven on my heart, and with the blessing of the gods we shall soon be united once more, and I will restore to you the throne you have given up for my sake, and you will bear me children to carry our name into eternity . . .'

THE BOOK OF TIME, A. M. HAYWOOD (1921)

Ten

⁂

The coffee was of the Turkish variety, the foreman said, the only worthwhile thing left behind by the Ottomans. He did not actually brew it himself; there was a small woman, in a shapeless dress and apron, who lit the small camp stove and measured the grounds in jerky little motions that suggested annoyance. The foreman hoped we liked it strong.

"The stronger the better," said Silverton. "And you, Miss Truelove?"

I said that I looked forward to drinking Turkish coffee for the first time.

Silverton turned back to the foreman. "Do you mind if I smoke?"

"Not at all."

Silverton drew out a chair from the table and offered it to me. I sat and watched him take the neighboring chair, settle his long legs, and withdraw his pipe and tobacco pouch from beneath the wide flap of his pocket. I wondered what else he kept there. The pistol, probably.

The table was long and rectangular and spread with what appeared to be blueprints, which the foreman now stacked hastily into piles at one end. "You will pardon the disorder," he said, in well-cultivated English. (His name, he had told us, was Vasilakis.) "Mr. Evans is presently away, and I have the entire site to manage."

"Oh? Where has Evans got to?"

"He has been called back to England and his collections at the museum." Mr. Vasilakis produced a box of matches from his pocket and bent over the paraffin lantern that rested in the center of the table.

"What a shame. I was hoping he could give us some news of our friend, who has not replied to our recent letters. There's been a death in the family, you see." Silverton assumed a sorrowful expression.

"My deepest condolences," said Mr. Vasilakis, also sorrowful. The wick caught slowly. He replaced the globe, shook out the match, and lowered himself into a chair on the opposite side of the table. "I have kept his post in my office. You are welcome to take it with you."

"I don't understand," I said. "Has something happened to Mr. Haywood?"

Mr. Vasilakis turned to me, blinking, as if he had quite forgotten I was there. Or perhaps he hadn't even noticed me to begin with. "Happened? Not that I am aware. Mr. Haywood left our company at the beginning of winter, and I am afraid we have not heard from him since."

"Left? Where to?" said Silverton.

"He did not say. If he had, we would have forwarded his post.

I understood he was to return. I presumed he was merely carrying out additional research for his studies."

The foreman's English was superb, his accent redolent of plum pudding and British public schools, only without the drawl that would have rendered it fully authentic. I glanced at his hands, which were ungloved and heavily calloused.

"His studies," said Silverton. "I see. Perhaps you had better start from the beginning, old man. I'm afraid I'm all at sea. What studies, precisely, was he carrying out here at Knossos?"

Mr. Vasilakis lifted his eyebrows. He glanced at me, and then returned to Silverton. "You are not aware of Mr. Haywood's area of specialty?"

His lordship's face was perfectly blank. "Are *you*?"

The foreman reached for one of the stacks of papers at the end of the table and thumbed his way rapidly downward. "I presume you are familiar with the history of Knossos," he began.

"Not at all," said Silverton, innocent as a babe. "Rather a dunce at history, in fact. Never could stuff another king inside the old noggin without an older one slipping back out the other ear."

Mr. Vasilakis had just pulled out a sheaf from his stack, and paused to impart an expression of utter disbelief: first at Silverton, who shrugged it away cheerfully, and then at me.

"It's quite true," I said. "He's perfectly useless."

Mr. Vasilakis turned to the woman at the stove, who was placing a series of demitasse cups on a battered enamel tray. He said something sharp to her, to which she replied just as sharply before carrying the tray to the table and setting it down in a rattle of angry porcelain.

"You will forgive me," said Vasilakis. "We do not often have visitors at this time of year."

The woman poured out the coffee in violent spurts. The air in the room—a tent, really, except for one wall made of ancient stone—reeked of damp canvas and turned earth, along with a faint hint of paraffin from the camp stove and the lantern on the table before us. I settled my nose into the steam rising from my cup and inhaled the nourishment of well-roasted coffee.

"You do not take sugar?" asked Vasilakis, surprised. His own teaspoon hung poised over his drink, having already done its work.

I looked at Silverton, who nodded sagely. "Sugar is much to be recommended in the case of Turkish coffee."

Mr. Vasilakis pushed the sugar bowl toward me, and I obediently emptied a spoonful into my cup. The drink was thick and black, and the sugar disappeared at once, as if it had never existed. I looked up again and found that the foreman now regarded me with considerably more interest, as if I were an artifact newly pulled from the earth.

I clinked the spoon against the side of my cup. "The history of Knossos, Mr. Vasilakis?"

"Yes, of course." He set down his cup and picked up the sheaf of paper he had plucked from the stack. "Here we have a map of the site. As you see, we have completed excavation of almost the entirety of the complex, and have now turned our attention to the problem of restoration. Once uncovered, you see, after so many centuries, the features of Knossos stand in very great danger of decay. For one thing, there is the winter rain, which is so often like the deluge of God."

I drew a tentative sip of the brew before me. The strength and bitterness shocked my tongue, and I reached hastily to retrieve the sugar bowl. "How long has all this taken?"

Mr. Vasilakis smiled in sympathy. "Mr. Evans began the purchase of the site from the native owners in perhaps 1894 or 1895, I believe, but it was not until the end of the civil war and the establishment of the independent state of Crete that he was able to begin excavation. That was five years ago."

"I say. Five years?" said Silverton.

Mr. Vasilakis glanced at Silverton with an upward roll of his dark eyes. "The work, as you can perhaps imagine, is painstaking. In that time, we have uncovered an entire complex of political and administrative buildings, which was built and rebuilt several times during the ancient period, and created de novo a chronology of the Minoan and later occupations—"

Silverton held up his hand. "Slow down, old man. Remember the sad state of my brains. Do you mean to say there were separate peoples occupying this place, one after the other?"

"Yes, at least. In the very early days of the excavation, we were fortunate to uncover tablets written in two distinct linear scripts, as well as an older hieroglyph system, none of which we have thus far been unable to decipher, though Mr. Evans finds many points of similarity between the Cretan hieroglyphics and the Phoenician alphabet in his great work, *Scripta Minoa*. Perhaps you have read it?"

Silverton gazed penitently into his coffee. "Afraid not."

Again, an expression of vague contempt from Mr. Vasilakis. "The two scripts we call Linear A and Linear B, as the former appears more ancient than the second. We have dated some tablets containing Linear B, in very approximate fashion, to the period just before the general collapse of Minoan civilization in the fifteenth century before Christ."

"How fascinating. Why did their civilization collapse?" I asked.

Mr. Vasilakis shrugged. "This is not known, I am afraid. There is evidence of earthquakes, fires. This was also the time of the spread of the Mycenaean culture, quite clearly evident in the stratigraphical record across the entire Mediterranean, so it is possible our Minoans were simply usurped, perhaps by force. Though, to be sure, the palace remains show no sign of armament or fortification." He smiled at me, showing his teeth, until I was compelled to smile in return. There was a bang of metal from the direction of the camp stove in the corner.

"All very well," said Silverton, "but where does my friend Haywood come into everything? I don't recall that he was ever particularly interested in Cretan comings and goings."

A small gust of wind shivered the canvas above us. Mr. Vasilakis folded his hands atop the map of Knossos while the light from the lantern stroked his face. He could not have been much more than thirty, and yet, despite his rough work clothes and careless appearance—hair grown out, black mustache a trifle ragged as it arched luxuriously over his upper lip—he exuded an air of polished responsibility. I could well imagine why Mr. Evans had seen fit to leave his beloved Knossos in Mr. Vasilakis's hands through the inhospitable winter.

"Mr. Evans called your friend to the site about a year ago, I believe," said the foreman, "because of his expertise in studying artifacts that—how shall I put this?—make no sense, from the archeological perspective."

"Make no sense? But from what you've just told us, very little of *any* of this makes proper sense." Silverton waved an arm to indicate the entirety of Knossos, and perhaps even the world.

"I mean from the perspective of chronology. Objects that do not fit—most profoundly do not fit—in the context in which they were discovered."

I had set down my satchel at the edge of my chair, and it rested now on the beaten dirt floor of the primitive room, slumped against one leg. *To be kept strictly confidential*, the duchess had written on the overleaf note to the photographs. But what about those who already knew about the frescoes? What about Vasilakis, who was intimately involved in the excavation and restoration of Knossos?

A quiet cough came from the corner of the tent, against the ancient stones, and I turned my head to the right and saw my father, sitting atop a camp stool, one leg crossed over the other. He was looking not at the men, nor the map Mr. Vasilakis held to the table with his fingers, but at me.

I pressed my thumbs into the curve of the porcelain cup before me, now nearly empty. The taste of the Turkish coffee filled my mouth, bitter and sweet and exotic.

"Don't fit?" said Silverton. "In what way?"

"I mean they are anachronistic. An object from one period is found where it should not—cannot—have existed."

"Oh, right-ho. I catch your meaning. But surely there's some logical explanation? Some native worker dropping his pocket watch into an ancient pit?"

"Usually there is," said Vasilakis. "But not always."

He lifted his hands from the map and pushed it toward us again. We bent forward eagerly, like a pair of schoolchildren. "We had already found a few such objects, which we duly recorded and set aside. But it was not until we began the restoration of the frescoes that we discovered something for which, it seemed, no possible explanation could exist." He tapped his finger on a small space on the map, indicating a room of some kind. "Right here, near the queen's bedchamber."

"The queen's bedchamber, eh?"

"Yes. It is a fresco depicting three figures in transit, of which the lead figure was holding an object that can only be described as a device of wholly modern invention."

"By God. Extraordinary," said Silverton, as if he had never seen the photographs in my possession. "And you called in my friend Max to sort it all out?"

"He arrived here last winter, and began immediately his work. He consulted the stone tablets, the other frescoes and mosaics, the objects we had found earlier. He conducted some additional excavation. I am afraid I am unfamiliar with the details of his investigation, as it was kept under the utmost secrecy. He consulted only with Mr. Evans. And his assistant, of course."

"His assistant?" said Silverton, and there was something about the way he asked the question that made me suspect, for the first time, he did not already know the answer. I glanced, from the corner of my eye, at the camp stool in the corner, and I thought I saw my father leaning forward, his finger pads pressed intently against each other.

"Yes, his assistant. A young Turkish student by the name of Anserrat, who I understand accompanies him in all his investigations."

His lordship lifted the coffee cup to his lips. If I believed in such things, I would say that a kind of electromagnetic ether had begun to gather around his figure, scintillating with invisible purpose. He bent his head back over the map.

"I see. And what did the two of them conclude?"

"I'm afraid I cannot answer that question. As I said, this particular investigation took place independently of our own work." He hesitated and pulled back the map. "They departed altogether at the end of December, and we have not heard from them since."

"And you have not made any inquiries?" I said.

Mr. Vasilakis stood and began shuffling the papers to his right. He slipped the map somewhere in the middle and said, "No, of course not. Why should I? It was not my business."

"But perhaps Mr. Evans has made inquiries."

"You will have to ask Mr. Evans himself."

"But Mr. Evans is currently back home at Oxford."

"You are welcome to make use of the telegraph machine."

Silverton had been staring curiously at the stack of papers, and now looked up, grinning his amiable grin. "The telegraph! I say. Bang up to date, aren't we?"

Mr. Vasilakis shrugged and returned a vague smile of his own.

"Where is the telegraph machine?" I asked.

"At the Villa Ariadne, where Mr. Evans is pleased to make himself at home when he is directing the excavation himself. Your friend, I believe, kept a room there, too. It's just back down the road, a few hundred yards, near the Little Palace. There is a housekeeper and a few members of the staff. They are frightfully bored at the present time, I suspect, and will be happy to assist you."

"I don't suppose they would object to putting us up for a night or two?" said his lordship.

"I beg your pardon?"

"We had some trouble obtaining rooms at the hotel in Heraklion." He presented an innocent aspect and spread his hands helplessly, as if he were quite incompetent either to understand the nature of this trouble or to resolve it.

Mr. Vasilakis blinked. "I don't see why they should not. Many of Mr. Evans's friends and colleagues have stayed there. It has something of the air of a boardinghouse, at times." He turned to the woman, who had dropped silently into a chair from which she watched us resentfully. He snapped out a few words, and she rose, black-eyed, and began to pile the coffee cups back on the tray. The camp stool behind her, I saw, was now empty of its brief illusion.

"If you will excuse me," Mr. Vasilakis went on, lifting the chimney to blow out the lantern, "I must return to my men before there is some colossal mistake."

Lord Silverton leapt to his feet. "We will not detain you for an instant. Miss Truelove?"

I rose more slowly, careful to avoid the wrathful tidying of Mr. Vasilakis's servant in the semidarkness. The wind whistled once more past the tent poles, making the canvas ripple.

"Very well," I said. "To the Villa Ariadne."

⟳

As soon as we were a hundred yards or so back down the road, map in hand and mule in train, I spoke up. "I suspect he may have been hiding something."

"Ah! Do you, now?"

"Also, I should like to inspect Mr. Haywood's area of investigation personally, when we have settled ourselves at the villa. Did you happen to notice the place on the map where the frescoes were found, before Mr. Vasilakis pulled it away?"

"I believe I can reconstruct the memory, if pressed."

"And of course we shall have to examine Mr. Haywood's old room at the villa. There are bound to be all sorts of clues lying around. If we're lucky, he may have left behind a note of some kind, or a travel itinerary."

"That would be smashing, wouldn't it? Back home in a week."

I breathed in the sharp air. The wind was still rolling briskly down the hills, smelling of clean rocks and vegetation, but it now struck me as invigorating rather than oppressive. "Perhaps *hiding* is too strong a word. Withholding, perhaps. He had additional information, which he did not see fit to deliver to us."

"And how did you arrive at this extraordinary conclusion?"

For an instant, I considered telling him the truth, or some version of it: the message my father had communicated to me—or rather, the message that my unconscious mind had communicated to me, through the illusion of my father—to *pay attention* to the map, to *pay attention* to the foreman's words.

Pay attention. How many times had I heard him say those patient words? *Pay attention, my dear. It is not the main subject, but the details that matter.*

"It was obvious from his manner," I said. We were turning from the entrance path—the Royal Road, according to the general site map Mr. Vasilakis had given us, which was of ancient origin—and onto the main highway. To the left, just past a crossroads, the partially excavated remains of another building rose up from the roadside, of which I had taken no notice during our approach, my attention having then been fixed on the ruins of Knossos itself. I consulted the map. "This must be the Little Palace."

"Palace, eh? How the mighty have fallen."

"So should you, after three thousand years."

"Touché, Truelove, as always. I say, I don't know about you, but I find all this tramping about has worked up a deuce of an appetite. Do you think a nice beefsteak is too much to hope for, in the heart of Knossos?"

Our footsteps echoed faintly among the stones. I glanced over my shoulder, where the mule plodded along, head bent to the ground, twitching his cross ears in an irregular manner, as if he meant to bolt at the first opportunity. I was not unsympathetic.

"I suppose, if the housekeeper is a female and reasonably sentient," I said, "you're likely to have no trouble convincing her to feed you whatever you like."

"Why, Truelove. I believe that's the kindest thing you've said to me thus far."

"It wasn't a compliment."

"Still." He paused. "Did you catch that, however? Beefsteak and Knossos, I mean."

"Amazingly clever."

"*I* thought so. Always chuffs a man up, to amaze his friends with a bon mot from time to time, as one's humble wits allow. Is this the villa, do you think?"

I gazed past a stand of trees to a rambling, square-built stone house, surrounded by plantings of cypress and palm that granted a distinctly exotic air, particularly now, in the last weeks of winter. The front steps were new and immaculate. "I suppose it must be. It's certainly not an excavation."

"My thought exactly." He looped the mule's lead rope over a nearby bush and straightened his cap. "Would you care to make the first introduction, or shall I do the honors?"

"I am perfectly capable of knocking on a foreign door and introducing myself."

"Then it's after you, my dear. And Truelove?"

"Yes, Silverton?"

"Do be nice."

I saw no reason to flatter this admonition—delivered, as one might expect, beneath the usual devastating wink—with a riposte. I marched up the stone steps and let fall the knocker on a thick wooden door, which opened in due course to reveal a woman of Mediterranean aspect, perhaps thirty years old, wearing an English-style uniform of black dress and white pinafore apron. A small lace cap adorned her hair. She gazed at me in perfect bemusement. "Madam?"

"Good afternoon. We are friends of Mr. Maximilian Haywood, who, we are given to understand, was a colleague of your master, Mr. Evans."

A faint groan disturbed the air behind me. The servant's two thick eyebrows knitted almost into one. She was, I suppose, a pretty sort of woman, if one happened to favor that sort of olive-skinned exoticism. Her hair was straight and glossy, arranged in a knot at the back of her head; her eyes were as large and dark as warm coals, and about as comprehending.

But she must understand me, I thought, *if she is Mr. Evans's servant.* Unless, of course, he had become accustomed to speaking to her in her natal tongue, which was not impossible. *Going native*, I believe, was the term: a common enough phenomenon among the sons of empire, who spent the greater part of their lives among remote populations.

I went on, a little more loudly, and enunciated my words with care. "We have not heard from Mr. Haywood in some time, and have come to Knossos to ascertain his whereabouts. Moreover, I am afraid we stand in some need of lodging and refreshment, as well as the use of your telegraph equipment." I paused. "My name is Miss Truelove, and this gentleman is his lordship, the Marquess of Silverton."

There was an astonished silence from the direction of the servant.

"Well. I suppose that about sums everything up," said Silverton.

The woman looked past my shoulder, and her expression of hostile befuddlement melted at once into the kind of look one sees on the face of a dog who has just caught sight of a rasher of bacon, left unattended.

"A very dear old friend, our Max," said his lordship. (I can only suppose his smile exuded its usual glamour.) "We'd be most abjectly grateful for any assistance you might be kind enough to offer."

The door opened wide. The servant stepped back.

"You are most welcome, of course," she said, in excellent English.

The Lady returned to the Palace, where she occupied herself in the preparations for the reception of the Athenian tribute. On the first night, a banquet would be served in the Hall of the Labrys, and on the second night, the Lady of the Labyrinth was to wash the feet of the Athenian youths in water taken from the sacred spring under the last full moon.

On the third night, according to ritual, the hunt would begin.

Though the Lady kept busy, still the hours came and went like the passage of a snail across a garden, and each minute apart from her love was an agony to her. She gave instructions to the servants to fill her husband's cup with wine at every draining, for she feared above all that the Prince would call her to his bed, while the seed of the Hero was still newly planted in her womb . . ."

THE BOOK OF TIME, A. M. HAYWOOD (1921)

Eleven

My mother was not a great beauty, but she *was* a coquette of tremendous charm. (You will conclude, I suppose, that my character must therefore resemble that of the man who fathered me, an assertion to which I would willingly subscribe, had I any idea who he was, or what he was like.) I know this fact not from my own personal recollection, but because her reputation has lived on so long after her corpse was laid in the damp earth of my early childhood.

Naturally, this interesting information did not reach my ears for some time after I came to live with my father—Mr. Truelove, I mean—at the Duke of Olympia's London town house. If it had, I don't suppose I should have properly understood the allusion. I do remember the first time someone spoke to me candidly on the subject. He was drunk, of course, which explains the candor. We were standing together on the outskirts of a party, a private musical evening hosted by Their Graces, to which they had kindly invited me, knowing my love of such things. The great soprano Tetrazzini had performed a series of splendid coloratura arias, and my whole being was so suffused with that euphoria which follows the experience of great art, I accepted a glass of champagne from a passing footman and drank it quickly and quietly, heedless of consequence.

The action did not go unnoticed, and I was immediately approached by a man of perhaps forty or forty-five years, who offered me a second glass of champagne and told me I reminded him of someone, a woman he had once much admired. Her name, he said, was Araminta, and she had married a man named Truelove.

"Then you must mean my mother," I said eagerly. (The champagne, you perceive, had gone straight to my head.)

His face transformed into an expression I now know well, but of which I was then entirely ignorant. "Ah, the great Araminta was your mother!" he exclaimed.

"Did you know her well?"

"I am happy to say I knew her very well indeed. The most *charming*, the most lovely woman. You have much the look of her." He winked.

"Do you think so? But surely not. I have seen her portrait, and while I suppose we share a certain superficial resemblance—"

"On the contrary, my dear, you're her mirror image." He stepped closer, and his voice dropped to a confidential murmur. "It makes one wonder what else you share with her."

"I'm afraid I cannot enlighten you, sir, as I hardly knew her. She died when I was only five years old."

"Only five years old! Then you must be . . . nineteen, perhaps?"

"Yes, sir. Nineteen next month."

"Charming." He glanced at my neck. "Perhaps, if you care to step outside for a breath of air, I will tell you all you wish to know about your dear mother."

"I'm afraid it's terribly cold."

"True. But your mother was just the sort of adventurous woman to disregard such little inconveniences, in the right sort of company."

At which point in this conversation I began to realize his meaning, I cannot say. I am ashamed to suspect that it was quite far along, because my father had sheltered me so absolutely from such men, and I was unused to the effects of champagne. I remember looking up at his face, which was of the sort that had once been handsome and now lay in incipient ruin, and feeling a kind of trepidation at the intensity of his expression. Then his arm appeared around my elbow, and the feeling became a flutter, and the flutter became a roil of dread.

But where were we? Oh, yes. My adventurous mother.

"I am afraid I am not quite so adventurous, by nature," I said. "I prefer a warm and well-lit room."

"Do you, now? Then perhaps the library will prove more to your taste. Your mother liked a quiet library very much."

I set down the second glass of champagne on a nearby table. "The library is closed to guests, sir, and I believe I must retire. I find I am—I am—" For a terrible instant, I couldn't remember the word, and for some reason this failure struck me as monumental. "Discomposed," I said at last, and I fled through the crowd, sick and small, terrified that he would follow me: not because I was afraid of him physically, but because I did not want to hear more. I could not remember my mother's face in life, but I did recall her gentle arms and her singsong laugh, and I didn't want to think that this horrible, ruined man had known them, too. I didn't want to think that he sought to know the daughter as he had known the mother, that Araminta's sins must inevitably become my own.

I didn't tell my father about this man. For one thing, he had already begun that decline in his health which would soon prove fatal, and for another, we scarcely ever spoke to each other on the subject of my mother. An odd, careful, unspoken agreement existed between us. She remained a mystery, a white void we never sought to fill, and I could not say whether our neglect arose because she was too sacred to us, or too profane.

But as I watched Lord Silverton beg the favor of a meal from Mr. Evans's pretty housekeeper—her name was Mrs. Poulakis, as his lordship readily discovered, though the title of *Mrs.* seemed only a dignity of her profession—and secure not only a pair of well-furnished rooms for our use, but the services of Mr. Evans's private telegraph machine as well, I began to understand a little of what the gentleman in that long-ago party meant by *charming*. After all, it's one matter to experience Silverton's powers of persuasion for oneself; to observe a third party, as she falls under his spell, is another perspective entirely.

"Is something the matter, Truelove?" asked his angelic lordship, spreading a soft English roll with butter. Mrs. Poulakis had just left to bring up another bottle of wine.

"Nothing is the matter, sir."

"Because you have that particular look of distaste on your face, which usually signals some kind of misbehavior on my part. Do you consider a proper meal a waste of time?"

"No. One's body requires nourishment, even in times of urgency."

"Wine not to your liking?"

"The wine is perfectly good, as one would expect, although perhaps not an *ideal* accompaniment to the concentration required of an investigation such as ours. I'm only thinking about how best to accomplish our objectives this afternoon, when the hours of daylight are in such limited supply."

"You sound like a general planning a military campaign."

"Is there anything wrong with that?"

"No, not at all." He gazed at the ceiling and rolled the wine in his glass, preparing to drink. "Are you suggesting we divide and conquer?"

"Why not? We might accomplish twice as much."

"I see. And which task would you have me undertake? The frescoes, or the villa?"

Like all Silverton's queries, this one was delivered as blandly as if the answer were of no significance at all. As if he were only making conversation. His Adam's apple slid up and down as he swallowed his wine, and when he put down the glass, he revealed an expectant smile.

"Which one would you prefer?" I said.

The door opened, and Mrs. Poulakis walked in, bearing a platter of sliced meat and ripe bosom, the latter of which balanced invitingly on the rim of the tray, flowing over from an inadequate bodice that had, in the course of her kitchen labors, unaccountably lost a pair of buttons.

"Dear me." I set down my wine. "Mrs. Poulakis appears to have misplaced her pinafore."

"A great shame." Silverton followed the parabola of her progress around the opposite end of the table, drawing away, away, and then coming near, nearer, until she reached the edge of his lordship's wineglass and leaned over to place her offering at his right hand.

"Some meat, sir?"

"Yes, please," said Silverton. "The breast, if I might."

"Among *polite* society," I said, as Mrs. Poulakis used a silver fork to lay the viand, slice by slice, on his lordship's plate, "we use the term *white meat*."

"Dash it all. I'm always forgetting these niceties. Thank you extremely, Mrs. Poulakis. Delicious, I'm sure."

Mrs. Poulakis simpered—as well she might—and made her way back around the table in my direction. "Not that I mind, particularly, Mrs. Poulakis," I said, "but in England it is customary to serve the ladies first and the gentlemen last."

"Oh! Sorry, madam."

"This is because, in civilized society, one naturally defers the choicest portions of each dish to the gentler sex. For example, Lord Silverton, in expressing a fondness just now for white meat over dark, was only being polite."

The fork wavered uncertainly over the platter. "Some meat, madam?"

"The dark, please. I shall not, of course, mention so *slight* an error to Mr. Evans, though I hope you will take my hint in good spirit. Something amuses you, Silverton?"

"Not at all, not at all. I am only laboring, so far as I am able, to decide whether my paltry talents are better employed in tramping about the ancient ruins where Max worked, or in conducting a thorough search of the villa in which he slept."

"Only you can determine that, your lordship."

His gaze slipped past my shoulder to Mrs. Poulakis's departing figure. "Hmm. Yes. And you have no preference?"

"After such a substantial and recuperative meal, I find myself equally prepared to do either."

'Then the choice is wholly mine, is it?"

"Wholly yours. You have only your own conscience to consult."

"Ah. My *conscience*."

"Your conscience, sir. If you have one."

Lord Silverton laid down his knife and fork and leaned forward. The table was large, and we sat exactly across from each other, parted by a wide snowfall of linen and a pair of brass candelabra, in need of polish. Against the backdrop of a new white plaster wall, his lordship's eyes shone an especially pungent shade of blue.

He steepled his fingers thoughtfully before his mouth.

"In that case, I fancy I'll ask that lovely Mrs. Poulakis to show me which bedchamber belonged to Max."

⁂

One hears often that anger is an unwholesome emotion: a moral failing, which it is one's Christian duty to overcome. I find I cannot quite agree. Properly channeled, anger is not merely useful but sublime.

As I tramped back up the Royal Road to the Knossos ruins, map secured between the gloved fingers of my right hand, the fury poured like melted steel through my limbs and rendered them invincible. Or perhaps it was the wine, of which I had, I confess, taken another glass. In any case, I marched along the old uneven paving stones so swiftly, I might have been born on a mountainside; I skirted the central area of restoration and approached Max's site like a slight female juggernaut.

Nobody stopped me. Perhaps nobody dared. Perhaps that liquid steel actually flashed and clanged fearsomely through my dress, so potent was its source material. A few crumbling steps appeared in my way; I climbed over them without hesitation.

My breath huffed from my lungs, damp and indignant and smelling of wine, and as I went on, I became aware of another set of lungs, huffing alongside mine with even more vigor, and I redoubled my effort.

"Slow down, you silly girl! Do you wish to kill me?"

"Impossible. You are already dead."

"There is no need whatever for this unsuitable display. I did, after all, warn you of his lordship's propensities. I warned you away from this ill-favored expedition altogether."

"I could hardly refuse, however."

"Yes, you could, if you had a little more nerve. A little more sense of what is suitable to a young lady's dignity." She spoke in self-righteous little puffs of air—*a . . . young lady's . . . dignity!*—and dragged her feet in metallic scrapes against the stone.

"There is nothing undignified about *my* behavior," I said.

"You're a fool. Did you really expect him to conduct himself differently? Did you expect him to alter his habits for *your* sake?"

I placed my hands on the top of a low stone wall and vaulted over, skirts and all. "Of course not. I have always viewed his lordship as a cross to be borne on this voyage. A voyage, I might add, that is of the utmost importance and urgency to a most prestigious, a most honored, a most *essential* peerage of Great Britain. A pillar of that empire you so ardently built and championed during your reign."

"He is a danger to your moral serenity." The word *serenity* ended in a grunt, as Her Majesty heaved herself after me. I had not troubled myself to glance in her direction, so I knew not what she wore, or how she handled herself over the obstacles in our path. I imagined her plump face must be flushed with effort, and her hair perhaps loose from a practical wool hat.

"He is no danger at all. I know what he is. I know what I am."

"You will end up like your mother, and then where will we be? In disgrace. *Disgrace*, Miss Truelove: profound and irrecoverable."

"I will not end up like my mother!" I shouted, and my left foot slipped right out from under me, causing me to slide down a pile of rubble and into the well of a stone doorway, shaded from the winter daylight.

"Excuse me," said a polite masculine voice above me. "May I perhaps be of some assistance to you, Miss Truelove?"

I looked up to see a familiar tanned hand stretched out toward me, connected to a wool-covered arm that belonged to the foreman, Mr. Vasilakis.

"Thank you." I took his hand and found myself instantly lifted to my feet, as effortlessly as I myself might lift a small child. "I'm sorry to trouble you. I am looking for this"—I held up the map, which bore a small black circle in the relevant quadrant—"the place where Mr. Haywood conducted his investigations."

"Ah! Where we found the frescoes, do you mean?"

"Yes."

Mr. Vasilakis nodded at the doorway. "The site is right through there, near a room we call the queen's library."

"Right through there?" I turned my head, looked down at the map, and lifted my gaze to the dark rectangle before me, leading into the ground.

"Yes. Perhaps you will allow me to escort you? The chambers and corridors, as one might expect, are difficult to navigate." He smiled, and his teeth were quite white and even, as if he visited a dentist regularly. How and where, I could not imagine.

"Of course. The labyrinth."

"The entire palace is a labyrinth, Miss Truelove. It is end-lessly fascinating. I have been working here since the beginning, five years now, and I sometimes feel I have not learned a tenth part of what is hidden here." He raised his other hand, which contained the same paraffin lantern that had rested on the table in his tent. "Would you like to see inside?"

I hesitated, and then imagined Lord Silverton at his ease in the Villa Ariadne, glowing with wine and food and the eager attention of Mrs. Poulakis.

I looked over my shoulder. Her Majesty had disappeared.

"Yes, of course," I said.

⁓

The lantern was already lit, and I followed its round glow down a number of stone corridors and rooms that led into one another. The walls contained decorations of all kinds, crumbling and faded but still visible, and the floors were stacked with artifacts: some in boxes, and others simply arranged in groups. From time to time, an open shaft appeared, channeling the meager light from the world outdoors. I paused before a kind of seat, built into the wall of one especially large room. "Is that a throne?"

"So we presume. It is of alabaster. You see the griffins painted on the wall behind?"

I squinted. "How beautiful! Have you restored them?"

"In fact, these required hardly any work at all. Mr. Evans discov-ered this room nearly intact, very soon after the excavation began, only a few inches below the surface. A miracle. We have since enclosed the chamber and many others, so that the rains and so on do not destroy in one season what three thousand years could not."

"So these are exactly as the Minoans painted them?"

"Yes. Other areas of the palace were not so lucky. We are beginning work on many of the frescoes. We have artists and chemists and so on. Sometimes there is nothing to go on but a few flakes on the floor."

"Then how do you know what they were? The images, I mean. How do you know that these griffins are, indeed, griffins?"

"Because there are certain—what is the word—motifs that repeat themselves elsewhere. The griffin is a symbol of divine power. It is not surprising to find them next to this throne. Elsewhere, there are many dolphins and such things. And of course there is everywhere the sign of the double ax—"

"I beg your pardon?"

"The double ax. Did you not see it, scratched into the rocks?"

"I— No. I hadn't noticed."

"Well, you must look more closely, Miss Truelove. Upstairs, there is an entire ceremonial chamber devoted to the symbol. In fact, the many replications of this double ax gave Mr. Evans his first belief that this palace was truly the genuine Knossos, the origin of the labyrinth. You see, in the Greek, the object is called a *labrys*, and its image, among other things, has the power to protect a person or an object from being destroyed."

As I stared at the alabaster throne, and the half-crumbled shapes on the walls behind it, I felt a sense of chill wash over my skin that had nothing to do with the dank air in the chamber around me.

"Is this—this symbol still in use today?" I asked.

"I don't believe so. It was primarily a relic of the Mycenaean Greeks, who conquered this island directly after the Minoan culture collapsed. Come along, now. It is likely to rain soon."

I turned and followed him out of the room. "I am a resident of Great Britain, Mr. Vasilakis, and quite accustomed to rain, I assure you."

He laughed over his shoulder. "Miss Truelove, I assure you this is not a gentle English rain we speak of. It is winter in Crete."

"But almost spring."

He did not reply, but went on turning corners before me, so swiftly I could scarcely keep up, let alone pause to examine the building stones for the double-ax motif.

I saw the object in my mind's eye, however, in strict detail: as a gold earring in the lobe of a man in the doorway of an Athens hotel room, bearing a strange-looking pistol in his hand.

"Here we come to one of the more interesting aspects of the palace," said Mr. Vasilakis, "which is the storerooms."

"Storerooms?"

"Yes. They are more in the nature of magazines, and very well engineered. Most of them are on this side of the palace, the western side, along with the domestic suites. The other wing, across the central court, has a more monumental scale. See here, however?" He squatted on the flagstones and pointed to the wall. "Here is a good example, almost whole. The double ax."

I knelt next to him and traced my finger along the rough and crumbling plaster. The image was etched to a mere hairline depth, and missing in pieces, but it could not be anything else: the double-bladed head of an ax.

"What is the word for it, again?" I asked.

"A labrys. So it is interesting, you see, that in English, fully three thousand years later, you have this word *labyrinth*, which we can translate to mean *place of the double ax*. And yet this site around us has only been discovered in the past thirty years."

"The true Knossos," I said in awe.

"This is our conclusion. An exciting one, if one is at all enchanted by the ancient myths."

I straightened and turned to face him. "I have heard it said that all myths have some origin in a grain of truth."

"I do not doubt it." His eyes were bright. "But come. Around the corner we have the curious frescoes that so intrigued your friend Mr. Haywood. I find myself eager to know your opinion on them."

Something in the tone of his voice caused the skin at the back of my neck to warm, but before I could ask him what he meant—why *my* untried opinion should matter, when there were so many experts to hand—he had turned and rounded the corner.

I followed him, breaking into a run to catch up, and then stumbling to a halt when he stopped abruptly, about halfway down a corridor, and ducked through a narrow doorway. For an instant I hesitated, for the room into which he had repaired was small and quite dark, such that the paraffin lantern, swinging luridly from the foreman's large hand, provided the only source of light.

But this was foolish. What had I to fear? I passed through the doorway, ducking my head reflexively just as Mr. Vasilakis had, though there was no danger to my own shorter stature.

"There we are." He raised the lantern and pointed to the back wall.

At first, the rough plaster appeared quite blank to me, and I thought that Mr. Vasilakis was mistaken and had turned into the wrong room. But as my eyes adjusted to the darkness, and to the shifting nature of the glow occasioned by the lantern, I began to see the familiar three shapes rise in relief from the gray surface of the wall.

"What do you think?" asked the foreman.

I took the lantern from his hand and held it close to the first figure. From some distance came the sound of a hard and sudden rain, drumming against the rocks, the way one imagines a monsoon. The air inside the chamber filled with damp wool and the oily reek of paraffin.

"It is curious," I said. I didn't want to touch the old paint, but my finger was irresistibly drawn to the small dark box in the hand of the first figure, the strap around the fingers, the perfect circle that might or might not form the aperture of an Eastman Kodak No. 1 Brownie camera. "Did you ever speak to Mr. Haywood about this?"

"I? No. He kept very much to himself."

"But you must have encountered him often, in such a relatively confined space."

"Mr. Haywood spent little time in this room itself, once his initial study of the fresco was complete. His chief task was to catalog the artifacts we had discovered, to see if any one of them might explain this anomaly."

"You mean finding something else that looked like a modern Brownie camera."

"Yes, I suppose that would be it."

I moved to the next figure, the woman, who was much smaller, and only reached the shoulder of the heroic figure before her. She was dressed in white, and wore an elaborate headdress. The man behind her had no head: that is, the upper part of his body had crumbled away. In real life, he appeared even more burly and thick-limbed than he had in the photograph, and his skin was a different color. Darker, and a little reddish.

My back was beginning to ache from stooping. I straightened and stepped back, taking in the whole of the work in the circular illumination of the lantern. "It's extraordinary. It's uncanny, and yet there's something else about it. I don't have the proper technical language, of course, but—" I stopped, because I could not articulate the nature of my intuition, nor the sour taste at the back of my tongue as I gazed upon those three enigmatic figures. I could not explain to Mr. Vasilakis my sense that these ancient persons were *alive*, even now, straining against the prison of paint that held them against the wall. That they wanted to turn their heads and tell me something.

"I am happy to hear this," said Mr. Vasilakis. "Happy, I mean, to hear that you perceive something unnatural about what we see on the stone before us."

I looked at him in surprise. "Why is that?"

"Because it is my personal opinion that this painting is a fake."

At last the hour of the procession arrived, and the Lady stood with her father the King and her husband the Prince at the entrance of the palace to await the arrival of the Athenian youths. Her heart began to misgive her, for those three days and nights in the great hall by the sea now seemed to belong to a dream, and the great strength and beauty of the Hero the offspring of her own imagination.

But when the cavalcade appeared around the curve of the dusty road, the Lady saw the fair head of the Hero towering above all, and his face turned to hers in the full sunshine of steadfast love, and so her courage returned to her.

By the Lady's side, the Prince saw also the beauty and magnificence of the Hero, and the lust boiled in his belly to see this perfect youth stripped and humbled before him . . .

THE BOOK OF TIME, A. M. HAYWOOD (1921)

Twelve

I returned to the Villa Ariadne through a drenching rain. Mr. Vasilakis had begged me to seek shelter in his tent until the storm passed—they are torrential, these downpours, he told me, but they do not last over an hour or two—but I was too eager to find Lord Silverton and communicate what I had discovered, this monumental news that made my fingers shake as I scrambled over the streaming rocks and paving stones toward the Royal Road.

This time, I didn't bother with the knocker, and simply let myself in. The surging notes of a piano wound around the corner of the entrance hall; I followed them to a large square room overlooking the back garden and found Lord Silverton seated before a magnificent ebony instrument, eyes closed in a kind of male rapture. Chopin. His hair spilled downward in a thick gold wave from his forehead. He broke off at my entrance and stood, scraping the legs of the bench against the wooden floor.

"By all that's holy, Truelove. Did you swim back, after all?"

I thought, *I will smack him.*

"I suppose you have no reason to realize that there is a torrential downpour taking place out-of-doors."

He looked at the window. "Is there, by God? I confess, I have been too deeply occupied to notice."

I snatched the pins from my hat and lifted it, dripping, from my head. "I daresay."

"Now, Truelove. I detect a certain accusation in your tone, which I feel I must parry at once. I have been *working*, I assure you."

"So I see." I turned away. "Regardless, we must leave here at once. I shall bathe and change first, if you don't mind. I am soaked through, to say nothing of chilled, and have been tramping about the ruins for the past two hours while you've been so *deeply occupied* inside the shelter of these rooms."

"Wait, Truelove."

But I was already hurrying down the hall. In the elation of discovery, I had forgotten all about nubile Mrs. Poulakis and the nature of Silverton's investigations inside the villa these past two hours. Now I recalled the reckless swoop of his lordship's golden hair, the languid Chopin, and my cheeks burned.

"Truelove!"

A large hand reached out and took my shoulder, forcing me to stop and turn. "You're cold," he said. "Cold and wet."

"Exactly, which is why I must rid myself of these clothes immediately." The words escaped my mouth quite without thought, and I regretted them at once.

He released me, took his jacket from his shoulders, and flung it about my shoulders.

"Change into what, Truelove? We haven't brought any spare clothes."

I pressed my lips together. "Then I'll simply wait until my clothes have dried."

"Nonsense. You'll catch a chill. I'll see if our dear Mrs. Poulakis has got something that might suit you."

"I will *not* under any circumstances wear—"

But he was already turning back down the corridor. "Only run yourself a bath, Truelove. I'll take care of the rest, never fear!"

❧

A glass of brandy awaited me in the room that had been reserved for my use when I returned, carrying my wet clothes and wearing a dressing gown I had discovered in the cupboard. Lord Silverton was present as well, sitting in an armchair, smoking his pipe and studying some papers. On the bed lay a dress of extraordinary plainness, which I ignored.

"You know, Truelove," he said, not looking up, "there's something odd about this fresco, and I don't mean the camera. I can't quite put my finger on it—"

"It's a fake," I said.

He looked up. "The photograph, or the fresco?"

"The fresco." I hung my wet clothes on the rack before the fire, which Silverton had built into a regular furnace, and sat down on a nearby chair to brush my hair dry in rapid strokes.

"And how did you come to this conclusion?"

"Mr. Vasilakis."

"Oh, you saw our old friend Vasilakis, did you?"

"Yes. He was tremendously helpful."

"I daresay."

I went on stroking my hair with the brush. The fire was so close and hot, it burned my knuckles. "I had the same intuition you did, that there was something wrong about the painting, though of course I lack any sort of experience or expertise in the field. But Mr. Vasilakis explained about the location of the fresco—not a domestic apartment or a ceremonial chamber, but a kind of storeroom—and various other aspects, which cast doubt on its authenticity."

"Such as?"

"Such as the fact that the male figure is in the lead. In the rest of the palace art, it is the females who occupy the dominant positions." I set down the brush and picked up the glass of brandy.

"Fascinating." Silverton watched me sip. "Anything else?"

"Oh, the colors. The pattern of aging, which seemed to him deliberate. The fact that the identity of the third figure—and the third figure only—is obliterated, in such a manner that does not suggest a natural deterioration."

"I see."

I lifted the brush again. "But that's not important, really. We haven't time. What matters is *why*. Why someone would take such trouble to create a false fresco: here, of all places."

"What do you think?"

The coals were a bright orange-red. I could not seem to get enough of their warmth. I thought, *we must pack, we must leave here at once*, but my limbs were so tired and heavy. "I think you know what I think."

"Someone wanted to lure Max here."

"Yes. Which means he was probably fleeing somebody when he left."

Silverton looked back at the photographs and sucked on his pipe. The room smelled comfortably of tobacco, of the coal fire.

The brandy fumes still filled my throat and mouth. In the sizzling heat, my hair was almost dry; I began to pin it up, using the hairpins I had laid aside before bathing.

"Possibly," he said at last.

"Possibly? What other explanation exists? Did you discover anything useful while I was gone, perhaps?"

"Hmm. Yes." He set down the photographs and rose from the chair. He approached me slowly, in the manner of a pensive leopard, wearing his spectacles low on the bridge of his nose. "I spent the first hour examining the villa itself, and the second hour going through the room that belonged to Max. It happens to be the room I was assigned as my own."

"A convenient coincidence."

"Yes. I found nothing of interest, however. According to Mrs. Poulakis, Max's assistant returned, a few days after their departure, and boxed everything up. It was sent, so far as she knows, to the apartment in Athens, though of course she cannot be completely certain."

"Max's assistant! And what happened to the assistant after that?"

"She doesn't know. He left, that's all." He knocked a little ash into the fireplace and rested his elbow on the mantel.

I jabbed the last pin into my hair and hurried across the room to my travel desk. "But don't you think that's suspicious?"

"Not in itself. Max may simply have been done with his work here, or was following another line of investigation. Mrs. Poulakis said there were no other visitors, menacing or otherwise, during his stay."

"It sounds as if Mrs. Poulakis has been most forthcoming."

"I can't complain, Truelove. But I find that most people are forthcoming when you're pleasant to them. Don't you?"

I had finished putting away the photographs. I locked the drawer and raised my head to stare at the window, which looked north toward Heraklion. Not that I could see very far; the rain had lifted, more or less, but the air was still too thick, and the day too advanced, to see beyond the terraced garden before me.

Two months ago, Mr. Haywood had set off down that hill and disappeared. What had happened to him? Was someone pursuing him? Had he left by boat? Where had he gone?

The urgency began to boil up again, filling my exhausted limbs with purpose. I turned around to face Silverton, who stood in exactly the same pose as before, nursing the pipe in his mouth.

"Naturally," I snapped. "So what do you propose we do now? I am most concerned about this development. We are now confronted with the renewed possibility that Mr. Haywood faced some sort of adversary, from whom he fled, or indeed was forced away. We must go the port at once and make inquiries."

Silverton shook his head. "He wasn't kidnapped, if that's what you mean."

"Why not?"

"No sign of struggle. Max would certainly have struggled. Mrs. Poulakis would have noticed."

"Perhaps Mrs. Poulakis has not been so forthcoming as you believe."

"Oh, she's forthcoming enough." He grinned.

"Regardless. The answer lies down the hill in Heraklion. Someone down there must have obtained him a boat and supplies for his journey. Someone must know *something*."

Silverton released a patient sigh. "Truelove, there are hundreds of fisherman scattered over the town. We shall have to spend days interviewing them all."

"Then we must start immediately!"

"A fool's errand. To the last man, they're all shut up snug in their houses by now, having dinner and making love to their wives, so they can be up at dawn tomorrow. There's no point. We stay here tonight." He tapped the end of his pipe on the mantel.

"So you can interview Mrs. Poulakis more thoroughly, perhaps?"

"Splendid idea. I'm sure we'll learn more from her than from some damned fisherman down in Heraklion."

I crossed my arms against my chest. "Oh, no doubt."

"Besides, Evans might reply to our telegram and sort out the whole matter for us." Silverton yawned and stretched his arms above his head. A faint blue line streaked lazily from the end of his pipe. I thought he looked lugubrious and magnificent and altogether too satisfied, and I turned away and pressed my fingers against the cold glass of the window. Already the darkness was falling down from the mountains behind us, as if to shroud us further from the truth.

"I don't like waiting like this," I said. "He's out there. He may be in desperate need of our help."

"And why the devil do you care so much? You don't even know the man."

"Because he is the Duke of Olympia."

"Ah, of course. I'd almost forgotten. And a lady always loves a duke, doesn't she?" I heard him pace across the floor in the direction of the door. "Buck up, Truelove. Perhaps some insight will simply arrive to us, during the night."

I could not be certain, but I thought I heard the devil wink.

⁓

Of course, he was right.

I took a tray in my room that evening, and fell asleep directly afterward, into an absolute void of exhaustion. As a result, I jolted awake at perhaps three o'clock in the morning, as if stung by an electric barb.

I lay with pounding heart, casting out the net of my senses, but I felt the presence of no unnatural illusion this night, either my father or Her Majesty. And yet something had awoken me, of that I was certain: whether the stimulus had come from the outside or the inside of my skull, I could not say.

Oh, very well. Perhaps I should confess something: I quarreled with Lord Silverton in the hour before dinner, and this quarrel, if I am honest, is the reason I suffered that mutinous tray of cold meat and bread, instead of a proper hot meal in the dining room.

The story, which perhaps does me little credit, goes thus: After Silverton left my chamber late yesterday afternoon, I had finished my brandy and, somewhat the better for courage, clothed myself reluctantly in the dress Silverton had obtained for me and wandered back to the drawing room, where I might locate his lordship.

I had found him without trouble. He was playing the piano again, but this time Mrs. Poulakis was with him, actually sitting on the bench by his side, exclaiming over his skill in the interpretation of Chopin (which, in itself, I could not deny). She had removed her pinafore altogether, and her hair was quite loose. She looked up insolently as I entered and did not rise from her seat.

"Mrs. Poulakis. Is it not time to prepare dinner?" I had asked sternly, and when she left, his lordship rose to his feet, propped one hand against the piano, and accused me—smiling, as if the idea amused him!—of jealousy.

I was not jealous, I insisted, only disappointed—*deeply* disappointed—that his lordship would so recklessly seduce a respectable young woman in the employ of his host.

"Are you implying that I have actually gone to bed with Mrs. Poulakis?" he had asked, incredulous.

"Let us say, since we are being frank, that I should not be at all surprised."

"Now, Truelove. Be reasonable. A proper seduction requires a great deal more time than the paltry two hours you allowed us this afternoon. I take pride in my work, after all."

His eyes twinkled at me, the beast, and I felt an anger so hot and instant and unreasonable that I am afraid I said something rash.

"Forgive my intrusion, then. I should hate to interrupt you in such an arduous task. Only imagine what you might extract from her with a few more hours of devoted labor."

"Truelove—"

"We must all stick to what we do best, after all," I pronounced, the triumphant last barb, and I turned and marched back down the hallway, expecting Silverton to follow once more and smooth things over, to assure me in his familiar jocular manner that he did not, in fact, mean to commit a transaction so amoral. That he would not place me in a position so awkward.

But the hallway behind me remained empty, and at seven o'clock I rang for a supper tray, determined to set the whole matter aside and concentrate my mind on the task that loomed before us in the morning.

But now, as I lay in my quiet room, attempting to judge the hour, while my blood coursed silently along my veins and my fingers sparkled in response to their unknown stimulant, I returned to that brief conversation with his lordship and saw how unjust I had been. After all, he was only attempting to extract information from her, using his extraordinary powers of persuasion; one must bring forth all the resources at one's disposal, in such a profession as his.

And he had not actually taken Mrs. Poulakis to his bed, by his own admission. He was not so ignoble as that.

An image flashed in my head and was gone: some glimpse of the dream from which I had just awoken. My chest ached, my lungs burned, and if I could have reached out my hands and clawed back the dream—or rather the memory of the dream—from the air, I would have done it. Whatever the dream contained, I craved it, the way one craves meat after famine.

And I did not even know what it was.

I thought, *I must apologize to Silverton.*

And then: *How absurd.* It was not yet dawn, and the message was hardly urgent. Indeed, I recognized the idea instantly as no more than an excuse. A reason—you see how brutal I am upon myself—to seek out another human being in this darkest hour of the night, so I would not exist in such profound isolation.

I would not succumb to this weakness. I would settle back to sleep and deliver my apology over breakfast.

But sleep did not arrive. My thoughts, once awakened, now bounced in all directions against the interior of my skull, like a rubber ball; my chest, once opened to longing, would not close. This, you see, is the familiar torture of solitude, and it does not lift easily.

I knew even then, from long experience, that I could not expect further sleep that night, and so I pushed aside the covers and forced myself out of the bed. Perhaps I could not seek out company to ease the burden on my spirit, but I could at least fill these wakeful hours with useful occupation, instead of wasteful contemplation. Work, after all, makes an admirable cure for dissatisfaction.

I switched on the lamp, went to my traveling desk, and pulled out the photographs, for perhaps the hundredth time. Were they taken by Mr. Haywood himself, I wondered, or had they been sent to him by Mr. Evans? Where did the fraud begin? According to Silverton, Mr. Haywood's assistant had removed all of his belongings, all the artifacts he had collected during his investigation. So there was nothing else, nothing to guide us. Not a single physical clue left behind.

I slumped back in my chair and allowed my arms to fall downward. The room around me was dim and shadowed, illuminated only by the single lamp now beside me. As a guest room, and a minor one, it was furnished simply, containing only the bed and desk, the wardrobe, and a small armchair. I had banked the fire before retiring, and the air had by now turned chilly, raising the hairs on my arms beneath the white linen of the shirt in which I slept. I rose to claim my dressing gown from the bottom of the bed.

As I did so, my toe caught a solid object, hidden among the thick folds of the counterpane where it touched the rug.

❦

Another confession. Hidden under my own bed in Belgrave Square, inside a pair of old trunks, lies a collection of penny-dreadful novels, of the sort that so-called *thinking people* love to scorn. (I suppose scorn makes one feel more clever, in the same way that indignation makes one feel more moral.) In the worn pages of these books, I have experienced great love and solved intractable mysteries, and I have learned many things that, perhaps, an unmarried young woman is better off not knowing.

I have learned, for example, that a lady really should not leave the shelter of her bedchamber in the dark hours of the night, particularly in a strange house, and *most* particularly in search of the bedchamber of a gentleman to whom she is not related, by blood or marriage.

In the excitement of discovery, however, I seemed to have forgotten this important lesson. Or perhaps the object that now lay in my hand, round and heavy, represented the excuse for which I had been unconsciously wishing: the excuse to seek out another human being, the excuse to seek out Lord Silverton.

As the novels often warn: be careful what you wish for.

~ ∞ ~

I found his lordship's bedchamber readily, even without a source of light, because the clouds had parted during the night, and a steady white half-moon now shone through the many windows of the Villa Ariadne.

Silverton did not respond to my knock, and I am afraid, in my haste and urgency, I thought nothing of trying the knob. As it proved, he had left the door unlocked, and I flung it open with rather more force than I intended, waking the occupants of the room.

I say *occupants* because there were two of them: Lord Silverton, who sprang to his feet at once, thoroughly naked; and Mrs. Poulakis, who only lifted her sleepy head from the sheets and flung out a long white arm, so that the moonlight spilled extravagantly over her bare and mountainous breasts.

In the manner of animals readied for slaughter, the Athenian youths were fed from bountiful plates, and perfumed with the finest extracts, and massaged with oils to make them tender. No one was allowed into their sacred quarters except for the slaves who waited upon them, nor were the youths allowed to leave except for the ritual ceremonies marking their sacrifice to come, to which they were led in blindfolds.

On the first night, a lavish banquet was held in the Hall of the Labrys, and the youths were seated on a dais while the Lady of the Labyrinth, dressed only in a simple white tunic and unbound hair, was required to serve them. The Prince watched her carefully as she performed her duties, and when they retired to their chamber, he said to her, 'Why does the first youth look upon you in the familiarity of lust? You know he is to be made sacrifice to my pleasure alone . . .'

THE BOOK OF TIME, A. M. HAYWOOD (1921)

Thirteen

Lord Silverton stirred the sugar into his coffee and gazed happily out the window of the breakfast room. "Splendid morning, isn't it?"

"Certainly the sun is shining," I allowed. I was eating my breakfast with great attention to detail, and only regarded my companion from underneath my downturned brow.

"You can see all the way down the hill to the harbor. There's the old Venetian fortress at the end. Marvelous stuff." He sipped his coffee, set down the cup, stretched magnificently, and pulled his watch from his waistcoat pocket. "A quarter past eight already! We should be off directly, I think. I find I'm bursting with energy today. A new man."

"I daresay."

"You know, Truelove, you might relax that expression of

prunelike disapproval on your face and consider the many bene-
ficial aspects of human love."

"I beg your pardon. Did you say *love*?"

"Lust, then, if you will. I was only trying to spare your blushes."

I laid down my knife and fork and lifted the napkin from my
lap to dab the corners of my mouth. "I'm afraid I am quite beyond
the range of blushes, and in fact, I find the subject of your noc-
turnal habits rather tiresome. Have you no opinion on the medallion I discovered in my room?"

"The medallion you thought so important, you rushed it to
my bed, unannounced, at three o'clock in the morning?"

"In my defense, I did not expect to find you entertaining company."

"In *my* defense, I didn't, either." He linked his hands behind
his head and grinned at the ceiling. "*Most* unexpected. But one
doesn't wish to be inhospitable."

"Your lordship. The medallion."

"Oh. Right-ho." Silverton straightened and reached for the
round bronze medal sitting near his plate, where I had placed it
that morning, just before his sunny arrival at the table a half hour
ago. Last night, you see, I had elected not to bring the object to his
attention after all, surmising that said attention was already entirely
occupied and quite possibly disordered; instead, I had returned to
my room without comment, without a single word, and crawled
under the bedclothes to turn the medallion over and over between
my fingers like a touchstone of great power. It was made of bronze,
about two inches in diameter, and on its face it bore the image of a
labrys—the familiar double-headed ax—in sharp relief. On the
back, there was a curious notch in the manner of a tunnel, and I
asked his lordship now what he thought of it.

"For a pin, I should say." He looked up, quite impossibly beautiful in the morning sunshine, and I had to concede that the act of human love appeared to agree with him. "A cloak pin. The pin is missing, of course, which is probably how it came free from the cloak itself."

"But where did it come from? I mean, from the ruins, obviously. But did it belong to Mr. Haywood, do you think? Was it one of his artifacts? I thought you had searched the rooms thoroughly."

"I didn't search *your* room, Truelove."

"Why not?"

"Why, because I thought it was improper." He winked. "If it was one of Max's baubles, however, it's strange that it turned up in your bed."

"*Under* my bed."

"As you say. Ah, there you are, Mrs. Poulakis! Perhaps you can assist us."

I looked up reflexively, and wished I had not. The housekeeper swept through the doorway, holding a coffeepot, and if Silverton looked well this morning, Mrs. Poulakis was positively radiant. Her cheekbones were stained a happy pink, and her skin looked as if it were sprinkled with fairy dust. She turned a pair of exceptionally bright eyes toward his lordship's side of the table and prowled forth, the way a lioness might lay claim to her kill.

When she arrived, coffeepot poised, face soft with adoration, Silverton returned her smile and nodded at me. "Very kind of you, my dear, but I believe Miss Truelove's cup stands empty."

Mrs. Poulakis looked up as if she had only just noticed my presence. I nudged my cup and saucer an inch or two in her direction.

When she had finished pouring the coffee, Silverton said,

"Now, Mrs. Poulakis. I wonder if you can tell us anything about this medallion, which Miss Truelove has found in her room."

"Hidden," I said. "*Hidden* in my room."

Mrs. Poulakis took the medallion from Silverton's fingers, examined it briefly, and shrugged. "Oh, it is like all the others. They have find many of these things, in the palace."

"Have they, now? Did it belong to our friend Mr. Haywood, do you think?"

"It is possible." She cast a quick glance at me. "You find it in your room?"

"Under the bed."

Another shrug. "He miss it, I think. When he is filling the boxes."

"The assistant, do you mean? Max's assistant?" said Silverton.

"Yes, yes."

"But how did it get in my room in the first place?" I said. "I thought Mr. Haywood occupied Lord Silverton's chamber. Has anyone in particular occupied mine, of late?"

Was it my imagination, or did a flicker of perhaps indecision cross Mrs. Poulakis's glowing face?

"Of late? No, no." She looked back at Silverton, and the expression of leonine satisfaction returned to her features. She held out the medallion. "Is a very common thing, this. They are finding them all the time."

Silverton took the object from her hand and as he did so, their fingers exchanged a subtle caress, causing a sour flavor to climb up the back of my throat, rather like the one I had experienced in the presence of the false fresco. I tossed down another mouthful of coffee and rose from the table.

"I shall make myself ready for the walk down to the harbor. Silverton, shall we meet in the hallway in fifteen minutes? I feel that time is of the essence. We ought to have left already, in fact."

"Oh, quite. Only say the word, Truelove."

I set my napkin alongside my plate and turned to leave.

"Just be sure to knock first!" called his lordship, over my head, and it was a very good thing for him that I had left my cup behind me, safe in its saucer, half-full of scalding black coffee.

⟋⟍

My bedchamber was already occupied.

"My dear, you are disturbed," said my father. He sat in the chair before the desk, one leg crossed over the other, wearing a plain gray suit that suggested walking. His hair was dark and shining, as if he had just bathed.

"I am not prepared to discuss the matter," I said crossly. I marched to the desk and reached past him to collect my hat and pins.

"It was really very foolish of you, to open his door without warning in the middle of the night."

I didn't bother asking him how he knew of the affair. I turned to the mirror on the wall and thrust my hat atop my head. "I knocked first. And it was foolish of him to leave the door unlocked, when he was engaged so privately."

"I thought you had already learned this valuable lesson, about opening bedroom doors at midnight."

My hands paused on my head, while the air of the bedchamber froze in place. I thought I could hear the ticking of my pocket watch, hanging by a chain against my skirt, but perhaps this was only my pulse. I resumed the careful insertion of the last hatpin. I turned my face to one side and then another, to ensure that no stray wisp of hair had come loose over my ears. "I don't know what you mean."

"Don't you? Well, perhaps I am mistaken."

I chanced a glimpse in the mirror to the space behind me, and saw that my father had uncrossed his legs and placed a palm on each knee. He was gazing at me thoughtfully, head tilted to the left, and for an instant our eyes met in the mirror: a glance of perfect and terrible understanding.

I stepped away to lift my jacket from the bed, which I had arranged neatly with my own hands before repairing to the breakfast table. I have always disliked the sordid appearance of an unmade bed.

"He was terribly casual about the whole affair, over breakfast," I said. "As if he were quite used to such escapades. Well, I suppose he is."

"It is not unlikely. He is a handsome fellow, and moreover he has the kind of manner that attracts people into intimacy."

"And I do not."

My father paused. "Does this upset you? Do you wish to enjoy love affairs, in the same manner as his lordship?"

"No, of course not," I said instantly. I flung the jacket over my shoulders and thrust my arms inside the sleeves, and without warning, the words burst from my lips: "But sometimes I am so bloody *alone*!"

"Not quite alone."

I buttoned my jacket.

"My dear Emmeline," my father said softly, "it is not hard to find a lover, if one is open to love."

The last button appeared through its hole. I smoothed away a wrinkle and settled the hem down over my hips.

"No, you're right about that," I said, and a sharp knock sounded on the door. I turned my head. "Who is it?"

"Your humble servant, bearing important tidings. Are you alone?"

I glanced at the chair, which was now empty. "Yes. Come in."

The door swung open, revealing Lord Silverton in full out-door kit: the same Norfolk jacket belted at the waist, sturdy shoes laced, leather gaiters fastened snugly about his calves. His cap shielded his golden hair from the light overhead, and the familiar field of electricity bristled about him.

"I thought I heard you speaking to someone," he said.

"Only muttering to myself. My buttons were stiff. Are you ready to leave?"

"Even better." He held up his right hand, which contained a strip of thin paper. "Firstly, that fine chap Evans has replied to our wire."

"What does he say?"

"Read it yourself."

I stepped forward and took the telegram from his gloved fingers. "WELCOME TO KNOSSOS STOP CONDOLENCES LOSS OF OLYMPIA STOP ASTONISHED HAYWOOD NOT THERE STOP EXPECTED RETURN BY JANUARY 15 LATEST STOP QUERY HORACE HIGGANBOTHAM BRITISH SCHOOL ATHENS STOP HAVE ALREADY SENT WIRE STOP GOOD LUCK." I looked up. "Who is Horace Higganbotham?"

"Some chap at the British School in Athens, I gather." He took back the telegram. "Perhaps he was in communication with Max. They're among the best classical scholars in the world, the British School. I've already wired him. But if Evans expected Max back in Knossos by the middle of January, he's hellishly late."

"He doesn't say why Max left in the first place, or where he went."

"Probably because he doesn't know." Silverton folded the telegram and placed in his pocket. "But that doesn't matter."

"Doesn't matter? Of course it matters! Are we simply supposed to wait to hear back from this Mr. Higganbotham? We might lose days!"

"No, we shan't. Because while you may disapprove of my methods, my dear Truelove, you can't possibly argue with the results."

"I will concede that you're in an excellent mood this morning."

"I don't mean my physical and mental condition, though both have never been better, since you're inquiring. I mean that the generous Mrs. Poulakis—now, don't roll those fine eyes of yours, Truelove—Mrs. Poulakis, after you left, was persuaded to relinquish a few interesting bits of information."

I folded my arms. "Persuaded?"

"I am a terribly persuasive chap, Truelove. People like to confide things in me; I can't imagine why. In any case, the first thing is, Max had a woman with him, the sneaky devil. That's who was in this room, you know."

I gasped. "A woman!"

"Heinous of him, wasn't it? And to make matters worse, he took her with him when he left. I'm shocked to the core. Shocked, appalled, the whole lot. But the point is, the medallion might possibly have been hers."

I said, in a low voice, "What sort of woman was she?"

"The good sort or the bad sort, do you mean?"

"You know very well what I mean."

"Why, I daresay she was the worst possible sort, Truelove. Let your imagination run rampant. I'm surprised they occupied separate rooms, though I always suspected old Max was a hypocrite at heart. Thalia said—"

"Thalia?"

"Mrs. Poulakis, I mean. She said the woman was very beautiful, quite tall, with dark hair. Also, she wouldn't speak. Haughty. Thought herself quite above our Mrs. Poulakis, which is *exactly* the sort of thing to rub a housekeeper the wrong way, you know, not that I'm casting any hints at present company."

"I see. And I suppose you rubbed her the *right* way?"

Silverton's face broke into a wide smile. "Why, Truelove! I never thought you capable of an improper bon mot. There may be hope for you after all. And yes, as it happens. I *did* rub her the right way, at every opportunity. If a thing's worth doing, it's worth doing well, I always say. In any case," he went on, over the top of my noise of outrage, "she told me another thing."

"I hardly dare ask."

He took my elbow and steered me out of the room. "She admitted, under duress—"

"Duress, is it?"

"Of the most acute kind. She told me that the night before Max left, he asked her if she knew any fishermen in the town. And as it happens, Truelove—this is the important thing—her own brother happens to be a fisherman. Her brother! And she was the very one who made the arrangements for Max's boat, a fact she was paid handsomely to conceal. No doubt that's why I had to go to such great lengths to win her trust."

We were halfway down the corridor. I stopped and turned to him. "Do you mean to say that Mrs. Poulakis's own *brother* supplied Mr. Haywood with his boat? That he might actually know where Mr. Haywood went?"

"That's it exactly!" His lordship beamed. "Straight down along the harbor in Heraklion, not five miles away."

A wild hope soared to life in my breast, lifting away the gloom
and oppression. I stared up at Silverton's pleased face. He was
wearing his spectacles now—more professor than lothario, hardly
even the same man I had glimpsed a few hours ago in the moonlight, in all his considerable glory—and instead of finding his gaze,
I saw my own twin reflections in the lenses, warped and wide-
eyed, dominated by two colossal noses.

"But that's—that's marvelous!" I exclaimed.

"Yes, I rather thought so. Not that I would expect your grateful thanks for my selfless labors on behalf of this investigation."

I grasped the sides of his cheeks with both hands, lifted myself
onto my toes, and planted a firm kiss on his astonished lips.

"Very grateful indeed," I said, and I danced down the corridor and through the entrance hall, toward the door that led out
into the road to Heraklion.

⁓

The sunshine fell on our shoulders with unaccustomed warmth,
a taste of the coming spring. I decided to look upon this as a
good omen after yesterday's downpour, which was still evident
in the long damp beds that ran down the length of the road. Silverton, leading the mule, took out his pipe and began to whistle
as he filled the bowl, juggling rope and pipe and tobacco pouch
with expert dexterity.

"Let me do the talking, now," he said, as we approached the
busy harbor, some hour or so before noon. Already the fishing
fleet was beginning to arrive back at the docks, swearing and
reeking, tossing out nets full of still-wriggling fish. The sunlight
glittered on the silver scales, and as the men's shouts rang through

the air, clashing with the squalls of the seagulls, I perceived that they were happy. A good day's catch, an early return.

I held my handkerchief to my nose. "I can't do anything else, really, since you're the one who speaks Greek."

"And yet I wouldn't be at all surprised to see you try." He knocked the pipe empty and replaced it in his jacket pocket, and then he handed the mule's rope to me. "I'm going to make inquiries. If you need me, just whistle."

"I don't know how to whistle."

"Then scream bloody murder." He shoved his hands in his pockets, hunched his shoulders, and sauntered off toward the docks, looking remarkably at ease among the nets of fish and the seagulls and the brackish stink. Across the harbor, the fortress rose high above the water traffic, so clear through the rain-washed air that the battlements appeared as little gray teeth against the blue sky.

The mule made a noise of disgust and strained against his halter. Our trunks were strapped to his back, one on each side, except that Silverton's was heavier and tended to list. I reached out my hand to push it back in place, but the mule's hindquarters moved away, leaving me to stagger after him in a ridiculous circle that ended, inevitably, in a heap on the cobbles.

I believe I may have sworn: the influence, no doubt, of a week spent in Lord Silverton's irreverent company. At least nobody could understand me, I thought, but as I struggled back to my feet, a gloved hand appeared before me, and a crisp British voice inquired after my welfare.

Not, I am sorry to say, the voice of Lord Silverton.

I considered the hand and the voice, and the state of my posterior upon the dirty stone quay. I considered the scent of mule and fish that hung about me, and my hat slipping down the side of my head, and the word that had just escaped my lips: a word I shall not repeat, out of respect for my readers' delicacy.

I gazed up and considered the face before me: dark-haired, brown-eyed, pale and handsome and finished off with a splendid, elegant moustache.

I shrugged my shoulders helplessly and said, "No English."

"How strange," he said. "You have such an English look about you." He took my hand and switched smoothly into what I believe was Greek. I levered myself to my feet and pretended ignorance to that, too.

"Well, then. What a charming mystery you are," said the man. He doffed his hat and made a polite little bow, which I returned. "*Parlez-vous français*, mademoiselle? *Auf deutsche*, perhaps?"

I shook my head. I feared my face was giving me away, hot with panicked shame. What had possessed me? But it was too late to back down.

"American?" he inquired.

I gave out an embarrassed laugh—this, at least, was not a pretense—and turned back to the mule, who stood scornfully by.

"Well, then, madam. I am happy to have been of service, and regret deeply that I am unable to express my pleasure at this unexpected and wholly delightful encounter. May we meet again, far from this latter-day Babel, in a place where we might understand each other with perfect ease."

It was a beautiful speech, and I would liked to have been able to acknowledge it with something more suitable than a quizzical smile. I offered him my hand instead. He shook it, touched the brim of his hat, and walked away: medium height, gray-suited, as slender and athletic as a tennis player. My shoulders sagged.

Just as the man looked back over his shoulder, the mule lifted his tail and evacuated his bowels.

❧

"Awfully sorry to be so long," Silverton said, sauntering up a half hour later and taking the mule's rope from my hand. "They're a suspicious bunch, these Cretans. But I think I've found our man."

"What a tremendous relief."

"I say. Are you quite all right? Not accosted or anything like that?"

"Nothing like that, alas."

I followed his lordship's broad and tweedy shoulders down the quay, toward a crumbling stone pier at the far end of the harbor, where a dark-bearded man was constructing a knot of elaborate dimensions with which to secure a boat to one of the pilings. I am no expert on the nautical sciences, as you have perhaps surmised, but it seemed to me that this particular craft basked no longer in the prime of her life. Her boards were warped, her rigging in some disorder. She smelled like the devil. But her net, still over the side, fairly burst with wriggling fish, and that was all that counted, wasn't it?

"Ahoy, there," said Silverton, and the man looked up. An expression of instant suspicion took over his features, which were thick and craggy and not inclined to good feelings to begin with. "Are you Mr. Poulakis?"

"*Naí, naí.*"

"Er, speak English, by chance?"

The man released the rope and picked up an object that might possibly have been a harpoon. "A little."

"Excellent, excellent. My name is Silverton, old fellow, and my companion and I were wondering if you might be persuaded to help us."

The man fingered the harpoon lovingly. "Help you what?"

"Help us find an old friend, as it happens. Haywood's the name. Maximilian Haywood. I understand he left this harbor in December, in company with a lady, in a boat he obtained by your good offices?"

Mr. Poulakis's face calcified into a silent stare. He glanced at me—up and down and then up again—and said, toward some point in my ribs, "Who say this to you?"

I opened my mouth to reply, since he seemed to be addressing this question to me, or at least to a fragment of my body, but Silverton's hand found the back of my waist and his voice interrupted me cheerfully.

"Why, none other than the housekeeper at the Villa Ariadne, up near Knossos. Your sister, I believe? Lovely woman. A pearl above price. She told us she'd made the arrangements with you personally."

Mr. Poulakis's gaze returned to Silverton and turned, if possible, more stony. "Maybe I do this."

"Well! Jogs a bit of the old memory, then, does it? Excellent. Because the thing is, our fellow's gone missing."

"Missing?"

Silverton snapped his fingers. "Gone. Disappeared. *Exafanístike.*"

I might have been mistaken, but it seemed that a small, worried line came into being between Mr. Poulakis's furry eyebrows.

"*Exafanístike?*" he said.

"*Naí.*"

The fisherman stood like a pillar, legs planted apart, as if braced for a gale. A tiny breeze tickled his forelock. He bent his face downward to inspect the point of his harpoon and said, "I know nothing."

"Oh, come on, old fellow," said Silverton. "British fellow, beautiful woman, sturdy craft acquired on the hush-hush. No doubt they paid you handsomely. Surely a bell rings somewhere inside that massive head of yours?"

The massive head flashed back up. "I mean I know nothing where they go."

"Ah! But you do remember setting them up and so on."

"They buy my boat. That is all." He shrugged and turned away, tossing the harpoon inside the craft as it rolled gently in the harbor wake. "They sail off, all three. They no say where is going."

"I beg your pardon," said Silverton. "Did you say *three*?"

"Yes, three! Two men, one woman. One man very big." He motioned with his hands. "Wear—what is word—" The hands fluttered around the head and shoulders.

"A hat?" Silverton suggested.

"No. *Mandýas*."

"Ah. A cloak."

"Cloak, yes." He turned and reached for his fishing net. "That is all I know. They go, that is all."

"Did anyone help them?"

"There was young man. Not in boat. He goes to villa, maybe."

Silverton turned to me. "Max's assistant, probably. So he knew what was going on, and probably where they were going. If only Thalia—"

Mr. Poulakis whipped around.

"*THALIA?*" he roared.

"I mean Mrs. Poulakis, of course," Silverton said hastily. "The honored Mrs. Poulakis—"

But the protest was wholly supererogatory. Comprehension had already dawned on that rugged face, followed by a full-blooded fraternal rage of the sort one rarely witnesses among the anemic races of the northern climes.

Mr. Poulakis struck out his long arm, secured Silverton by the collar, and with a thick right fist delivered his lordship a cracking blow exactly in the middle of his perfect left jaw.

And, to be perfectly honest, I can't say I blamed him.

⁓⁓

"I could easily have fought back, of course, and avoided the blow," said Lord Silverton, nursing a loin of beef to his cheek and a cup of strong hot Turkish coffee to his lips. "But a sense of honor compelled me to submit. Do stop gloating, Truelove."

"I am not gloating."

"I took my punishment like a gentleman, that's all, and furthermore it was worth the beating."

"*What* was worth the beating? The crime itself, or the information gained from it?"

"Well, both. But particularly the former."

"Unrepentant, I see."

"Well, I could hardly refuse a lady in extremis, could I? Not gallant at all." He lifted away the beefsteak. "How does it look?"

"Ghastly."

He tossed the meat on the worn wooden table between us. We were sitting in a sort of restaurant, across the street from the familiar arched façade of the Hotel Alabaster, which seemed to model itself on the style of the Parisian café, presumably in the hope of winning the Heraklion tourist trade, such as it was. The tables were round, the walls a lurid crimson. I had asked for coffee and sandwiches and the beefsteak for Lord Silverton's jaw; we had already eaten the sandwiches, and the coffee had at last arrived after a long delay. I frowned at his lordship's face, which now sported an interesting purple swelling, and wondered whether the jaw was actually broken. (He had claimed not, on the grounds that he was perfectly familiar with the sound of a snapping bone.)

Silverton turned his head away to stare at the hotel entrance across the street. "At least we know Max made it off Crete alive, and in the company of a beautiful woman. That's something."

"I suppose, in your view, that's everything."

"Company *is* everything in these little escapades, I find." He finished his coffee. "Our trouble now, of course, is that there are perhaps a thousand islands in the Aegean to which he might have repaired, to say nothing of ports beyond."

"Then his enemies will have as much trouble discovering him as we will, I believe."

"An excellent point, Truelove. You're getting the hang of all this quite exceptionally well. The problem remains, however." He was still staring out the window, and a frown had begun to develop on that wide mouth, insofar as it could bear any expression at all at the moment.

I followed his gaze. "Is something the matter?"

"I don't quite know." He reached into his waistcoat pocket and produced his spectacles. "How are your eyes, Truelove?"

"My eyesight, do you mean? Perfect."

"Of course it is." He drew the glasses over his nose. "Hmm. Yes. Tell me what you think of that fellow lingering around the second column from the left."

I peered about, not seeing anyone, until I moved closer to Silverton and a man appeared in view, leaning against the column in

question, hands shoved into his pockets. He was wearing a dark
suit and a low hat, and his head swung back and forth as he observed
the leisurely flow of traffic in the street.

"He seems to be waiting for someone," I said at last.

"Yes, I thought so, too. And whom do you think he might be
waiting for?"

I was about to reply that I could have no idea, could I, but as the
man turned his head again, I thought I detected something familiar
about his posture and profile. My pulse tripped over itself. I curled
my fingers around the edge of the table, waiting for him to move
again, and when he did, gazing for just a moment at the restaurant,
seeming for all the world as if he saw right through the windows to
our small round table with the beefsteak in the center, my breath
caught in a gasp in the back of my throat.

The sunlight glinted on the lobe of his right ear.

"Us?" I said, rather more thready than I intended, but I suppose
I should have been grateful that I retained any power of speech
whatever.

Silverton rose from the table. "We think on identical lines,
Truelove. I shall return in half an hour. In the meantime, I suggest you order yourself another cup of coffee."

Throughout the next day, the Lady hoped to send a message of warning to the Hero, but to no avail, for the Prince kept a jealous watch on her at every minute. That evening, when the youths were led under blindfold to the Hall of the Labrys, the Prince stood before them and explained that, in defiance of custom, the hunt would begin that very night, once the Lady of the Labyrinth had washed their feet and anointed their skin with oil.

The Lady was distressed, for she had no time to send word to her brother, but she did as her husband commanded and washed the feet of the youths, and anointed their skin with oil. When she came to the Hero, she took care to avert her eyes from his beauty, but as she bent to spread the oil across his forehead, she whispered that he was not to fear, for she would find a way to locate him in the intricate chambers of the palace.

Yet when she finished the ritual, the Prince dismissed all the retainers, and with his own hands placed a blindfold over the Lady's eyes, and said to the youths, 'This night shall the Lady of the Labyrinth join the hunt with you, and if any of you seek to escape your fate, her life shall be forfeit . . .'

THE BOOK OF TIME, A. M. HAYWOOD (1921)

Fourteen

I had protested, of course. I ought to go with him; could there be any act so singularly unprofitable to our investigation as that of sitting at a table, drinking coffee?

He would not hear of it. I had no training or experience in these sorts of confrontations, nor had he any time to prepare me.

I had demanded particulars: What was his lordship planning to do? Did he mean to catch the man? Interrogate him?

What if he didn't return in half an hour? What if something happened to him?

"My dear Truelove," he said, tugging a few coins from his pocket and laying them on the table, "I have promised to return to you in half an hour. I do not break my word."

And he had turned and left, as if that settled the matter.

During the course of our conversation—I will not call it an argument—the man with the earring had straightened himself away from the column and ducked into the hotel itself, so quickly that I nearly missed the maneuver. But Lord Silverton had not. He crossed the street nimbly, paused, and went around back through the narrow alley between the Hotel Alabaster and a neighboring tavern, where I lost him from view.

I checked my watch briefly—seven minutes past one o'clock—and continued for some time to stare at the columns forming the shallow portico of the Hotel Alabaster, as if I might actually conjure some vision of what was occurring within. But the exterior of the hotel remained somnolent, in the manner of a Mediterranean town in the middle hours of the day, even in winter, and after twelve minutes (having checked my watch a second time, and dropped it with exasperation back into my jacket pocket) I raised the first two fingers of my right hand and signaled the waiter for more coffee.

Six excruciating minutes later, during which the front portico of the Hotel Alabaster remained wholly complacent, a waiter arrived bearing the coffee, a welcome distraction. He removed Silverton's empty cup and raw beefsteak with an air of decided distaste. I added two teaspoons of sugar, and had only just taken the first tentative sip when the door opened and a man walked in, wearing a gray suit and a familiar black moustache.

Very quietly, I turned my chair away.

"Beg your pardon," the man said to the waiter, "but I don't suppose you could spare a plate of sandwiches?"

"Sandwiches?"

"Yes. Famished. I've just arrived off the boat from Piraeus, and the hotel doesn't seem to be serving yet."

I shrank into my collar and bent my head over my coffee cup. The waiter appeared not to understand him—he hadn't understood us very well either, until Silverton had switched to Greek—and the Englishman tried again, this time in the local tongue. An animated discussion ensued, during which I finished my coffee and disappeared further into my clothes. I had just begun to measure the distance to the door when the man's voice switched abruptly from incomprehensible patois to a sound, sharp, unmistakable English. *Damn!*

The word made me jolt, a fatal error. I faced the window, and could not see the Englishman directly, but a certain airless quality shaped the silence that followed, instructing me that I had won his attention.

I sat absolutely still, in the manner of a stag caught in the open.

"Oh, I say," the Englishman said, so softly I might have missed him, had I not been straining every nerve underneath my outward petrification. He said something in Greek to the proprietor, who responded in kind, and an instant later his footsteps sounded briskly on the paved floor, approaching me.

When I was perhaps eight, I had been caught in a small lie; I can't remember what. Something to do with missing cake, I believe. The crime itself was not important. It was the concealment that disturbed my father. We all commit transgressions, he told me gravely. It is the manner in which we conduct ourselves afterward that marks our true character. And the trouble with a lie, Emmeline, is that you shortly discover you must continue in a series of further lies to support the first, until you end inevitably entangled inside a massive skein of falsity, which you must slice through with a knife in order to free yourself, in an act altogether more painful than the snapping of a single thread.

Yes, Papa, I had said dutifully, and I meant it. I have passionately defended the truth ever since. But every so often, I find myself in what the duke's London housekeeper used to call a fix: a skein of falsity, the fault (I'm afraid) not of some deliberate and cold-blooded lie, but only my own pride.

I don't know why I pretended not to understand the Englishman on the quay, but I suspect I was ashamed: flat on my posterior on the cobbles, leading a mule, swearing like a common fishwife. If I spoke to him, I should have had to explain myself. Now, as his footsteps drew closer, I remembered my father's advice, and thought, *I should come clean at once.*

The Englishman stopped next to my chair. Courtesy obliged me to look up.

"What a charming coincidence," he said. "Are you a visitor to Heraklion, too?"

My lips flailed for response.

"Ah, damn." He removed his hat and pushed a hand through his hair, which was thick and dark, a pleasing shade of walnut brown. "Let me see. Vis-it-or?"

Come clean, Emmeline. (Quite stern.)

I opened my mouth and said, "Vis-it-or?"

The man's face brightened. "Exactly! So am I. Not for pleasure, alas, but—well. Do you mind if I join you?" He motioned to the other chair.

As I nodded a reluctant acquiescence, it occurred to me that this man's appearance might not prove a coincidence at all. If so fearsome a man as the earring-wearer lurked about the hotel, waiting for our return, perhaps he had a less-threatening accomplice to search the rest of the town?

You see? I was right to disguise my nationality. Silverton would certainly approve. Now I had only to continue the subterfuge until his lordship returned, or else the Englishman departed in—so I hoped—utter frustration.

I bent my head once more over my cup and studied the man while he settled himself across the table, hitching up his trousers slightly as he crossed one leg over the other, straightening his sober jacket. His hair had been brushed back with pomade, and his moustache was precisely trimmed. The sign of a villain, or simply a man of exact grooming? He dropped his hat on his knee and smiled benignly at me, in the style of a grandparent trying to think of something to say to a child. He patted his pockets. "Dear me. I wish I had a notepad with me. We might communicate in pictographs."

I stole a glance through the window. No sign of activity at the Hotel Alabaster. Where the devil was Silverton? If only Silverton would turn up. On the other hand, if this man were dangerous, then it was best if—

"Ah! Are you staying at the Alabaster?" said the Englishman.

I shrugged noncommittally.

"Al-a-bas-ter? Yes?" He patted his pockets again, and again the expression of illumination spread across his regular features. His eyes were brown and soft and heavy-lidded, and as he lifted his brows in anticipation of whatever idea had just occurred to him, I conceded that he looked rather handsome. He produced a small book from his pocket, a rumpled red Baedeker's guide, and unfolded a map from the inside cover. "Now, see here. Suppose you point to that part of the world where you're from, and chances are, I'll know at least a few odd words of the language. What do you say, eh?"

I looked at his face, and down at the map. I suppose I must have appeared terrified.

"There's no harm, I assure **you**. **Are** you from Romania?" He pointed to a small blue spot on the map.

I shook my head. His finger moved. "Bulgaria? East Prussia? Denmark, perhaps?"

I glanced desperately at the hotel and back at the map. The Englishman was now working his way doggedly through Scandinavia, and as his finger slid east into Finland, I nodded, just to stop him.

"Finland! What luck! *Vietin kaksi kuukautta Suomessa, kun olin kahdenkymmenen vuotisista.*"

His smile was broad and encouraging. I dropped another spoonful of sugar in my coffee and stirred, stirred. "Eh?" I said at last.

"*Ei, se on totta. Olen pahoillani minun Suomi ei ole parempi. Ymmärrätkö minua?*"

"Neh?"

"Oh, dear. I'm afraid I'm sadly out of practice. I only wish to— Look. I haven't even introduced myself." He held out his right hand. "Horace Higganbotham, British School at Athens."

As luck would have it, I had just begun to drain the last of my oversweet coffee, hoping to hide my expression of dismay. I coughed it up at once.

"Dear me," said Mr. Higganbotham. "Are you all right?"

He took out a handkerchief and pressed it into my hand, and when a few more barks failed to halt the spasm, he rose from his chair in concern and came around to deliver a solid thump to the middle of my back. The coffee rose up the channel of my throat and into the cavities of my nose. I made a noise of distress that ended in a choke.

"Hey there! What the devil are you doing?"

I looked up through watery eyes to find Lord Silverton, at

last, standing at the door of the restaurant, quite unharmed and looking as if he meant to debone someone in order to make the evening's soup.

"Oh! Hello!" Mr. Higganbotham straightened away from me. "You must be Lord Silverton."

His lordship formed his hands into fists and roared, "Never mind who *I* am. Who the devil are *you*, and what *in God's name* do you think you're doing with that woman?"

"Oh. Right. Horace Higganbotham, British School, Athens. This dear young lady has had a spot of trouble with her coffee, that's all." Mr. Higganbotham leaned forward and tapped his temple. "A little bit slow, I suspect. I don't suppose you happen to speak Finnish?"

I shall spare you the scene of humiliation that followed. Suffice to say that his lordship nearly disgraced himself from laughing, and it was quite some time before we could get a sober word from him. When we did, it was only to learn that he had not been able to find the man with the earring, though he searched the hotel diligently.

"But I saw him go in," I said.

"So did I. Regardless, he's given me the slip, which is dashed confounding. Makes a chap wonder if he's lost his touch."

"I don't mean to interrupt," said Mr. Higganbotham, "but am I to understand that we stand in some sort of physical danger at the present time?"

"Yes. Do you object?"

The sandwiches had arrived a moment ago, and Mr. Higganbotham had already finished the first. At Silverton's casual *yes*, however, he set down the remaining crust and turned a little pale.

"Dear me," he said.

"Quite." Silverton drummed his fingers on the table, which had grown much too small with the addition of the two men. His lordship's long legs stretched halfway across the room, crossed at the ankles, for the singular purpose of showing off his unnatural height to the smaller man.

Or so I suspected, as I observed the laconic scowl that had settled upon his ordinarily amiable face in the wake of his laughter: a face made infinitely more fearsome by the purple bruise on the side of his jaw. From time to time, he cast a watchful glance through the window, though he had taken off his spectacles, and was now removing his pipe from his jacket pocket as if he meant to settle in for a comfortable afternoon's conversation.

Mr. Higganbotham swallowed. "I see. Well, since you ask, I don't suppose I *can* object to a bit of danger. I am, after all, a party concerned."

"So I understand," said his lordship. "And how, exactly, are you concerned in the matter? You were corresponding with my friend Max, isn't that right?"

"Oh, yes. He sent me a letter last October, inquiring into various aspects of classical mythology. My particular area of study at the school, you understand. I have had regular conversations with Mr. Evans and his colleagues, over the course of the past five or six years." He gained a little confidence as he spoke, straightening both his shoulders and his moustache.

"I see. Most useful of you. And what sort of inquiries did Max have for you?"

"Well, to do with Minoan myth, primarily. The story of King Minos and the labyrinth, and the defeat of the Minotaur by Theseus, familiar to every schoolboy. He was well aware of the general features of the legend, of course, but in fact there are numerous variations on the details, as one might expect, with the Athenians having it one way and the Mycenaeans having it another, and even Plutarch, in his avowedly factual history of Theseus, coming up with an odd twist or two. Mr. Haywood asked me, in the first place, to lay out, in an orderly fashion, all the different variations and their sources, which took quite some time, I can tell you." Mr. Higganbotham shook his head.

"I can well imagine," I said.

"And then what?" said Silverton. "You sent him this—this compilation of myths. Did he have any further questions?"

"Oh, yes. He kept me busy, I can tell you that. He then wished to know more about the known facts of Greek history, dates and so on, which are of course only approximate, particularly in the period before what we call the classical age, Socrates and Plato and the Persian wars. He found that frustrating, I'm afraid, although it's something to which a classical scholar is long accustomed."

"No doubt." Silverton's fingers resumed drumming.

"Indeed," Higganbotham went on, gathering enthusiasm, "it's part of the whole work, really. Comparing history with myth, and applying a chronology to events previously deemed fantastic. We are beginning to understand from Mr. Evans's work, for example, that there existed a specific civilization that we might call Minoan, existing in Crete and indeed the Aegean as a whole in the centuries before the dominance of the Mycenaean Greeks. Mr. Haywood wished to speculate with me what the cause of this transformation might be. Whether the Mycenaean simply defeated the previous inhabitants, as so often happens, or whether some specific event might have precipitated the transfer of power." He lifted another sandwich from the plate. "Forgive me. I haven't eaten since a very inconsequential breakfast on the ship from the mainland."

"No need for restraint, I assure you."

"I set off at once, you see, after I received Mr. Evans's telegram yesterday. I have been concerned about Mr. Haywood for some time."

"Had you? Why?" I said eagerly.

"Why, because we had arranged a meeting in December, and he never appeared." Mr. Higganbotham filled his mouth with sandwich, chewed, and swallowed.

"He never appeared? But why didn't you say something?"

"Well, I had his note. I simply assumed—"

"His note? Where?"

The patting of pockets again, and then a nod. "I left it back in Athens. But—"

Without warning, Lord Silverton sprang from his chair and leapt for the door.

"What on earth—" began Higganbotham, astonished, but I was already out of my own chair and heading for the door, flinging it open again to find Silverton racing across the street in pursuit of something only he could see.

I raised my arm to shade my face against the bright winter sun. Silverton disappeared between the columns of the hotel portico, and after an instant's hesitation, I started after him.

"Where are you going?" exclaimed Mr. Higganbotham, from some district just over my shoulder, but I didn't pause to satisfy his curiosity. I ran across the cobbled roadway, struggling against the heaviness of my skirts, and slipped through the portico to where the hotel doors stood open to the warming air.

Once inside, I had no trouble discovering Silverton's where-abouts: he stood behind the front desk, holding the clerk's lapels by the fistful, having evidently given up his philosophy of gentle persuasion.

"He's gone up to Knossos," Silverton said, "and taken our mule, too, the cheeky bastard."

Mr. Higganbotham flinched at the word *bastard* and glanced at me. "Sir, there's a lady present."

"Where? Oh, do you mean Truelove? She doesn't mind. Do you, Truelove?"

We sat in a private back room of the Hotel Alabaster, overheated by an entirely unnecessary fire; or rather, Mr. Higganbotham and I were sitting, and Lord Silverton was pacing, pacing, a glass of the local liquor in one hand and his pipe in the other. The landlord had been persuaded to give up the room in exchange for his clerk. The *tsikoudia*, I believe, cost extra.

I folded my hands in my lap and said, "I suppose I am resigned to his lordship's habits of speech. I should like to point out, how-ever, that the mule was not ours. He belongs to the hotel, which had every right to hire him out to this man."

"It's a piece of damned cheek, is what it is. However, I shan't complain, as the mule is presently bearing him farther away from our location at every step. Ha! I should like to see his face when he arrives at Knossos, only to find out we've got the jump on him again."

"Still, it doesn't give us much time, does it?"

"No, that's true." He turned to Mr. Higganbotham. "Sir. I believe you were telling us something about my friend Max."

"Was I?" Mr. Higganbotham looked alarmed. "I thought I'd told you all I know already."

"My attention was diverted during the last bit. Something about the Minoans and the Mycenaeans that so vexingly captured Max's attention, and you had arranged to meet him—"

"No, no. It was Mr. Haywood who asked for the meeting. He wrote me in December. He had found something terribly interesting, he said, but it was all quite sensitive and he wanted to bring it to me personally."

"Did he say what it was?" asked Silverton.

"No. But he asked me not to discuss it with anyone; not to mention, in fact, that he had been in touch with me at all, or to disclose any of the arrangements for our meeting."

"Once more with the hush-hush." Silverton drained his glass and set it on the mantel. "Most immensely valuable object, one must conclude."

"I gathered there was somebody else involved," said Mr. Higganbotham. "Someone else, whose motives were venal rather than scholarly, from whom he was trying to conceal this object, whatever it was."

"So you agreed to meet him."

"Yes. I must confess, I was too intrigued to refuse. I arrived at the appointed lodging on the appointed day, but in the end there was only a note, and even that was unsigned. Something had come up, he said, and he would write again when it was safe for us to rendezvous. And I should remain silent about the entire matter until he gave me the all clear."

"How lucky for us, then, that you've elected to break Max's edict."

Mr. Higganbotham rose from his chair and met Silverton with a gaze that had turned decidedly steely. "When I learned yesterday that no one else had heard from Mr. Haywood since that day, I was naturally concerned. I hope my trust has not been misplaced."

"It has not," I said.

He looked at me. "Thank you. And now I expect you will want to track him down there, won't you? His last known abode."

Silverton brought a fist down on the mantel. "Back to bloody Athens again. A needle in a haystack."

"Athens?" Higganbotham looked back and forth between us. "Who said anything about Athens?"

For a moment, neither I nor Silverton made a single sound. I remember how we stared mutely at Mr. Higganbotham's well-kept moustache, waiting for his lips to move again and cure our perplexity; how—at least to my eyes—his brow seemed to take on the radiance of an oracle.

I leapt to my feet. "He didn't meet you in Athens?"

"No, of course not. He wanted to avoid Athens, above all. No, he asked me to meet him rather more remotely, on an island in the Aegean. He would sail there himself, he said, though I told him that was madness, at this time of year. But he insisted that he was an experienced sailor, and the matter could not wait until a more auspicious season."

During the course of this speech, Silverton had removed his spectacles and wiped them with a handkerchief, and was now replacing them on his nose in precise movements. His blue eyes, I thought, were terribly bright; but then my own heart was beating so quickly, I felt almost dizzy.

"Which island?" asked Silverton, very low.

"Well! That, you see, is what I found so intriguing, as a student of classical mythology." Mr. Higganbotham smiled, first at me and then at Silverton, as if it were Christmas Eve and he'd just presented us with an especially pleasing gift. "He asked me to meet him at Naxos."

Now the Lady was blindfolded, she had no advantage over her husband the Prince in her knowledge of the Labyrinth, so she tore a thread loose from the hem of her tunic and unspooled it behind her as she raced through the maze of chambers in the heart of the Palace. But the Prince soon caught her, and the Hero, hearing her cries, followed the sound to the chamber where she was chained. 'Release her,' he said to the Prince, 'and I will submit to whatever torture you require.'

So the Prince chained the Hero, but instead of releasing the Lady he removed her blindfold and said, 'She will first witness your suffering at my hand, for I know she has lain with you and carries your seed in her womb, and if that seed bears fruit, I will repeat this revenge on your innocent babe.'

The Hero roared and fought against his chains, but even his great strength could not wrest the iron free . . .

THE BOOK OF TIME, A. M. HAYWOOD (1921)

Fifteen

W e must leave at once," I said. "Mr. Higganbotham, do your
duties require you to return to Athens immediately, or
can you spare a few days to assist us in Naxos?"

"Truelove—" began Silverton.

"I am at your service, of course," said Mr. Higganbotham.

I strode to the door. "Then I shall find the landlord and have
him retrieve our luggage, and send word to the ship to build steam.
There's not a moment to lose. Silverton, do you think—"

"Madam," said his lordship, in a voice of such deadly certainty
that I stopped my hand on the very knob and turned my head toward him. "A word."

"Silverton, there isn't time to plan the details. That awful
man will come thundering back down the road in short order,
and in the meantime the *Isolde* cannot be ready to depart without
at least some advance warning—"

"Truelove!"

I blinked in astonishment at the thunder in his voice. My hand, shocked into obedience, began to fall away from the knob, and then I remembered myself and straightened. "You have some concern, perhaps? Some *better* plan?"

Silverton's gaze met mine, as raw and hazardous as an electric current. I thought I felt it sizzling the atoms of my skull. In the familiarity of our frequent intercourse, I had forgotten how tall he was, and his height now returned to me: so towering that his hair nearly brushed the ceiling, and his shadow might have sheltered an army.

"Mr. Higganbotham," he said quietly, "will you be so good as to allow me a moment or two of private conversation with Miss Truelove?"

"Of course." Mr. Higganbotham walked toward me, and I stepped back from the threshold as he approached. "I shall be just outside, should you require my assistance," he said, directing his words to me rather than to Silverton, and then the door closed behind him.

"I call that extremely rude," I said.

"Rude? I call it prudent. We don't know the first thing about this Higganbotham fellow, only that he turned up conveniently beside you in a tavern while I was off tracking down a man who means to kill you."

"Us."

"Yes, *us*, though I'm rather more concerned about *your* welfare, Truelove, since you haven't the least bit of training and, what's more, are apparently reckless enough to invite strangers along on an expedition fraught with murderous—"

"Oh, if you're going to go throwing around words like *fraught*—"

He strode up to me and took me by the shoulders. "It *is* fraught, damn it all. It's bloody dangerous, and I can't for the life of me imagine why the duchess sent you along in the first place. To be a millstone around my neck, I suppose. The fly in my ointment, the last damned straw to break my back!"

A knock sounded on the door behind me. "Miss Truelove. Is everything all right?"

I looked up fearlessly into Silverton's blazing face. "Quite all right, thank you, Mr. Higganbotham," I called.

His lordship's hands dropped away. "And there you are. The proof, right on the other side of this door, of your reckless judgment. We have no reason at all to believe that Higganbotham isn't behind this himself."

"He isn't. He's a scholar."

"Scholars are some of the greediest devils I know. Convinced of their superiority to the rest of humanity, and then jealous of the riches that accrue to those who prefer to act instead of study—"

I began to laugh. "I've never heard anything so unreasonable."

"Because you haven't stepped outside that Belgrave Square library long enough to know the world and the men who inhabit it."

"Is *that* what you think? You think I'm *sheltered*?" I pointed my finger out the window. "Do you have any notion of the sorts of men I've encountered, in the course of my duties? I have performed a man's job since my father's death, Lord Silverton, enjoying scarcely a single day to myself in all those years. I have dealt with rich men and poor men, yachtsmen and merchant sailors, City bankers and country farmers, and yes, I have met many scholars. And in my experienced judgment, Mr. Higganbotham is genuinely concerned about his friend, and genuinely curious about this mystery in which Mr. Haywood was embroiled: not because he lusts after riches, but because he is a decent fellow.

And that"—I adjusted the stab of my finger, so that it pierced the center of Silverton's capacious chest—"*that*, I suppose, is what you don't recognize. *Decency*."

In the course of this outburst, Silverton's face had lost all expression. The electricity of his gaze died away, breaking its circuit with mine, retreating to an ordinary blue behind the screen of his spectacles. His fingers, which had been gathered into fists, relaxed at his sides, and he said, quite reasonable now, "Very well. We will follow your judgment in the question of Mr. Higganbotham, since you feel so passionately on his behalf."

"Hardly *passionate*—"

"And since he has so thoroughly gained your trust, I shall leave you under his expert protection while I nip back up to Knossos before we leave. A great relief to my mind, in fact."

I thought, for a moment, that I hadn't heard him properly. My mind fastened on a single word and turned it over, several times, to ensure it was genuine.

"Knossos! You can't go to Knossos!"

"My dear Truelove, have you forgotten that a certain innocent young woman, who has so generously assisted our investigation, lies in the direct path of a dangerous man who will stop at nothing to gain the information he requires?"

"Do you mean Mrs. Poulakis?"

"Yes."

"I beg your pardon. I was thrown off by the word *innocent*."

"Another piece of wit. How clever you've become, Truelove." He turned away to knock the remaining ash from his pipe and replace it in his pocket. "Regardless. I'm heading up now. I find myself in the grip of an irresistible urge to confront this fellow before he begins to make an actual nuisance of himself."

"Confront him? Are you mad?"

"Not at all. I do this sort of thing all the time, or had you forgotten?" Silverton had sat down in front of the desk in the center of the room, and was now rummaging shamelessly through its drawers. He made a triumphant noise and withdrew a sheet of writing paper and a fountain pen.

I watched him with gathering alarm. *This sort of thing.* What sort of thing was that? Did he mean to kill the man? What if Silverton himself were killed? "This is impossible. We don't have time for you to—to do whatever it is you do. We've got to leave for Naxos immediately. Had you forgotten about Mr. Haywood? He stands in far greater need of your help than Mrs. Poulakis."

"You needn't wait for me. Leave as soon as the ship is ready. Brown's on board; give him this note. He'll know what to do, if I'm not back in time."

"But how will you get to Naxos?" I asked, bewildered. Silverton's head was bent over the paper, on which he scribbled furiously.

"I'm a dashed good sailor, Truelove. Didn't you know that? Here." He folded the paper and held it out to me. "Don't worry. I'll be back in time, likely as not."

His face had resumed its ordinary expression of congenial beauty, impossible to penetrate. You could not react in fury to a manner like that, any more than you could argue with the wagging tail of a Labrador retriever.

I took the note between my fingers and asked feebly, "But what if something happens to you?"

He rose from the desk and replaced the pen carefully in its holder. The smile came out, as burnished as ever, if somewhat distorted by the nearby bruise. "Why, Truelove. You know better than that. I am the favorite of the gods, am I not? And, as I'm sure Mr. Higganbotham will happily explain, those immortal chappies never allow their protégés to come to harm."

౼ಎ

In his lordship's absence, I took charge of the arrangements, as swiftly and efficiently as I had learned to do, throughout more than six years of service to so exacting an employer as His Grace, the Duke of Olympia.

A note was dispatched to the *Isolde*, instructing her crew to make ready for an immediate departure, and our luggage was brought out from the windowless room in which we had stored it yesterday morning. The cart and horse already stood waiting by the door, and a man who might be described as a porter, had he not reeked so strongly of the stables, began to load our trunks inside.

"Wait a moment," I said, bending over my traveling desk, which rested atop the single trunk that belonged to me. I pulled on the small handle of the bottom drawer, which opened without impediment, and examined the lock. "It's broken!"

"What's broken?" asked Mr. Higganbotham.

"My desk. Someone has broken the lock. Where's the landlord?"

Mr. Higganbotham jiggled the drawer. "My God, it's outrageous! Did you keep anything valuable inside? Has anything been taken?"

"Only some papers, and photographs that Mr. Haywood had sent to my employer. By good luck, I brought them with me to Knossos instead of leaving them here." I stared at the gaping drawer, and my breath went cold in my chest. The man with the earring, perhaps? Or someone who worked at the hotel, hoping to find valuables?

The landlord, summoned by Mr. Higganbotham, threw up

his hands and insisted he had no knowledge of this, no knowledge at all, and the door had been locked throughout the entirety of our absence. By now, the cart was fully loaded and the minutes ticked by. "I suppose we've got to leave it at that," I said reluctantly, and we climbed into the cart for the short journey to the quayside, where the *Isolde* waited for us, fires stoked, boilers heating impatiently.

"What sort of photographs?" Mr. Higganbotham asked as the cart bounced along the cobbles.

"They are of a certain fresco that was discovered in the Knossos ruins, which is what led Mr. Haywood to his investigation in the first place."

"I say. You don't mind if I take a look, do you?"

I hesitated only an instant. "No, of course not."

I found the photographs in my satchel and handed the first one to him. He took it eagerly and held it up at an angle, so that the image found the afternoon light. I thought perhaps I should tell him about Mr. Vasilakis's conclusion—that the painting was not native to the Minoans—but some instinct made me hold back the words. Perhaps it was the way Mr. Higganbotham held the photograph: with the possessive appetite of a scholar contemplating his particular field of study.

"Interesting," he said. "What is that object in the first man's hand?"

"An excellent question. We are equally puzzled." I made a motion with my fingers to take back the photograph, and he relinquished it to me.

"Perhaps you will be so good as to allow me to study the image at greater length, when time permits," he said.

"Of course."

He looked out the side of the cart, up the hillside toward Knossos itself. "It's curious. I have visited the excavation many times, of course, and I thought I was familiar with all of its frescoes. Most have similar themes, you see, but this one is entirely different."

"Is it? I wish we had had time to see more." I followed his gaze. We could not see Knossos itself, of course; the passing buildings kept obscuring the view, and the details were too far away to distinguish in any case. But it was there, weighing against the base of the mountains. What had it looked like, three thousand years ago? Who had lived there?

And what scenes were playing out between those half-crumbled buildings now?

⌒⌒

But I would not think about Silverton. There was no point. What could I do to help him, after all? My duty lay to the dowager duchess and to Mr. Haywood.

The ship and crew had made nearly ready to depart, the captain informed me. I had only to give the order. The tide was on the point of turning, which would assist our passage out of the harbor in Heraklion.

"We are traveling to Naxos, and a cabin must be made ready for our guest," I said, with all the authority in my power.

"Will Lord Silverton be accompanying us?"

"I hope so. He has been detained at the ruins. If he has not returned in an hour, we shall have to leave without him, I'm afraid." As I said the words, their full import struck me in the chest. *Leave without him.* Leave without Silverton: did I really mean to do that? I added quickly, to cover that instant of panic, "Is his lordship's valet about? I have a message for him."

The captain's mouth registered a flicker of distaste for Mr. Brown, but he informed me readily that the valet was to be found in Silverton's own cabin, supervising the arrangement of the trunks.

Down I went to the main deck, where Silverton's stateroom existed in solitary luxury amidships, but before I reached it, Mr. Brown himself came barreling around the corner of the grand staircase, looking as if someone had spat on his dinner.

"Mr. Brown—" I began bravely.

"Where is he? Why has you left him behind, you nasty b—h?" (I shall not attempt to render his singular accent in any sort of phonetic accuracy.)

"*I* haven't left him behind. He left himself behind." I held out Silverton's note, still folded. "This is for you."

Mr. Brown snatched the note with his right hand—the one that still existed—and opened it.

I inspected the backs of my fingers. "I feel compelled to add, for the sake of clarification, that there is a woman concerned."

Mr. Brown looked up bleakly. "Ain't there always?"

"This sort of emergency is a regular occurrence, then, in his lordship's service?"

As soon as I said the words, I knew I should not have asked. To ask was to imply that Silverton's habits mattered to me.

But Mr. Brown took my curiosity in a matter-of-fact sigh. "There's no woman born can resist him, miss, nor no woman he can resist her wanting of him."

"Ah. He does it all out of the goodness of his heart, does he? So the poor little things won't be disappointed. Dear me, what a cross he bears."

Mr. Brown's eyes rolled heavenward, as if expecting to discover his lordship strumming a harp among the angels, somewhere above the low, flat ceiling of the ship's corridor. "That's it exactly, miss."

"I don't mean to shock either of you, then, but I beg leave to observe that *I* have resisted him without difficulty."

Mr. Brown turned his gaze back down to humble earth and squinted one eye at me. "So far."

I pointed to the note, still in his hands. "Are there any special instructions? How long are we to wait for him, before we depart?"

"That's between me and his lordship, miss. You carry on. He'll be back before we're off, though, or my name ain't Aristophanes Brown."

I took a second or two to absorb this information. Mr. Brown regarded me cryptically, one eye still squeezed shut, while a current of dry wind down the corridor set his left sleeve shivering around the hook.

"I beg your pardon. Did you say your name was *Aristophanes*?"

"Maybe it is and maybe it ain't. We'll find out soon, won't we? Now stand aside."

I was too startled by his bluntness to do anything except step obediently back against the wall, and the valet brushed past me to stomp up the main staircase like a man much put-upon.

❧

Within the hour, Captain Merriwether informed me that the *Isolde*'s steam was fully up, and she lay poised to sail upon my command. I stood on the promenade deck, near the entrance to the deckhouse, and watched the sun drop behind the jagged spine of the mountain range to the west. The quayside was quiet, except for the irregular slap of water against the vessels and the harbor walls; the fishing fleet was secured to the pilings in preparation for the coming dawn, and the fishermen had disappeared into the whitewashed houses and tavernas of the town.

By my side, Mr. Higganbotham leaned his arms against the railing and inhaled the briny air. "I suppose he'll have to catch us up in Naxos."

"So it seems."

The captain waited patiently, a few feet away, but I couldn't quite bring myself to give the order. My eyes strained against the flattening light, trying to detect some sort of movement in the streets below that might belong to a madcap marquess with the devil at his heels. He had left on horseback, looking quite at home and having paid a small fortune for the privilege; would he return the same way? Mr. Brown stood near the bow, pacing and peering. In a moment, I thought, he would jump overboard with the force of his distress.

"Miss Truelove," the captain said, in a voice rich with respect. "Shall I give the order?"

The streets were quiet, the dying sun orange against the western ridge. A last surge of anger filled my throat: Why did he risk himself for her? Surely our need was greater. Surely our claim on his talents was stronger.

Why *her*?

I thought how the gathering sunset would look on his hair, and I turned to the captain and said, "Very well. There's not a moment to be lost, after all. I'm sure he will catch us up soon enough."

Captain Merriwether returned a brisk nod and strode off to the deckhouse. A moment later, a short blast of steam issued from the funnel, and then another. Mr. Higganbotham frowned and covered his ears. The grind of the engines vibrated the wooden boards below our feet, and then came the shouts as the ropes were cast off, and the sense of disorienting motion as we slid away from the dock.

"There is something triumphal, isn't there, about having an entire steamship at one's command," said Mr. Higganbotham.

"It isn't mine, however. It belongs to Mr. Haywood."

Mr. Higganbotham turned to me, astonished. "To Mr. *Haywood*?"

"He is now the eighth Duke of Olympia."

"I *say*! I had no idea." A shocked pause, and then: "He never said a thing." Still another pause, while the wedge of dirty water widened between ship and quayside. "Are you quite sure?"

"Quite sure." I tore my gaze away from the untroubled line of buildings on the western edge of the quay, from which a man hurrying down to the harbor from the southern hills might be expected to emerge, and faced my awestruck companion. "Presuming, of course, we can find him."

The awfulness of this pronouncement struck me anew, and before Mr. Higganbotham could part his lips to reply, I turned away and walked down the larboard railing as the ship began its turn, swinging about to head out of the harbor mouth. The air, which had warmed so considerably during the sunlit day, was now turning to chill, and a sharp breeze had picked up from the northeast. I had changed clothes in my own cabin, into a sensible skirt and neat striped shirtfront, belting a thick woolen cardigan over all, and as the cool majesty of the Venetian fortress edged into view from the other side of the deckhouse, I slid my fingers deep into the pockets.

I thought, *Perhaps if he is killed, he will come to visit me.*

The sea wall crawled past on my left, angling out toward the fortress. Already I was beginning to feel the telltale slosh in my head, the vertigo of seasickness. I fought back, fixing my gaze on the fortress walls ahead, thinking that I could not go to my cabin until Crete went out of sight behind us. The cold draft swept along my temples. I gripped the rail with my two hands. A few yards away at the bow, Mr. Brown seemed to sense my approach and half turned, eyes wide, shouting some alarmed question to me.

"Quite all right," I called back, just before I leaned past the rail and emptied my stomach over the side.

Mr. Brown came by my side directly, no doubt to tender me the usual handkerchief in my distress, but I am not the sort of person to enjoy company in misery and motioned him away. As I lifted my head, however, he did not step back. His attention was fixed not on me, in fact, but at some point in the distance, directly opposite.

I blinked my watery eyes. Mr. Brown let out a thundering halloo.

The few last orange bars of sunlight glared back at me. I lifted one hand to shade my eyes, and an object came into view, moving along the sea wall: a galloping horse, bearing an over-long man whose hair burned like a fireball in the setting sun.

The nausea fell away from my belly, or perhaps I only ceased to notice it. I ran shouting to the deckhouse: *Stop! Stop! It's Silverton! On the sea wall!*

A commotion erupted at once. Captain Merriwether barked out a few terse commands, and the officers flew about the deckhouse. From the bowels of the ship came a massive grinding noise, causing the deck to shudder and the crew, hurrying along the sides, to stagger and grab the rails. They were going to send a boat out; someone was already climbing up to tear off the canvas cover and swing out the davits.

I returned to strain over the rail. Our forward momentum had carried us almost to the fortress, and Silverton and his horse disappeared from view behind the walls. I cupped my hands around my mouth and shouted his name, over and over, as if that could conjure him back.

A faint echo sounded across the water, like a horseshoe striking stone.

Or like a gunshot.

And then there came movement along the fortress walls, along the battlements like little teeth. A golden head popped up, and an arm that waved vigorously in reply to my shouts.

Another crack, and the figure paused, ducked, raised. What the devil was he doing?

He climbed to the edge of the stone battlement, fully visible, outlined by the last burst of sunset, and lifted his arms away from his body to form a cross.

I thought, *My God, he is going to dive.*

And he did.

☙

"You are a bloody fool," I told Silverton, an hour later, as we steamed northward through the inky night.

"What appalling language, Truelove. Someone has corrupted you utterly. I can't guess whom, but I imagine he must be a thorough rascal."

He stood next to the wall in his stateroom, having bathed and changed into a heavy dressing gown of dark green brocade, and had just lit his pipe. A glass of brandy sat familiarly on the dresser nearby, half-empty. He was smiling. His blue eyes shone with unnatural brightness, unencumbered by the spectacles. The shimmer of exhilaration still rippled from his body.

"You might have been killed. If I'm not mistaken, somebody was shooting at you, not that I blame him."

"Oh, there's no doubt about that. I was luring him away from Knossos, you see, with fiendish cleverness." He tapped the mouthpiece of his pipe against his temple. "I only regret I hadn't the means to kill him outright, but the wretch wouldn't give up his gun, and I hadn't the time to quarrel over it."

"And now he knows we've left, and he'll find a way to follow us. So you've accomplished absolutely nothing, except to distract him from troubling your paramour. And if he thinks to double back and question her about our destination, you haven't even done that."

"I could not do less than I did, Truelove, in all honor. In any case, I've alerted her brother to her predicament, and we already know he is her ardent defender." He touched the ugly bruise on his jaw. "What a price one pays for one's pleasures. Even my shoes now lie at the bottom of the harbor, though I daresay I've got a spare pair packed away somewhere in these trunks."

"My God, how can you be so cavalier? You nearly lost your own life, and jeopardized our own investigation into the bargain. And all for a woman!"

"Not jealousy again, is it, Truelove? You'll have me dreaming impossible dreams."

"I'm not jealous! I only—only—" I made a noise of frustration and turned away, so he might not see how my eyes stung with fury.

"Ah. I see. You were *worried* about me, weren't you?" His voice was soft.

"Not worried. It was a great strain, that's all. Having to take charge of everything, and not knowing what had happened to you. I am not accustomed to enterprises of this sort, you know. I have no experience in physical adventure."

I did not hear his approach until the last instant, when his hands folded around my upper arms, and the weedy smell of tobacco enveloped us both.

"You valiant thing, holding everything up. Aren't you supposed to be seasick, or something?"

"I *am* seasick. As soon as I've finished scolding you, I shall go straight to my berth and never get up."

"I'm flattered to the core, Truelove. Here you are, alone with me in my cabin, battling sickness, battling your own notions of propriety, just to deliver me a richly deserved scolding from the goodness of your heart, while I stand here guilty as sin in my dressing gown, and naked as an ape underneath—"

I lurched forward, but his hands would not give way. "Let me go."

"Admit it, my dear. You *like* me."

"I'm glad you're still alive, if that's what you mean." I saw his pipe from the corner of my eye, clasped between the first two fingers of his right hand and not quite touching my shoulder.

"Is that what I saw on your face, when I got to the top of that rope you so kindly threw over the side for me?"

"*I* didn't throw the rope. It was much too heavy. Mr. Higganbotham assisted me."

"The good Higganbotham." His breath was damp on the top of my head. "Well, I'm grateful. To be perfectly honest, I was just as happy to see you. You're a good face to find at the end of an escapade, did you know that? You've a certain look of safe harbor about you."

"If that's meant to be a compliment—"

"It's meant to make you want to kiss me."

This time, I did succeed in breaking away. I spun around to face him, at a safe distance of several feet, my back almost to the wall. The room, I thought, was altogether too warm. "To kiss you!"

"Yes. Why not?"

"Because it's improper!"

He replaced the pipe in his mouth and smiled around it. "But not because you don't *want* to, eh, Truelove?"

"I can't imagine what's come over you."

"What comes over every man after a spot of derring-do. Are you not aware?"

"Then it's a shame Mrs. Poulakis isn't aboard."

Silverton stepped forward and touched my chin with his thumb. "Mrs. P again. Why this preoccupation, Truelove?"

"*I'm* not preoccupied with her. *You're* preoccupied with her."

He shook his head slowly. "My dear, I invite you to think long and hard about how—and most especially *why*—I came to admit the good Thalia to my bed the other night."

"*Last* night."

"Odd. It seems like an age. But the critical point is this, Truelove: When we speak of sexual congress, it is not simply that the act itself gives one pleasure. It is the afterward that matters. It is the sense of relief that arrives with connection to another human being. The illusion, however fleeting, that one is actually and truly loved."

I cannot say why, at that point, I had not already left the room. Certainly it was not proper to remain, and certainly I had no wish to initiate any sort of connection (as he called it) with his lordship, beyond that which was necessary for the success of our joint mission.

Certainly, by then, I knew better than to stake my all on so dubious a wager as a restless English aristocrat.

I can only ascribe my lethargy to shock, or to the extremity of emotion to which I had recently been subject. My nerves were stretched so thin by the anxiety of life and death, they would not now respond to the more ordinary alarm of Lord Silverton attempting to work his expert sexual hypnosis upon me, almost as if I were the sort of woman he preferred to seduce.

When I did not reply, his lordship continued in his soft voice: "There *is* a cure, my dear Truelove, for what ails us."

"For what ails *you*, you mean. I am only seasick."

"And I am sick of life." He brought his hand up to his forehead. "No, that's not true. I'm sick of something else, and I can't quite put my finger on it, but when I look at *you*, Truelove, I can almost—almost glimpse—"

I stepped forward and reached for his spectacles on the dresser, next to his brandy glass. "Here you are, sir. I expect these will help you glimpse whatever you like. And now, if you will excuse me—"

He caught my arm. "Wait."

He had chosen his moment well; our faces were only inches apart. For a brief time, my sluggish nerves paused at the brink. I may even have glanced down at his lips, which until then I had hardly ever dared to do, for I remember thinking how unexpectedly full they were, parted and damp with brandy.

Then the ship began to tilt, and I staggered queasily sideways a step or two, before recovering both my balance and my good sense in the same instant.

"Your lordship," I said, "I believe I am going to be sick," and it was a very good thing that Silverton's private lavatory lay close by, for sick—thoroughly and at length—is exactly what I became.

The Lady closed her eyes and prayed to the gods for their intercession, and at that instant a new roar came to her ears, which she recognized as that of her brother the Beast, for the Hero had kept his promise to her and obeyed those instructions she had given him, and gone first to the chamber in which the Beast was kept to free him from his confinement.

The Prince fled at once at the sight of the Beast, and together the Hero and the Beast contrived to loosen the chains from the walls. When he and the Lady were both freed, the Hero wished to pursue the Prince and sink his own dagger into the Prince's cruel heart, but the Lady said, 'No, remember our plan, and leave my husband to the vengeance of the gods.'

So the Beast concealed himself in a storeroom, while the Lady and the Hero followed the thread until the Lady knew her surroundings, and found the King in his chamber, imbibing the juice of the poppy as the Prince had made his habit. Said the Lady, 'This Hero has killed the Beast your son in the heart of the labyrinth, and therefore the annual tribute from Athens is forfeit . . .'

THE BOOK OF TIME, A. M. HAYWOOD (1921)

Sixteen

❦

I naturally declined dinner in the dining saloon, and instead crept into my familiar brass-railed bed on the starboard side. I know not at what hour I fell asleep, but I woke sometime shortly after dawn, to the sound of a knock on the door of my stateroom. The ship, I realized, was pitching and rolling with unusual vigor.

In retrospect, I should not have presumed that my visitor was Lord Silverton. After all, his last sight of me had not been a salubrious one, though he had behaved like a gentleman, given the circumstances. He had found a washcloth and dampened it at the faucet; he had poured me a little brandy (which I did not dare to drink) and helped me to my own cabin by his own arm, in order to spare me the embarrassment of ringing for a steward. *Shall I come inside and tuck you in?* he had asked, all wicked smiles, and I replied that he had better not, if he had any regard for the beauty of his dressing gown.

But I knew this gallant offer was intended only to prop up my flagging self-regard, for when I hazarded a glance in the mirror before retiring, I hardly recognized myself. I sank into bed in a misery of humiliation, and if I had given myself a moment to gather my logic, I should have known straightaway that the hand behind that eager knock the next morning could not possibly have belonged to Lord Silverton.

I am afraid my surprise—I will not call it disappointment—showed on my face.

"Only me," said Mr. Higganbotham, flushed with high color. "I beg your pardon for the early hour. Are you well enough to speak?"

"Of course. Please come in."

I was not feeling very well, in fact, and it occurred to me that this was the second time in twelve hours that I had entertained a gentleman in the privacy of a steamship cabin, while one of us wore only a dressing gown. Once loosened, my principles apparently meant to remain flaccid.

Or perhaps it was only the effect of sea air, and our distance from England.

Mr. Higganbotham walked in briskly, in the manner of a man who had already breakfasted well and enjoyed no ill effects from the raucous motion of the ship. I rather wanted to smack him. Instead, I said, "I hope you are well, Mr. Higganbotham, and have no bad tidings for me."

"Bad tidings? Why, no. Not at all." He gathered his hands behind his back and looked grave. "I understand you have been subject to *le mal de mer.*"

The *Isolde*, as if to emphasize his words, lurched drunkenly to port. I flung out my hand to catch myself against the wall, while Mr. Higganbotham merely braced his legs and rode out the movement.

"Yes," I said. "Have you happened to take note of the weather this morning? I'm afraid I haven't dared to look outside the porthole."

"It seems a trifle tempestuous."

The ship pitched again. I clutched the corner of the dresser. "Mr. Higganbotham, I regret very much that I must ask you to be brief."

An expression of alarm overtook his face. "Oh. Indeed. Brief I shall be. I only wished to ask whether I might have another look at those photographs of yours. The ones taken of Mr. Haywood's fresco."

"I—well, I suppose so." For some reason, I found myself hesitating.

"Of course, if you'd rather not—"

"No, of course you may see them."

"Because I have no wish to cause any trouble between you and Lord Silverton."

I was staggering toward the writing table on the opposite wall, where my traveling desk had been placed the previous evening. I glanced back, over my shoulder. "Trouble? Between me and Silverton? Why on earth?"

Mr. Higganbotham turned to gaze out the porthole, behind which a dim and monotonous steel-gray ocean met an equally monotonous steel-gray sky. "I had the impression that his lordship does not entirely trust my motives."

"His lordship is naturally suspicious. Suspicion is essential to his work, after all." I turned back to the desk and opened the bottom drawer. "I disagree with him on this matter, of course, and I told him so."

"Thank you for that. I assure you, your trust is not misplaced."

He took the photographs from my outstretched hand, and, in a noble show of restraint, managed to avoid examining them at once. Instead, he fingered the edges, turning them upside down before righting them again. "The reason I asked is because— Forgive me, but I don't wish to be indelicate—"

"Indelicate? In what way?"

Mr. Higganbotham discovered something interesting in the weave of the rug at his feet. "I had the impression that there is a kind of—of mutual—*understanding*, between you and his lordship."

"An understanding? Between me and his lordship?"

"Am I wrong?"

Mr. Higganbotham looked up from the rug, and his eyes were so hopeful, his lip so uncertain beneath his moustache, I felt the warmth of kindness soften my bones.

"Quite wrong, Mr. Higganbotham. I assure you, Lord Silverton and I are merely colleagues, bent upon a similar goal. We share a certain degree of friendship, but nothing more, and I would go so far as to say that his lordship is hardly the sort of man to whom I could *imagine* myself offering anything more."

The entire aspect of Mr. Higganbotham's face brightened, from hope to gratitude, and even in my discombobulated state, I could not help feeling the transformation as a compliment. Not that I had any designs on the gentleman, of course—goodness, no—but there was a certain small wound in my chest, a little open sore that was soothed by Mr. Higganbotham's relief at the news that my affections were not in any way engaged by Lord Silverton.

"Thank you, Miss Truelove, for your frankness." He clutched the photographs to his chest. "And now I see that you would rather be left in peace, so I shall not detain you another instant. I hope to find you shortly recovered from your malady, thought I must say"—here he wove his way carefully to the tilting door—"judging by what I have seen of the weather this morning, the prospects for a steadier sea are not altogether good."

❦

To say the least.

I spent the rest of the morning in misery, trying to fix my gaze on some object that might have the courtesy to remain still, but even when I shaded the lights and closed my eyes, the sense of vertigo continued, as if I were spinning in the center of God's palm while he carried me about, swinging his arms as he went.

At noon I forced myself to rise and dress. I could not face lunch, but I wanted to step outside for a short time to assess the weather, and then perhaps to find the captain and discuss our progress (or perhaps our lack of it) toward Naxos.

"What the devil are you doing out here?" demanded his lordship, as the door banged shut behind me.

"The same thing you are! Taking the air!"

I had to shout, because the wind snatched away my words at the very instant they left my mouth. I gazed out to the angry sea, and I could not believe this was the same world I had known yesterday. The deck slanted at an impossible angle, and a flume of water exploded into the air a few yards away, stinging my face with a hundred tiny pieces of cold salt shrapnel.

"Go back inside!" Silverton shouted back, but his words had the opposite effect, and determined me to stay. I staggered to the rail and gripped it with both fists, gloved in leather, while my small woolen hat strained against the draft. And yet, I did not feel any worse. The fresh air, the mighty pitch of the ship, seemed to breathe new life into me.

Silverton's hands appeared next to mine. "Aren't you sick?"

"I shall manage."

"You're a damned stubborn thing, Truelove. Hold on."

The ship found a particularly towering wave, and I lost my breath in the crash of water against steel, the groan of rivets, the tilting climb and weightless descent. I thought of the painting in the Duke of Olympia's morning room, the tiny frigate on the wide ocean, and though I would never have said the words aloud, I was glad for the solid weight of Silverton's woolen forearm nearby, and his large leather hand sharing the rail with mine.

"How much farther to Naxos?" I shouted.

"Another couple of hours, I should think. We should be there by now, if it weren't for this damned weather!"

"But how will we land?"

"Damned if I know. Watch out!"

We rode out another wave, and this time Silverton threw out an arm to steady me, or rather to steady us together, against the greedy tug of the sea. "I apologize," he said, into my ear.

"Apologize for what?"

"For my—" Another sharp pitch. "For my conduct last night. There is a surge of elation after these adventures, which—"

"I can't hear you very well!"

Without warning, he took me by the arm and dragged me inside the deckhouse. He had to fight the door with both hands in order to close it. We stood in the corridor, panting a little, wet and reeking of salt and ozone. Silverton took off his hat and shook it, sending off a fine spray into the glossy white wall.

"You see, Truelove," he said, examining the hat, "when a man fights his enemy and then escapes with his life—"

"You *fought* him?"

"A short struggle. But as I said, after he fights back the possibility of death, he naturally craves life." He looked up, somber eyed and repentant. "An intense biological desire. Do you see what I mean?"

"I suppose so."

He replaced the hat on his head. "I gave offense. It won't happen again, I promise you."

"I quite understand. You were overwrought. I am not angry with you about that."

"But you're angry with me for going back to Knossos in the first place, aren't you?"

I shrugged. "It was a matter of honor to you, having committed the act in the first place."

"I see. But I would have gone back anyway, Truelove, whether or not I had gone to bed with her. She had given us the information, you see. *That* was the act of trust I was bound to return."

"But she gave you the information because you *had* spent the night with her."

There must have been something in my voice, because he peered at me, beneath a disturbed brow. "Did it really pain you so much?"

"Because it was thoughtless! Because it placed us both in danger!"

He was frowning, patting his pockets as if he meant to pull out his pipe, and I had the impression that he wanted to say something more. The ship pitched, and we crashed together against the wall, and when we had mutually untangled, muttering overlapping apologies, we found ourselves doing so under the stern gaze of the *Isolde*'s captain.

(To be sure, Silverton was much the taller man, but such was the natural schoolmaster's authority of Captain Merriwether that he seemed to tower over us both.)

"What ho! Any news, sir?" said Silverton cheerfully, straightening his jacket, as if he had not just been discovered in a stormy corridor, enjoying the close embrace of a female passenger.

"I regret to say that we are unable to make a perfect reckoning of our location at the present time, given the force of the storm," said Captain Merriwether, in the dark tones of a man who has certain other regrets, which he is too discreet to mention, "but I expect we shall reach the proximity of Naxos within the hour. We shall, however, be unable to enter the harbor under the present conditions."

"But the matter is urgent!" I said. "We have others in pursuit, and we cannot allow them to find Mr. Haywood first!"

"Not at the cost of the ship, madam, or your life."

I turned to Silverton. "Can we get a boat in, do you think?"

"A boat?" He shrugged. "Why not? I did enjoy a spot of sculling in my university days."

Captain Merriwether started in shock. "With respect, sir, I must urge you forcefully to wait until conditions are calmer. I cannot answer for your safety if you attempt the land in a boat."

"And how long until conditions are calmer, do you think?"

"I can't say. These Mediterranean blows are damned unpredictable. It might be over by tonight, or it might last several more days. My Marconi man is attempting to contact the station in Naples to gather any reports on the possible size of the storm."

Silverton considered me from the corner of his eye. "What do you think, Truelove? Wait here, or chance it in the boat?"

"I don't wish to put you in any unnecessary danger . . ."

"But you're itching to land before our fellow with the earring beats us to it." He nodded. "Very well, Captain Merriwether. Make the boat ready, if you will."

"But, sir!" The captain was appalled.

The ship began its familiar climb, and I braced my arm against the wall, waiting for the inevitable slow fall. My stomach lurched queasily, whether because of the ship's motion or dread of the ordeal to come. We crested, and when I stumbled once more against the corridor wall, despite my best efforts to remain standing, Silverton's shoulder was already there to cushion the impact.

Oh, the fellow had more faults than I could name, but I could not deny that his lordship was a good man to have at one's back.

I straightened from the wall and turned my head to meet Silverton's gaze.

Are you with me? I asked silently.

"No doubt we shall be killed," said Silverton, as cheerfully as ever, "but they do say drowning's the best way to go."

❧

"This is madness," gasped Mr. Higganbotham, as we lurched from wave to wave through the darkening water. "I can't even see the island!"

"That's because it's behind you," I said. I was sitting in the boat's stern, holding the rudder, while Silverton and Mr. Higganbotham pulled for shore. At the time, I was not an expert on the steering of a vessel, even one so small as the *Isolde*'s tender, but Silverton had assured me that it was as simple as guiding a bicycle. Which I had not done, either, to be perfectly honest, but I cared not to mention this to his lordship at such a precarious moment.

In fact, the storm had steadied somewhat since the middle of the day, or else we might not have attempted this landing at all,

even for the sake of outrunning our enemy. The captain thought
it might blow over by morning, and we might as well wait, but I
could not. I could not stand off Naxos throughout the rest of the
afternoon and all night, while the answers to all our vexing questions lay within sight. So now I sat on a plank of wood in the tender's
narrow stern, directing a tiller by I know not what instinct, ignoring
the churn of my belly and my head as we fought the current and
tilted past the harbor entrance, filling our lungs with rain at every
breath.

Ahead, the smudges on the horizon began to resolve into individual buildings, though I could not tell them apart as they bobbed
in and out of view around the laboring heads of Lord Silverton and
Mr. Higganbotham. Silverton's *spot of sculling*, as it turned out,
encompassed the Henley singles championship for Oxford two
years running (or so the captain had reverently confided in me),
and under his brief instruction, Mr. Higganbotham now pulled
with remarkable dexterity, if not exactly ease. As we cleared the
mouth of the harbor, my spirits began to lift, despite the wind and
rain and waves and nausea: I thought, *We might actually make it.*

But the harbor was not the open water, and the storm had
brought every vessel into port. The fishing boats strained at
their moorings, cavorting about like horses on picket lines, and
it fell to me to avoid the capricious twists and swings of each
craft as we passed, the vicious eddies that formed and disappeared around these obstructions.

Mr. Higganbotham was tiring fast, and even Silverton's teeth
were now bared with the effort of fighting a current that wished to
dash us against the ancient stone wall protecting the harbor. I had
to brace both hands on the tiller, which shuddered under my grip,
and the surge of hope that had filled my limbs as we crossed into the

port now turned to panic. The force of the current shoved us to starboard, so vengefully that I could scarcely maintain my hold on the tiller, and in a minute, in two minutes, even Silverton's great strength could not save us. The landing was too far away. The forward motion was no match for the lateral.

Beware the lee shore, my father used to warn me, speaking metaphorically, and now I saw in literal fact that he was right.

Silverton must have seen our conundrum reflected on my face. His bared-tooth animal expression turned into a grin—*Never fear, Truelove, we shall fight our way clear of this*—and when I tried to yell back that I couldn't do it, that I simply could not battle the tiller one single instant longer, he seemed to understand. He leaned forward and muttered something into the tiring Higganbotham's ear, and Mr. Higganbotham dropped his oars and dove forward to take the tiller from my hands.

"The rope!" shouted Silverton. He nodded downward at his own feet, while his arms heaved at the oars.

I crawled forward along the bottom of the boat, clambering over Mr. Higganbotham's seat, until my hands encountered the coil of rope against his lordship's shoe, the one that was meant to moor us to the dock, except that we were at least a hundred yards from our goal, a hundred yards that might as well be a hundred miles.

"Find us a piling!" shouted Silverton.

"A what?"

"A piling! Look around you!"

I struggled upward and craned my neck. "I don't—I don't—"

"Look!"

In the heavy gray light and the tangle of shipping, I could hardly distinguish one shape from another. The rain streamed down my face and into my soaked clothes. I steadied myself on the heaving edge of the boat, and for an instant, beyond the shadow of a small cutter, I thought I saw a faint glow.

I blinked my eyes to clear them of rain, and when I looked again I saw her, standing imperiously atop the water, next to a narrow black post to which a pair of vessels appeared to be moored. Her hands were planted on her plump hips, and her smooth dark hair did not stir so much as a millimeter in the gale. She seemed to be wearing a white sash across her breast. I could not see her face, but I had the idea that she was frowning through the rain.

I flung the knotted end of the rope toward her, as far as my strength would reach.

For ten days and ten nights the Hero searched for the Prince among the intricate chambers of the Palace of the Labrys, but to no avail. At last the Lady went to him and said, 'Let us give up the Prince to the vengeance of the gods and sail to Athens as you vowed to me, for I am sick of the sight of this palace and cannot abide here another day, and my brother longs to see the sight of sunshine.'

So the Hero agreed and gathered together the Athenian youths, and together they boarded the waiting ships, where the Beast was waiting for them in the darkness of the hold, wherein he had concealed himself.

As the Hero and the Lady stood on the deck, he returned to her the Medallion of the Labrys she had given him as a guard against death, and the Lady said, 'This medallion has proven its worth, and indeed I shall now have need of its protection myself, for I am with child by your love of me . . .'

THE BOOK OF TIME, A. M. HAYWOOD (1921)

Seventeen

"The most extraordinary thing I have ever witnessed," said Mr. Higganbotham, cradling his glass of brandy to his lips as if it were his mother's milk. "I thought you should never throw the rope half that distance, and there it went! Settling over the piling as if the hand of God had guided it."

I cast down my eyes so he could not read their expression. "They say one is capable of almost anything, at the instant of crisis."

"Yes, I suppose that's true. One could never expect a female to throw a rope so expertly, in ordinary circumstances. Wouldn't you say so, your lordship?"

Silverton turned from his contemplation of the view from the window. "What's that?"

We were sitting in the private parlor of a certain inn in Naxos, the proprietor of which had been astonished beyond measure to find us banging on his door in the middle of a February gale. His hospitality had equaled his astonishment, however, and in short order we were bundled into this snug room in the company of a bottle of good French brandy and three sets of fresh clothes, which did not fit properly—Silverton, in particular, looked as if he were wearing a suit meant for an adolescent—but had the inestimable virtue of being dry.

"Miss Truelove's marvelous feat of strength, in the harbor," said Mr. Higganbotham. "Were you not amazed?"

Silverton moved away from the window and went to the fire, which he poked restlessly with an iron from the set to the right of the mantel. His hair was still damp, though brushed back neatly from his face, exposing both the perfect angle of his cheekbones and the lurid bruise left behind by the housekeeper's brother.

"Not particularly. I'm accustomed, by now, to Miss Truelove's extraordinary abilities, when she is called upon to exercise them." He turned the corner of his face to me and smiled privately. "More grateful than amazed."

"This is all quite ridiculous," I said. "It was a lucky throw, that's all. I believe we have God's providence to thank for our salvation, and of course your unflagging efforts, Lord Silverton, in manning the oars and maneuvering us to safety once we were secured to the piling. I can only apologize for putting us all in such danger. If I had known how just treacherous the harbor waters would be—"

"Oh, never mind that, Truelove. It's always best if we don't know the dangers first, or we should never attempt anything important. Isn't that so, Mr. Higganbotham?"

"Oh. Quite."

His lordship stuck the fire iron back into its stand with perhaps more force that was strictly necessary. The sleeves of his jacket ended a full two or three inches above his wristbones, giving the action a comical air of youthful rebellion. I thought how he had hauled in the boat to the dock, securing bow and stern with another rope, and then hoisted us both to the solid wooden surface by his own arms in the calm and competent manner of a man ferrying passengers across a millpond.

Outside the window, an unruly dusk had settled over the town, and the wind and rain still battered the stone buildings. We had been lucky to find the inn at all—Mr. Higganbotham's memory was not precise, and we were shivering and wet and exhausted after our ordeal—and the thought of heading back out into that forbidding climate made my bones ache.

But as Silverton straightened from the fire and turned to face us both, he showed no sign of fatigue. He clasped his hands behind his back and said, "In any case, we've almost certainly achieved an advantage of considerable length over our adversary, which was, after all, the point of the exercise. And if the two of you will excuse me, I mean to press home that advantage directly."

"Why, where are you going?" I asked.

"To have a few words with our landlord, my dear, and any other likely persons I can find wandering about. That plump young lady who fetched our brandy, for example, looked as if she knows a great many valuable things, and I mean to coax every last one of them out of her." He winked, bowed, and left the room.

"I say. What a curious fellow he is," said Mr. Higganbotham, gazing at the closed door as if it might produce some clue to solve the riddle that was Lord Silverton.

"I'm afraid I have grown used to his little jokes, by now. But he's quite right to begin questioning the staff. We should find out everything we can before starting our search tomorrow morning, or else we shall end up wasting a great deal of valuable time." I obeyed the command of my aching muscles and settled back in my armchair, which was plump and substantial, the most comfortable chair in the world at this particular moment. The fire had done its work well, and the room now seethed with warmth, replacing a chill in my bones that I had begun to think was permanent. *You must get up*, I told myself. *You must join Silverton in questioning the staff.* But I couldn't move. I closed my eyes, because they left me no choice.

"Yes, of course," said Mr. Higganbotham, and I had to think back to recall what, exactly, he was agreeing to. I heard him sit down on the sofa nearby, the old springs creaking, and I forced my eyes to open again.

"And you, Mr. Higganbotham? What do you remember of this hotel, and the circumstances of your earlier visit?"

"Not much, I'm afraid." He toyed with the glass in his hands, which was nearly empty. "May I ask how Lord Silverton came to accompany you on your search for Mr. Haywood? If you will forgive me, he hardly seems the most logical choice to be entrusted with the protection of a young and—you must allow me to say it—charming lady."

"I think you're under a misapprehension, Mr. Higganbotham. I am not so young as you imagine, and I am not a lady accustomed to gentle protection. I am—or rather, I *was* the personal secretary of the Duke of Olympia, Mr. Haywood's great-uncle, and I am quite capable of guarding my own person."

"Yes, of course. I didn't mean to imply otherwise."

"As for his lordship, he was a friend and colleague of the late duke, who has traveled widely and is familiar with the—well, with these sorts of adventures. I don't admire his manner of living, perhaps, but he has supplied the most invaluable assistance through-out. Don't you agree?"

Mr. Higganbotham glanced at his palms, which were red and blistered from his labors with the oars. "Oh, yes. Beyond doubt." He paused. "In one of his letters, Mr. Haywood mentioned that he was setting up some sort of institute, back in England, to do with his studies."

"Yes, that's true. His uncle the duke, in fact, was very much involved in its organization, which is why . . ." I allowed my words to trail away. Had not Her Grace enjoined me to secrecy? But I had already shown this man the photographs, and Mr. Haywood himself had trusted him.

Silverton, however, did not.

"Which is why . . . ?" Mr. Higganbotham said gently.

"Which is why his disappearance is all the more frustrating. Are you quite sure you can't remember any details? He said noth-ing about the nature of this circumstance that prevented him from making the rendezvous?"

"No. Only the note. According to the landlord, he had not even stayed the night. He only stopped by the previous day, left the note to my attention, and departed at once." Mr. Higgan-botham glanced at the door. "Really, I can't think what his lord-ship hopes to discover."

"Was there anyone with him? A woman, perhaps?"

"The landlord didn't say, and I'm afraid I didn't inquire. At the time, I was disappointed, but I imagined nothing sinister."

"You didn't ask anyone in the harbor how he had arrived, or whether he had left?"

Mr. Higganbotham shook his head. "I did not. If I'd known . . ."

"Yes, of course. In the morning, at daybreak, we shall go down to the harbor together and investigate, while Silverton makes inquiries in the town. I'm sure we shall find out soon enough. He can't have simply dissolved into thin air."

"You are a terribly determined woman, Miss Truelove."

"I only do what I must."

He smiled and leaned forward, placing his forearms on his knees. The fire cast a warm glow on the side of his face. "Allow me to observe that you do it very well indeed. You are an immense credit to a sex I already revere."

It was a beautiful compliment, far more elegant than Silverton's casual assertion that—what was it?—that he was accustomed to my extraordinary abilities. I opened my mouth to say something suitable in reply, and as I did so, I happened to notice the small, plump, blue-robed figure now sitting in the armchair opposite me, her feet propped up on a cushion. Upon her miniature torso she displayed the same white sash as before, in the harbor, but this time her face shone with approval.

"Mr. Higganbotham," I said, "do you think we might persuade the landlord to bring us a tray of tea?"

Her Majesty wasted no time. "*This* is more the thing," she announced, clasping her hands in her lap. "Exactly what I have intended for you."

I pitched my voice just above a whisper. "Madam, I must entreat you to leave at once. You cannot simply *appear* here like this."

"Ha! You were grateful enough to see me in the harbor. Don't think for an instant that it was your own humble strength that got that rope over the piling. Or do we still pretend I am only an illusion?"

"As his lordship said, I am capable of extraordinary ability, when I set my mind to the task."

"Hmph. Stubborn girl. You are entirely unworthy of the trouble I take on you. I sometimes wonder why I bother."

My fingers tightened around the arms of the chair. "An excellent question, madam. Why, exactly, do you bother?"

The Queen extracted her right hand from the neat pile on her lap and extended the forefinger. "That hardly matters, does it, since you continue to deny my existence, and to ignore my excellent advice. You have allowed Silverton to charm his way into your affections, when I have warned you repeatedly that he is not the sort of man to bring any woman happiness."

"I beg your pardon. I have not allowed Silverton into my affections at all."

The royal finger wagged. "Do you think me unaware of what transpired in his lordship's stateroom last night?"

"Nothing at all transpired in his stateroom. We hardly touched."

"Oh, but the *electricity*." Her voice was scathing. "The very air between you two. You must remember that you are the susceptible sort, Miss Truelove. You are the kind of woman who enjoys bedsport, who is tempted and allured by the promise of pleasure."

I jumped to my feet. "How do you know this?"

"Because I am that same sort of woman, of course."

I was too dumbfounded to reply. I gazed at the razor parting of her hair, exactly down the middle, as if Moses himself had stood on her forehead and commanded the two sides to separate. At her round little figure, and the bosom that swelled beneath the sleek blue wool of her gown, divided by a white satin sash.

"One does not conceive nine children in rapid succession unless one is either *excessively* dutiful, or intensely passionate. And

I am not so dutiful as *that*, I assure you." The Queen formed her lips into a self-satisfied smile.

"Your Majesty, this is all quite—quite—"

"We kept a lock on our door, my husband and I, when he was alive, which we could operate from the bed itself. One is so often embarrassed by the early entrance of servants into one's room, you know. And those precious minutes at dawn, when one has just woken up inside the embrace of one's husband, are, in my opinion, the time when one's passions run warmest."

I put my hands over my face, to block out the sight of her animated expression. "Good God," I muttered between my fingers.

"I have shocked you. Good. The trouble, of course, is that coition leads to a much less desirable condition: that of being with child, which I always found extremely disagreeable. To say nothing of the tedium of laboring to bring that child into the world, and all its attendant miseries and humiliations. And then there is the babe itself, a red squashed little thing. I never could understand this instant worship of motherhood. I did not become interested in my children until they were old enough to ask questions, and even then I found them frequently tiresome and altogether too inclined to disregard my authority." She paused and drew breath. "But while we quarreled often, my husband and I were most happy in our marriage, and I would wish the same for you, Miss Truelove. I would wish you the happiness that derives naturally from a marriage of two devoted minds, who are wholly and utterly faithful to each other."

I let my hands fall away, into the folds of the unfamiliar dress of navy wool that draped like a sack over my body. "I have no thoughts of marriage, madam."

"Mr. Higganbotham would be ideal. He is a gentleman pursuing a genteel profession. He has a small but secure fortune with which to keep you. You might live a virtuous and unexceptionable life, in a part of the world in which your mother and her past are quite unknown."

"My mother! What has my mother to do with any of this?"

"We are well aware that you have experienced embarrassments, from time to time, from certain men who were once acquainted with her." She had reverted to the plural, as she liked to do when she meant to impress me with her importance.

"I don't know what you mean."

"Don't you? I suggest you think very hard, Miss Truelove, about the future that awaits you when you return to England. Whether or not you discover the whereabouts of the new duke, you cannot continue as a personal secretary to a young and comely man who is a stranger to you. It is most improper, to say nothing of impractical. What will you do?"

"At the present time, I am only concerned with finding Mr. Haywood and ensuring his safe ascension to the title that rightfully belongs to him. I have no time for any other considerations."

"Well, you should do. And I urge you forcefully to consider how a union with Mr. Higganbotham might render you far happier than any other of the possible courses open to you."

"How utterly inspiring."

"I only speak the truth." She lifted her prim eyebrows. "For surely you don't imagine that a man of Lord Silverton's rank would wish to *marry* you?"

I lifted my chin and stretched my spine to its greatest possible length. "What I don't understand, madam, is why a woman who has accomplished so much, who led our great British nation for the greater part of a century, should see marriage as the greatest height to which a female might aspire."

The round blue eyes narrowed at me. "Because, my dear. Unlike me, you have a choice in the matter. I suggest you choose wisely. That is all."

A knock sounded on the door. I turned my head and said, "Come in."

A maid entered, bearing a tray, and I remembered that I had sent Mr. Higganbotham away to order a tea that I hadn't really wanted. I motioned to the table behind the sofa, and the young woman gratefully eased her burden on the wooden surface. I searched for Mr. Higganbotham, but he had not accompanied the maid back into the room.

The other armchair was now empty, as if the illusion had never appeared.

"Do you know where Mr. Higganbotham has gone?" I said to the maid.

She looked at me helplessly and shrugged her shoulders.

"Mr. Hig-gan-both-am." I raised one hand a few inches above my own head, palm down, to approximate the height of a male companion. "The man who was here with me."

She shrugged again, bequeathed me an apologetic smile, and then bobbed what might be called a curtsey and left the room.

I went to the tray and lifted the lid of the blue-and-white china pot. My hand, I realized, was trembling very slightly. The contents were not tea at all, but thick black coffee, still hot. I poured a cup and sipped it, considering the now-empty chair and the gloomy windows, and the liquid that burned my empty stomach.

More hungry than thirsty, I realized, and that was my excuse to leave the cozy room and go in search of my companions.

The hallway was silent, almost eerily so, and much cooler than the snug parlor in which I had spent the past hour. I walked past the rough white walls, clicking my ill-fitting shoes against a floor made of worn stone, and tried to retrace our earlier steps back to the common room.

As I drew closer, I heard the reassuring patter of low voices, and I followed the sound to the large room at the inn's entrance. A pair of men, dark-haired and wet, sat at one of the tables, drinking from a set of small glasses. They looked up in astonishment as I appeared in the doorway. I pretended not to see them, and instead spread my gaze extravagantly around the room, which seemed to serve equally as foyer, tavern, and dining room.

But no one else was there.

A flush crept upward from the shelter of my collar, burned there by the unwavering inspection of the two strangers, whom I still feigned not to notice. Where the devil had Silverton and Mr. Higganbotham gone? It wasn't a large inn, and surely they would not have ventured back out into the storm at this late hour, having neither dined nor informed me of their intentions.

One of the men spoke a few words, presumably in Greek, and began to rise from his seat. He had the leathery skin and broad hands of a fisherman. Beneath his dark beard, his expression was kind, almost soft, but for some reason the action filled me with alarm. I backed away from the doorway and into a solid human chest.

"Silverton!" I turned in relief.

But the chest did not belong to his lordship. It was the landlord, who explained to me in halting English that Silverton had left the premises a quarter hour ago in the company of the inn's lovely barmaid.

⁓

Dinner, carried up to my room by the landlord himself, consisted of a fragrant vegetable soup, fish, bread, and pickled olives, accompanied by wine.

"A great shame," said Mr. Higganbotham, for perhaps the dozenth time in the past hour. He sat back in his seat and sloshed the wine about in his glass, inspecting the results with a keen eye. "I might have expected better from a man of his parts and stature, but I suppose these aristocrats simply cannot help themselves."

I picked at my fish and agreed that this tendency to amour represented an unfortunate weakness on his lordship's part, but I expected he would return by daybreak. He would never willingly jeopardize the investigation.

"Wouldn't he?" Mr. Higganbotham released a sigh and shook his head at his empty plate. His disappointment, thank goodness, had not affected his appetite.

"No. And it's entirely possible that he thought the girl had some useful information."

"And *this* is his means of interrogation?" Another shake of that well-tended head. His hair was terribly thick and waved just so at the temples, so that I couldn't help wondering if nature were perhaps receiving some sort of friendly assistance. "How sorry I am, Miss Truelove, that a mind so delicate as yours must be exposed to such corruption."

My room at the inn was not large, and when Mr. Higganbotham had swung down the stairs and directed our dinner to be served here—the common room, he said, was far too public a stage for a lady of good English breeding—I had considered objecting. Mr. Higganbotham had placed his chair so close to my bed that his elbow rested, from time to time, on the corner of my pillow; my own chair sat only inches from the whistling fireplace and the rack from which hung my drying clothes. The entire effect was one of forced intimacy, and I had the distinct idea that if I turned, I would see my father standing by the mantel, attending closely to our conversation.

But then I relented, because anything was less awkward than having dinner with Mr. Higganbotham in his own room, and *here*, at least, I was in command.

I thought of the Queen's earlier words, or rather those words I had imagined the Queen to say. "I am not *quite* so delicate as that, Mr. Higganbotham," I said crisply.

"Not by circumstance, perhaps. But surely by *nature*." Mr. Higganbotham set down his wineglass and leaned toward me, over the dinner that had been set so carefully on the small wooden table in my room. "I am grieved, Miss Truelove, *grieved* that this crisis has forced you to witness all the degraded aspects of human nature, when you should be safely home in England, surrounded by a loving family."

"And yet, it's the strangest thing. When I pause to reflect, I find I'm rather enjoying myself, Mr. Higganbotham, except for the anxiety over Mr. Haywood's welfare. And the inclement weather, of course. I begin to think that adventure agrees with me."

"You've hardly eaten."

"Only because of my present concern."

Mr. Higganbotham reached across the table, and I withdrew my hand just in time, so that he was forced to divert himself to the stem of his wineglass at the last instant.

"I only wish I could relieve your *every* concern, madam," he said quietly.

"Very kind of you, I'm sure, but where would we be without our concerns? An awfully bland sort of existence, I should think. What did you think of the photographs?"

He blinked. "Photographs?"

"The snaps of Knossos. The ones you were so ardent to study, you arrived at my stateroom door at seven o'clock in the morning."

"Yes, that's true." He dropped his gaze and shifted in his seat, as a schoolboy might when questioned about the contents of his desk. "They were—well, that is to say, they proved very much as I suspected from the beginning."

"Dear me. Suspected what?"

Mr. Higganbotham looked up mournfully. "I'm sorry to have to break such untidy news, Miss Truelove, but I fear these particular frescoes are not genuine. I mean, they are frescoes right enough, but they cannot possibly have been painted during the period during which the palace was occupied." He paused to take his lower lip under his teeth. "Can you tell me—do you think Mr. Haywood had truly based his studies on their discovery?"

"Ah," I said.

"Ah?"

"Nothing. Yes, this is disappointing news. How extraordinary. Are you quite certain?"

"I cannot be certain, of course, without seeing the paintings in situ. But the subjects and the style are all quite wrong, and what is more, it makes no sense."

"In what way?"

He was leaning forward again, but this time the animation in his expression had nothing to do with his concern for my delicate mind. "Because we are meant to interpret the three figures as the triptych of the labyrinth—Theseus, Ariadne, and the Minotaur—and yet they are positioned in such a way that defies every single known recounting of the myth."

Was it my imagination, or did a swift intake of breath occur in the small space behind me? A gasp: but not of surprise, I thought, though I could not have said why I knew this.

Not of surprise, but dismay.

"I am afraid you have lost me. Did you say the fresco depicts Theseus and Ariadne?"

"And the Minotaur." Mr. Higganbotham nodded vigorously. "Or so we are meant to believe, although the artist—whoever he may be—has chosen not to portray the actual head of the beast. But merely *placing* such an illustration inside what is deemed to be the palace of Knossos would naturally lead the viewer to assume that it represents the actual myth for which Crete is famous. Just as the repeated depiction of the labrys throughout the ruins leads us inevitably—almost *too* inevitably, if you understand me—to conclude that these buildings were, in fact, the Knossos of legend." He tapped his forehead. "The human brain, you see, craves these connections. We want *sense* in our world; we want things to fall neatly into place. We want a guiding hand. Fate, or God himself."

"Are you saying the palace *isn't* Knossos?"

"I only mean that we *assume* it is. It may well be, but how do we know for certain? And yet we pretend this is fact. In the same way, your average fellow sees a certain fresco on a wall at Knossos—assuming, as he does, that this building is the true Knossos—and he will say, at first sight, *Ah! These three figures must certainly be the great Knossos myth come to life; there can be no other explanation.* But the painting, I am afraid, does not make sense."

"Why not?"

"Oh, a hundred small things. In the first place, it is Theseus leading Ariadne out of the labyrinth, when we know it was Ariadne's own ball of string that allowed Theseus to escape after having slain the beast. It is *Ariadne* who reigns in the labyrinth, *Ariadne* who leads, because of her love for Theseus."

Mr. Higganbotham's eyes were bright with passion, and he was now arranging olives on his plate, demonstrating the relative positions of his mythological characters. His fingers were long and white, the nails neatly trimmed, and they maneuvered the olives with a certain capability, a tensile strength that mesmerized me. In the harbor, I had dismissed him as so much ballast in our struggle to make landing, but here he stood athwart his element. He had transformed from the miniature to the colossal.

"And there is the Minotaur. Why is his head hidden from us?"

"Because that part of the fresco did not survive."

"But why? It's a damned coincidence, that everything else in the painting shows up beautifully, but the most interesting part—the Minotaur's head—doesn't survive. And then there's the matter of that camera in the hand of Theseus."

"You noticed it?"

"Miss Truelove, I'm wholly familiar with Mr. Haywood's field of interest. I naturally assumed that some anachronism would exist in this fresco that so fascinated him. And there it was, so obvious as to be laughable. No, the fresco is obviously a fraud, the unskilled effort of a mediocre artist who retains only a superficial understanding of his subject."

"But why? Why go to such trouble?"

Mr. Higganbotham gave up his olive and nudged the plate

away. "If it weren't for the question of Mr. Haywood, I should say it was a hoax. You would be surprised, Miss Truelove, to see the lengths some men will go for a silly joke." His eyebrows expressed exactly what he thought of silly jokes.

"But because of Mr. Haywood, you think it's something more sinister."

"Bait," he said succinctly.

The same conclusion to which Silverton and I had arrived earlier, but I wanted Mr. Higganbotham to say it on his own. "Bait?" I said innocently. "Bait for what? Why would anyone want to lure Mr. Haywood to Crete?"

"There you have me." He paused. "Of course, now that I understand he's been made a duke, it casts a different light on the matter."

"He wasn't *made* a duke. He simply inherited the title when his great-uncle . . ." I felt as if an icy palm had just been laid against my neck.

"When his great-uncle died," Mr. Higganbotham finished for me.

"Yes. When the previous duke died."

I thought, *Maybe this isn't about Knossos at all. Maybe we have all been fools.*

"Miss Truelove? Are you all right? You look rather pale."

"Only tired, I'm afraid." I passed my hand over my eyes and thought, *I must speak to Silverton. I must speak to him at once.* "Such an exhausting day."

"My God, yes. What an ass I am. Here I sit, rattling on about old myths and frescoes, when you have faced down death today." He folded his napkin and laid it next to his plate. "I will leave you in peace. Shall I call the maid to clear away the dinner things?"

"Yes, please."

He smiled and rose from the table. "Do try to eat a little more first, Miss Truelove. You are too slight already."

I agreed that I would, and Mr. Higganbotham straightened his cuffs and his collar and turned for the door. I stared at my plate. The cold hand had lifted from my nape, but the chill remained under the skin, making my head ache. I lifted my fingers to rub my forehead, and as I did so, I realized that Mr. Higganbotham had not left the room, but instead stood arrested, while his hand gripped the back of the chair.

"Is something wrong, sir?"

He shook his head, as if coming out of a trance. "Nothing, nothing. It's just—for an instant there— No, no. It must be the strain of the day."

The cold hand returned, exerting an icy pressure on the base of my skull. "For an instant—what?"

"Well, for an instant, I thought I saw a woman, standing there by the hearth, looking rather dismayed." Another shake of his head, and he stepped to the door. His borrowed jacket hung over his shoulders, a bit too large. He put his hand on the knob and looked back, and the smile he gave me was small and rueful.

"Obviously, I was mistaken."

⁑

As the door closed, I felt a renewed and desperate need to speak to Lord Silverton. I rose from my chair and peered out the single tiny window, but there was only darkness outside, a thick and restless night I could not penetrate, and the glass, when I pressed my fingers against it, was as cold as ice.

A moment later, the landlord himself arrived to clear away the dinner tray. I inquired after Lord Silverton, and he replied that the English lord had not yet returned to the inn, nor the barmaid with whom his lordship had departed. He said this in a voice just above a growl, which did not bode well for Silverton's health when he did reappear.

"No doubt he will turn up smiling at the breakfast table," I said, and in the privacy of my own head I added, *Where I shall happily poison his coffee.*

For two days, the ships sailed north toward Athens under a hot blue sky, while the Lady and the Hero gave thanks to the gods for the blessings that had come upon them, but on the third day the wind grew mighty, and the rain rolled across the sea, and the green waves washed over the decks of the ships.

As the storm tossed the fleet about, the Lady was taken much ill, and so great was her misery that the Hero, fearing for her life and for the tiny babe that grew in her womb, ordered the ships to put ashore on the nearest land, which proved to be the island of Naxos, cradle of Zeus . . .

THE BOOK OF TIME, A. M. HAYWOOD (1921)

Eighteen

I woke just before dawn, as suddenly as if I had been dropped from a cliff. The fire had gone out during the night, and the room was damp and chilled. I rose and went to the window to inspect the charcoal world outside. The storm had died away, but the sun had not quite risen, and the nearby rooftops were oily with rain. Around me, the walls and floors of the inn stood still in expectation of daybreak.

I dressed hurriedly in my own now-dry clothes, pinned my hair, and crept down the silent corridor to Silverton's room. There was no answer to my soft knock. I tried again, but he was either absent or heavily asleep.

The barmaid, I knew, was really quite lovely. Like Mrs. Poulakis, she had had dark hair and eyes, and that smooth golden-olive skin, as if she were bred for the sun, though she was taller and less bountifully made, and wore a shapeless brown dress. She had not flirted with Lord Silverton, however. I remembered thinking that she was a modest young woman, who kept her eyes cast low and her shoulders straight. She hadn't spoken as she fetched the brandy and set out the glasses, and we had taken very little notice of her.

Well. It seemed Silverton had taken notice of her after all, and she had not objected to his interest. The women, it seemed, rarely objected to Lord Silverton.

Did he remember them all? I wondered. Or, over time, did they all blend and merge in his memory, faces and breasts and bottoms all converging into some pleasurable feminine mean, an Ur-woman he could address conveniently in his thoughts by a single name?

Was he still with her? It was a chilly morning, in the dissolution of the storm. I thought again of the Queen's words, and the effects of waking in your lover's embrace in the early dawn. The intimate warmth of someone's skin against yours. The scent, not of perfume or soap or tobacco, but of a man's genuine smell, the salty familiar musk of a human body. I could almost taste it at the back of my throat: the flavor of longing.

I turned away from Silverton's door and marched down the back stairway. I found the common room empty, but the landlord seemed to hear my entrance, for he appeared a short moment later, wiping his hands on the oversized apron that covered him from breast to knee.

His expression was dark. No, the Englishman had not returned, and if the landlord was not mistaken, my other companion had also walked out the door, not ten minutes ago.

Would madam be pleased to break her fast?

I was not pleased, but I sat down anyway. The landlord returned shortly with coffee and fried cakes and dates, and as if the food itself had found voice and summoned him, Mr. Higganbotham blew through the entrance a moment later.

"Ah! Breakfast," he said.

"Where have you been?"

He sat down heavily in the chair opposite, smelling sharply of the outdoors, and grasped the coffeepot. "Why, making inquiries. The lads out back, I thought, would know where Silverton's gone. That is to say, they'll know where to find this pretty barmaid of his."

"Were you right?"

"Yes." He was piling his plate. "She lives in a cottage just outside of town with her brother, and I shall go there directly after I've had a bite to eat."

"You?"

He peered up from his work. "Should we send someone else, do you think?"

"I meant that I should go with you."

"Go *with* me? Miss Truelove!"

"You object?"

Mr. Higganbotham gathered his composure in a mouthful of date, chased down by an enormous gulp of coffee. When he spoke, his voice had taken on the reasonable cadence of a father explaining to a greedy child why he cannot have a second slice of cake. "I could not live with myself, Miss Truelove, if I were to expose you to the sordid scene we are likely to encounter at the house of this *barmaid*." (As he might say *harlot*.) "Moreover, she is not worthy to have the honor of your notice."

"Rubbish. I have met his lordship's paramours before, and the experience has had no lasting effect on my moral constitution. Moreover, we have not a single moment to waste on such idiotic considerations."

"Idiotic? Oh, Miss Truelove—"

"Yes, idiotic. I assure you, my delicate mind is quite up to the task of rousting his lordship out of bed with a wanton barmaid."

Mr. Higganbotham turned quite pale, and for a moment I thought I should have to call for another bottle of brandy, or perhaps a vial of smelling salts, if such a thing were to be had on an ancient island in the Aegean, peopled by a race long accustomed to hardship.

And do you know, I found it all rather satisfying. If you had told me two weeks ago that I should say such a thing to a man of Mr. Higganbotham's undoubted decency, I should have said it was impossible. But I *had* said it—*roust his lordship out of bed with a wanton barmaid*, good heavens, very brazen—and what was more, I had *relished* the words. I took a mild but unmistakable glee in the expression of pale horror that disfigured poor Mr. Higganbotham's face.

My God, what was happening to me?

I finished my coffee and rose from the table, causing Mr. Higganbotham to throw down his napkin and shoot reflexively upward, as a gentleman ought.

"If you'll excuse me," I said, quivering with the joy of rebellion, "I shall just fetch my jacket."

༄

The town was not large, and Mr. Higganbotham had armed himself with a map. At this early hour, the streets were quite empty, though when I looked down the hill to the harbor I saw that the fishing fleet had already left. The *Isolde*'s tender bobbed by the southernmost mooring, looking somewhat chastened after its bad behavior the previous day.

"How far outside of town does this barmaid live?" I asked Mr. Higganbotham, as we tramped up the narrow and winding street. The houses were all pale and plain, facing the harbor, and while the air was now light, the sun had not yet reached above the eastern hills to touch the rooftops.

"About a half mile, or so I understood. Beyond the citadel, to the northeast." He paused, and said reluctantly, as if the information were somehow shameful, "Her name is Desma."

"How lovely."

"We must, after all, have something to call her by."

In the wake of the storm, the air was mild and damp, and the cobbles still wet. The town seemed to be waking up from a long sleep. I walked by Mr. Higganbotham's side, brisk and silent, past the clustered houses and around the shoulder of the hill, until the buildings began to thin and I happened to look down again and see the small islet to the north, connected to the harbor by a narrow causeway, and I stopped short.

"What is that?"

Mr. Higganbotham followed the direction of my pointing finger. "That? Oh, it's the Portara, the lintel of a temple to Apollo that was never finished. Rather extraordinary, isn't it? A single white rectangle, all by itself."

"How old is it?"

"I believe it was built by the tyrant Lygdamis, in about the sixth century BC. He was overthrown before he could finish it, poor fellow. In any case, this was all perhaps a thousand years after our Minoans flourished on Crete."

I resumed walking, though I craned my head from time to time, not quite able to leave the sight behind. "What a glorious setting, too. On that little island, like a teardrop."

"As it happens, the island is not without meaning to our own concerns," said Mr. Higganbotham. "According to legend, it's where Theseus landed with Ariadne, when bad weather forced them into Naxos."

I looked back again. "And he left her there."

"So the myth has it. Then Dionysus happened along, fell in love with her, and brought her up to heaven to marry her. Although according to certain accounts, old Bacchus had already fallen in love with her by the time they reached Naxos, and it was he who ordered Theseus to abandon Ariadne."

"Leaving the lady no choice in the matter, of course."

Mr. Higganbotham craned his neck northward. "Homer even has it that she was already married to Dionysus at the time of her elopement. That Theseus only deserted her because Dionysus caught up with them and accused her of adultery."

"I suppose every generation of storytellers must fit the myth to serve the particular needs of the audience," I said. "Unlike the study of history, there's no need to convey truth."

"Why not?"

"Why, because it didn't really happen. It's all made up."

Mr. Higganbotham didn't reply, and for some time we walked in a comfortable silence, while the Portara disappeared from view behind us. A mild breeze struck my cheek, hinting of spring, but for some reason I could not seem to warm myself properly. Inside my chest, the chill of foreboding had taken hold, and the higher we climbed, the more uneasy I felt, until all at once we came free of the buildings and rounded the shoulder of the slope. The sea stretched off to the left, impossibly blue, while before us meandered the gray-white road, bordered by green grass and the occasional small villa.

I paused to secure my hat more firmly on my head, for the breeze now came briskly off the water. "I presume the lady inhabits one of these houses?" I said, in so detached a voice as I could manage.

"So I understand."

"Which one?"

"I believe it stands to the right, facing the sea, and there is a distinctive outbuilding, made recently of stone."

We resumed our walk. The houses looked snug and comfortable, each one trailing a thin, pale stream of smoke from its chimney. The air smelled of salt and grass and burning wood, and the track was still damp and muddy in patches. At one point, a torrent of water had actually washed away a section of road, creating a small ditch of mud and debris. I picked my way around this obstruction, accepting Mr. Higganbotham's assistance for the sake of his pride, and as the short heels of my boots sank into the mess, a thought occurred to me.

I stopped, turned my head to peer behind me at the outskirts of the town, and frowned.

"Is something the matter?" asked Mr. Higganbotham.

"I was only wondering . . ."

"Wondering what?"

"Wondering why Lord Silverton would have put himself to the inconvenience of traveling a mile along a dark and unknown road, in the middle of a midnight tempest, instead of simply repairing upstairs with his companion." I returned my body to its ordinary forward posture. "Particularly when he had only just dried out from our earlier adventure."

Mr. Higganbotham shifted his feet and stared into the distance, where our destination presumably lay. "For the sake of discretion, perhaps?"

"Perhaps."

"She is, I'm told, an especially beautiful woman."

I resumed walking. Mr. Higganbotham fell in beside me. I said, "But are we not making the same sort of assumption as the scientists at Knossos? Because the barmaid is beautiful, and Silverton is, well, *Silverton*, we accept without question the suggestion that he has gone with her for the sake of pleasure."

"By God." Mr. Higganbotham lengthened his stride.

I matched his speed, and then increased it. "And he's been gone for hours now. Nor have we encountered him on the road, returning to town."

Mr. Higganbotham swore under his breath, unaware, perhaps, of the clarity of the atmosphere following the storm.

We took the next quarter mile almost at a run, until a small white house appeared to the left of the road, set back about fifty yards, flanked by a square structure made of gray volcanic stone. A roof of clean red shingles topped this outbuilding, and Mr. Higganbotham said, wheezing slightly, "This must be it."

"Yes, that roof looks new, the one on the outbuilding." I raised my hand to my brow. The sun had risen over the mountains now, white and determined against the blue sky directly ahead.

"It seems rather lifeless, don't you think?" said Mr. Higganbotham. "There's no smoke from the chimney."

"Perhaps they haven't awoken yet," I said acidly, but my heart wasn't in it. I struck down the muddy path from the road to the house, not pausing to confirm whether Mr. Higganbotham followed me.

The door was old and thick. I pounded on it with my fist. "Hello! Silverton! Hello!"

There was no answer, no sound at all.

I pounded again, and this time Mr. Higganbotham's cries joined mine, calling Silverton's name in an urgent chorus made to shake the heavens.

"Shall we try the door?" said Mr. Higganbotham, when our efforts died away into silence.

I didn't answer, but rather placed my fingers on the handle of the door and pushed. To my surprise—or perhaps not—the portal yawned easily open, unbolted.

"Well, there's a lucky stroke," said Mr. Higganbotham.

Inside, the house was chilled and damp, the fire unlit. Through the eastern window came a square of pale sunlight, the sole source of illumination, which reflected efficiently against the whitewashed walls to give the impression of great and fleeting lightness.

The room in which we stood contained the necessities of life, and nothing else: a hearth at one end, surrounded by various implements intended for the preparation of food, and a rectangular table at the other, bearing a pair of candles and served by four rush-seated chairs, all of which had been pushed in snugly, as neat as a pin.

I knelt before the hearth, removed one glove, and passed my hand over the pile of ashes therein. Not a trace of warmth remained.

"There's a bedroom back here," called my companion, and I rose and turned, replacing the glove over my fingers. He was standing in the narrow doorway at the opposite end of the room— it was not large, this living chamber, perhaps twelve feet square— as if he had not quite made up his mind whether it was proper to step inside.

I had no such scruples. I nudged him aside and slipped through the opening, and though my heart beat fast and my head felt a little dizzy, I saw at once that I had no need for embarrassment. The narrow bed lay empty and neatly made, exhibiting not the slightest sign of recent passion.

"It's empty," I announced, though unnecessarily, as Mr. Higganbotham had stepped in behind me and now stood, frowning, turning his head from one side of the room to another. "And I don't believe anyone slept here, either."

"Unless she—or they—rose early and returned to town by another route than ours."

I placed my hand atop the flat quilt. "I don't think so."

"But how do you know?"

I could not quite explain this to Mr. Higganbotham. How could I sensibly describe the scent that remained in the air, the peculiar metallic salt, after recent human habitation? How could I represent, in words of logic a scholar might comprehend, the lingering electricity of the human spirit, which was not something to be seen or heard or smelled or touched, but rather to be felt in the marrow of one's bones, in the folds of one's brains?

This bedroom was empty of both.

"I just do." I turned away, and as I did, I caught sight of a small, leather-covered trunk in the shadow beneath the window.

A trunk of some sort was to be expected in a bedroom, particularly in the absence of a wardrobe or a chest of drawers. I should not have given the object a second glance. And yet it drew my gaze irresistibly back, though I could not have said why.

A leather trunk, secured with a pair of brass buckles, perhaps two and a half feet wide: a compact space, speaking for the parsimony of its owner.

Or else because it is a traveling trunk, I thought. An English traveling trunk, nearly identical to the one I owned myself, down to the small brass plate in the center of the lid that would—if, in fact, the trunk *were* identical to mine—bear the owner's initials.

"Wait a moment," I said to Mr. Higganbotham, who had already turned to leave. I stepped to the window, which faced south toward the slope of a green hillside, and bent over the trunk. Though the light was dim, I could read the Roman letters perfectly well, for they were etched in a deep and confident type:

AMH

"My God!" I exclaimed. "We've found him!"

But I was not to know Mr. Higganbotham's immediate reaction to this news, for the last word was swallowed by the decisive bang of the front door, and a Greek voice demanding to know who the devil we were.

(Or so I deduced, for the Greek language remained a mystery to me.)

The Hero carried the stricken Lady ashore in his own arms, and found shelter for her among the caves. In the morning, the storm had cleared and the Lady was much improved, yet she was loath to revisit the sea while still so delicate, and told the Hero, 'Return to your ships so that the King your father will have news of your safe redemption, and the mothers of your companions may embrace their sons and daughters once more, and I will wait for you here in Naxos as a bride awaits her bridegroom.'

The Hero made protest, for his love for the Lady did each day grow a hundredfold, from the proof of her bravery and her loyal heart, but she held her hand to his lips to silence his grief, and said, 'Do not fear, for I swear by my love for you, and by our child that grows in my womb, that you shall find me faithful in these caves when you return, and my arms will open for you as the flower opens for the bee.'

So the Hero embraced the Lady tenderly and left her with such food and drink as he could spare, and set off for Athens with heavy heart, as fast as the wind could carry him . . .

THE BOOK OF TIME, A. M. HAYWOOD (1921)

Nineteen

At the sound of the intruder, Mr. Higganbotham's startled eyes met mine. Of course I hadn't thought to bring a weapon, and I very much doubted that he had, either.

But his manhood quickly asserted itself. He gathered himself upward, held up one strong, gloved hand, mouthed a muscular *Stay here!* in my direction, and strode through the doorway to the main chamber.

I followed him directly.

A man stood outlined near the entrance of the cottage, dressed in a thick woolen jacket and a cap drawn low over his forehead. The sunlight struck the side of his face, and I thought he looked familiar, though I could not quite place the point of recognition.

Mr. Higganbotham addressed him in Greek, and when the intruder gruffly replied, glancing at me from beneath a dark and stony brow, I realized who he was.

The innkeeper.

"Why, what are *you* doing here?" I exclaimed.

Mr. Higganbotham lifted his eyebrows and spoke dryly. "I believe he asks the same question, more or less, of *us*."

I addressed the landlord directly. "*Us?* We're here because your barmaid went off with Lord Silverton last night, and he hasn't turned up again, and here's Mr. Haywood's own trunk, right here in her house—"

"And my Desma has not come to the inn this morning! So I ask you, what sort of man is this English lord, and what is he doing with my Desma?"

"I rather thought that was obvious," I said.

He shook a fist. "She has not done this before! She is a good girl."

"They're all good girls, aren't they? Until they're not."

The landlord turned to Mr. Higganbotham and spoke in fluid Greek, something with a great many details and flourishes, until I tapped Mr. Higganbotham on the shoulder and demanded to know what they were talking about.

"I beg your pardon. It seems he's genuinely worried about the girl. She's never done anything like this before, lives here quietly with her brother, virtuous as the day is long."

"Her *brother*! I don't understand. Does he mean Mr. Haywood?"

"So I presume."

"But Mr. Haywood hasn't got a sister, and in any case, where would he sleep?"

The innkeeper pointed to the window, and I followed the direction of his finger to the small stone outbuilding, just within view. "*There?*" I said, astonished.

"Yes, there! But *he* is not inside, either," the man said. "Something is happen, and is all because of this English lordship!"

I thought of the trunk inside the bedroom, bearing Mr. Haywood's monogram. *Brother*, indeed. But if the innkeeper spoke the truth, and he slept by himself in a tiny and presumably unheated shelter, then why on earth had he gone to so much trouble and secrecy to elope with this Desma? If, indeed, Desma was the woman in whose company he had left Knossos.

And if she *was* that woman, and Mr. Haywood had been living here with her all this time, why had the innkeeper claimed yesterday to know nothing of Mr. Haywood's whereabouts?

And, good heavens, if Silverton *had* indeed actually discovered Mr. Haywood's whereabouts last night—had perhaps even *met* him, within the walls of this very house—then why hadn't he sent us word?

Mr. Higganbotham was frowning pensively. I turned back to the innkeeper, whose eyes had formed into suspicious dark slivers beneath his thick eyebrows, examining first me, and then my companion, as if we were a pair of spiders that had wandered into his kitchen.

Rather than the other way around.

"You seem to bear a great deal of concern for this girl," I said. "*And* for her brother. Perhaps you can tell us more about them? Our friend Silverton, after all, seems to have involved his fate with theirs."

Mr. Higganbotham shot me an amazed look, and then returned his gaze to the innkeeper, whose lips had compressed in an expression of stubborn silence. My blood raced along my limbs, light and keen, anticipating the thrill of discovery. I folded my arms.

"I believe he knows something," I said.

"Knows something? Knows what?"

I said to the landlord, "She's not your barmaid, is she?"

She had arrived at the inn on a windswept day in early November, when the weather had just begun to cool, the landlord told us reluctantly: illiterate and incomprehensible, dressed in pale summer clothing. In exchange for the beautiful gold bracelet she wore on her left arm, he had given her warm clothes and shelter. Her confusion and her modest demeanor had soon enlisted his chivalry—such as it was—and he returned the bracelet. Eventually he had ascertained that she came from Crete, and helped her book passage to Heraklion, where he thought she might rejoin her friends.

At this point in the narrative, the landlord stopped, turned to us, and tapped his temple with his forefinger. She was not in her right mind, he had thought at the time. He could understand a few of her words, but as if they were passed through a meat grinder first: all jumbled and misshapen. She was perhaps struck on the head.

"Ah! Very interesting! Can you perhaps describe the nature of her particular dialect?" said Mr. Higganbotham, leaping across a gleaming puddle to land at the man's side. For the past half hour, we had walked swiftly along the road that paralleled the northern coast, leaving the town and the barmaid's cottage well behind us. I still did not quite understand where the landlord was taking us, and could only hope that the tale he spun now—strange, full of odd and gaping holes—might somehow make the point of our journey more clear. My gaze kept shifting to the left, toward the sea, and the muscles of my abdomen clenched with urgency.

"Hang her dialect," I said. "Where has she *gone*? And what has she to do with Mr. Haywood?"

The landlord spun about and launched himself determinedly forward. "I have already said. She is his sister."

"But he's English!"

"That is what she say. *Brother*, she say."

"Miss Truelove," said Mr. Higganbotham, sotto voce. He brought a tactful fist to his mouth and coughed into it. "Surely it does not need further explanation."

I looked sideways at Mr. Higganbotham, who had found some point of interest on the distant hills, and then at the back of the landlord's rigid head. My cheeks grew warm. "Of course. I *mean*, how did they—? That is, to what extent is he—?" I cleared my throat. "How did he come to Naxos with her?"

The landlord shook his head. "She leave here alone, in December, and then I send her to Crete, where she from. She return a week later, with her brother, except they have some fear. They say to me, *We must hide, you must find us a shelter outside of the town, you must say nothing to any person who ask.*" He glanced toward me at last, and his face bore the same stony-browed glare as before. "And now this English lord come and take her away."

"He has not taken her away," I said. "He's a good, sensible, reliable fellow, and only wants to help. I should say it's the other way around, and she has taken *him* off somewhere, for whatever purposes of her own."

The landlord grunted his doubt. His stride lengthened, eating up the ground with remarkable efficiency for so stocky a man.

"In any case, Mr. Haywood has left with them, and we know already that he is attached to her, and has gone to great effort to keep her from harm."

Another grunt. "He has not left with them."

"What's that?" I said, panting a little.

"She come to the inn, last night, in the storm. She say that her brother has gone to the caves, that he has not return. She ask for help. So I say to her, we will go in the morning, she must stay the night at the inn, she cannot stay at her house alone."

"Very sensible," said Mr. Higganbotham.

"What caves?" I demanded.

The landlord raised a fist in the air. "And then she go off with the English lord! Into the night!"

Mr. Higganbotham said cheerfully, "Now, now. It isn't all that bad. He's an honorable fellow, I assure you."

"Yes, but *what* caves?" I halted in the middle of the road and crossed my arms across my chest. "I won't go another step until somebody explains what's going on. Who *is* this woman, and where did she come from, and where are these caves to which you're leading us?"

The landlord stopped and turned, making a broad gesture with his right arm, corresponding roughly to the sweep of the sea down the cliffs. He said, in the kind of gruff, impatient voice that suggested I was an imbecile, or at the very least inattentive: "The caves of the myth! The caves where the Lady of the Labyrinth rise to heaven with her husband."

I don't know at what age I first realized that my parents were not in love. (Love, I mean, as the poets and the composers had it; love such as Antony felt for Cleopatra, or Tristan for Isolde, or Des Grieux for Manon. The unselfish agony such as Radamès feels for Aida, when he realizes she inhabits the tomb with him, and all the might of his strong arms cannot force the stone away to free her.)

I had never seen any sign, for example, of a passionate courtship. When I was still quite small, but yet old enough to remember such things, my mother announced that she was to be married, and shortly afterward the deed was done: a visit to a church in London, a brief wedding breakfast at a magnificent marble house I now know to be that of the Duke of Olympia, and then a rattling train journey the next morning back to East Sussex. "Now we will be perfectly provided for," my mother said—I recall this very well, for there was something terribly momentous about the way she said it, all glossy and radiant in a rose-colored traveling dress, while her new ring sparkled on her finger—and she was right. I never wanted for a single thing, so far as my memory serves. My father came down from London to stay with us every weekend, and repaired to a bedroom he shared with my mother, who remained a breathtaking beauty—so I am told, for I can't quite picture her face, only the shape of her hair around it—even in her pastoral seclusion from the worldliness of London. One day, in fact, when I was nearly six, Mama and my father sat down with me and told me with great delight that I was going to have a little baby brother or sister.

So we were very much a family, and yet while I observed many instances and gestures of affection between them, there was not that magnetic power I later understood from books and from stage. My father treated Mama with tender respect, and I believe he would have died for her: but he would have laid down that life because of duty, not because of passion.

I don't know why that should have made any difference to me, but I believe it must have. For when I was fifteen, and my father took me to Covent Garden for the first time to watch a performance of *Siegfried*, I knew a kind of despaired young yearning as Brünnhilde awoke to the embrace of her hero: as if I had just discovered the gaping existence of a hole in my breast that could never, in this modern world made of steel rails and monstrous engines, be filled.

"But surely he doesn't mean the *actual* cave," I whispered to Mr. Higganbotham, as we trudged along the road behind the landlord.

"I beg your pardon?" Mr. Higganbotham appeared to be lost in some sort of scholarly firmament high above, for his face was turned up to the watery sun, and his eyes had filmed softly over.

"The *caves*, sir. The caves to which this man is leading us. He can't actually *believe* these are the caves of Ariadne, that she really existed here. That these mythical events"—I gestured to the sea, much as the landlord himself had done a short while ago—"truly took place, three thousand years ago, on this soil."

"Oh, I expect he does. That's the splendid power of myth, you know. It's marvelously flexible, allowing anybody to interpret events as he pleases." He paused to negotiate a small rockslide obscuring the roadway. "Did you ever play that game as a child, in which you whispered a statement of fact into somebody's ear, and that friend passed it on to another, and so on?"

"Yes, and the friend at the end of the line announced what had been uttered in *her* ear—"

"And it was entirely different from the statement at the beginning, eh? Well, that's myth for you. Handed along from mouth to ear for millennia, until somebody wrote it down at last and made it fact. But what really happened? We haven't a clue." He nodded to the road ahead. "Something interesting may very well have happened at these caves. Obviously our friends think so."

"You mean the landlord?"

"I mean Mr. Haywood and his female companion."

"But what could it be? What could possibly be so important that it's worth risking one's life for?"

Mr. Higganbotham considered. "Treasure, perhaps? A very great deal of treasure often tempts men into extraordinary deeds."

I fell silent, because this was not the answer I craved, and I could not speak this yearning aloud. Above us, the sky had turned a brilliant morning blue, and the air was almost spring-like, smelling of damp stone and new grass and sunshine. I removed my jacket and slung it over my shoulder. My shoes were beginning to pinch.

"How much farther?" I asked Mr. Higganbotham.

He called obediently to the landlord, who turned his head and shouted something back.

"Ah, I see," said Mr. Higganbotham.

"What did he say?"

"Six or seven miles." He cleared his throat. "Or perhaps eight."

"Eight miles!"

But it was no use protesting. There was too much distance already behind us to turn back, and so we marched on, pausing only briefly to eat the bread and the hard sheep's cheese that the landlord had taken from the cupboard in the cottage. The terrain became rockier, the cliffs more sheer. The sun reached its zenith and began to fall slowly to earth, and a series of clouds scudded into view from the southwest, before a strengthening wind.

Mr. Higganbotham examined the sky. "I do hope it's not a scirocco."

"A scirocco?"

"It arises from the Sahara at this time of year. Nasty sort of wind, carrying dust along, stirring up trouble. There is a whole category of study devoted to its effects." He tapped his forehead. "It's been known to do things to one's mind."

The heel of my shoe slipped into the crack of a rock, and I nearly fell to the ground. Mr. Higganbotham's arm reached out to steady me, which for some reason I rather resented. I drew away and, to cover over the ingratitude, said, "To think I once imagined the Mediterranean climate as a dry, sunny, salubrious sort of thing."

"Oh, no," he replied cheerfully. "You have been grossly misinformed, I'm afraid."

Contrary to Mr. Higganbotham's stated hopes, the wind picked up briskly, and a haze of ominous dust filled in the gaps between the clouds. The landlord muttered to himself and increased his pace, though the light was starting to fail. In the distance, a headland was taking shape, and I could not see whether the road went around its face, next to the sea, or crossed the steep and rocky neck.

The landlord marched on, as if he were quite sure of his route. As if he had made this voyage several times before.

I leaned toward Mr. Higganbotham. "Something's wrong. I cannot believe that Silverton and the woman traveled this road last night, in the dark, during the storm."

"It seems improbable."

"We should have stopped him. We should have refused to go, or at least sent some message back to the *Isolde*. Nobody knows where we are."

He didn't reply.

I thought, *But we had no choice. We have no choice but to follow him.*

The headland grew in detail, rocky and forbidding. I could not tear my gaze away. Something about the shape of it, which seemed to resemble that of a man's head, bearing an enormous bony nose and a chin that disappeared into the cliffs below, encoded some deeper meaning that transfixed me.

Without quite realizing that I did so, I eased my hand into the pocket of my jacket and ran my fingers around the slim, ridged rim of the Knossos medallion. An image arose in my head—Lord Silverton, leaning against a rocky wall, smiling very slightly at one corner of his mouth, while his blue eyes remained narrowed and serious—accompanied by a rush of longing so intense, I buckled beneath it.

"Why, what's wrong?" asked Mr. Higganbotham, starting toward me.

I braced one hand against the boulder on which I had sunk, while the other hand remained in my pocket, clutching the medallion. "I don't know," I gasped.

Mr. Higganbotham turned to the landlord and whistled.

"No, it's all right." I lifted my eyes to the headland, and again the wave struck, except that this time I was expecting it, and did not flinch. "Let's press on."

"We can't. You're not well."

"But Silverton—"

"Hang him." He turned to address the landlord, who had come up grudgingly, wearing an expression of thunderous impatience. They exchanged a few phrases in rapid Greek, while I fought down the emotion clawing at my ribs and examined the headland, and its strange formation of rock, with the dispassion of a scientist.

"Are the caves inside there?" I asked the landlord, interrupting the exchange. I lifted my hand and pointed toward the rocks.

He glanced over his shoulder. "Yes! We cannot stop now."

"But night will be falling soon, and we have been walking all day," said Mr. Higganbotham.

I rose from the boulder. "Our friend is right, Mr. Higganbotham. It would be foolish to stop so close to our goal. I am more than equal to finishing the journey."

"Nonsense. You're done in."

"My present vigor, whether small or large, is quite irrelevant. I am deeply concerned for the safety of Lord Silverton, to say nothing of Mr. Haywood, and both men have every right to expect our most strenuous efforts to discover them." I turned back to the landlord, who stood akimbo, gazing fiercely at us both, and said firmly, "Lead on, sir, if you will."

Less than half an hour later, the main road began an inland curve to the right, declining the harsh edge of the headland. The wind now blew steadily, warm and just slightly damp, as if, like a thirsty cloth, it had soaked up a fine layer of seawater along its journey from the African deserts. A bit of dust caught in my throat, and as I coughed, I thought in wonder, *This is the dust of the Sahara.*

The landlord shouted impatiently and waved his hand.

"He has left the road," I said to Mr. Higganbotham.

"So he has."

The man was about fifty yards ahead, and as we drew closer, I saw that he had taken a faint path, almost invisible in the stony landscape, that forked away from the main road, toward the sea.

Mr. Higganbotham and I had both slowed our steps. The wind blew against my back. "Do we follow?" he asked, in a low voice.

I gazed at the landlord, silhouetted against the monstrous gray spine of the headland. His black hair twisted angrily in the wind beneath the edges of his woolen cap, and his eyes had narrowed into slivers against the African dust, giving him a wild and exotic bearing. Behind him grew the cliffs, silent and impervious to so temporary a condition as a common Mediterranean scirocco, showing no sign of recent human activity. The longing swelled again in my chest, holding down my breath.

He is hiding something, I thought, and then I said aloud, with great effort, "You may certainly turn back if you like, Mr. Higganbotham. You are under no obligation whatever, and have put yourself in enough danger already. But I'm afraid I must go on."

He sighed heavily, because of course he had to go with me; no man of any character could allow a lady to proceed into peril and forbear to accompany her. But he didn't like it, didn't like it at all; and furthermore, neither did I.

Yet the scirocco was at my back, and propelled me forward to this strange and massive formation of rock. A prickly pear stood by the fork in the road, where the new path beat through the stones toward the cliffs, and at the exact instant that we turned down the narrow track, a gust of wind struck the tree, making it shiver and bend and whistle.

The landlord, seeing that we had obeyed his summons, turned and resumed his march, and I struggled into a half run, in order to catch up with him. My mouth filled with dust.

"I say!" exclaimed Mr. Higganbotham, hurrying up behind, but the energy had returned to me, and I kept on striding, while the heels of my low boots slid on the stones and my right hand, still in the jacket pocket, clutched the medallion.

We had almost reached the first craggy face of the rising rock before I saw it: a small lean-to, built of stone and nestled into a fold of the escarpment.

The landlord, still several yards ahead, plunged inside without hesitation. I heard Mr. Higganbotham calling behind me, but I was now wholly gripped by that same urgency that had

lured me onward from my first sight of the stern profile overlooking the sea. I ducked under the lintel, half expecting to be
crushed on the head by a primitive club, but instead saw only the
landlord, turning about in the murky darkness.

"They are not here," he said, sounding bewildered.

Outside, Mr. Higganbotham was shouting something. I narrowed my eyes and peered into the shadowed corners of the shelter, but the room was quite small, and I could easily perceive that
it contained only a straw pallet, a few blankets, a small hearth for
a nonexistent fire, and a locked wooden chest. The air smelled of
stale smoke and damp stone, of the scat of curious animals.

"No one has lived here for some days, at least," I said.

"How do you know this?"

I considered how to reply to this reasonable question, but before
I could open my mouth, a loud bang shattered the air outside.

"Mr. Higganbotham!" I exclaimed, turning for the door.

But the way was already blocked by a man's broad shoulders, and
by the persuasive heft of the large pistol he gripped in one hand.

So the Lady remained hidden in the cliffs by the shore, attended only by the Beast, who had also come ashore to protect his sister in the absence of her beloved. Their days passed quietly in the heat of the late summer, and as the time for harvest approached, and the nights grew longer, and the babe began to quicken in the Lady's womb, the two of them watched the horizon for the approach of the Hero's ships.

But the long weeks came and went, and the air grew cool, and still no black sail appeared over the edge of the sea to answer the Lady's hopes. Their stores of food, though carefully husbanded, began to dwindle, until at last nothing remained of the supplies the Hero had left behind for the nourishment of his Lady.

One morning the Beast said, 'I will disguise my monstrous form under a cloak and hood, and I will take this gold bracelet into the nearest village and exchange it for bread and meat. But you must hide yourself carefully while I am gone, and do not reveal your face to any man until I return, for we know not what dangers may lie around us . . .'

THE BOOK OF TIME, A. M. HAYWOOD (1921)

Twenty

A scream rang out, which I recognized as my own, calling Mr. Higganbotham to my aid.

But he did not reply, and in the next instant, I launched myself desperately in the direction of the pistol, reaching with both hands to dislodge it from the man's grip. He was motioning to the landlord, and did not notice my movement for the first split second. He turned his head, and I had just grasped the air, inches from the pistol, when he brought it up and down heavily on my shoulder, sending me spinning to the dirt floor.

The impact stunned me, and I have only the most confused recollection of the next few seconds. There was a struggle of some kind, a short argument in Greek, and as I attempted to rise, a strong hand closed around my arm, jerking me upward.

"Who are you?" I demanded.

The man replied with another jerk, dragging me outside into

the swirl of the wind, where Mr. Higganbotham stood stiff under the pressure of an arm locked about his throat. The arm belonged to a stout, well-muscled man, clean-shaven, whose skin was quite pale except for a few incongruous freckles across the bridge of his nose, and whose hair burst forth from his head in a shock of ginger.

The two men signaled to each other. "What's going on?" I gasped out to Mr. Higganbotham, and my captor shoved the pistol into the small of my back, urging me forward toward the edge of the cliffs.

The other man released his hold on Mr. Higganbotham's neck and prodded the poor man with a large fist. "Get going!" he growled, in a rough American accent, and Mr. Higganbotham stumbled forward to my side.

As we started on in tandem, encouraged by the butt of the pistol, he said to me, somewhat scratchily, "I gather it's an ambush."

⌒

As it happened, I had some experience with ambushes. One can hardly avoid them, as a young and unattached female in a massive household such as that of the Duke of Olympia. Their Graces did their best to protect me, of course, and I soon learned how to protect myself. How to maneuver against the unexpected capture. I developed the instincts of a deer, vigilant and suspicious: vigilant especially against those who laid the more artful snare, the one baited with my particular weakness.

But I had also once been caught, and I learned from this painful entrapment the most valuable lesson of all.

You must not, at first, attempt to break free. You must bide your time. You must lie in wait, just as he has; you must gather your strength for the moment when his own defenses have softened, and he is not expecting a blow.

When at last you strike back, your engagement must be total.

Of course, I could not explain this principle to Mr. Higganbotham, as we stumbled along the darkening path toward the edge of the cliffs, whipped by the African wind and by the stern commands of our captors. But it didn't matter; he seemed to have accepted his defeat, and went along by my side, rubbing his abused neck from time to time, and clearing his throat of both dust and abrasion. I noticed he was limping, but I could not tell whether this came as a result of some wound, or because of the miles of uneven road over which we had passed today.

"Why, where's the landlord?" I asked suddenly, because I had just realized he was missing.

"Ah, yes. I believe I saw—" He cleared his throat again, for his voice remained raspy, as if he had swallowed a number of sharp pebbles. "Believe I saw him bolt past, just before the spots appeared before my eyes. And then you, with the big fellow and the pistol."

We spoke in low tones, though the two men were right behind us and could, I suppose, have understood what we said.

"How did it happen?"

"Why, I don't properly know. One moment I was straining to catch up with you, because I didn't like the look of that shed he was hustling you into, and the next moment I had someone's arm about my neck." He rubbed it again.

"Hey!" said the man with the pistol. "Shut the f—— up, do you hear?"

"Sir!" Mr. Higganbotham exclaimed. "There's no need for that sort of—"

A blow landed on the back of his shoulder; I am not sure which man delivered it.

"—in front of a lady," Mr. Higganbotham finished, in a sulky mutter.

We rounded the curve of the headland, and the bright sea spread out before us, held in place by a pale and aging sky. By now, I no longer noticed the marine scent of the air, but as we approached the cliffs, the brine began to tickle my nose anew, together with the desert dust. The slow crash of the waves struck against the rocks below, and to the left stretched a gigantic golden beach, nurtured into magnificence by the shelter of the ancient headland.

A hand nudged mine. "Look there," whispered Mr. Higganbotham.

"Where?"

"The sea."

I lifted my gaze to the flat horizon, and at first I didn't see anything, except the white-laced heave of the water under the scirocco's hand.

And then an object moved, in tandem with the waves, and I realized it was a ship: a long, graceful craft, perhaps a half mile out to sea, trailing a faint smudge of white smoke from the funnel at the center of its upper deck.

My lips moved. *Isolde*, I said silently.

But what was she doing here, so far from her station on the western side of the island? Right here, at the exact spot where we made our way along the edge of the headland, along a path that now sloped downward, as if to reach the shore itself?

And—my God!—how could we win her attention?

It was the worst kind of agony. I returned my gaze to the path before me, but my eyes kept shifting quietly northward, to the instrument of our salvation hovering nearby, metal-clad and mighty, so tantalizingly close and yet as far away as the moon.

I could not signal. Anything I did would bring instant retribution from our captors, and—worse—would reveal the ship's proximity, and possibly even our relation to it. We might be dead before a boat could even be readied for our rescue.

I could only hope that someone's glass was trained upon this shore. That the *Isolde*'s appearance here was not a coincidence.

The path was now barely that. We were forced into single file as the track narrowed to perhaps twenty-four inches, along the throat of the old man embodied in the rocks, while the sea washed his collar fifty or more feet below. The spray stung the tender skin of my cheek and fell upon my lips. I licked them and tasted salt, and I realized I was horribly thirsty.

I walked in front, measuring my steps carefully, for the trail was strewn with small rocks. I no longer looked out to sea; the traverse demanded my full attention. To my left, the cliff dropped vertiginously away. I had been clutching the medallion in my pocket, but now I released the talisman and lifted my right palm to steady myself against the rock face as we descended.

"Where are we going?" I shouted back boldly, over my shoulder, because the two men could not possibly do any worse to us.

"I said, shut the f——up!"

I planted my feet and made a half turn. "I refuse to go any farther—"

But the blast of a pistol cut off my words, shattering the rock nearby. A spray of tiny shrapnel stung the back of my neck.

"Next time," the man said, "I'll be aiming at your f——ing head. Or his."

"I say—!" began Mr. Higganbotham, shocked.

"Just another fifty feet," said the other man. "You'll see it."

My ears rang; my body shook. The sting at my neck turned into a trickle that traveled down my collar. I turned, almost unable to breathe, and moved my wobbling legs another step, and another, though my head swam and my vision had reduced to a narrow tunnel.

"You're bleeding," said Mr. Higganbotham.

"I'm all right." A little courage returned to me as I uttered the words.

The path made a slight turn inward, revealing a wider section, flat and overhung by a large ledge that I realized must be the man's nose. As we reached this shelter, an opening became visible in the rock face beneath the ledge, rather like a nostril.

"Here we are," said the man with the pistol. "In we go."

"In *here*?"

"You heard me, didn't you? Or are you deaf? Get going." He waved the pistol.

I looked at Mr. Higganbotham's pale face, and again at the pistol. I hardly dared glance at the faces of the men who drove us, but then I didn't need to; their hard glares bore down upon us, filled with a will and determination I could not begin to comprehend.

The caves, the landlord had said. *The caves of the legend*. But surely a myth of three thousand years' distance had no power to lure men into murder. What was the inducement? Was there perhaps a treasure of some kind hidden inside?

"I don't understand—" I began.

"For f——'s sake!" he roared. "You don't need to *understand*! Just go in the f——ing cave, and shut your mouth."

"Just tell me one thing," I whispered. "Tell me whether Lord Silverton is inside. Tell me if he's alive."

His aimed the pistol at the crown of Mr. Higganbotham's head. "*Go!*"

I turned and ducked into the cave.

❧

I sensed a third presence in the cave well before the pulse of Mr. Higganbotham's breathing had lapsed into somnolence, but I said nothing. The poor man had been subject to shocks enough today.

In fact, our prison was rather more comfortable than I might have expected from an opening in a cliff face, miles from any civilized encampment. Mr. Higganbotham presently snored beneath a pair of thick woolen blankets, and two more lay across my own shoulders, as I stared into the blackness and listened to the distant percussion of the sea. The floor was covered with straw, reasonably clean, and we had eaten bread and drunk water. I had even been allowed a moment of relief, in a private crevice of rock that seemed perfectly designed for such an emergency.

So my pulse soon returned to a semblance of its ordinary rhythm, and I lay on my makeshift couch counting its beats while I waited for Mr. Higganbotham to enter the deepest chasm of his sleep. I had no personal inclination for slumber. Each time I closed my eyes, the unaccountable ache swelled in my breast, as if some foreign person had taken advantage of this vulnerability to slip inside my skin, to wriggle herself inside me like fingers into a glove, transferring her own urgency into mine. My hands turned cold and trembled, and my lips moved in the shape of someone's name—Silverton, perhaps?—and I opened my eyes again and thought, *I must find him.*

I must find him.

"I don't mean to say I told you so," began Her Majesty.

"But you will, nonetheless."

"Did I not warn you against this expedition, from its very inception? Did I not caution you at every turn? And still you would not heed me. Oh, no. Sensible Miss Truelove knows best, doesn't she? She can manage herself perfectly, all on her own. Clever girl."

I turned my head in the direction of the voice. At the corner of the chamber hovered a faint glow, in the center of which I could just make out the outline of her small and queenly figure. "I must beg you to whisper," I said.

"He is fast asleep, I assure you."

"Nonetheless. He has borne enough already, considering how innocently he has entered into our investigation."

"He cannot hear me."

"He can hear *me*, replying to you."

Her Majesty stumbled upon my logic and pursed her lips. The glow around her shifted in tint, from blue to very faintly red.

I turned my head back to the space above. "And I'm sure the guard outside isn't asleep, is he?"

No answer.

I closed my eyes and let out a long and vaporous breath. "Why did you come? Only to castigate me for my foolishness?"

She said grudgingly, "I suppose your intentions were noble."

"Thank you for that."

"But you *have* got yourself in a wretched muddle, haven't you? Do you have any notion of trying to escape?"

"I have been trusting that the opportunity might arise, at some point, if I remain vigilant."

The Queen made one of her little harrumphing noises. For some reason, the sound gave me comfort. So predictable, in this strange and perilous corner of the globe, into which fate and foolishness had led me.

"Do you have any notion what's happened to Lord Silverton, perhaps?" I said. "Since you are fortunate to possess such extraordinary powers of perception."

"Ha! Can it be? Are you actually allowing that I might represent something more than your own fevered imagination? This is progress indeed."

"I am only grasping at whatever hope remains to me."

She made another noise, much softer, and for a moment there was only silence between us, beating its slow wings. I became aware of another light floating against the rock above me, blue again, as faint and transparent as a child's dream, and it seemed that the tide of brutal longing receded an inch or two. I thought, *It doesn't matter if she's real or not. She is here.*

When she spoke again, the tone of her voice had also softened, though the vowels remained as imperious as ever. "My dear, I have only ever wanted what is best for you. I have only ever wanted your happiness."

"My happiness, for the moment, is most intimately bound with the survival of my companions."

She sighed. "I thought as much."

I felt as if I were choking. I turned on my side to relieve the pressure, and said, "Can you not give me a hint of some kind? Do you not even care what becomes of him?"

"Not particularly. He is nothing to me. It is *you* who matter."

"But *why?*" I spoke a little too loudly, and from the opposite wall of the cave, a few yards away, Mr. Higganbotham stirred. "Why do I matter to you? Why do you insist on persecuting me like this?"

The Queen said sharply, "That is our own concern."

I was too angry to reply. I closed my eyes, this time with determination, and *pushed* with all my might, forcing everything out, every tingling awareness, every thought and sensation and perversity, until I lay limply under my blanket, a hollow sack, empty of all my power.

After all, there was nothing I could do. I lay imprisoned in a dark, damp cave on the edge of the sea, blind, exhausted. I had no weapon, no insight into my condition, no idea even why I was being held prisoner.

I believe I must have drifted into sleep, for I next experienced a sense of awakening, though I have no memory of any dream. The Queen was gone, the trace of her spirit quite extinguished, and yet I still perceived, when I opened my eyes, a transparent blue glow floating against the rocky ceiling.

I lay quite still—I had turned on my back, it seemed, during the time I was insensible—and regarded this hint of radiance for several minutes. I still possessed a feeling of comfortable and blessed emptiness, each muscle quite slack beneath the two thick blankets, which seemed to pin me to the earth as efficiently as an anvil, and my unusual calmness of mind made every sense acute.

Something had woken me, I realized. A sound.

I waited patiently, because I had no choice. I had lost all will to move. My hands and feet were too warm, my limbs too loose.

Tap tap tap.

There it was, almost too faint for human ears, regular and metallic.

I went on staring at the dim radiance above me. I thought, *I will wait until I hear it again*, and then it came, just above the whoosh of Mr. Higganbotham's sleeping breath: *Tap tap tap.*

As I heard the sound, I realized that the glow on the ceiling was not uniform. If I watched carefully, if indeed I absorbed the sense of the glow rather than watched it, I became aware that it was concentrated—if a light so transparent can be said to concentrate—on that corner of the cave near which the Queen had earlier been sitting.

And if I transferred the whole of my attention to that corner of the cave, I observed that the light produced just enough illumination to disclose a series of regular ruts ascending the cave's wall, ending in black shadow.

I blinked several times and narrowed my eyes, because I wasn't quite sure that I had really seen this extraordinary pattern, or whether it was simply a trick of the light. The closer I peered, however, the fainter the glow became, until at last it winked out entirely and left the cave in darkness.

I thought, *I will not get up. I cannot get up.*

I was too tired, and the cave was utterly dark, and it was all an illusion in any case.

Tap tap tap.

This time I noticed—quite against my *will* to notice—that the sound came from the strange anomalous corner of the cave, and if I were completely honest with myself, I had to acknowledge that the sound drifted down from above.

From the black shadow on the rock ceiling.

I closed my eyes—they were no use, anyway—and in that instant the ache returned at full force, crushing the bones of my chest, leaving me gasping for breath.

I must find him.

I lifted my hands and pushed at the blankets, but even when they were gone, and the chill air drenched my clothes, the weight still sank against me. I sat up and turned on my hands and knees, trying to cough and not succeeding, while the vivid certainty of someone's presence up above me, inside that black shadow at the uppermost corner of the cave, drilled into my every nerve.

He's there, I thought. *He must be there.*

The longing increased, too intense for expression, and while I couldn't find the balance to rise in that sightless chamber, I crawled across the rocky floor, scraping my knees and my palms, until I found the edge of the wall and spread my hands over its rough surface, searching for the ruts I had seen—had I really seen them?—a moment earlier.

"Hello?"

A male whisper drifted downward, and my fingers froze against the rock.

"Hello? Who's there?"

I tilted my head upward. *It's me!* I whispered back. *I'm coming!*

There was no reply, and I resumed my scrabbling, frantic now, until at last my fingernails dragged against a horizontal bar, cut into the rock, to a depth of perhaps two inches.

A foot above it, another bar.

I climbed upward in blind triumph, feeling for each bar in the ladder, slipping twice and still pushing on, until my head reached the place where the ceiling should be and plunged straight through, into a cold blackness suffused with the presence of life.

"I'm here!" I called out, in a whisper. "Where are you?"

"Against the far wall."

I hoisted myself through the hole in the ceiling, to land on my stomach like a fish, legs waving wildly, hands grabbing for some sort of purchase on the uneven floor.

"Careful. The ceiling is low."

The whisper was wet and exhausted. I levered myself up at last and crawled across the ground in the direction of the words.

"Silverton! Are you all right? What have they done to you? What's going on?"

I reached him in a few short yards: found his prone legs stretched out, his two large feet covered by his boots, both still whole by the grace of God. I covered the leather with my hands and sank over his toes in relief.

He was alive, at least. As long as he was alive, the rest of it didn't matter.

"Silverton?" The voice was now bewildered. "I'm afraid—*Lord* Silverton?"

I lifted my head. My hands traveled up his legs, his torso, his shoulders, until at last I held his face in my palms, his massive jaw, his cheeks covered by thick foreign stubble.

I fell back. "You're not Silverton!"

"Of course not," he said. "My name is Haywood. Who the devil are you?"

Again the Lady waited, deep inside the shelter of the cave, while the Beast her brother searched for food and water to sustain them until the Hero's return. On the second day of his absence, a great storm grew outside and the wind whistled mightily along the rocks. She abased herself on the ground and prayed to the gods that her brother had found shelter, and that the Hero's ships were not even now upon the sea in search of her, for they would surely be wrecked in the surf.

When the storm cleared, the Lady ventured outside in great anxiety, and magnificent was her delight at the sight of a fleet of ships safely at anchor nearby, and boats even now landing upon the beach below. She flew down the path from the cliffs, animated with joy that she would soon be gathered into the embrace of the Hero, from whose arms she vowed she would never allow herself to be parted again.

But as she reached the golden sand, she stopped short, for she saw that the man leading his party ashore was not the Hero at all, but her husband the Prince . . .

THE BOOK OF TIME, A. M. HAYWOOD (1921)

Twenty-One

Y our Grace," I whispered, into that hole in the darkness occupied by the stranger. His boots drove painfully into my side, and I shifted to my knees, taking care for the low ceiling of which he had warned me.

There was a faint rattle of metal. "No," he said slowly, "you're mistaken again. My name is Haywood. Max Haywood. A private gentleman only."

"I'm afraid not, sir." I gathered my breath, for I was shaken to my bones, and my brain spun madly within. "I am Emmeline Truelove, secretary to the late Duke of Olympia. I have been sent by the family to find you."

"The *late* duke?"

"I am grieved, sir, most deeply grieved to inform you that His Grace passed away last month."

The man did not reply. I could hardly blame him; the shock of it struck me afresh. I said his name firmly to myself—Maximilian, Duke of Olympia—and still I could not quite comprehend that he sat before me at last, the new and rightful duke, the object of our expedition.

How had he come here?

"My God," he whispered. "It can't be true. He— I thought he was immortal."

"Yes. I believe we all did."

"How did it happen?"

"An accident on the estate. He—well, it appears he lost his step along a footbridge, and drowned in the stream below."

He made a disbelieving noise. "That hardly seems like Olympia."

"It was January, and the bridge was icy."

He absorbed this information quietly. "God rest his soul," he said at last.

"Indeed. The service—the interment—I am so sorry you missed them. They were all—his friends were all—it was all quite, I hope, as you would have wished, had you been there." My voice was failing me. I brought my hands together on my knees and went on: "You are therefore, of course, the new Duke of Olympia, and Her Grace—the dowager duchess, I mean—has been much concerned for your welfare. We hadn't heard from you in some time."

Another rattle of metal. "I have been otherwise occupied, it seems."

"What's that? That noise?"

"Ah. Those are the chains, Miss Truelove, that hold me to this wall."

"Dear God!" I reached forward and found his wrists, which were covered by a pair of thick iron manacles, and followed the chains to a heavy iron bolt in the rock nearby. "How long have you lain like this?"

"I don't quite know. A day or two, I think. It's hard to tell, in the darkness."

"But who did this? And why?"

"The same fellows, I imagine, who have imprisoned you here as well."

"And Lord Silverton? Are they holding him as well?"

The duke paused. "Silverton? Do you mean the marquess?"

"Yes. His lordship was good enough to accompany me, in search of you. You haven't seen him?"

"No, I have not."

"Oh, heavens," I whispered, and sat back. My eyes stung. I thought, *I will not cry.* There was no point in crying, here in the dark, in front of a man I had only just met, and whose face remained a mystery to me.

Simply because he was not the man I hoped to find here.

"There is a woman," the duke said softly.

"I beg your pardon?"

"I don't suppose you know anything about her? She accompanied me to Naxos some weeks ago, and I am very much afraid for her safety."

"Do you mean Desma? The barmaid at the hotel?"

"She is no barmaid, Miss Truelove," he said gravely, but without offense. The chains clinked again, as he shifted position, and I had the impression that he was leaning closer to me. "Have you heard any news of her?"

"I met her briefly, at the hotel—"

"Yes, I told her to stay there, until I returned."

"I am afraid, however, that she left last night, during the storm,

in the company of Lord Silverton. We set out after them this
morning, but her cottage was empty, and the landlord—"

"I beg your pardon," said the duke. "Did you say *we?*"

"Yes. I have lately been accompanied by your friend Mr. Higganbotham, from the Athens School."

"Higganbotham."

"Yes. From the British School at Athens. You wrote to him
earlier, if you'll recall, and arranged to meet him here on Naxos,
except—"

"Miss Truelove," he said, in the manner of a man accustomed
to having his patience tried by inferior intellects, "perhaps you
had better start over again, from the beginning."

∽

No doubt you have noticed that Lord Silverton and I both persisted, throughout our journey, in calling the new Duke of
Olympia by his previous name, even though Maximilian Haywood was entitled to the full style of that splendid rank from the
moment of the old duke's death. I am not quite certain why. Perhaps we felt too much respect for the great lion to hand off his
name so cavalierly to another.

Perhaps we were simply afraid to tempt Providence.

In any case, he remained plain Mr. Haywood, in my mind
and (I am afraid) in my heart. What other man could possibly
deserve the name Olympia? Who was worthy to follow the
grand old duke, who had held each crowned head of Europe in
his palm, at one time or another? (In the case of its female sover-
eigns, quite often literally.) Who else had bestrode the great
empire like a silver-haired colossus, never asking so much as a
gram of treasure in return, and yet richer in mind and body than

any petty potentate he had outwitted and outmaneuvered in his long, illustrious life?

No, I could not name Maximilian Haywood by his proper title. I could not bear to think of this stranger walking the earth as the Duke of Olympia.

And yet.

Here we sat at last, improbably and intimately, on the damp rock floor of a cave hidden in the cliffs of distant Naxos. And I could not see him, could not even make out the shadow of his shape in this black hole, and the air was cold and smelled of despair.

But as I crouched next to him, explaining the history of our expedition in a hushed voice that rose only just above a whisper, while he listened earnestly and without interruption, I found that I addressed him, from time to time, as *Your Grace*, in a style of newfound reverence. I found reassurance in the measure of heat that issued from his body, from the indomitable stillness with which he sat against the wall, from the olympic patience in his manner. In his demeanor, I discovered an intense familiarity, so real and pungent that I nearly forgot I was attending the present duke, and not the former.

Near the end of my story, he stopped me. "There was no sign of their presence in the shelter? No indication whatever that Silverton and my friend had reached these caves?"

"None at all, I'm afraid. We saw no trace of them anywhere."

"I see. I suppose I may take some comfort in that. Silverton is a resourceful fellow, and largely trustworthy."

"Only largely?"

"He has his little weaknesses, as I'm sure you've discovered. And then you were brought here, I presume, and placed under guard."

"Yes. They gave us a little food, and one of the men remained behind to prevent our escape. In any case, it was too dark to make an attempt, on such a treacherous slope."

"Yes. I hope you were not hurt."

I touched the back of my neck. "No."

"No?"

"A trifle."

"I see," he said again, nothing more.

I cleared my throat. "I have told you what I know. Perhaps you have some idea what is to be done? Mr. Higganbotham and I stand at your service. Surely we can defeat these two men, if we can conceive a sound plan."

"Yes, I think so. The prospects are altogether brighter than they were an hour ago."

I waited for more. My feet had begun to grow numb, under the weight of my crouching body, and I shifted position, accidentally encountering his knee. "I don't mean to intrude on your private affairs," I said at last, "but I confess we have been at a loss to explain your actions since December. Perhaps you can explain some part of this mystery? Who these men are, I mean, and why they have pursued you with such extraordinary persistence?"

"Me? I am afraid you mistake the matter. It is not *me* these men wish to capture."

"Who, then?"

"Her," he said, but the word was smothered under the weight of a loud noise from below: an explosion that sounded very much like the firing of a pistol.

"Mr. Higganbotham!" I exclaimed, and started for the opening in the rock.

But the air that drifted up from the cave below already rang with shouts. "Wait!" said the duke, and I hesitated, straining to pick out the voices, while my pulse pounded thunderously in my ears.

But the shouts tangled together, a melee of oaths and grunts and thumps, a howl of pain. I pressed one palm against the wall and leaned over the edge, desperate for news.

"Who is it?" demanded the duke, just as the words *Up your bloody a——!* carried upward, loud and distinctly British.

My breath caught.

Then came a sound between a shout and a squeal, a word I did not recognize, from a throat that could only belong to a female, or else a very young male.

The latter possibility, I decided, was distinctly remote.

I turned to Olympia. "There's a woman."

The duke let out a low roar, and the chains rattled in fury. The noise distracted me only a few seconds, but in that short time the tide of battle seemed to shift, and as I turned back to the opening, I saw that a light was growing below, illuminating the charcoal walls of the cave, and the sounds had grown loud and immediate.

I fell back, just as a golden head thrust upward from the hole.

"*—shall rip your filthy b——locks from your ar——e with my own bare—*"

But his sentence was cut short, as the rest of his body flew over the edge of the opening like a breaching whale, arms and legs bound together with rope, and slid a few feet across the rock, knocking me on my back.

I scrambled away, while the man before me lifted his head and squinted his eyes upward.

"Why, Truelove!" he said. "Dash it all. I was counting on you to ride to our rescue."

Our reunion was short-lived, to the tune of perhaps four seconds.

"I'd watch out, if I were you," Silverton said cheerfully, "for I expect the chap who sent me up—"

A large figure burst forth from the opening. His legs and arms were quite at liberty.

"Ah! There he is now."

From the shadows, the Duke of Olympia shouted, "Where is she, man? Where's Desma?"

Silverton turned his head. "Who the devil's that?"

"It's Haywood, you damned fool. What have you done with her?"

"Haywood! I say! We've been looking for you. There's beastly news, I'm afraid."

"Where is she?"

"Why, Desma? She's down below, old boy, and in much better condition than I am. For some reason these fellows seem actually to value her life, unlike that of your poor humble servant."

During the course of this conversation, the man behind him climbed out of the hole and rose to his feet. In the new glow around us, I saw it was the ginger-haired fellow, bearing his familiar pistol in one hand and a curious electric torch in the other, which he cast about the walls until the light fell upon the figure of the Duke of Olympia, no longer recumbent but crouching like a predator about to spring, at the far limits of his chains.

"So, b——ch," said the man. "Looks like we found her after all, without your help. What do you think of that?"

"I don't know what you're talking about."

I shall not repeat the oath uttered by the newcomer; I have, I believe, given you enough flavor of his conversation. He gave voice fluently, and then said, "Come on, man. It's over. We've got the woman. Time to start talking, okay? Nice and slow, so we don't miss a thing."

"You are mistaken," said the duke. "Wasting your time."

The man hadn't seemed to notice me, kneeling next to the fallen Silverton, a few feet away. Men usually didn't, did they? A woman was nothing to be afraid of, nothing to take into account, except perhaps as a useful pawn. A chip with which to bargain.

I found my feet, one by one, and edged around the far side of Silverton's body.

The duke made no sign that he had seen me. He lifted his arms and rattled the chains. "Release me, or there will be the devil to pay. I assure you, I have powerful friends, who will pursue you with the full might of the British crown behind them."

The man laughed and jerked his head at Silverton's bound limbs. "Powerful friends like this one, right? I'm shaking in my boots."

"I say," Silverton said, in an offended voice.

"The thing is, you've got no idea what I am, right. No idea *who* I am. You can brag all you want about your powerful friends, but to me and my crew, they're dead and gone. Dead and—"

I brought up my fist and knocked the torch from his hand, and in the instant of his shock, I grabbed for the opposite hand, the one with the pistol.

At the same instant, Silverton rolled like a dervish, crashing into his ankles, and the pistol slipped into my hands. I grasped it properly, as Silverton had shown me, and flipped back the safety latch.

The man swore and launched himself at me, but I had already taken aim, and my finger squeezed the trigger just before the blow landed.

We fell together in a heap, to the sound of splintering metal. His weight crushed me into the rocks. He swore in my ear, and his rank breath smothered my face as he attempted to heave himself up, but I wrapped my legs around his, tangling us both in the folds of my dress and petticoats.

"Ugh! You f——ing b——ch!"

He was trying to land a blow of some kind, but we were too closely entwined, and I had the advantage because he required the use of his arms to hoist himself up. I grabbed a fistful of ginger hair and yanked it. The word *b——ch* transformed into a howl of anguish. He whipped his head backward, trying to dislodge my hand, but I held on viciously while his fingers grasped for my throat and his thumbs found my windpipe.

All of this took place over the course of a few frantic seconds, though my sense of time, in the manner of such moments of crisis, seemed to stretch out into an infinity. The black spots appeared before my eyes, and I thought, *I must hold on, hold on to his damned hair*, even as my fingers weakened and his pale image blurred in front of my eyes.

And then he disappeared entirely, and I thought I was strangling to death. A roar built in my ears—from the lack of air? impending unconsciousness?—that grew in fury until, in a flash, the pressure on my neck flew away. In the next instant, the man's body went with it.

I swung dizzily to my side and tried to sit up. The torch still burned from the nearby ground, providing the necessary minimum of illumination, showing the ginger-haired man dangling from the chest of the Duke of Olympia, who held him there with a double loop of chain.

My aim, it seemed, had proven true.

"Damned fine shot, Truelove," said Lord Silverton, and I turned my head and saw him, too, still lying on the ground with his cheek to the rock. I could not see his expression in the shadows, but as I took in the familiar outline of his cheek and jaw, the congenial bulk of his cinched-up body, I felt a sense of profound solace settle on my chest, an antidote to some unsuspected poison, traveling warmly along the vessels near my heart.

I have found you.

I crawled toward him and found the rope securing his wrists. The knot was tight but familiar—a double square, hardly expert—and I forced my stiff fingers to work the lines apart until his hands loosened and then fell free.

"Ah, God!" he said in relief, stretching out his palms and rubbing them together. "You're an angel. Damned inglorious, to lie trussed up like a Christmas goose, while some scoundrel attempts to strangle my Truelove on the ground nearby. Now the legs, if you will?"

But I was already at work on the knot at his ankles. A few yards away, the duke gave the ginger-haired man a last experimental tug and allowed him to slide to the ground: quite unconscious, if not dead. I tried to call out to him, but my wounded throat allowed only a whisper. "Almost done!"

The duke didn't notice. He stepped over the fallen American as if he were a pile of rubbish, picked up the pistol, and tucked it into the waistband of his trousers. "Follow me," he said, and strode not toward the two of us, Silverton and me, but toward the opening that led to the cave below.

"What are you doing?" I tried to shout.

"The knot, Truelove!" said Silverton. "Quickly!"

"But what's going on?"

"He's gone to get Desma, no doubt."

Desma, I thought angrily. I tugged at the rope, which proved even tighter than the first, though the knot was exactly the same. Silverton was flexing his fingers, shaking them, attempting to work the sensation back into his nerves. "But who is she?" I rasped.

"Poor Truelove," he said. "You sound dreadful. Honey and lemon, that's the ticket, and perhaps a rinse of salt water."

"Do you mind answering my question? Who *is* this woman?"

"Desma? I'm not quite certain, to be perfectly honest. She speaks a dashed odd dialect. Cornered me at the inn, gave me to understand that she knew where Max was, but he had fallen into some sort of imminent danger, so off we went into the tempest on a pair of recalcitrant mules, and that was only the start of— Ah! Here we are. I could kiss you for that."

His legs fell apart. I unwound the rest of the rope while he rubbed at his trousers, one calf and then the other, and then braced himself on the ground and attempted to rise.

"Damn it all," he muttered. "Give us a hand, will you, Truelove?"

I ducked under his shoulder. The duke had already disappeared down the hatchway, into an explosion of shouts and thumps that had now gone inexplicably and ominously still.

"Quickly! These damned legs."

"But you can't be thinking of going down there, like this!"

"My dear, I don't believe we have a choice. Give me a lift, now."

I supported him upward, and together we staggered to the opening in the rock. Silverton lurched forward and braced himself on the opposite wall, then swung his legs down until he sat on the edge, breathing hard. "Right-ho," he said, and looked up at me. "Awfully sorry about all this, Truelove. You ought to have stayed in England, after all."

Then he slid free and dropped to the floor below.

Someone shouted out a warning. I peered over the edge in time to see Silverton on his feet, braced against the wall, perfectly still, staring warily at the scene before him.

"Bloody damn," he said.

Behind me, the American groaned roughly. I turned and found the discarded rope, and before he could stir further, I grabbed his wrists and tied them together. "It's known as a double gunner's knot," I told him in my scratchy voice, giving the hemp a last ruthless tug. "You shall probably need a knife to open it."

I rose and found the torch, which I switched off and slid into the pocket of my skirt. *Down we go, Truelove,* I muttered, and without another thought, I lowered myself to the edge of the opening and dropped to the floor of the cave below.

At the sight of the Prince, the Lady turned and fled, but the new roundness of her form slowed her steps, and he soon caught her and held her fast. 'My love,' he said gently, 'do not struggle, for you have nothing to fear. I have seen how grave were my sins against you, and I now ask only your forgiveness, and a return to that dear love we once shared on our bridal couch.'

The Lady answered, 'Then you have traveled here without gain, for I tell you now that I first wed you only by the command of the King my father, and have since known only loathing for your base cruelty and your gross habits. I have renounced that false vow I made at our nuptials, and the gods have rewarded me with a true Hero for my spouse, and a child sired by him in my womb which was barren until now.'

The Prince howled with rage and took out his knife, and he swore he would cut out the bastard babe from her belly with his own hand. But as the dagger touched her skin, a roar sounded all down the length of the beach, and the Beast her brother emerged from the rocks in a fury . . .

THE BOOK OF TIME, A. M. HAYWOOD (1921)

Twenty-Two

The shock of impact traveled up my feet and into the bones of my legs. I staggered forward, and an arm snaked out to catch me just before I fell. Silverton. I recognized the bass note of his grunt.

"Holy sh——," said a new voice, one I didn't recognize, "another lady drops by. How about that. Should have worn something nicer."

I lifted my head and gasped. A man stood near the entrance to the cave: not the other American, the one who had accompanied us to the cave, but a wiry fellow of medium height, brown-haired and clean-shaven, who held a woman in one arm and a knife in the opposite hand, which he held in a perfect horizontal line against the center of the lady's long, pale throat.

"Don't move," the man added, "or the b——ch gets it."

I looked at her face, which I scarcely recognized, even though I knew it must belong to the not-barmaid, Desma, who had occasioned all this trouble. She was handsome rather than beautiful, bones strong and eyebrows thick, and her lips were voluptuously red and full, as if she had been sucking on lemons. Her dress was that of a peasant, loose and rough-textured. I wondered if I was gazing upon the next Duchess of Olympia.

I said hoarsely, "I beg your pardon? *Gets* it? Gets what?"

"Meaning I cut her throat."

Like the others, he spoke in that plain, flat-voweled voice I have come to recognize as American, though it was not at all the sort of American accent—thank goodness—spoken by the Dowager Duchess of Olympia. No, there was something else about him, a foreign aspect to which I could not quite place a name.

I glanced around the cave, at the men standing arrested at this extraordinary spectacle, which was lit by a powerful lantern that now hung from a hook near the entrance. The second man stood next to Mr. Higganbotham, securing him with one thick arm; the Duke of Olympia held a wary stance a few feet away, as if he had been on the point of launching himself at the American and stopped himself just in time. By my side, Silverton kept his arm at my waist, in a gesture that soon drew the American's curious gaze.

I stepped away from his lordship and said, "Very well. We are at an impasse. What are your demands?"

The American nodded at the Duke of Olympia. "He knows what we want."

"You're mistaken," said the duke. "I have not the slightest understanding what you want from me, and never have. I am a scholar, nothing more. I thought I made that quite clear."

The American seized his prize even closer to his chest, and she cried out and grasped his arm. Her loose dress flattened against her body, revealing the round curve of a secret I had not suspected.

"But she's with child!" I exclaimed.

"Indeed," the duke said quietly.

I looked back and forth between them, and compassion spread inside me like a spill of oil, replacing my earlier resentment. "Sir," I said firmly to the American, "you are a blackguard of the worst sort, and I demand that you release this poor woman at once, or you will one day answer to a far mightier judgment than ours."

He chuckled. "*Blackguard.* Now that's a good one. I don't think anyone's ever called me that before. *F——ing asshole*, maybe."

"I'm afraid I don't know what that means."

"He means *ar——e*, I believe," said Silverton. "*Ar——ehole.* Americanism."

"My apologies," the man said. "F——ing ar——ehole."

I held out my hand. "Give me that knife."

He tilted his head to one side. He seemed to be smiling. "You know, I think I'm starting to like you, Miss—?"

"Truelove," said Silverton. "Miss Truelove. I rather like her, too."

Something was afoot, that much was clear. I could tell by his lordship's easy, jocular manner—even more easy and jocular than usual, I should say—which seemed designed for some special purpose. To put the American off his guard, perhaps? To distract him?

Because of course Lord Silverton possessed a plan. He had his faults—all too many, in fact—but in a tight corner like this one, Silverton always had the angle on the way out.

If only I knew what it was.

Follow his lead, I thought. *Just follow his lead.*

"Why, thank you, your lordship. I confess, I had no notion of your esteem."

The American laughed again. "Listen to you. Jesus. It's like watching f——ing *Downton Abbey*."

"Downton Abbey? Where's that?" said Silverton. "Never heard of the place."

My heart was beating quickly, and my eyes remained fastened on that wicked knife, which had not budged from its position against Desma's naked throat. I said, "Perhaps he means Doncaster Abbey, in Lancashire. Though it's half-ruined, and the baronet hardly welcomes guests. Particularly not the American sort."

"What, Sir Cedric? Hasn't the old rascal died yet?"

"Still hanging on."

"By God. He must be ninety at least."

"And he hunts all season long, just as he always did," I said. "The abbey might be falling apart, but the Doncaster kennel remains a palace. Olympia used to go down every November and ride for a week, until the duchess made him stop."

The young woman gazed at us in utter bewilderment.

"Ah, splendid lady, the duchess. Is that what you meant, my good man? *Doncaster* Abbey? Good hunting, rubbish accommodation?"

"Actually, I don't give a sh——. What I want is for *him* . . ." The American turned his head slightly, in the direction of Maximilian Haywood, and his mouth fell open. "The *f*——!" he shouted, and the knife flew away from Desma's throat at last, flailing at the empty air while the Duke of Olympia coolly fired his stolen pistol at the man's head.

✑

I am afraid the next few moments have somewhat blurred in my memory, though I recall they seemed quite clear at the time of the event itself. I once discussed the matter with an eminent student in the field of psychological analysis, and he explained that my reaction was quite normal in instances of violent attack. The mind, you see, wishes to protect itself from the effects of traumatic experience, and buries (if that is the proper term) the sensations so deep in the regions of memory, they are sometimes never properly recovered.

In any case, the duke's bullet did find its mark, and the impact of such a powerful weapon on a frail human skull was spectacular, though the immediate postmortem image is—thankfully—long since lost to me.

I do remember a vague sense of appalled shock, followed by an instant or two of disorganized shrieking, and then the crisp voice of Lord Silverton as he issued the necessary orders to unbind Mr. Higganbotham's hands (this task he delegated to me, I believe) and evacuate the cave in a rapid yet orderly fashion.

But what I still remember most precisely (perhaps because I found it so curious) was Desma's frantic weeping, and her reluctance to leave the cave at last. In the end, the duke was forced to hand his pistol to Lord Silverton and carry her out of the cavern himself, and even then she struggled and beat her fists against his chest, as if he were bearing her away not from mortal danger, but from life itself.

⟆

I recovered some degree of mental composure during the walk down the cliff path, toward the beach, which flickered in and out of view according to the turnings of the path, broad and bright and golden in the light from the morning sun. The scirocco had died down, and already the air bore a calm and springlike warmth, such that I could almost hear the shooting of tiny new plants upward through the damp soil, and smell the peculiar greenness of young vegetation. The scent of hope.

The Duke of Olympia went first, carrying his precious double burden, and the pistol was tucked back into the waistband of his trousers. Perhaps the child would be a boy (I thought, as I watched the muscles of his back dampen his stained white shirt) and therefore the next heir to the dukedom. Or perhaps a girl, who would take her place in London society, wearing a beautiful white gown and one of the delicate family tiaras suitable for a debutante. There would be music and champagne, and all this hardship would be forgotten, and the child's illegitimate beginnings lost to all but the most distant memory.

Mr. Higganbotham followed directly behind me, and Silverton last of all, urging us forward. I wanted to stop and ask why we drove along in such hurry, when our foes lay vanquished behind us, but I perceived that this was not the moment for lengthy explanation. I merely asked, over my shoulder, "Where are we going?"

"The beach, down below. I believe I see the good old *Isolde* plying the waters to the north. We can signal her from there, and I daresay the jolly boat can easily land on all that sand and ferry us to safety."

"But what is the *Isolde* doing there to begin with?"

"Why, because I had the presence of mind to send a message to the lighthouse before I left the hotel."

"The lighthouse?"

"Yes. They've got a Marconi device, you see. The only one on the island." His voice was rich with self-satisfaction. "One of my first inquiries, when we arrived."

"How clever."

"Experience, Truelove. Experience and training. Enough of those, and you don't need any brains."

"That's fortunate for you."

"Isn't it?"

Down the path we marched, while the beach grew in scope below us, and the blue sea sparkled to our right. Under the effects of relief and of Silverton's bright conversation, I was beginning to feel an unreal and almost demented levity. In a moment, I thought I should perhaps laugh aloud.

We had done it. We had recovered the missing duke and brought him to safety. We had even secured his chosen bride and an heir to ensure a new generation of the illustrious line, presuming an Anglican minister could be hastily summoned in Athens to legitimize the union.

How all this had come about, I couldn't quite say. I studied the movement of the duke's shoulders before my nose, the flop of Desma's despondent legs at his side, and I realized I knew almost nothing more about either of them than I had known the day before. Not even the most basic questions: why they were so doggedly pursued by these strange, ill-mannered men; what, exactly, they had been doing here in Naxos for the past several weeks.

Well, all that could wait until we were safely aboard the ship and steaming back toward the civilization of Athens. The Duke of Olympia was alive; he was uninjured, unimpaired in faculties, and even now on his way back to England to claim that noble birthright to which he had succeeded. The dukedom was secured from ruin by the licentious younger brother. The planned institute in East Sussex—goodness, I had almost forgot its existence, during the series of emergencies that had engulfed us—was no longer in doubt.

As for my own future? I supposed that remained to be seen. But I rather thought I had acquitted myself well, if this expedition could be said to constitute a trial for the position of personal secretary to the new Duke of Olympia.

The path was beginning to flatten and fill with sand. Desma had stopped sobbing, and her dark head was now tucked into the hollow of the duke's shoulder. He was saying something to her, but I couldn't hear the words, and I had no wish to disturb their privacy. I held back a step or two, lengthening the distance between us, and Mr. Higganbotham, who had maintained a petrified silence since the terrible scene inside the cave, grunted as he adjusted his own pace down the uneven track.

"Easy as she goes, now," Silverton said cheerfully, and then, "Hello! Who's that fellow?"

My head snapped up.

Just ahead, the duke skidded to a stop and made a half turn, as if to shield Desma from sight by the width of his own body. I peered around him to the wide beach beyond, almost expecting to see the familiar shape of my father, seated upon a boulder in the morning sunshine, with his neat black jacket folded over his arm. I don't know whether I dreaded the sight or welcomed it.

But it was not my father who occupied the beach before us.

"Get back," the duke ordered, depositing Desma on the ground, where the last jagged rocks of the cliff staggered onto the beach. He withdrew the pistol from his waistband and stepped forward to drop one knee in the sand.

Silverton was already brushing past me. In his right hand he gripped the same knife that the American had held against Desma's throat. "Stay here, for God's sake," he shouted as he went, and I wasn't quite sure whether he directed those words at His Grace or at me, Mr. Higganbotham having already ducked to the ground next to Desma's crouching body. He continued on, plowing through the sand in his leather shoes and gaiters, a British madman set loose on a foreign beach, toward the four men who approached down the grassy slope from the south.

He's creating a diversion, I thought, and I opened my mouth to scream *No!*

But as I started forward, the duke flung out his hand to stop me. "Take her out of here," he said. "Not the cave, the road. There's a beach around the other side of the headland. Try to signal the ship, to get a boat out. Higganbotham, go with them. Now!"

"But Silverton!"

"For God's sake! Do it!"

The duke's dark eyes blazed with desperation, as if he were trying to communicate something more: all those things he had not yet told us. That he was prepared to die for this woman. I looked down at Desma, who was already rising from behind the boulder, bracing herself with one hand and pointing her round belly upward for better leverage. The sunshine suited her olive skin and her strong bones, and her dark eyes that had narrowed into crescents, determined and terrified at once. A pair of silver lines tracked down her face, from the inner corners of her eyes, past her nose and mouth.

Next to her, Mr. Higganbotham rose from the ground and dusted the sand from his trousers. "Let's go," he said.

I took her other hand. "Come along!" I cried, over the gathering shouts from the beach, and I drew her around the boulders, to the rocky slope that hugged the side of the cliff.

"Wait!" said the duke.

I turned.

He stepped toward me and pressed the pistol into my hand.

"There are four bullets left, I believe, if it was fully loaded before. Use them wisely."

"But then you've got nothing to defend yourself with!"

"Neither will you, without this. Now go." He pushed my shoulder and turned away.

We had to tug Desma along. She didn't want to leave. Our feet scrabbled in the gravel, for there was no path here, no surface in which to find purchase along the slope of tiny stones that had eroded in their millions from the ridges above.

"Hurry," I gasped, more to myself than to Desma, who could not understand me. Her hand was warm and strong, and her steps surer than mine, but she kept turning her head to view the scene behind us, causing her feet to falter. Like Orpheus, I thought, and I tried to tug her again, but she cried out and stopped, and I was forced to turn, too.

I saw Silverton first, whether because his furious golden head stood out from the rest, or because I could not help seeing him, any more than you can help seeing your own coat hanging on a peg in a crowded cloakroom. He was fighting two men at once, wielding the knife and his bare fist, and his body moved so fast, like quicksilver, that I could not follow every action: a thrust, a spin, a punch, a kick, all gathered into motion that reminded me of a steel machine pounding the air, while the two men bobbed and ducked fearfully around him. One staggered back as a blow landed on his chin, and Silverton whirled and slashed at the other without a pause.

So transfixed was I by this electrifying spectacle that I did not, in those first few seconds, notice how the other men had disposed themselves, until Desma clutched at my arm and cried out.

The duke had emerged from the boulders and was now running, unarmed, toward the combatants at the top of the beach.

One of the men had detached himself from the others and stepped deliberately in the duke's direction. He raised his arm, and a puff of white smoke exploded from the barrel, a single instant before the air shattered in an almighty bang, and I flinched and ducked, turning my body in a kind of instinct to shield Desma, though she was not the object of the bullet.

The duke staggered, spun, and dropped to his knees in the sand.

At the instant of his falling, Desma screamed and started forward, and in that brief space of time I hesitated, because I did not know my own duty. Did I come to the aid of the Duke of Olympia, as the dowager duchess herself had charged me, or did I protect this woman and her unborn child, for whose innocent sakes he meant to lay down his life?

As I hovered, as the seconds stretched out into an eon of indecision, I experienced the strangest sensation. The effect is almost impossible to describe. It was as if I had acquired a separate being, which flew to a point of vantage perhaps fifty feet above my own head, from which I could see my surroundings in three hundred and sixty perfectly simultaneous degrees of arc, in addition to the scene presently visible from my two earthbound eyes.

I saw the Duke of Olympia pick himself up, lower his head, and rush again at his approaching attacker.

I saw the knife fly out of Lord Silverton's hand, flashing in the sunshine as it tumbled end over end through the air.

I saw the fourth man (pistol in hand) charge up the stony slope toward the three of us—Desma and Mr. Higganbotham and me—who were still turned toward the Duke of Olympia and quite unprepared for his arrival.

I saw a boat, manned by six sturdy sailors and an eager coxswain whom I knew to be Mr. Brown, pulling hard for shore at a distance about halfway between the *Isolde*'s place of anchor and the outermost point of the beach on which we stood.

I gathered all these pieces of information together and realized, in helpless despair, that it wouldn't do. That the attackers would reach us long before the boat breached the sand; that, furthermore, we had not the smallest chance of holding out against them until our friends arrived.

I wanted to call out to my own figure, standing in the sand, and warn her of the armed villain scattering the rocks nearby, but the throat of this second all-seeing Truelove, floating above the beach, was frozen shut. She had no voice. She could only watch as the real living Truelove heard the approaching man at last, turned in shock, and lifted the pistol.

The bullet struck the man's shoulder and made him grunt, but it did not halt his progress. Desma now turned—the duke was down in the sand by now, wrestling with the third man and stained with blood—and stumbled back in shock, falling to the ground. She picked up a fistful of gravel and flung it toward our attacker. Mr. Higganbotham, recovering from his shock, did the same. The tiny stones struck the attacker on the side of his face, and he swore loudly, losing his footing for a brief instant.

But by now the first two men had broken free of Silverton's furious attack, and charged up the slope in their companion's wake. Silverton followed them at a run, but he was favoring one leg, and he clutched his left arm, bracing it against his side at a stiff angle. I fired again and missed—the sun was directly in my eyes—and then the hammer clicked on an empty chamber.

The gun had not been fully loaded, after all.

I bent down and picked up a rock. I threw it with all the strength in my slender arm, and it struck the man's temple, knocking him sideways, but again he recovered, like a child's toy that bounces back upward every time it is batted down.

The other Truelove, observing this scene from above, beat her helpless arms against the air and noticed, for the first time, that another man had accompanied the four aggressors to the beach this morning. Until now, his huge body had been obscured by the combat with Lord Silverton, for he was bound by the arms and hobbled at the ankles, and had been tossed in the sand when the fighting began.

But he was not helpless, as the floating Truelove was. He was crawling on the sand, though his shirt was bloody, and his head appeared to have been badly injured. As I watched the progress of the *Isolde*'s boat, and Silverton staggering up behind the men who attacked us, and the first man reaching us while the earth-bound Truelove beat him with the butt of her pistol, I also saw the prisoner's object, a few final feet away.

Silverton's knife.

The man grabbed my battering pistol and threw it away. He swung his fist and hit me in the jaw, hard enough that I staggered back and fell into the rocks, while the other two men pounded up the slope, and the fourth man struggled in the sand with the Duke of Olympia, fighting for possession of the gun.

But the prisoner had now crossed the last few feet of sand and maneuvered his body around to grasp the knife in one hand and saw, thread by thread, at the rope that secured his wrists.

I watched the progress of this fascinating operation closely, at the same time as I fought and kicked and scratched at the man who had now held me to the ground with his booted foot and pointed a gun at my head.

Perhaps I had some notion what my other self observed from

the air, for I remember thinking, *I must hold him off somehow, I must prolong this struggle to its last possible second.*

But I knew I was too late. I had failed, for one of the men—I had lost count of them, in my earthbound mind—had taken hold of a shrieking Desma, and now held the barrel of his gun directly at her temple.

A cry of despair split the air in two, just as the prisoner sawed apart the last filament of rope, and freed his hands.

"Drop the gun, motherf——r," called out the man who held Desma, in a loud and carrying voice.

Across the beach, the Duke of Olympia, who had succeeded in wresting the pistol from the hand of his opponent, stood with his legs apart and howled again at the injustice of his predicament: having fought so hard, against impossible odds, and so nearly won. The left shoulder of his white shirt was dark with blood.

Fifty yards away, the prisoner applied the knife to the rope that hobbled his feet. It had been secured at a circumference just wide enough to allow him to shamble along with his jailers, and by the stiffness of his movements, he seemed to have been shambling for many miles already. How he had done so, bearing such terrible and disfiguring injuries, I could only imagine. But he was young and strong—his strength rippled from his giant frame, and from the wide muscles that animated him—and perhaps that had served him well.

Silverton had stopped, too, but unlike the others, his attention had fallen on me. My heart, already sick, seemed to wither in my breast. His face was bruised and cut, and something was wrong with his left shoulder, which emerged from its socket at an unnatural angle. His trousers were dirty and slashed, and a stream of blood came down his right calf to stain the sand below. He watched me steadily, from those eyes I had once thought too blue, as if he were trying to communicate something vital.

His latest plan, perhaps.

"Let her go, Anserrat," growled the Duke of Olympia, in a low and restrained voice that was nonetheless perfectly audible to us, a hundred feet away.

The man holding Desma shook his head and spoke in the same flat American voice as the others, except tilted at the vowels by an accent that suggested some corner of the Levant. "Where's Tom? What happened in there?"

"Mr. Henderson is dead," said the duke. "Let her go."

"*Dead?* Sh——." Anserrat glanced upward at the cave and squinted his eyes. The barrel of the gun pressed hard against Desma's temple, forming a round impression on her skin.

"You see? There's no point. Just let her go."

Anserrat returned his attention to the duke. "What do you mean? No f——king point. This is not just about Tom, man. It's all of us. Don't play dumb. You know what we want."

"I haven't the slightest idea, any more than I did in Knossos. You're mistaken about me. I'm just a scholar."

"Do you not understand I will f——ing *kill* her?"

"Then I will kill *you* with my bare hands, and you'll still not have what you want from me, because I don't have it."

"Yes, you *do!*" Anserrat paused, and his tone grew calmer. "I know you do. I've got proof."

"Proof of *what*? I haven't done anything!"

And this Anserrat, whoever he was, actually smiled—*smiled!*—just as if he were not holding a gun to the head of a helpless and visibly expectant woman, as if he knew the secret of the universe.

"Don't you get it? It's not what you've *done*, b——ch. It's what you *will* do."

Down the beach, the prisoner had cut through the rope binding his ankles, and now rose to a towering height.

"You're mad," I said, and my captor tightened his arm against my ribs, nudged the gun against my head, and told me to shut the f—— up.

My eyes flew back to Lord Silverton, not because I was terrified (though I admit that I *was* terrified, that terror suffused every particle of my body) but because I detected a familiar and invisible change coming over him, as the impasse wore on. He was still watching me, and his eyebrows had flinched as the gun worked closer into my temple, but the fury in his face had now smoothed away into the pretty mask in which I had first come to know him.

And then he yawned.

"By damn. Are we going to carry on like this much longer? Because I could do with a spot of breakfast. How about you, Truelove? Has anyone here troubled themselves to arrange for a morning feed?"

"Shut up," said Anserrat. "Dave, watch him."

"Oh, Dave needn't bother himself." Silverton yawned again. "Feeling a bit faint, actually. Loss of blood and all that."

And then—well, it was as if that second Truelove, the one hovering above, came back to earth, hurtling herself back inside the corporeal Truelove in a thud of understanding.

I knew, without looking, that the prisoner on the beach was now circling around behind us, keeping just out of sight among the rocks and the brush that rimmed the sand. That he had drawn close, while Silverton was chatting on amiably, and when

Silverton fell forward, directly after saying the word *faint*, causing an instant of confusion, he would strike.

And he did, roaring in such a bestial manner as I have never heard from a human throat. He flew between us and launched himself upon Anserrat, and I did not even see the slash of that knife as it sliced open the man's helpless throat.

But I saw the blood, pints of it, as it gushed over the rocks to the sound of Desma's keening wail.

And I will never forget the sight of that beast, his terrible misshapen head, as he raised himself triumphantly from his kill, teeth bared, and turned toward me.

I screamed, and the man who held me released his grip and lifted the pistol. He fired once, into the center of that animal-like face, and the blast of the nearby gun erased all sensation of sound from my ears.

The beast fell, and so did his killer, and it was not until I looked up and saw Mr. Brown running toward us at full tilt, leading a pack of the *Isolde*'s best men, holding a smoking pistol in his one good hand, that I realized the valet had fired a shot of his own—a bullet that had penetrated the chest of my captor—directly after the explosion that had deafened me.

For many minutes the two men fought, while the Lady searched for the knife in the sand, where it had fallen. But the Prince's men soon recovered from their shock and advanced to protect their patron, and the Lady knew that they would show her no mercy if he were killed, for they had enjoyed many hours of drink and debauchery under his command, and worshipped him almost as a god.

At last the blade came under her fingertips, and she seized it in her hands and cried, 'The next man who steps forward will see this dagger in his belly, and the man who touches me will know the vengeance of the Beast my brother, who protects me, for I wear the medallion of the Labrys on my breast as a shield against death.'

The Prince's men halted in fear, for the Lady spoke in a terrible voice, and her eyes and her hair were wild with fury. And then before their eyes, the three figures blurred and then disappeared, and the men later swore that the Lady and the Prince had ascended together into the heavens, while the Beast ran off into the hills and was nevermore seen by man . . .

THE BOOK OF TIME, A. M. HAYWOOD (1921)

Twenty-Three

o you really believe that?" I asked. "That this wretched, deformed man was the actual Minotaur?"

"That depends, I suppose, on what you mean by *Minotaur*. In any case, it is the least of the mysteries that surround us, at the present moment." The duke turned a leaf in the portfolio of papers I had given him to review. "Is it really necessary to maintain twelve different country houses, scattered throughout the length and breadth of the British Isles?"

"Most of them are let."

"Under what terms?"

"Long, in most cases. The estate's standard lease extends for ten years, paid in advance with an option for renewal at five years, a sum then invested in government bonds at a similar maturity. The income provides for upkeep and a reasonable profit." I paused and fingered my pen. "Your business manager, of course, will be happy to provide you with further detail. The previous duke took an active role in all the duchy's financial affairs."

"I daresay." He turned his head toward the March sun, which shone bravely through the portholes as we steamed north toward Athens. He occupied the sofa, on the strict order of the doctor in Naxos who had attended his wound—the bullet had only grazed his shoulder, but it was a nasty, open slice, requiring twenty-four sutures and a magnificent dressing that had to be changed twice daily for a week—and rather overwhelmed the poor furniture, in my opinion. He was not so tall as the towering seventh duke, only just reaching six feet, but he was a burly man, each bone manufactured to a high load-bearing specification that seemed intended by God for feats of strength rather than scholarship. Beneath his dressing gown of dark blue paisley, the bandage made a shocking lump on both sides of his right shoulder, giving him the look of prize-fighting hunchback. The brooding expression on his face did little to dispel this impression.

"It is not so bad as that, sir," I said quietly. "You will have an immense and talented staff to assist you, and the duchess, I am sure, will be a great comfort."

"The duchess?"

"I mean the lady below, sir, who will become your duchess in a matter of days."

"Yes, of course."

I sifted through the papers in my desk. "I have here the telegraphed reply from Reverend Armitage in Athens, who will be honored to perform the marriage service at our convenience." I looked up. "The sooner the better, I should think. When is the—er, the happy event expected?"

"June, I believe."

"Very good. She's in deep mourning, of course, so I'll make the arrangements as simple as possible, but I believe a small wedding breakfast is in order, don't you think, to mark the occasion? She will be the Duchess of Olympia, after all."

"Very small, Miss Truelove, and very simple. I should like to stay aboard the ship, in fact, and to set off for England immediately afterward. Silverton can give her away," he added, as an afterthought.

I made a note on the paper before me. "Of course."

"And I suppose you will have to be bridesmaid."

"It will be my honor to do so. I have already made inquiries for a dressmaker. She will have a number of suitable articles ready upon our arrival, which will require, I hope, only a minimum of alteration."

"You are a miracle, Miss Truelove." He rose from the sofa, wincing very slightly, and walked across the room to the coffee service on the side table. I started to rise, but he waved me down and asked if I would like coffee.

We were only twelve hours out to sea, and my stomach was not quite at peace. "No, thank you," I said.

He lifted the silver pot—a little awkwardly, for he was forced to use his left arm—and apologized that there was no tea. He would order it tomorrow, if I preferred.

I thanked him.

He set down the pot and reached for the sugar. "You have not troubled me with a great many questions."

"It is not my place, sir."

"Isn't it? You risked your life, after all."

"I have only done my duty."

"You have done far more than that." He added a few drops of cream and stirred briskly. "I have the impression that you don't fully credit Desma's tale."

I hesitated. "I have the greatest regard for the lady. She has a noble heart, and she will do you honor as your duchess."

"But you don't believe she is whom she claims to be."

"Do you?"

He walked—or rather stalked, for his limbs moved at an animal-like rhythm in spite of his injuries—to one of the portholes, which overlooked an eastern sea turned gold by the new-risen sun. "The story itself is impossible either to prove or disprove. I will say this. When I first met her in Knossos, she was reluctant in the extreme to tell me anything at all. And I have never in my life encountered a dialect so strange as hers. It was scarcely even recognizable as Greek. I had to transcribe every word in the beginning, until I could understand her at the most basic level. Even then, I don't believe I properly gained her trust for many weeks. We were in Naxos before she revealed anything of import."

"But you didn't arrive in Naxos until December," I said.

"Yes, the end of December."

"But—" I wet my lips and looked down at the smooth wooden desk before me. "You will excuse my indelicacy, but your child will be born in June."

"Miss Truelove, the child is not mine."

"Oh!"

"Good Lord, did you really think—?"

"I—well, I merely presumed, since you—your obvious devotion—"

"My devotion to her is absolute," he said softly, "but her heart was never mine to win."

The sea was calm, and the sun was warm, and the ship made not a wobble as we slid across the water. The engines ground comfortably beneath our feet. The ducal suite sprawled across the width of the upper deck, separated from the wheelhouse by the same corridor in which I had taken shelter with Lord Silverton on the morning before our tempestuous landing at Naxos a fortnight ago, and the view stretched from east to west almost without interruption, if one happened to be standing near the portholes, as the duke did, sipping his coffee. His attention was fixed on some point outside, and the sun struck his skin like a whitewash.

"I am sorry, sir," I whispered.

"She has done me the honor of agreeing to become my wife, however, and the child will never know that he is not mine by blood as well as affection. I can do no less for the man who fathered him."

I could think of no answer to this.

The duke turned to me. "Well, Miss Truelove? Are you not curious?"

"It is not—"

"Your place to ask," he finished for me. "And in any case, it's too much to believe, I suppose."

I stared at my hand, which still held the pen, poised and ready for service. My hands were my mother's, smooth-skinned and long-fingered. A valuable inheritance indeed, for which I was vain enough to be grateful. "Does it matter, though? Whoever he is, he's lost to her now."

"So it seems. We spent weeks waiting at the caves, looking for some sign of his appearance, and hoping that the men who had tracked us down in Knossos would not discover our trail to Naxos. By then I had discovered that it was my own personal secretary who had painted those frescoes in order to lure me to Crete, who had searched my belongings and betrayed me to his friends—that was why we left the villa so precipitately, you see, while I told Anserrat we were bound for Athens instead of Naxos, in order to buy us at least a little more time. But I still cannot understand his purpose, and the ferocity of his pursuit. What can they possibly have had to gain? Even if Desma *is* the lady of myth, what use is that? There is no tangible treasure, except perhaps to display her like a circus curiosity, and that was not what they wanted."

I thought of the hundred and fifty drachmae left behind in the flat in Athens. "No, it was not. But how did they know who Desma really was? What she might be, I mean?"

"I have no idea whatsoever, except that they believed most profoundly that she *was* the true Ariadne, to use the mythical name."

Was Ariadne, I thought. And the child in her belly sired by an ancient Theseus.

But the notion was too absurd. A fevered fantasy, the most impossible thing in the world. People did not close their eyes and wake up three thousand years in the future. Science and religion both rose up and forbade the very idea; such a brazen act had no place in a logical universe.

On the other hand, there were many things that ought not to exist in a logical universe.

When I was perhaps eleven or twelve, my father took me on a visit to the Tower of London. It was late autumn, and the trees were bare, and the air smelled of soot and damp earth. I remember examining the Crown Jewels and the messages inscribed by prisoners into the stone walls of the Beauchamp Tower, and the warmth of my father's hand as we climbed the endless winding staircases, each step worn down at the middle by the passage of infinite feet.

At last we arrived on the Tower Green, and my father led me to the exact spot where, according to tradition, the infamous scaffold had once stood: the one on which Anne Boleyn had been beheaded. The sky was cold and blue, and I thought that this was the very same sky under which that unfortunate lady had met her end. That my eyes, running over the gray walls and the turrets and the million blades of grass, viewed much the same scene as had pressed a final earthly image upon the eyes of the queen. That she had existed in this precise spot, had stood and breathed, had spoken a few words and had bared her brave neck and had died.

That the only thing separating us was time. The long, unstoppable beat of centuries: a thing, a mystery you could not hold in your hand and examine, a power that existed inside the memory of inanimate objects.

These stone walls knew Anne. And as I stood where she had stood, I knew her, too. I would have sworn that she was there.

According to legend, it's where Theseus landed with Ariadne, when bad weather forced them into Naxos. Then Dionysus happened along, fell in love with her, and brought her up to heaven to marry her.

I lifted my head. "What does Mr. Higganbotham say?"

The duke turned away from the porthole and walked back to the side table to pour himself another awkward cup of coffee. "I am afraid Mr. Higganbotham is ready to believe any word that falls from her mouth."

"And Lord Silverton?"

His Grace's eyebrows rose above the rim of his cup. He set the vessel back in its saucer, shook his head, and said, "Miss Truelove, I have the impression that, upon this earth, there lives only a single person who has the power to discover his lordship's true thoughts on any subject."

"And who is that?"

"You."

⁂

I found Lord Silverton in the main saloon, quite in opposition to the strict instructions of the Naxos doctor who had, in the manner of Humpty-Dumpty, put him back together again.

He sat in his favored armchair, leg propped on a cushioned footstool, and tossed a cricket ball in the air with one hand while he smoked his pipe with the other. The air of the saloon was fragrant with warm tobacco. Across from him, the next Duchess of Olympia perched on the edge of the sofa, and I am sorry to report—for I fear it does neither of them any credit—that the lady was actually smiling.

"I beg your pardon. Am I interrupting?"

Silverton craned his head to the doorway. "Why, Truelove! There you are. Secretarial duties all finished?"

"For the moment. Is that Caruso?"

"Indeed it is. I was just attempting to explain to Desma what he's going on about in this little ditty, and I'm afraid the essential bits may have been lost in translation."

I flinched at the words *little ditty.* "So it seems. How lovely, nonetheless, that you were able to amuse the poor lady, so early in her bereavement."

"Laughter cures all, I always say."

"How true." I turned to address the lady herself, taking care to speak slowly. "Desma, my dear. The duke presents his compliments, and asks if you will do him the honor of attending him in his stateroom."

The smile faded, and Desma gave me rather a blank look. Silverton cleared his throat. "Allow me."

He explained the situation in careful Greek, illustrating with his hands and his pipe, and Desma nodded and rose from the sofa. She sent me a regal nod and a rather odd pair of words that, after a few seconds' consideration, I recognized as *thank you*.

"Of course, madam," I replied, and then, as she made her way to the door, I exclaimed, "Oh! Wait a moment."

She turned, and I put my hand in my pocket and hurried toward her. "Here," I said, drawing out the medallion we had discovered under the bed in Knossos. "I believe this belongs to you."

Her dark eyes grew huge. She looked into my face, and then returned to the object in my hands.

"I'm terribly sorry I haven't returned it already. In all the fuss, I had quite forgotten its existence. I discovered it in the pocket of my jacket this morning." I pressed the disc into her stunned hand. "I believe it's meant to protect the owner against death, in which case it seems to have performed its work admirably."

She did not understand me, of course. She stared down at the medallion for some time, and when she lifted her gaze at last, her eyes were wet, and her nod of thanks was no longer regal but heartfelt.

"Well done, Truelove," Silverton said, when I sat down on the armchair next to him.

"How are you?"

"Absolutely tip-top. That dear fellow the doctor dispensed me a most marvelous bottle of pills for my sins. Hardly feel a thing."

He gazed at me, all blue sky and sunshine, despite the assortment of bruises and half-healed abrasions adorning his face. He wasn't wearing his spectacles, and as he continued to toss the cricket ball into the air and catch it unerringly, I wondered whether he possessed some sort of extra sense.

"I'm glad to hear it," I said.

Silverton caught the ball and set it down on the table between us, beneath the glow of the lamp, though his fingers remained to trap the object in place. "And you, Truelove? Rather a bad show, back there on Naxos. The worst show I think I ever saw, though there was a wretched balls-up in Seville once that I shouldn't care to repeat."

His voice was tender, and the corners of my eyes responded like a child's, filling with wetness.

"I am quite recovered," I said.

"Oh, Truelove." He lifted his hand, allowing the cricket ball to roll off the table and onto the rug, and leaned forward to grasp my fingers. "What a damned stoic you are. Do you know something? I don't think there's anyone I'd rather have at my back in a tight spot like that."

"A tight *spot*?"

He stuck his pipe in his mouth, reached into his pocket with his other hand, and gave me a handkerchief. I dabbed at my eyes while he smoked in that observational way of his. He went on, "I am quite in earnest. You've the spine of a Cossack. You're colossal. There you stood, a gun to your head, cool as you please, telling the poor bloke just what you thought of him. I said to myself, Silverton, old boy, if by some miracle you make it out of here alive, you have got to marry that woman."

I blew my nose. "You needn't joke."

"I am not joking, Truelove."

I looked up in surprise, into a pair of serious blue eyes.

"I am not joking," he said again. "I want you to marry me."

I set the handkerchief on the table, where the cricket ball had rested in the moment before it rolled off.

Silverton released my hand and continued, in a quick voice that was not his own. "I'm afraid I'm quite incapable of going down on one knee at the moment, though I'm willing to try if you require that sort of thing. Bended knees. Flowers, rings, kisses. I'm damned good at all of that, you'll find, especially the latter." He paused. "What I'm saying, I suppose, is that I should do my uttermost to make you happy."

I couldn't speak. The ship steamed along, the sunlight darkened for an instant and then reappeared, and I couldn't say a word.

"The thing is, Truelove, I have been lying around these past few days, according to the doctor's orders, and I have been thinking that you will go off this ship when we're back in England and become somebody else's very efficient and capable personal secretary, the duke or some other immensely fortunate fellow, and I am not at all certain I can survive that. I am not at all certain, I mean, that I *want* to survive that."

I looked up helplessly at the ceiling and thought of Mrs. Poulakis.

"Dash it, Truelove. *Say* something."

I thought of Silverton poised against the sunset at the top of the fortress in the Heraklion harbor, arms outstretched like a human cross, ready to jump. The ceiling seemed to be rotating around its central glass dome: first clockwise, and then counterclockwise, as if it could not quite make up its mind which hemisphere it belonged to.

"You'll be a duchess one day, if that's any consolation."

I leaned forward and put my face in my hands. "I'm afraid I'm going to be sick."

∽

My father's fatal illness was of short duration, a matter of a few months. I understand from the doctors that it had something to do with his heart; he began to weaken, and to suffer pains in his chest. He could no longer walk without stopping for breath, and one day, to his great annoyance, he could not rise from his bed.

He called for his lap desk, which I brought to him, and then he asked me to sit by the bed while he worked. I poured him tea and arranged his pillows. At half past twelve I went to see about a tray for lunch, and when I returned, he was dead. He had suffered a final attack, the doctors said, shaking their heads—and the Duke of Olympia had paid for the best medical men in London, he had spared no expense whatever for his loyal secretary—and there was nothing anybody could have done for him.

And perhaps that's true, but I still cannot forgive myself for allowing my father to die alone. During those nights when sleep comes reluctantly, I lie in my own bed and imagine how helpless he must have felt, in the grip of that painful attack, and how seized with despair that this moment was his last, and he had not even said good-bye.

E muoio disperato . . . E non ho amato mai tanto la vita . . .

And I die in despair, and I have never loved life so much.

Over my own objections, Lord Silverton had carried the phonograph to my cabin and installed it there—*Nobody else appreciates the racket the way you do, Truelove*—and I was too listless to change the record for another. Eventually the last song

ended, and I stared at the ceiling while the needle scratched use-
lessly at the edge, and then gave up at last to leave me in silence.

But not alone.

I became aware, as the turntable slowed and stopped, and the
scratch of the needle faded into quiet, of a presence in the room,
like the placing of a warm hand atop my heart. I whispered, to
the ceiling, "Would it be so dreadful a mistake, do you think?"

"My dear, do you love him?"

"I don't know." I pressed my fingers together over my stomach. "Yes. He enchants me. But is that enough?"

"Marriages have been made with less."

"I have been enchanted before, and it was a terrible mistake."

"But this is a different man."

"But alike in one respect: he cannot remain faithful."

My father paused, and my stomach turned, as it always did
when he did not answer immediately, because I was afraid the
illusion had dissolved back into the ether.

"Are you certain of this?" he said at last.

"No doubt he'll make a tremendous effort. But it cannot last,
can it? If I am with child, or away in the country, or some woman
of great allure casts herself in his path. He cannot resist that. He
admits it himself."

"Would this be so terrible? A straying husband is hardly
uncommon, particularly in his lordship's class of society."

Again I considering lying to him, but to what end? I said the
truth: "I would die."

He must have heard the pain in my voice, for he made a noise
of almost soothing pity. "You have always had the most tender
heart, my dear. You are so easily wounded. "

"That's not true. I am *quite* self-sufficient."

"Because of your tenderness. You are self-sufficient because you're afraid of betrayal."

I closed my eyes. "Yes."

Again there was a long and stomach-churning pause. I listened to the bass pitch of the engines and thought, *I will never board a ship again. This sickness, it's not worth the beauty of travel.*

My father spoke. "You would, of course, have a particular consolation. You would have the comfort of knowing that, of all these women, he has chosen to marry you."

"But not because he loves me."

"My very dear Emmeline," he said, full of pity, and I believe he meant to say more, for I felt a strange warmth encompass my hand and travel up my arm, but at that instant a knock sounded on the door, and the sensation retreated.

"Hello?" I gasped.

The knock repeated itself, and I swung my legs from the bed and made my way to the door. Opened, it revealed the figure of Desma, straight-backed and smooth-haired. She held a book under her arm, and her expression was wrinkled and thoughtful.

I stepped back. "Please come in."

I didn't quite know how to address her. I supposed *Desma* would have to do. In a series of gestures and words, I offered to ring for tea. She declined and set her book on the table. An illustrated history of Greek mythology, obtained no doubt from the ship's library.

Oh dear, I thought.

She did not waste time in small talk. After all, she had none. She opened the book and flipped through the pages with her long and sturdy fingers, and I observed that her pregnancy became her.

The size and shape did not overwhelm her; she did not draw to her belly any unnecessary attention, and yet its perfect round curve contained the sensual fascination of a bosom, so freely and unself-consciously fecund, beneath the sober green wool of the dress she had found in Naxos.

She began to slow and to study each page before she turned it, as if searching for something particular. I stepped closer and craned my neck to gaze over her arm at the bright illustrations, the neat paragraphs of text, flashing into view and disappearing beneath her nimble fingers. For a moment I felt the return of that vertigo that had assailed me earlier in the saloon, and in my mind I caught the scent of Silverton's pipe.

I gripped the back of the armchair, wanting to sit. But how could you occupy a chair, while a woman stood nearby who was heavy with child?

Desma did not notice my dilemma. Her concentration fixed ferociously on the book before her, until at last she came to a stop and rested one spread palm atop the left-hand page, while the forefinger of her right hand tracked across the spine and landed in the center of an illustration. I leaned near, and saw that it was a man of enormous size and muscular breadth, clinging to the edge of a cliff, naked except for a white cloth swathed precariously across his chest and around his middle.

The caption was partly obscured beneath Desma's wrist, but I hardly needed to read it.

"Yes," I said. "That's how he met his end, according to myth. Pushed off a cliff by a rival king."

Of course, she did not understand me; at least, she couldn't translate my literal words. But the expression on her face, as she turned to me, contained all the agony of genuine grief, and her finger stabbed at the white cloth that protected the modesty of Theseus.

"I'm sorry," I said. "On the other hand, it *is* only myth. We have no proof that he died like this."

She must have understood my sympathy at least, for she nodded. But the nod was an impatient one, and she pressed her finger again into the page, as if she meant to rub a hole in the illustration, to demolish the fact of her lover's death.

And I was sorry for her, and I did understand her agony, for had I not myself bled for the loss of love? But mixed in my pity, I found a trace of anger. I took the corner of the book in my own hand and slid its heavy weight a few inches to the east. I flipped back a page or two, until another illustration lay exposed, which I had noticed earlier: Theseus and the Amazon queen Hippolyta.

And another: Theseus and Phaedra, the sister of Ariadne. Phaedra knelt before her towering husband, and her robes flowed richly around her, and her arms opened upward in supplication. The artist had rendered her in lifelike and loving detail. Her breasts curved forth from her gown, and her shoulders were bare and white. I did not need the caption here, either. Phaedra knelt in the very act of accusation, telling her husband Theseus that his son Hippolytus—his son by the Amazon queen—had raped and dishonored her, and though her tale was a false one, Theseus would then go forth from his nuptial chamber to kill the unhappy Hippolytus, whose only crime was to worship the chaste Artemis instead of vengeful Aphrodite.

"He is not worth your grief," I said. "He is not worth another living thought."

Desma plucked my hand from the page, without hostility, and smoothed her palm across the paper.

"Anyway, it's just stories. Stories handed down by men, told by men. You are welcome to imagine it's all true. You're welcome to imagine whatever you please. But it will not return to you this lover of yours, whoever he is. You're much better off getting on with your life. We shall arrive in Athens in a matter of hours, and you will be married by nightfall."

Married by nightfall: the words sounded so final. Perhaps Desma understood more English than I realized, for her fingers made a kind of spasm on the page, as if the hand had received an invisible wound.

My God, I thought. *The poor duke.*

I continued, "You'll be a mother soon, after all. You've got what you needed, a husband to make you respectable in the eyes of the world, and it's turned up trumps for you. Don't waste any more tears. I daresay he hasn't wasted many for your sake."

She turned the page again, back to the death of Theseus, and her forefinger traced the line of his profile. A single tear rolled down her pristine cheek, and leapt from her chin to the back of her hand.

Una furtiva lagrima. Caruso's voice. *Negli occhi suoi spuntò.*

"You're mad. Poor dear, it's all an illusion. But the duke is quite real, and I'm sure he will make you as happy as he can. He will at least—"

She turned to me. "Go," she said. Her eyes were wild.

"Go?" I said, in affront. "But it's *my* cabin!"

She jabbed her finger at the illustration. "Go!" she said again, quite desperate.

I frowned and peered again at the page. *Plate no. 127. The great hero visits the island of Skyros, where the king Lycomedes, afraid that his guest plans to overthrow him, tosses the unsuspecting Theseus from a cliff. He perishes and is buried in obscurity, until his remains are discovered and returned to Athens in 475 BC by the conquering king Cimon.*

"My dear girl," I said, "you are about to be married. You must relinquish these morbid thoughts at once."

A single blast of the ship's horn vibrated the wall of the cabin.

"You see? We've sighted the port already. The good reverend awaits. Indeed, I should begin giving orders directly for the preparation of the main saloon for the ceremony, and the cook is already making the cake ready, or I shall have his—"

"Go!" said Desma.

"—hide," I finished.

She slammed the book shut and tilted her chin, and the look she gave me from within those lustrous dark eyes was nothing short of imperious.

"Go. Skyros." The fist came down on the front cover. "Now."

The next day, the Hero's ships arrived at last on the beach below the cliffs, and his heart quickened with fear when he saw no sign of his Lady awaiting him on the sand, nor in the caves in which he had left her. For many weeks he searched the island, sending out his men far and wide to inquire after her, but he found only the rumor that a great Prince had come to Naxos to seek his beloved, who was mourning another man, and they had disappeared together.

In despair, thinking the Lady had betrayed her promise, the Hero returned to Athens and ruled the city with great wisdom for many years, though he was never again to find a true and faithful love among the many women he took in bed and in marriage. It is said that he died by the hand of Lycomedes in Skyros, and that his bones were returned to Athens a thousand years later, though there are those who whisper that he met a different fate altogether . . .

THE BOOK OF TIME, A. M. HAYWOOD (1921)

Twenty-Four

My first love affair ended not by some dramatic quarrel, but in tranquil and agonizing neglect. (If, indeed, anything so brief and undignified can be properly called an affair.) I remember the helpless period of his silence, for of course I could not write to him; I remember how I would lie awake, conceiving and discarding various schemes by which I would encounter him accidentally, on a London street or at some musical performance, or even inside His Grace's study while waiting for an appointment. It came to nothing, and now I am glad I did not. He was cruel to ignore me, but perhaps his kindness would have been worse in the end.

Inevitably, we met again. Our world—the world, that is, of the Duke of Olympia—is not small but actually minuscule, and twelve months after our final hasty assignation, we quite literally bumped into each other while queuing for tea at Covent Garden, during the second intermission of *Il Trovatore*. (Our initial conversations had flourished over a shared passion for Verdi.) I had prepared a curt remark for this stranger whose elbow had intruded so carelessly into my arm, and I had looked up and seen his familiar smooth cheek and hooded eye, and the remark had died on my lips. His irritated expression brightened into genuine pleasure. "Why, Emmeline! It's uncanny! I was *just* thinking I should see you here tonight."

My first thought was that he was not quite so handsome as I remembered. My second was that *I*, by contrast, had not considered the possibility of encountering him at all; I had not, in fact, thought about him in many weeks, and perhaps this inattention meant I hadn't really even loved him to begin with, that I had only imagined my attraction to him was love, because I so badly wanted to love and be loved. This revelation occurred in an instant, over the course of his single sentence, and it gave me such a sense of my own power that I was able to answer, with perfect composure, "Why, good evening, Mr. M——d. It must be true; one sees everyone at the opera."

We exchanged the usual pleasantries. He insisted on buying my tea, and I allowed him because I thought it would be more particular to refuse than to accept. As we parted, I had the idea that he wanted to continue the conversation, that I had regained just enough novelty to be interesting again.

But I was a year older and a century wiser, and I gave my farewell firmly, though his dark and hooded eyes, for a single instant, seemed to hold their old magic. And I remember feeling, as I took a cab home to the Duke of Olympia's house in Belgrave Square, that this was how all love affairs should end. That one should never try to regain what was lost, because it no longer existed. Like a pair of rocks reshaped by the passage of time and tide, you no longer fit together the way you once had. Only the four walls that had sheltered your secret could recall that connection.

I had not allowed myself to think about that moment of farewell in some time, but I thought about it now, as the island of Skyros took shape before us. I stood near the bow of the *Isolde*, next to Desma on my left side and Lord Silverton on my right, inhaling the comfortable scent of his lordship's pipe as it mingled with the sunny draft.

"I don't suppose she's mentioned what she hopes to gain from this little expedition," Silverton said, quite as if the lady in question were not standing a few feet away, breathing the same marine air.

"What every woman does, I expect. She wishes to make a proper farewell to the old love before she begins her life with the new one."

"Poor old Max."

I hazarded a glance at the railing on the opposite side of the bow, where the Duke of Olympia was engaged in close conversation with Mr. Higganbotham over the flapping ends of a map. "He seems to be taking the challenge in the proper spirit," I observed.

Silverton pulled the end of the pipe from his mouth. "Ah, don't let his military mien fool you, Truelove. He may look as if he's planning a campaign of imperial invasion, but in reality he's just an ordinary lovestruck blighter, trying to make some slight impression in the heart of the bird he adores."

I chanced a sidelong glance at the bird in question, who seemed not to notice the subject of our conversation or, indeed, our very existence by her side. She gripped the rails with two fierce, gloved hands, and her shoulders tilted forward, as if she could, by the strain of her own muscles, propel the ship faster along the water. Her eyes were narrow against the draft.

"I hope she understands her good fortune," I said. "I hope she doesn't mean to throw aside her own future happiness for the sake of a past passion."

"But hers isn't just any old passion, Truelove. It's one of the great passions of all time."

I turned in surprise. "But surely you don't believe that!"

"Why not?"

"It's impossible! You must be mad, to believe in such a thing. For God's sake, you're a mathematician, not a fantasist."

Silverton replaced the pipe in the corner of his mouth. "The more one studies mathematics, my dear, the more one realizes what an elegant mystery it all is, this vast universe around us. Have you heard of a chap called Einstein?"

"I've heard something about him, yes."

"Lives in Vienna. Published a few scientific papers last year. Audacious stuff. Time and space and matter and all that." He let out a long curl of smoke from between his lips, which the wind whisked instantly away.

"And?"

He turned to face me, leaning one elbow on the railing. The bruises, I realized, were already fading from that lusty skin. His eyes behind his spectacles were blue and warm. "And it seems, quoth the Bard, that there are indeed more things in heaven and earth than are dreamt of in Truelove's philosophy. We are as insubstantial as a dream, you and I and everything else, composed of little bits of stray electricity, and if one chances to find something solid to hold on to in this whole damned unstable mirage, why, one had better reach out boldly and grip it with both hands."

We landed on Skyros a short while later. Following the calculations of Mr. Higganbotham and the Duke of Olympia, the *Isolde* dropped anchor not in the main harbor, but near a headland to the northwest, and we went ashore in the tender. The suspicious gaze of Mr. Brown followed us across the water to a narrow strip of pebbled beach, and I could not say I blamed him.

The sky was warm and tranquil. We had eaten a brief luncheon before we left, and carried water in glass bottles that hung in slings from the shoulders of the men. "She wishes to see the place where he died," the duke said to me, as we climbed carefully up the side of the hill, where the slope was gentler than the cliffs to the north.

"But how can we know for certain? These events—if they really occurred—happened three thousand years ago. The hills have no doubt shifted, the vegetation has regrown. And even if everything *were* the same, we still would have no idea at which exact point the king made the fatal push."

"Mr. Higganbotham has spent the past two days studying the various texts." The duke nodded at the eager figure climbing the hillside a dozen yards ahead. "Plutarch on Theseus, and the *Achillead*."

"What, Achilles?"

"The account of his time on Skyros at the court of Lycomedes, just before his departure for the Trojan War, is exceptionally detailed."

"I see. And Mr. Higganbotham has scoured these tea leaves for the true and correct notch upon the cliffs?"

"You are skeptical, Miss Truelove."

I concentrated on the path before me, which was now growing rough and steep. "Mine is not to question why," I said.

"But you believe it is all a devil of a waste of time."

I paused and turned to him. "It is my personal opinion that we are better off returning to England and resuming our proper lives, sir, but I understand the peculiarities of your position, and that the whims of a lady in a certain condition are to be indulged whenever possible. I am only concerned, sir, *deeply* concerned by the cost to yourself."

The duke paused, too, resting one foot on the boulder obstructing our path. His breath, unlike mine, was not remotely troubled by the exertion of our journey, and the wind tufted the dark hair on his forehead. He had yesterday exchanged the bulky dressing on his shoulder for a smaller one, and the transformation was startling: you would hardly know he was injured at all, except for a certain stiffness of movement. He set a hand on his burly knee and said, "I am moved by your sense of duty, Miss Truelove. But you must understand that I do not make this detour solely for the sake of Desma's whims, as you put it."

"What, then?"

He gestured with one hand. "There's a great mystery here, an enigma of such breadth and power that it takes my breath away. It has been chasing me all my life. It has driven men to their deaths, out of lust for it. And I find I should like to undertake this final attempt, before I resign myself to the life that God in his wisdom has apparently ordained for me."

He was wearing a tweed suit almost identical to the one worn by Silverton, except gray-toned rather than brown. The color suited his square dark features and pale skin. I thought he looked as if he were made of the same stone as the island around us, rugged and ascetic, and that God was perhaps mistaken: this man did not belong in England at all.

"There is another thing," he went on, glancing down the hill, where Lord Silverton, a cane hooked over his elbow, was assisting the lady Desma over a patch of rubble. "I cannot bear to see her unhappy."

"As you like," I said.

The duke's eyes narrowed as he watched the progress of his beloved. He reached into his pocket and said, in a low voice, "I am, however, more than a little concerned for her."

"She should not attempt such a climb, in her condition."

"It isn't that. She's as strong as a mountain goat, I assure you. But she gave me this last night." He held out his hand and opened his fingers, and upon his palm rested the medallion from Knossos, the one I had returned to Desma two nights ago, flashing in the sunshine.

"But that's hers! A protection against death. Would she not want to keep it for her own safety? Carrying a child?"

"I am afraid, Miss Truelove, most *deeply* afraid that she means to leave me here, and join her lover."

"*Join* him? But he's—" I looked into the duke's grave eyes and comprehended him. "Surely not. Surely she would not end her own life, and that of her babe."

With his thumb, he turned the medallion over, revealing the double ax etched into the metal. "I have not touched her," he said quietly. "I have offered her nothing but friendship and respect, though my true desire is, at times, almost impossible to suppress."

"Perhaps if she knew the nature of your devotion . . ."

"She loves him." He shook his head and replaced the medallion in his pocket. "She loves him with a tenacity that cannot be turned, or even dented. It is ageless. She would die for him without a second thought, and such is my—my *admiration* for her, I would allow her to do it. Because to do otherwise is to condemn her to a lifetime of unending sorrow." He turned and levered himself easily up the boulder, extending his good left arm to assist me in following him. "But *you* will keep an eye on her for me, won't you, Miss Truelove?"

I took his hand and climbed up beside him. "I will do whatever you ask of me, sir."

"Good. Now head up that path and ask Mr. Higganbotham how much longer we are to tramp along before reaching our destination. And *I* shall go back to make sure she gets up this damned path without giving birth along the way."

⁓

"According to Plutarch," said Mr. Higganbotham, rearranging his maps, "Lycomedes pushed Theseus directly off the cliff and into the sea. Now, my best calculation places the ancient palace somewhat to our south and east, making this headland the obvious place to take one's unsuspecting guest for a doomed afternoon walk . . ."

I turned to Silverton and whispered, "We're on a fool's errand, aren't we?"

"My dear Truelove," he whispered back, "the truth is immaterial. We have only to convince the lady that we have reached the exact spot of the poor bloke's demise."

"You would deceive her?"

He tilted the glass bottle over his tin cup and allowed a stream of water to fall inside. "It's not a deception. He might just as well have plunged off here as anywhere. Water?"

"Thank you." I accepted the cup from his hand and shifted my eyes to the figure of the duke, who was pacing along the cliff path nearby, turning over an object in his pocket that I knew to be the medallion. I had done much the same trick, hadn't I, as we walked along the road in Naxos.

But you *will keep an eye on her for me, won't you, Miss Truelove?*

I returned my gaze to the point in which I had last noticed Desma. She was still there, sitting upon a solitary boulder, staring out to sea. Her gaze was steady and unblinking, and her hair was loose, moving in the breeze. The falling sun turned her face to gold.

"She is beautiful," I murmured.

"Desma? Oh, yes. Quite." Next to me, Silverton fidgeted with the bottle, spinning the glass slowly between his large hands. His injured leg stretched out stiffly before him, and his cane lay across his thighs. I sensed a turn in the subject of his thoughts, and before I could rise and walk away, he said, "You have not given me an answer, you know."

For an instant, I considered saying, disingenuous: *An answer to what?*

I lifted the tin cup and drank thirstily. "I miss your pipe, at a moment like this. Did you leave it on board?"

"Yes. But I thought you disliked my pipe."

"The human spirit can grow accustomed to anything, it seems."

"Am I to take hope from this?"

I looked again at the duke, who had come to a stop and now stood on the dusty earth, perhaps thirty yards from where Desma sat on her boulder. His head was bowed, and his fist clutched the medallion in his pocket. The gentle afternoon light outlined his shoulders, so that he seemed even broader than before. Nearby, Mr. Higganbotham fussed with his map, stood, and sat down again. The breeze was picking up, mild and dulcet, alive with salt and greenness. My heart seemed to be straining in my chest: for what, I could not say.

"A new wife may not look kindly on her husband's female secretary, after all," said Silverton, when I did not reply.

I laughed and finished the water. "I doubt this particular young wife will care one way or another."

The duke took a hesitant step, and another. He seemed to be scrutinizing the ground before him for some unknown object. He had taken off his hat, which he clutched in his left hand, while the right fist was still balled in his jacket pocket, where he kept the medallion. I found myself mesmerized by his movements, which were uncharacteristic of him: small and jerky, as if he were not quite in control of his own limbs.

"Would *you* care?" Silverton asked softly.

"I suppose that depends on the husband."

"Me, for example?"

My heart beat at a ferocious pace, crashing against the wall of my chest as if to shatter my ribs. Ahead of me, the duke kept moving forward in that curious marionette way, still examining the ground, still gripping the medallion. My mouth had gone quite dry, and the warmth of the sun on my face turned suddenly oppressive.

"In that case, I should care very much indeed. But you knew that already. You know my fatal jealousy."

He hesitated. "If you want to call it that. I was rather gratified that you gave a damn. But I assure you, in future—"

"There is no point in making assurances you cannot keep. I am jealous by nature, and you are promiscuous by nature."

"Oh, I say—"

"So we are unsuited in the most fundamental point of marriage."

The duke kept moving. In a moment, I realized, he would reach the edge of the cliff. The tin cup slid from my fingers, into the dust.

"Dash it all, that's not true. For God's sake, I don't go to bed with women because I can't help it. I go to bed with them because—"

I leapt to my feet. "Look to the duke!" I screamed.

❧

Now I come to the crux of my story, on which hinges all the rest of my life.

You will possibly not believe me, when I tell you what came next. I should not have believed it myself, if I encountered the incident in a book or a play, and indeed I don't know how to describe the sequence of events in a manner that properly communicates their double nature: a physical reality that is etched in minute and exquisite clarity in my memory, and an agency that can only be described as supernatural.

I shall stick to the facts.

At my cry of warning, my companions sprang into movement. Silverton, whose reflexes were naturally the sharpest, reached the duke first, in an athletic blur of his long and golden limbs that stirred the very dust from the rocks. He reached for Olympia's shoulders, but they were no longer there: the duke was falling forward, arms outstretched, to land on his knees at the extreme edge of the cliff, his muscular frame supported by I know not what unseen force.

To my left, Desma released an inhuman shriek. Mr. Higganbotham ran toward the two men, but I was there before him, wrapping my arms around the duke's waist while Silverton took hold of his left shoulder.

As I have said before, the Duke of Olympia was a burly, well-built man, but between my efforts and those of the exceptionally strong Lord Silverton, we ought to have dragged him from the brink at once.

We could not.

I dug my heels into the pebbly earth and strained with all my might; above me, Silverton wrapped his arm across the duke's chest and heaved backward. But it was as if gravity itself had taken on a mighty new strength, holding His Grace at the cliff's dizzy edge, and though I could see very little from my vantage, I felt that the duke was straining, too. That his outstretched arms contained an object of immeasurable weight, and it was this unknown mass—not the duke himself—that drew us inexorably forward, until the cool, vast emptiness of the chasm beneath us struck my forehead, and my heels skidded against the rock.

"He's slipping!" I gasped, and I thought my arms should pop from their sockets, so great was the burden upon them. Silverton roared with effort, or perhaps the pain in his injured limbs, unable to loosen his grip in order to achieve a better point of leverage. I remember the texture of tweed against my cheek, the briny scent of the sea crashing below us, the taste of dirt in my mouth, the horrible scrape of my shoes against the rock. The stretching pain in the muscles of my upper arms and in the joints of my fingers, which I had locked together against the duke's hard belly, so I would not lose hold of him.

A weight dropped next to mine on the rock, and for an instant I thought it was Mr. Higganbotham. But the bones were too small, and the panting that came from its lungs was shallow and high in pitch, and as she gasped out desperate words in a strange tongue, I realized the body belonged to Desma. She was reaching for something just beneath the edge of the cliff, something I couldn't see, and I tried to tell her to go back, that she was going to crush the child in her womb, she was going to tumble from the cliff to her death, but I was too tired to speak, too exhausted of oxygen to form the words.

My fingers began to slip against the wool. Next to me, Desma was making urgent noises, repeating words in a desperate, aching cry; she maneuvered her clumsy body to the farthest possible point and grasped frantically into the air.

My God, I thought, *maybe she loves him after all*.

And then, without warning, the balance shifted.

For an instant, I thought that a gust of wind had drafted upward from the sea and caught the duke, forcing him from the brink. The effect was so sudden, I found myself tumbling backward, drawing His Grace with me. Silverton uttered a surprised oath as the duke fell back on his chest, and we dropped together in a heavy, panting, sweating tangle: limbs and breath and bones all crushed atop each other, while I lay stunned at the bottom, unable to move.

"Get off her!" shouted Silverton, and the weight shifted, the limbs untangled. I found fresh air and sucked it into my lungs. The final body lifted from mine and I rolled to my side, wheezing and grateful.

Desma was keening softly in her foreign tongue, repeating a single word, over and over. My eyes were closed, the lids too heavy to lift, and so I did not, in that first moment, realize the extraordinary truth.

I heard Silverton's voice above me, saying softly, *My God*.

And Mr. Higganbotham, answering, incredulous: *Who is he?*

Befuddled, I thought that perhaps some native walker had stumbled upon our party. At the outside edge of my perception, I heard a male voice, unusually deep, utter a few guttural noises that might have been words. Desma seemed to be answering him.

Someone moved heavily on the ground next to me.

It can't be, whispered the Duke of Olympia.

I opened my eyes.

A man lay before me, enormous in size, wearing a simple tunic made of a dirty homespun cloth. His skin had the dark, leathery cast of an ancient tannery; his hair, shorn to no more than a half inch in length, was nobly dusted with gray. His neck was so thick and muscular, ribbed with tendons, that I was reminded of the trunk of a tree.

But it was his head that drew my fullest attention: not because of his arresting features, or because his eyes were now blinking in a kind of disordered shock, but because his face was framed by Desma's two loving hands, and she was pressing a kiss upon his lips that, in the manner of a fairy tale, brought him inevitably back to life.

Epilogue

We remained nine days on Skyros. On the morning of our departure, I woke early and walked along the cliffs, near the headland where Tadeas had first appeared, contemplating the vast froth of the sea as it encountered the rocks below.

The weather had grown warmer and steadier as each day passed, and though I wore my cardigan jacket of thick worsted wool, I left the buttons undone, and the ends flapped against my legs as I walked. The morning breeze was sweet against my cheek. Presently I found the opening of the path that we had taken up the hillside, the steepening of the track as it met the cliffs. There was the ledge on which I had sat with Lord Silverton, just before the strange miracle unfolded in my arms; there was the boulder that had borne Desma. I leaned against it and folded my arms.

"It is really most ill-advised for a young lady to walk by

herself, so early in the morning, and among a foreign people," said a voice behind me.

I did not bother to turn, nor even to soften the squarish set of my shoulders. "What a very great relief," I said. "I'd begun to fear that you had discovered some other fortunate young lady to torment."

"I assure you, if I had any choice in the matter, I should be comfortably home in England."

"Any choice? You have all the choice in the world, haven't you? You're hardly obliged to inflict yourself on me."

"Well, you are quite wrong there."

She said this in a subdued voice, not her usual stately pronouncement at all, and curiosity provoked me to turn around and look at her. She was wearing a sensible walking costume of gray tweed jacket and matching skirt, and she had settled herself on the ledge, though her short legs did not quite reach the ground, giving her an almost childlike aspect. I admired her hat, made of gray wool felt and a single black feather, which tilted just an inch or two to one side and beautifully suited her soft, round face. Her cheeks were pink with exercise, and she appeared to be a trifle winded, though her bulbous Hanover eyes shone as blue and bright as the promising spring sky above us.

"I don't understand," I said.

"Don't you? You're a clever, impertinent sort of girl. Surely you realize that *you* are the one who calls me to attend you."

I am not often struck dumb—the phenomenon seemed to have afflicted me more frequently in this single journey than in all my preceding years—but as the Queen's words passed into the soft Aegean air, I found myself speechless. I fastened my attention on the single black feather that wavered above Her Majesty's hat, and my hands tightened around my elbows.

"I have been thinking about your mother," she went on.

I opened my mouth and filled my lungs. The briny air returned some measure of vigor to my limbs.

"What about my mother?"

"How, despite sharing so many of your more disagreeable traits—her stubborn impertinence perhaps the least among them—she was at last persuaded to do the sensible thing. Marrying your father, I mean. I believe she had found some measure of peace when she died."

"Indeed. She expired as soon as she became happy. An inspiring moral, don't you think?"

The Queen sniffed and looked away. "Would you rather she had died unhappy?"

"No. But I think it hardly matters whether we are happy or unhappy. It's all the same, in the end."

"I suppose that's true." She heaved a little sigh and arranged her hands in her lap. She wore a pair of black kid gloves, somewhat worn. "Regardless, we have, upon reflection, reconciled ourselves to the prospect of your union with his lordship, and are prepared to offer you our most sincere wishes for your contentment in that fruitful institution to which, above all, God commends us."

"I beg your pardon. I have not agreed to Lord Silverton's proposal of marriage."

"My dear girl. You can hardly refuse."

"Can't I?"

"In the first place, you are unlikely to receive a better one. In the second, you may be able to do him some good, which is no small consideration in the eyes of Providence—"

"Do *him* good? What about my own inclinations? Are those not to receive any consideration at all?"

"As to that," she said, a little more softly, "I believe I have your own moral welfare in mind, most of all."

"My moral welfare."

"You are, of course, fatally in love with him."

I pushed myself away from the rock and turned to the sea. "I will admit to a certain personal inclination, but that is easily overcome."

"How? For what purpose? What else are you to do with your life?"

"I will continue to work for the Duke of Olympia, of course, if he will have me."

Her feet landed on the ground behind me. "Impossible!"

"Impossible? Why?"

"How can you ask such a thing? You have seen what he is. You have seen the immeasurable danger of this power he possesses."

Her footsteps crunched over the dirt and gravel toward me. I looked down at the tossing white foam below, the perilous sharp edges of the rocky shore.

"I don't know what you mean."

She came to stand next to me, though her image exuded no living warmth, no breath of any kind. "Of course you know what I mean. We cannot ignore what occurred here."

"But that's the thing," I whispered. "I don't know. I don't understand what happened at all."

"I think you do, however." Her voice was unexpectedly kind. "You saw for yourself that he summoned a man through an abyss of time."

"But it's impossible! The duke cannot have been the *agent* of his appearance!"

"Miss Truelove, I doubt that Almighty God much cares *what*

a single, overclever young woman believes is possible or impossible. In any case, you're better off washing your hands of the entire affair, even if such an escape requires you to unite yourself in marriage to one of the most cheerfully promiscuous reprobates in England."

I made a sound of frustration.

"Come now," she went on. "You have seen for yourself the continual jeopardy in which this agency places the poor fellow. The moral burden he bears, to say nothing of the lust other men harbor for the immeasurable power he controls. Why, you were nearly killed yourself."

In spite of the growing warmth of the sun, I began to feel chilled in the core of my belly. I drew together the ends of my cardigan and folded my arms under my breasts. The wind, picking up strength, blew against my ears.

"And yet he has done good," I said. "The joy that now belongs to Tadeas and Desma, it is almost beyond bearing."

"Of course he can do great things. That's the marvelous thing about power. But there is a price, Miss Truelove; there is always a price. To the duke himself, and to anyone who shares his life."

I bowed my head.

"Well?" said the Queen. "What is it?"

"I don't know what to do. I don't know which is worse."

She stood by my side, without speaking. I believe she only reached so far as my shoulder, and yet her presence cast an enormous shadow over me, as if to smother me with a will that was not my own.

I don't know how long we hung there, poised over the sea. I lost count of the beating waves, the cries of the dirty seagulls, and I remember thinking, *I might be anywhere; there is nothing*

here that anchors me to the century to which I belong, no sign that it is
1906 and not a thousand years past, or a thousand years in the future,
so perhaps I too have passed into another time.

"Hullo there," said Lord Silverton.

By good fortune, he had put his hand out to touch me, or I might
have fallen over the brink. I leaned into his arm for an instant,
regaining my balance, and straightened. The Queen had gone.

"Not as bad as all that, is it?" he said.

"What's that?"

"You looked as if you meant to jump."

The most cheerfully promiscuous reprobate in England, the Queen
had called him, and yet he hadn't acted like a reprobate at all
during the past nine days. He had held us all together, as if rescuing ancient Greek heroes from the clutches of fate was all part of
his life's work. While the rest of us staggered in shock, he had
sorted out every practicality, limping about with his cane and his
battered face. He had taken Tadeas in hand, man-to-man, and
found the two travelers a cottage of their own, and hunted down a
doctor, and calmed down Mr. Higganbotham into the proper
spirit of inquisitive cooperation. Once the duke had recovered
from the physical enervation that had rendered him almost helpless in the immediate aftermath of the fateful event, to say nothing of the several burst stitches in his right shoulder, Silverton had
taken him out for a long and apparently merry night at the taverna
in Molos, in order to recover him spiritually.

I remembered hearing them arrive back at our hostelry, roaring with song, and how I lay on my bed and smiled at the ceiling.

The next morning, I had asked Silverton how he did it. How
he had known exactly what to do, how he hadn't seemed surprised or wrong-footed for even an instant. *Why, training, True-*

love, was his answer, tapping his temple. *Expect the unexpected, that's what they pound into our skulls.*

Expect the unexpected, I thought, and I smiled a little, because I could smell him now, that curious combination of pipe tobacco and soap and sunshine, as *unexpectedly* pleasurable as the scent of my bedroom at home.

I said, "I assure you, my lord, I am not the sort of person who leaps off cliffs."

"*My lord?* Just what have I done to deserve that?"

"Nothing." I turned to face him. His height came as a surprise after the short Queen; my gaze traveled for some time, up his chest and neck until I reached his unsmiling face. A trace of fear tingled my nerves at the sight of this unaccustomed gravity, and I asked if something were amiss.

"No, no. Have just been making my farewells to the happy couple, who seem to have accepted their miraculous lot with remarkable fortitude. Higganbotham was there, administering another lesson in Modern Greek. I don't believe they give a tinker's damn at the moment, but I daresay he will keep trying until it sinks in."

"It's good of him to stay on and help them."

"On the contrary, I think he would have stayed on whether they agreed or no. He's like a chap with a new bride." Silverton paused to turn pink.

"Yes," I said. "About that."

"Don't say it like that."

"Like what?"

"Like you're about to tell me *no*."

The breeze was ruffling his hair, and the sun found his cheek. By now, the bruises had largely faded. Except for a few red marks left behind by the more serious lacerations, his beauty was back in possession of his face, thoughtlessly perfect. He wasn't wearing his spectacles, and his eyes were blue and earnest, crinkled with worry at the corners. I reached up and brushed a speck of imaginary dust from his broad right shoulder.

"I wasn't about to say no," I said. "But—"

He caught my hand, just before it left his shoulder, and held my fingers against his chest. "But?"

At the sight of his relief, and the warmth of his breath on my face, I had forgotten the substance of my conditional clause. "But I—but before we—"

Silverton leaned closer. His hand tightened around mine. "Before we *what*, Truelove?"

"Before you—that is, I think—"

He lifted his other hand and touched his finger to my lips. "Oh, let's not have any of this thinking business, Truelove. If you think any more, I daresay you'll probably change your mind, and my last hope for earthly redemption will be shattered."

He is going to kiss me, I thought, and then, in wonder: *And, by God, I believe I am going to let him.*

His hand moved to lie against my cheek, and such was the length of him, his fingertips rested on the crown on my head, while his wrist touched my jaw.

"If you wish to remain untouched before your wedding night, Truelove," he said, smiling a little, "you had better speak up now."

His head moved closer, while my ears sorted through his words. His eyelids sank, and I closed my own eyes. Just before his lips touched mine, I heard myself say, "But I am not untouched."

Silverton paused, a millimeter away.

A second passed, and another. I opened my eyes.

"What did you say?" he asked softly.

I don't think I answered him aloud; I don't think I was able to say the words again, not while his eyes were open, and mine, too.

"Yes," he said at last. "As I thought."

He did not release my hand, but he straightened away from the imminent kiss. A bird screamed overhead.

"We should be getting back," I said. "The ship leaves soon."

~

We were almost halfway back to the village before his lordship spoke again.

"Listen, Truelove. I'm afraid something's come up, and I'll be parting ways with you in Athens."

I examined the toes of my dusty shoes as they descended the path. "What has come up, pray?"

"A telegram from the duchess. I'm afraid I can't say more."

"No, of course not."

"It's just a routine little annoyance. I shall be back in England by the first of May at the latest."

"A routine little annoyance, is it? The sort of thing that happens all the time in your chosen profession?"

"Yes, as a matter of fact."

He swung his cane as he walked, a little flourish at each step, as if to disguise the slight limp that impeded his stride. The red-tile peaks of the village rooftops had begun to take shape over the next rise.

"I see," I said.

Our footsteps crunched along the path, which was strewn with pebbles. The sun was now high and warm, and the smoke from the village chimneys mingled with the scent of the sea.

"Can you tell me his name?" asked his lordship.

"No, I will not."

He released a small sigh. "Very well."

In another half hour, we reached the door of the hostelry. Silverton opened it and waved me inside. "Aren't you coming in?" I asked.

He shrugged. "A few loose threads to tie together."

"Then I will see you on board the ship," I said, and turned away.

His hand found my arm. "Wait, Truelove."

"Yes?"

He was frowning down at me, one foot lodged on the step below. "We will continue this conversation in England, when I return. Do you understand me?"

From within, I heard the scraping of a chair leg against a stone floor. A voice called my name: "Ah, Miss Truelove! There you are at last. May I have a word with you?"

"You'll excuse me, Lord Silverton," I said, withdrawing my arm from his lordship's grasp. "The duke has need of me."

"Are you quite all right, Miss Truelove?" asked His Grace, when we were alone in the small and rustic chamber that had been allotted to him. "You're rather pale."

"Quite all right, I assure you."

"Very good. I am sorry to call you into service at such a hurried moment, but I have been thinking a great deal about this institute, and about my uncle's enthusiasm for the project, and your own capability."

"My capability?"

"Yes, Miss Truelove." He handed me a promised cup of tea

from the tray on the table. "I should like to put a proposal before you. You needn't answer at once, of course; I am happy to wait until the conclusion of our voyage before you make your decision."

The duke was looking much better than he had nine days ago, when we had carried him, half-dead, down the track by the seaside, and brought him to this very chamber. The next day, he had regained the better part of his senses, and the day after that, he had risen from his couch and begun, without the slightest suggestion of sentimentality, to assist Lord Silverton in making arrangements for Desma and Tadeas to live quietly together in Skyros. He had insisted on a ceremony of marriage, which the couple carried out in a kind of dazed bewilderment, and gave the bride away from his own arm. He had then immersed himself in the duchy papers, firing endless questions at me and then taking long walks of contemplation along the seaside, holding his injured limb stiffly at his side. He had avoided any turn of the conversation toward the events of that fateful day. On the morning after his night out with Silverton, he had woken at his usual hour and called me in to breakfast, and though his face was perhaps a trifle more haggard than usual, he betrayed no sign of indisposition.

No sign, indeed, that his heart had been irretrievably broken.

I stirred my tea and said, "What is your proposal, sir?"

He propped himself on the table and picked up his own teacup. "Before the extraordinary turn of events here in Skyros, I confess I had approached this notion of an institute for the study of anachronisms with a certain degree of skepticism. I suppose I offered my cooperation only to appease my uncle, who had recently developed such a passionate interest in my work."

"Yes, I remember it well."

"Do you happen to have any idea *why*, Miss Truelove? I only ask because—well, because everything has taken on a different cast, now. Now that we know the truth."

I set my teacup in its saucer. "That you are the instrument of miracles."

He did not answer at first. He was sitting near the window, and the light struck the left half of his face in a white and almost smoky blur. Were his eyes always so grave and dark, I wondered, or had they acquired their gravity recently? But I had only known him a fortnight. The breadth and depth of him remained a mystery to me.

I heard the Queen again, as if she had returned and stood now by my side: *You have seen for yourself the continual jeopardy in which this agency places the poor fellow. The moral burden he bears, to say nothing of the lust other men harbor for the immeasurable power he controls.*

"Yes," he said. "So it would seem. It explains a great deal—why, for example, Anserrat and his companions were so determined to gain control of me, though we can only speculate how they came to learn of this power, when I—at the time—had no idea of it."

"Have you any theory at all?"

"None that makes any logical sense. And you?"

The duke made this query without thought, as if asking my opinion were the most natural thing in the world. I fingered the handle of my teacup and said, "It seems to me—you will forgive me, sir, for I speak only from my own feeble intuition—it seems to me, as I look back on the encounter in Knossos, that these men did not . . ." I hesitated, looked at my lap, and looked up again. "They did not quite seem to belong to our own age."

"Ah. I confess, Miss Truelove, the same idea has lately occurred to me."

"Of course, it's impossible, unless we suppose you are not the only man invested with this power. Or else how might they have found us, in our present century?"

The duke swung his leg and glanced out the window. "I was thinking of something Anserrat said, just before the end. How he had proof of my power, and that it wasn't something I had already done . . ."

"It was something you *would* do."

"Yes."

The tea was finished. I set it aside. "Is there any news of the other man? The one we left tied up in the cave?"

"No word at all. He appears to have vanished." He turned to the papers on the table behind him and lifted a slip of paper. "And the only man among them to survive the attack on the beach has, I'm afraid, now died of his wounds."

He handed me the telegram, and I glanced over the words. "So we have no one left to interrogate."

"I'm afraid we must be content to live with the mystery, Miss Truelove, unless some solution presents itself in the future." He paused to take back the telegram from my outstretched fingers. "Furthermore, I believe, for the time being, we must keep this knowledge strictly to ourselves."

"Sir, I have never considered otherwise."

"Of course not. I knew at once that I could trust you, thank God, which is why I have asked for your help in this matter."

"I will do whatever I can for you."

"No, don't say that. You must not obey me out of a sense of duty, for God's sake. You must enter into this partnership freely."

At the word *partnership*, my heart stopped. "What do you mean?"

"I mean that I can think of no better person—no other person at all, in fact—to run this institute on my behalf, Miss Truelove, except you."

My heart resumed its course, except perhaps at an accelerated pace, as if to make up for lost ground. "I see. This is indeed a position of great trust."

His Grace set his cup and saucer on his knee and turned his head to the window. "You see, Miss Truelove, I have always been of a curious cast of mind, and when I encounter a problem of any sort, my instinct is to gather as much information as I can on the subject. And this—this *problem* of mine, it seems to me, is the reason God placed me on this earth. It is the great purpose of my life, and it is my duty to discover why, exactly, he has chosen me for this particular task."

"Of course. I quite agree."

The duke turned his gaze back to me. "I want you to give this a great deal of thought, Miss Truelove. It is no small task I have asked of you; you must perceive that."

I rose to my feet and carried my cup and saucer to the table, where I placed them on the tray. "There is no need for further consideration, sir. I am quite willing to devote myself to this mystery, in any capacity you require."

"There may, of course, be some danger involved in this position," he said.

"I am equal, I hope, to any challenge that may present itself."

He regarded me without expression. I was close enough to see the lines about the corners of his eyes, the bruised shadows beneath them, and my chest filled with compassion.

There is always a price, Her Majesty had said, the duke was already paying it.

"There is one other matter," he said. "I hope I do not intrude on your privacy."

"Not at all."

"You see, I had some concern that you would dismiss my proposal out of hand." The slightest suggestion of color came to the tip of his nose, and the outer edges of his thick cheekbones. "I thought there might perhaps exist some prior engagement."

"A prior engagement?"

"Between you and my friend Silverton."

I confess, I was surprised to hear this. I had thought this subject would have been thoroughly covered by the two of them by now; certainly after such a night of manly comradeship as had occurred the day before last. Had the question of Emmeline Truelove's affections not been raised at all?

And yet, why should it? Nothing had been settled, after all. I had not given Silverton an answer. He hadn't pressed me for one.

I turned my head to the window, which overlooked the village square. The white sun blinded me, but I could still make out the shapes of the central statue, the wandering townsfolk. Silverton among them, no doubt, swinging his jaunty cane, chewing his pipe, tying up his loose threads.

With Silverton, I supposed, there were always loose threads.

I have few clear memories of my mother; they are mostly of the dreamlike variety, bedtime kisses and the scent of her skirts and something to do with paper dolls. Even the image of her on her sickbed is lost to me. But I do have this: a visit to the village confectionary, a much-anticipated reward for some childish achievement. I remember looking at the rows of sweets in an agony of indecision. I gazed back and forth between a glossy fruit marzipan—I can still see the luscious purple curves of the grapes, perfect in every detail—and a round chocolate bonbon, containing a brandied cherry, and I burst into tears, because to have one was to relinquish all hope of the other.

And my mother bent down next to me and put one warm arm around my shoulders, and she didn't scold. "Emmie, darling," she said, "every day of your life you will have to make choices, and you can't waste a single precious minute mourning what you have lost. Only be grateful for what you have gained."

I remember the comfort of her words, though at the time I did not fully understand them, and as I stood there in that simple room in the center of the Aegean, contemplating the new spring sun, I thought I could feel my mother's arm upon my shoulders once more, and smell the scent of her dress, as if she were standing again beside me.

I returned my gaze to the Duke of Olympia and smiled gravely.

"In fact," I said, "I am quite at liberty."

A Most Extraordinary Pursuit

BY JULIANA GRAY

Discussion Questions

1. *A Most Extraordinary Pursuit* begins with the death of the Duke of Olympia, a fictional titan of the Victorian Age, and Emmeline links the duke's death to the death of the nineteenth century itself. What changes do you think took place during the turn of the twentieth century? How do you think Emmeline feels about them? How do these themes play out in the book as a whole?

2. What were your initial impressions of Lord Silverton? How did they change during the course of the narrative? Do you think he would make a good match for Emmeline? Why or why not?

3. Do you think the ghosts of Queen Victoria and Mr. Truelove are "real," or simply figments of Emmeline's imagination? What role do they play in the story? What is the nature of the Queen's apparent bond with Emmeline, and vice versa?

4. Were you surprised to discover that Emmeline has a lover in her past? Why do you think she held this information back from the reader for so much of the narrative? Do you think Emmeline is a reliable narrator? Why or why not?

5. Emmeline is a woman holding down a man's job in 1906, executing those duties competently and holding her own against her male companions, and yet at many points in the book she expresses traditional views about social, economic, and sexual politics. Do you find this contradictory? Why do you think she feels this way? What kinds of internal conflicts might Emmeline be experiencing, other than those she tells us about?

6. What did you think of the "retelling" of the myth of Theseus and Ariadne? Do you believe that myths and legends originate from real historical events? What role do you think myth and storytelling play in human society?

7. Max Haywood, the new Duke of Olympia, doesn't appear until the last section of the book. What impression did you have of him before he finally entered the story? Were your expectations realized or confounded? How does he compare to Lord Silverton?

8. How would you cope if you discovered you had Max's power? Would you use that power in some way, or leave it aside? Why?

9. What do you think of the possibility of time travel? Would you be afraid of affecting other events through the domino effect? Or do you think those effects are already "written" into history?

10. Do you think Emmeline made the right decision at the end of the book? Do you think Lord Silverton really loves her? Which man would you choose?

LOOK FOR THE NEXT JULIANA GRAY BOOK
FEATURING EMMELINE TRUELOVE,
COMING FALL 2017 FROM BERKLEY BOOKS.

Dear Reader,

You might know me by another name. As Beatriz Williams, I write historical fiction set primarily in that tumultuous center of the twentieth century, after the First World War blew apart the remnants of Romanticism and ushered in the modern era. A Hundred Summers *dissected the habits and family secrets of a New England beach community during the summer of the hurricane of 1938, while* The Secret Life of Violet Grant *introduced Vivian Schuyler, a dashing 1960s Manhattan career girl uncovering the scandalous history of her long-lost Aunt Violet. In* Tiny Little Thing, *Vivian's older sister Tiny tells her story as a photo-perfect political wife hiding a devastating mistake in her past, during the telegenic age of Camelot.*

But Tiny and Vivian have another sister, Pepper, who's the most tortured—and the most beautiful—of the Schuylers. She's pregnant with the child of a prominent (and very married) United States senator, from whose savage political ambition she needs a refuge. She finds that refuge in the form of a rare vintage Mercedes Roadster, whose previous owner takes Pepper under her protective wing. As Annabelle Dommerich's story of passionate young love in 1930s Europe unfolds alongside Pepper's search for safety and redemption on the 1960s Florida coast, the two women forge a deep and complicated bond.

I hope you'll enjoy this excerpt from Along the Infinite Sea, *a novel that took me on a profound emotional journey through a historical moment that has no equal for human heartbreak and fortitude. When I finished this book, I felt it was my best yet, and I can't wait for you to meet Annabelle and Stefan, Johann and Florian and Pepper, and the rest of the Schuyler family.*

Happy reading!
Beatriz

KEEP READING FOR A SPECIAL EXCERPT FROM

Along the Infinite Sea

BY BEATRIZ WILLIAMS

Overture

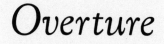

To see all without looking;
to hear all without listening.

CÉSAR RITZ
King of Hoteliers, Hotelier of Kings

Annabelle

Paris ❦ 1937

All you really need to know about the Paris Ritz is this: by the middle of 1937, Coco Chanel was living in a handsome suite on the third floor, and the bartender—an intuitive mixologist named Frank Meier—had invented the Bloody Mary sixteen summers earlier to cure a Hemingway hangover.

Mind you, when I arrived at Nick Greenwald's farewell party on that hot July night, I wasn't altogether aware of this history. I didn't run with the Ritz crowd. Mosquitoes, my husband called them. And maybe I should have listened to my husband. Maybe no good could come from visiting the bar at the Paris Ritz; maybe you were doomed to commit some frivolous and irresponsible act, maybe you were doomed to hover around dangerously until you had drawn the blood from another human being or else had your own blood drawn instead.

But Johann—my husband—wasn't around that night. I tiptoed

in through the unfashionable Place Vendôme entrance on my brother's arm instead, since Johann had been recalled to Berlin for an assignment of a few months that had stretched into several. In those days, you couldn't just flit back and forth between Paris and Berlin, no more than you could flit between heaven and hell; and furthermore, why would you want to? Paris had everything I needed, everything I loved, and Berlin in 1937 was no place for a liberal-minded woman nurturing a young child and an impossible rift in her marriage. I stayed defiantly in France, where you could still attend a party for a man named Greenwald, where anyone could dine where he pleased and shop and bank where he pleased, where you could sleep with anyone who suited you, and it wasn't a crime.

For the sake of everyone's good time, I suppose it was just as well that my husband remained in Berlin, since Nick Greenwald and Johann von Kleist weren't what you'd call bosom friends, for all the obvious reasons. But Nick and I were a different story. Nick and I understood each other: first, because we were both Americans living in Paris, and second, because we shared a little secret together, the kind of secret you could never, ever share with anyone else. Of all my brother's friends, Nick was the only one who didn't resent me for marrying a general in the German army. Good old Nick. He knew I'd had my reasons.

The salon was hot, and Nick was in his shirtsleeves, though he still retained his waistcoat and a neat white bow tie, the kind you needed a valet to arrange properly. He turned at the sound of my voice. "Annabelle! Here at last."

"Not so very late, am I?" I said.

We kissed, and he and Charles shook hands. Not that Charles paid the transaction much attention; he was transfixed by the black-haired beauty who lounged at Nick's side in a shimmering silver-blue dress that matched her eyes. A long cigarette dangled from her fingers. Nick turned to her and placed his hand at the small of her back. "Annabelle, Charlie. I don't think you've met Budgie Byrne. An old college friend."

We said *enchantée*. Miss Byrne took little notice. Her hand-shake was slender and lacked conviction. She slipped her arm through Nick's and whispered in his ear, and they shimmered off together to the bar inside a haze of expensive perfume. The back of Miss Byrne's dress swooped down almost to the point of no return, and her naked skin was like a spill of milk, kept from running over the edge by Nick's large palm.

Charles covered his cheek with his right hand—the same hand that Miss Byrne had just touched with her limp and slender fingers—and said that bastard always got the best-looking women.

I watched Nick's back disappear into the crowd, and I was about to tell Charles that he didn't need to worry, that Nick didn't really look all that happy with his companion and Charles might want to give the delectably disinterested Miss Byrne another try in an hour, but at that exact instant a voice came over my shoulder, the last voice I expected to hear at the Paris Ritz on this night in the smoldering middle of July.

"My God," it said, a little slurry. "If it isn't the baroness herself."

I thought perhaps I was hallucinating, or mistaken. It wouldn't be the first time. For the past two years, I'd heard this voice every-where: department stores and elevators and street corners. I'd seen its owner in every possible nook, in every conceivable disguise, only to discover that the supposed encounter was only a false alarm, a collision of deluded molecules inside my own head, and the proximate cause of the leap in my blood proved to be an ordi-nary citizen after all. Just an everyday fellow who happened to have dark hair or a deep voice or a certain shape to the back of his neck. In the instant of revelation, I never knew whether to be relieved or disappointed. Whether to lament or hallelujah. Either way, the experience wasn't a pleasant one, at least not in the way we ordinarily experience pleasure, as a benevolent thing that massages the nerves into a sensation of well-being.

Either way, I had committed a kind of adultery of the heart, hadn't I, and since I couldn't bear the thought of adultery in any form, I learned to ignore the false alarm when it rang and rang and rang. Like the good wife I was, I learned to maintain my poise during these moments of intense delusion.

So there. Instead of bolting at the slurry word *baroness*, I took my deluded molecules in hand and said: *Surely not.*

Instead of spinning like a top, I turned like a figurine on a music box, in such a way that you could almost hear the tinkling Tchaikovsky in my gears.

A man came into view, quite lifelike, quite familiar, tall and just so in his formal blacks and white points, dark hair curling into his forehead the way your lover's hair does in your wilder dreams. He was holding a lowball glass and a brown Turkish cigarette in his right hand, and he took in everything at a glance: my jewels, my extravagant dress, the exact state of my circulation.

In short, he seemed an awful lot like the genuine article.

"There you are, you old bastard," said Charles happily, and *sacré bleu*, I realized then what I already knew: that the man before me was no delusion. That the Paris Ritz was the kind of place that could conjure up anyone it wanted.

"Stefan," I said. "What a lovely surprise."

(And the big trouble was, I think I meant it.)

First Movement

Experience is simply the name
we give our mistakes.

Oscar Wilde

Pepper

PALM BEACH * 1966

1.

The Mercedes-Benz poses on the grass like a swirl of vintage black ink, like no other car in the world.

You'd never guess it to look at her, but Miss Pepper Schuyler—that woman right over there, the socialite with the golden antelope legs who's soaking up the Florida sunshine at the other end of the courtyard—knows every glamorous inch of this 1936 Special Roadster shadowing the grass. You might regard Pepper's pregnant belly protruding from her green Lilly shift (well, it's hard to ignore a belly like that, isn't it?) and the pastel Jack Rogers sandal dangling from her uppermost toe, and think you have her pegged. Admit it! Lush young woman exudes Palm Beach class: What the hell does she know about cars?

Well, beautiful Pepper doesn't give a damn what you think about her. She never did. She's thinking about the car. She slides her gaze along the seductive S-curve of the right side fender, swooping from the top of the tire to the running board below the door, like a woman's voluptuously naked leg, and her heart beats a quarter-inch faster.

She remembers what a pain in the pert old derrière it was to repaint that glossy fender. It had been the first week of October, and the warm weather wouldn't quit. The old shed on Cape Cod stank of paint and grease, a peculiarly acrid reek that had crept right through the protective mask and into her sinuses and taken up residence, until she couldn't smell anything else, and she thought, *What the hell am I doing here? What the hell am I thinking?*

Thank God that was all over. Thank God this rare inky-black 1936 Mercedes Special Roadster is now someone else's problem, someone willing to pay Pepper three hundred thousand dollars for the privilege of keeping its body and chrome intact against the ravages of time.

The deposit has already been paid, into a special account Pepper set up in her own name. (Her own name, her own money: now, that was a glorious feeling, like setting off for Europe on an ocean liner with nothing but open blue seas ahead.) The rest will be delivered today, to the Breakers hotel where Pepper is staying, in a special-delivery envelope. Another delightful little big check made out in Pepper's name. Taken together, those checks will solve all her problems. She'll have money for the baby, money to start everything over, money to ignore whoever needs ignoring, money to disappear if she needs to, forever and ever. She'll depend on no one. She can do whatever the hell she pleases, whatever suits Pepper Schuyler and—by corollary—Pepper Junior. She will toe nobody's line. She will fear nobody.

So the only question left in Pepper's mind, the only question that needs resolving, is the niggling *Who?*

Who the hell is this anonymous buyer—a woman, Pepper's auction agent said—who has the dough and the desire to lay claim to Pepper's very special Special Roadster, before it even reaches the public sales ring?

Not that Pepper cares who she is. Pepper just cares who she *isn't*. As long as this woman is a disinterested party, a person who has her own reasons for wanting this car, nothing to do with Pepper, nothing to do with the second half of the magic equation inside Pepper's belly, well, everything's just peachy keen, isn't it? Pepper will march off with her three hundred thousand dollars and never give the buyer another thought.

Pepper lifts a tanned arm and checks her watch. It's a gold Cartier, given to her by her father for her eighteenth birthday, perhaps as a subtle reminder to start arriving the hell on time, now that she was a grown-up. It didn't work. The party always starts when Pepper gets there, not before, so why should she care if she arrives late or early? Still, the watch has its uses. The watch tells her it's twenty-seven minutes past twelve o'clock. They should be here any moment: Pepper's auction agent and the buyer, to inspect the car and complete the formalities. *If* they're on time, and why wouldn't they be? By all accounts, the lady's as eager to buy as Pepper is to sell.

Pepper tilts her head back and closes her eyes to the white sun. She can't get enough of it. This baby inside her must have sprung from another religion, one that worshipped the gods in the sky or gained nourishment from sunbeams. Pepper can almost feel the cells dividing in ecstasy as she points herself due upward. She can almost feel the seams strain along her green Lilly shift, the dancing monkeys stretch their arms to fit around the ambitious creature within.

Well, that makes sense, doesn't it? Like father, like child.

"Good afternoon."

Pepper bolts upright. A small and slender woman stands before her, dark-haired, dressed in navy Capri pants and a white shirt, her delicate face hidden by a pair of large dark sunglasses. It's Audrey Hepburn, or else her well-groomed Florida cousin.

"Good afternoon," Pepper says.

The woman holds out her hand. "You must be Miss Schuyler. My name is Annabelle Dommerich. I'm the buyer. Please, don't get up."

Pepper rises anyway and takes the woman's hand. Mrs. Dommerich stands only a few inches above five feet, and Pepper is a tall girl, but for some reason they seem to meet as equals.

"I'm surprised to see you," says Pepper. "I had the impression you wanted to remain anonymous."

Mrs. Dommerich shrugs. "Oh, that's just for the newspapers. Actually, I've been hugely curious to meet you, Miss Schuyler. You're even more beautiful than your pictures. And look at you, blooming like a rose! When are you due?"

"February."

"I've always envied women like you. When I was pregnant, I looked like a beach ball with feet."

"I can't imagine that."

"It was a long time ago." Mrs. Dommerich takes off her sunglasses to reveal a pair of large and chocolaty eyes. "The car looks beautiful."

"Thank you. I had an expert helping me restore it."

"You restored it yourself?" Both eyebrows rise, so elegant. "I'm impressed."

"There was nothing else to do."

Mrs. Dommerich turns to gaze at the car, shielding her brows with one hand. "And you found it in the shed on Cape Cod? Just like that, covered with dust? Untouched?"

"Yes. My sister-in-law's house. It seemed to have been abandoned there."

"Yes," says Mrs. Dommerich. "It was."

The grass prickles Pepper's feet through the gaps in her sandals. Next to her, Mrs. Dommerich stands perfectly still, like she's posing for a portrait, *Woman Transfixed in a Crisp White Shirt*. She talks like an American, in easy sentences, but there's just the slightest mysterious tilt to her accent that suggests something imported, like the Chanel perfume that colors the air next to her skin. Though that skin is remarkably fresh, lit by a kind of iridescent pearl-like substance that most women spent fruitless dollars to achieve, Pepper guesses she must be in her forties, even her late forties. It's something about her expression and her carriage, something that makes Pepper feel like an ungainly young colt, dressed like a little girl. Even considering that matronly bump that interrupts the youthful line of her figure.

At the opposite end of the courtyard, a pair of sweating men appear, dressed in businesslike wool suits above a pair of perfectly matched potbellies, neat as basketballs. One of them spots the two women and raises his hand in what Pepper's always called a golf wave.

"There they are," says Mrs. Dommerich. She turns back to Pepper and smiles. "I do appreciate your taking such trouble to restore her so well. How does she run?"

"Like a racehorse."

"Good. I can almost hear that roar in my ears now. There's no other sound like it, is there? Not like anything they make today."

"I wouldn't know, really. I'm not what you'd call an enthusiast."

"Really? We'll have to change that, then. I'll pick you up from your hotel at seven o'clock and we'll take her for a spin before dinner." She holds out her hand, and Pepper, astonished, can do nothing but shake it. Mrs. Dommerich's fingers are soft and strong and devoid of rings, except for a single gold band on the telling digit of her left hand, which Pepper has already noticed.

"Of course," Pepper mumbles.

Mrs. Dommerich slides her sunglasses back in place and turns away.

"Wait just a moment," says Pepper.

"Yes?"

"I'm just curious, Mrs. Dommerich. How do you already know how the engine sounds? Since it's been locked away in an old shed all these years."

"Oh, trust me, Miss Schuyler. I know everything about that car."

There's something so self-assured about her words, Pepper's skin begins to itch, and not just the skin that stretches around the baby. The sensation sets off a chain reaction of alarm along the pathways of Pepper's nerves: the dingling of tiny alarm bells in her ears, the tingling in the tip of her nose.

"And just how the hell do you know that, Mrs. Dommerich? If you don't mind me asking. Why exactly would you pay all that money for this hunk of pretty metal?"

Mrs. Dommerich's face is hidden behind those sunglasses, betraying not an ounce of visible reaction to Pepper's impertinence. "Because, Miss Schuyler," she says softly, "twenty-eight years ago, I drove for my life across the German border inside that car, and I left a piece of my heart inside her. And now I think it's time to bring her home. Don't you?" She turns away again, and as she walks across the grass, she says, over her shoulder, sounding like an elegant half-European mother: "Wear a cardigan, Miss Schuyler. It's supposed to be cooler tonight, and I'd like to put the top down."